For Valentine's... Forever!

Celebrate the most romantic day of the year
with three stunning Valentine's stories
from favourite authors Barbara Dunlop,
Trish Wylie and Caroline Anderson

Escape for Valentine's

BARBARA DUNLOP

TRISH WYLIE

CAROLINE ANDERSON

MILLS & BOON

All the characters in this book have no existence outside the imagination
of the author, and have no relation whatsoever to anyone bearing the
same name or names. They are not even distantly inspired by any
individual known or unknown to the author, and all the incidents are
pure invention.

Mills & Boon, an imprint of Harlequin (UK) Limited, Eton House,
18-24 Paradise Road, Richmond, Surrey TW9 1SR

ESCAPE FOR VALENTINE'S
© Harlequin Enterprises II B.V./S.à.r.l. 2012

Beauty and the Billionaire © Barbara Dunlop 2008
Her One and Only Valentine © Trish Wylie 2007
The Girl Next Door © Caroline Anderson 2000

ISBN: 978 0 263 89714 2

011-0212

Harlequin (UK) policy is to use papers that are natural, renewable
and recyclable products and made from wood grown in sustainable
forests. The logging and manufacturing processes conform to the
legal environmental regulations of the country of origin.

Printed and bound in Spain
by Blackprint CPI, Barcelona

BEAUTY AND THE BILLIONAIRE

BARBARA DUNLOP

Barbara Dunlop writes romantic stories while curled up in a log cabin in Canada's far north, where bears outnumber people and it snows six months of the year. Fortunately, she has a brawny husband and two teenage children to haul firewood and clear the driveway while she sips cocoa and muses about her upcoming chapters. Barbara loves to hear from readers. You can contact her through her website at www.barbaradunlop.com.

For my editor, Kathryn Lye,
who has the uncanny ability to track me down
anywhere in the world.

Prologue

A one-night stand only lasted one night. Sinclair Mahoney might be far from an expert, but she could guess that much.

So, while Hunter Osland's bare chest rose and fell in his king-size bed, and a door slammed somewhere in the far reaches of the mansion, she pushed her feet into her low-heeled black pumps and shrugged into her pinstriped blazer. She was only guessing at the protocol here, but she suspected it wasn't a lingering goodbye in the cold light of day.

Peacefully asleep in the gleaming four-poster, Hunter had obviously done this before. There were three brand-new toothbrushes in his en suite, along with half a dozen fresh towels and an assortment of mini toiletries in a basket on the marble counter. He had everything a woman needed if she wanted to make a simple, independent exit—which was exactly what Sinclair had in mind.

Last night had been good.

Okay, last night had been incredible. But last night was also over, and there was something pathetic about hanging around this morning hoping to see respect in his eyes.

So, she'd washed her face, brushed her teeth, and pulled her auburn hair into a simple ponytail, glancing one last time at the opulent cherry furnishings, the storm-tossed seascape that hung above his bed, and two potted palms that bracketed a huge bay window. It was nearly 8:00 a.m. She had just enough time to find her twin sister in the maze of the rambling Osland mansion. She'd say a quick goodbye before hopping a taxi to the Manchester, Vermont, airport and her flight to JFK.

She had a planning meeting at noon, then a conference call with the Cosmetics Manager at Bergdorf's. There were also two focus-group reports on Luscious Lavender beauty products tucked in her briefcase.

Last night was last night. It was time to return to her regular life. She squared her shoulders and reached for her purse, her gaze catching Hunter's tanned, toned leg. It had worked its way free from the tangled ivory sheets, and she followed its length to where the sheet was wrapped snugly around his hips.

She cringed at the telltale tightening beneath her ribs. His broad shoulders were also uncovered, along with the muscular arms that had held her tight into the wee hours of the morning. At five foot seven and a hundred and fifteen pounds, she wasn't used to feeling small and delicate in a man's arms. But she had in Hunter's.

In fact, she'd felt a lot of things she hadn't expected for a one-night stand.

Her friends had talked about them. But Sinclair had only imagined them. She always assumed they'd be stilted and awkward, each party self-conscious and trying to impress the other, while convincing themselves it wasn't tacky and shallow to sleep with a near stranger.

She'd been wrong about all of it.

There was an edge of the forbidden, sure. But Hunter had mostly been sweet and funny. At first, his intelligence had challenged her. Then his smile had enticed her. His touches and kisses had been the most natural things in the world. By the time they were naked, she felt as if she'd known him for years instead of hours.

In fact, standing here on the brink of goodbye, she could feel the heady sensations all over again. She wanted to turn back the clock, climb into the big, soft bed, taste those lips, run her fingertips over his skin, inhale the clean, woodsy scent of his hair.

She took a reflexive step forward.

But he shifted in the bed and she froze, appalled to realize she was about to hop in for round three. Or was it four? She supposed that depended on whether you counted his orgasms or hers.

He stretched his arm across the bed, and his expression drew taut in his sleep. He felt around and frowned.

Any second now, he would open his eyes. She knew somewhere deep down in her soul that if she was still standing here when he woke up, she'd be flat on her back in an instant. He knew his way past her defenses, knew a hundred ways to make her gasp and moan, knew all the right things to growl and whisper in her ear.

Her palm closed around her purse strap, and she commanded herself to back off.

He gave a bleary blink, and she grasped at the doorknob.

Before he could focus, she was out in the hall, shutting the door behind her and striding for the staircase.

It was over.
It was done.
Her best hope was to never see him again.

One

Hunter was here.

Six weeks later, Sinclair's stomach clenched around nothing as he strode into the Lush Beauty Products boardroom like he owned the place.

"—in a friendly takeover bid," Sinclair's boss, company president Roger Rawlings, was saying. "Osland International has purchased fifty-one percent of the Lush Beauty Products voting shares."

Sinclair reflexively straightened in her chair. Good grief, he *did* own the place.

Could this be a joke?

She glanced from side to side.

Would cameramen jump out any second and shove a microphone in her face? Were they filming even now to record her reaction?

She waited. But Hunter didn't even look her way, and nobody started laughing.

"As many of you are aware," said Roger, "among their other business interests, Osland International owns the Sierra Sanchez line of women's clothing stores across North America, with several outlets in Europe and Australia."

While Roger spoke, and the Lush Beauty managers absorbed the surprising news, Hunter's gaze moved methodically around the big, oval table. His gaze paused on Ethan from product development, then Colleen from marketing. He nodded at Sandra from accounting, and looked to Mary-Anne from distribution.

As her turn grew near, Sinclair composed her expression. In her role as public relations manager, she was used to behaving professionally under trying circumstances. And she'd do that now. If he could handle this, so could she. They were both adults, obviously. And she could behave as professionally as he could. Still, she had to wonder why he hadn't given her a heads-up.

The Hunter she'd met in Manchester had struck her as honorable. She would have thought he'd at least drop her an e-mail. Or had she totally misjudged him? Was he nothing more than a slick, polished player who forgot women the second they were out of his sight?

Maybe he didn't e-mail because he didn't care. Or, worse yet, maybe he didn't even remember.

In the wash of her uncertainty, Roger's voice droned on. "Sierra Sanchez will offer Lush Beauty Products a built-in, high-end retail outlet from which to launch the new Luscious Lavender line. We'll continue seeking other sales outlets, of course. But that is only one of the many ways this partnership will be productive for both parties."

Hunter's gaze hit Sinclair.

He froze for a split second. Then his nostrils flared, and his eyebrows shot up. She could swear a current cracked audibly between them. It blanketed her skin, shimmied down her nervous system, then pooled to a steady hum in the pit of her stomach.

Hunter's jaw tightened around his own obvious shock.

Okay. So maybe there was a reason he hadn't given her a heads-up.

There were days when Hunter Osland hated his grandfather's warped sense of humor. And today ranked right up there.

In the instant he saw Sinclair, the last six weeks suddenly made sense—Cleveland's insistence they buy Lush Beauty Products, his demand that Hunter take over as CEO, and his rush to get Hunter in front of the company managers. Cleveland had known she worked here, and he'd somehow figured out Hunter had slept with her.

Hunter's grandfather was, quite literally, forcing him to face the consequences of his actions.

"So please join me in welcoming Mr. Osland to Lush Beauty Products," Roger finished to a polite round of applause. The managers seemed wary, as anyone would be when the corporate leadership suddenly shifted above them.

It was Hunter's job to reassure them. And he now had the additional duty of explaining himself to Sinclair. God only knew what she was thinking. But, talking to her would have to wait. He refocused his gaze on the room in general and moved to the head of the table.

"Thank you very much," he began, smoothly taking control of the meeting, like he'd done at a thousand meetings before. "First, you should all feel free to call me Hunter. Second, I'd like to assure you up front that Osland International has no plans to make staffing changes, nor to change the current direction of Lush Beauty Products."

He'd mentally rehearsed this next part, although he now knew it was a lie. "My grandfather made the decision to invest in this company because he was excited about your product re-development—such as the Luscious Lavender line—and about your plans to expand the company's target demographic."

Hunter now doubted Cleveland had even heard of Lush Beauty Products before meeting Sinclair. And Cleveland would be a lot less excited about the product redevelopment than he was about yanking Hunter's chain.

"Osland International has analyzed your success within the North American midprice market," Hunter told the group. "And we believe there are a number of opportunities to go upscale and international. We're open to your ideas. And, although Roger will continue to manage day-to-day operations, I'll be hands-on with strategic direction. So I want to invite each of you to stop by and see me. I expect to be on site several days a month, and I believe I'll have an office on the twentieth floor?"

He looked to Roger for confirmation.

"Yes," said Roger. "But if any of you have questions or concerns, you should feel free to use me as a sounding board."

The words surprised Hunter. Was Roger telling them not to go directly to Hunter?

"We'll try to make this transition as smooth as possible," Roger continued in a silky voice that set Hunter's teeth on edge. "But we understand some of you may feel challenged and unsettled."

Oh, great little pep talk. Thanks for that, Roger.

"There's no need for anyone to feel unsettled," Hunter cut

in. "As far as I'm concerned, it's business as usual. And my door is always open." Then he looked directly at Sinclair. "Come and see me."

An hour later, Sinclair took Hunter up on his invitation. On the twentieth floor, she propped herself against the doorjamb of his airy corner office. "This," she said, taking in the big desk, the credenza piled with books and the meeting table that sat eight, "I have *got* to hear."

He straightened in his high-backed chair and glanced up from his laptop, a flash of guilt in his eyes.

Ignoring the way her heart lifted at his reaction, she took two steps inside and closed the door behind her. He cared that he'd blindsided her. At least that was something.

Not that she cared about him in any fundamental way. She couldn't. They were a brief flash of history, and nothing more.

"It was Gramps," answered Hunter. "He bought the company and sent me here to run it."

"And you didn't know about me?" she guessed.

"I didn't know," he confirmed.

"So, you're not stalking me?"

He hit a key on his computer. "Right. Like any reasonable stalker, I bought your company to get close to you."

She shrugged. "Could happen."

"Well, it didn't. This is Gramps' idea of a joke. I think he knows I slept with you," said Hunter.

"Then there's something wrong with that man." And there was something frightening about a person with enough economic power to buy a four-hundred-person company as a joke. There was something even more frightening about a person who took the trouble to actually do it.

"I think he's losing it in his old age." Then Hunter paused

for a moment to consider. "On the other hand, he was always crotchety and controlling."

"Kristy likes him," said Sinclair. Not that she was coming down on Cleveland Osland's side. If Hunter was right, the man was seriously nuts.

"That's because he's batty over your sister."

Sinclair supposed that was probably true. It was Cleveland Osland who had helped Kristy get started in the fashion business last month. And now her career was soaring.

A soaring career was what Sinclair wanted for herself. And what she really wanted was for Hunter not to be a complication in that. She had a huge opportunity here with the planned company expansion and with the development of the new Luscious Lavender line.

She advanced on his wide desk to make her point, forcing herself to ignore the persistent sexual tug that had settled in her abdomen. Whatever they'd had for that brief moment had ended. He was her past, now her boss.

Even if he might be willing to rekindle. And she had no reason to assume he was willing. She was not.

She dropped into one of his guest chairs, keeping her tone light and unconcerned. "So what do we do now?"

A wolfish grin grew on his face.

All right, so maybe there was a reason to assume he was willing.

"No," she said, in a stern voice.

"I didn't say a word."

"You thought it. And the answer is no."

"You're a cold woman."

"I'm an intelligent woman. I'm not about to sleep my way to the top."

"There's a lot to be said for being at the top."

"I guess you would know."

He leaned back in his chair, expression turning mischievous. "Yeah. I guess I would."

She ignored the little-boy charm and leaned forward to prop her elbows on his desk. "Okay, let's talk about how this works."

"I thought we'd pretty much demonstrated how it worked last month."

She wished he'd stop flirting. It was ridiculously tempting to engage. Their verbal foreplay that night had been almost as exciting as the physical stuff.

"Nobody here knows about us," she began, keeping her tone even.

"I know about us," he pointed out.

"But you're going to forget it."

"Not likely," he scoffed.

She leaned farther forward, getting up into his face. "Listen carefully, Hunter. For the purposes of our professional relationship, you are going to forget that you've seen me naked."

"You know, you're very cute when you're angry."

"That's the lamest line I've ever heard."

"No, it's not."

"Can you be serious for a second?"

"What makes you think I'm not serious?"

"Hunter."

"Lighten up, Sinclair."

Lighten up? That was his answer?

But she drew back to think about it. Could it be that simple? "Am I making too much of this?"

He shrugged. "I'm not about to announce anything in the company newsletter. So, unless you spread the word around the water cooler, I think we're good."

She eyed him up. "That's it? Business as usual?"

"Gramps may have bought Lush Beauty Products for his own bizarre reasons. But I'm here to run it, nothing more, nothing less. And you have a job to do."

She came to her feet and gave a sharp nod, telling herself she was relieved, not disappointed, that it would be easy for him to ignore their past.

"See you around the water cooler, I guess," she said in parting.

"Sure," Hunter responded. "Whatever."

Despite the casual goodbye, Hunter knew it would be hell trying to dismiss what they'd shared. As the office door closed behind her, he squeezed his eyes shut and raked a hand through his hair. Their past might have been short, but it was about as memorable as a past could get.

For the thousandth time, he saw Sinclair in the Manchester mansion. She was curled in a leather armchair, beneath the Christmas tree, next to the crackling fireplace. He remembered thinking in that moment that she was about as beautiful as a woman could get. He'd always had a thing for redheads.

When he was sixteen years old, some insane old gypsy had predicted he'd marry a redhead. Hunter wasn't sure if it was the power of suggestion or a lucky guess, but redheads were definitely his dates of choice.

The flames from the fire had reflected around Sinclair, highlighting her rosy cheeks and her bright blue eyes. Her shoulder-length hair flowed in soft waves, teasing and tantalizing him. He'd already discovered she was smart and classy, with a sharp wit that made him want to spar with her for hours on end.

So he'd bided his time. Waiting for the rest of the family to head for bed, hoping against hope that she'd stay up late.

She had.

And then they were alone. And he had been about to make a move. She was his cousin's new sister-in-law, and he knew their paths might cross again at some point. But he couldn't bring himself to worry about the future. There was something intense brewing, and he owed it to both of them to find out what it was.

He came to his feet, watching her closely as he crossed the great room. Her blue eyes went from laughing sapphires to an intense ocean storm and, before he even reached her chair, he knew she was with him.

He stopped in front of her, bracing a hand on either arm of the chair, leaning over to trap her in place. She didn't flinch but watched him with open interest.

He liked that.

Hell, he loved that.

"Hey," he rasped, a wealth of meaning in his tone and posture.

"Hey," she responded, voice husky, pupils dilated.

He touched his index finger to her chin, tipping it up ever so slightly.

She didn't pull away, so he bent his head, forcing himself to go slow, giving her plenty of time to shut him down. He could smell her skin, feel the heat of her breath, taste the sweet explosion of her lips under his.

His free hand curled to a fist as he steeled himself to keep the kiss gentle. He fought an almost overwhelming urge to open wide, to meet her tongue, to let the passion roar to life between them.

Instead, he drew back, though he was almost shaking with the effort.

"Stop?" he rasped, needing a definite answer, and needing it *right now.*

"Go," she replied, and his world pitched sideways.

With a groan of surrender, he dropped to one knee, clamping a hand behind her neck, firmly pulling her forward for a real kiss.

There was no hesitation this time. Their tongues met in a clash. She shifted in the chair to mold against him, her breasts plastered against his chest while desire raced like wildfire along his limbs.

Her hair was soft, her breath softer, and her body was pure heaven in his arms.

"I want you," he'd muttered.

"No kidding," she came back.

His chuckle rumbled against her lips. "Sassy."

"You know it," she whispered in the instant before he kissed her all over again.

The kiss went harder and deeper, until he finally had to gasp for air. "Can I take that as a yes?"

"Can I take that as an offer?" she countered.

"You can take it as a promise," he said, and scooped her into his arms.

She placed her hands on his shoulders and burrowed into the crook at his neck. Then her teeth came down gently on his earlobe. Lust shot through him, and he cursed the fact that his bedroom was in a far corner on the third floor.

A knock on his office door snapped him back to reality.

"Yeah?" he barked.

The door cracked open.

It was Sinclair again.

She slipped inside, still stunningly beautiful in that sleek ivory skirt and the matching blazer. Her pale-pink tank top molded to her breasts, and her shapely legs made him long to trail his fingertips up past her hemline.

"Since it's business as usual," she began, perkily, crossing the room, oblivious to his state of discomfort.

"Right," he agreed from between clenched teeth.

"I have something I'd like to discuss with you."

At the moment, he had something he wished he could discuss with her, too.

"Fire way," he said instead.

She took up the guest chair again and crossed her legs. Her makeup was minimal, but she didn't need it. She had a healthy peaches-and-cream glow, accented by the brightest blue eyes he'd ever seen. Sunlight from the floor-to-ceiling bay window sparkled on her hair. It reminded him of the firelight, and he curled his hands into new fists.

"I have this idea."

He ordered himself to leave that opening alone.

"Roger's been reluctant to support it," she continued.

She wanted Hunter to intervene?

Sure. Easy. No problem.

"Let's hear it," he said.

"It's about the ball."

Hunter had just read about the Lush Beauty Products' Valentine's Ball. They were going to use it to launch the Luscious Lavender line. It was a decent idea as publicity went. Women loved Valentine's Day, and the Luscious Lavender line was all about glamming up and looking your best.

"Shoot," he told her.

"I've taken the lead in planning the ball," she explained, wriggling forward, drawing his attention to the pale tank top. "And I've been thinking we should go with something bigger."

"A bigger ball?" He dragged his attention back to her face. They'd rented the ballroom at the Roosevelt Hotel. It didn't get much bigger than that.

Sinclair shook her head. "Not a bigger ball. A bigger product launch. Something more than a ball. The ball is fine.

It's great. But it's not…" Her lips compressed and her eyes squinted down. "Enough."

"Tell me what you had in mind," he prompted, curious about how she conducted business. He'd been struck by her intelligence in Manchester. It would be interesting to deal with her in a new forum.

"What I was thinking…" She paused as if gathering her thoughts. "Is to launch Luscious Lavender at a luxury spa. In addition to the ball." Her voice sped up with her enthusiasm. "We're going after the high-end market. And where do rich women get their hair done? Where do they get their facials? Their body wraps? Their waxing?"

"At the spa?" asked Hunter, trying very, very hard not to think about Sinclair and waxing.

She sat back, pointed a finger in his direction, a flush of excitement on her face. "Exactly."

"That's not bad," he admitted. It was a very good idea. He liked that it was unique, and it would probably prove effective. "What's Roger's objection?"

"He didn't tell me his objection. He just said no."

"Really?" Hunter didn't care for autocracy and secrecy as managerial styles. "What would you like me to do?"

Whatever it was, he'd do it in a heartbeat. And not because of their history. He'd do it because it was a good idea, and he appreciated her intelligence and creativity. Roger better have a damn good reason for turning her down.

"If you can clear it with Roger—"

"Oh, I can clear it with Roger."

Her teeth came down on her bottom lip, and a hesitation flashed through her eyes. "You agreed awfully fast."

"I'm agile and decisive. Got a problem with that?"

"As long as…" Guilt flashed in her eyes.

"I'm reacting to your idea, Sinclair. Not to your body."

"You sure?"

"Of course, I'm sure." He was. Definitely.

"I was going to approach New York Millennium." She named a popular spa in the heart of Manhattan.

"That sounds like a good bet. You need anything else?"

She shook her head, rising to her feet. "Roger was my only roadblock."

Two

"Obviously," Roger said to Sinclair, with exaggerated patience. "I can't turn down the CEO."

She nodded where she sat in a guest chair in his office, squelching the lingering guilt that she might have used her relationship with Hunter as leverage. She admitted she'd been counting on Roger having to say yes to Hunter.

But she consoled herself in being absolutely positive the spa launch was a worthwhile idea. Also, Roger had been strangely contrary lately, shooting down her recommendations left and right. It was all but impossible to do her job the way he'd been micromanaging her. Going to Hunter had been her option of last resort.

Besides, Hunter had invited all the employees to run ideas past him. She wasn't taking any special privilege.

"I'm not holding out a lot of hope of you securing the Millennium," warned Roger.

Sinclair was more optimistic. "It would be good for them, too. They'd have the advantage of all our advance publicity."

Roger came to his feet. "I'd like you to take Chantal with you."

Sinclair blinked as she stood. "What?"

"I'd appreciate her perspective."

"On…" Sinclair searched for the logic in the request.

Chantal was a junior marketing assistant. In her two years with the company, she'd mostly been involved in administrative work such as ad placement and monitoring the free-sample program.

"She has a good eye," said Roger, walking Sinclair toward the door.

A good eye for what?

"And I'd like her to broaden her experience," he finished.

It was on the tip of Sinclair's tongue to argue, but she had her yes, so it was time for a strategic retreat. She'd figure out the Chantal angle on her own.

Her first thought was that Roger might be grooming the woman for a public relations position. Sinclair had been lobbying to get an additional PR officer in her department for months now, but she had her own assistant, Amber, in mind for the promotion, and Keely in reception in mind for Amber's job.

"Keep me informed," insisted Roger.

"Sure," said Sinclair, leaving his office to cross the executive lobby. First she'd set up a meeting at the Millennium, then she'd sleuth around about Chantal.

Three days later, Sinclair lost the Millennium Spa as a possibility. The President liked Lush's new samples, but he claimed using them over the launch weekend would put him in a conflict with his regular beauty products supplier.

She'd been hoping the spa would switch to Luscious

Lavender items on a permanent basis following the launch. But when she mentioned that to the spa President, he laughed and all but patted her on the head over her naiveté. Supply contracts, he told her, didn't work that way.

Chantal had shot Sinclair a smug look and joined in the laughter, earning a benevolent smile from the man along with Sinclair's irritation.

Then the next day, at a pre-Valentine's event at Bergdorf's on Fifth Avenue, Chantal earned Sinclair's irritation all over again.

It was twelve days before Valentine's Day and the main ball and product launch. Sinclair had worked for months preparing for both events.

For Bergdorf's, she'd secured special space in the cosmetics department, hired top-line professional beauticians, and had placed ads in *Cosmopolitan, Elle* and *Glamour.* She'd even talked Roger into an electronic billboard in Times Square promoting the event. Her spa plan might have fallen flat, but she knew if they could get the right clientele into Bergdorf's today for free samples and makeovers, word of mouth would begin to spread in advance of the ball.

The event should have come off without a hitch.

But at the last minute Roger had inserted Chantal into the mix, displacing one of the beauticians and making the lineups unnecessarily long. Amber, who had already heard about Chantal's appearance at the spa meeting, was obviously upset by this latest turn of events. Sinclair didn't need her loyal employee feeling uncertain about her future.

The result had been a long day. And as the clock wound toward closing time, Sinclair was losing energy. She did her hourly inventory of the seven makeover stations, noting any dwindling supplies on her clipboard. Then she handed the list to Amber, who had the key to the stockroom and was in charge of replenishing.

She reminded the caterers to do another pass along the lineup, offering complimentary champagne and canapés to those customers who were still waiting. The cash register lineup concerned her, so she called the store manager on her cell, asking about opening another till.

The mirrors on stations three and six needed a polish, so she signaled a cleaner. In the meantime, she learned they were almost out of number five brushes and made a quick call to Amber in the back.

"How's it going?" Hunter's voice rumbled from behind her.

She couldn't help but smile at the sound, even as she reflexively tamped down a little rush of pleasure. They hadn't spoken in a few days and, whether she wanted to or not, she'd missed him. She twisted to face him, meeting his eyes and feeling her energy return.

"Controlled chaos," she mouthed.

"At least it's controlled." He moved in beside her.

"How are things up on the executive floor?" she asked.

"Interesting. Ethan gave me a tour of the factory." Hunter made a show of sniffing the back of his hand. "I think I still smell like a girl."

"Lavender's a lovely scent," said Sinclair, wrinkling her nose in his direction. She didn't detect lavender, just Hunter, and it was strangely familiar.

"I prefer spice or musk."

"Is your masculinity at stake?"

"I may have to pump some iron later just to even things up."

"Are you a body builder?"

Even under a suit, Hunter was clearly fit.

"A few free weights," he answered. "You?"

"Uh, no. I'm more of a yoga girl."

"Yoga's good."

"Keeps me limber."

"Okay, not touching that one."

"You're incorrigible."

"My grandfather would agree with you on that point."

A new cashier arrived, opening up the other till, and the lineup split into two. Sinclair breathed a sigh of relief. One problem handled.

Then she heard Chantal's laughter above the din and glanced at the tall blonde, who wore a cotton-candy-pink poof-skirted minidress and a pair of four-inch gold heels. She was laughing with some of the customers, her bright lips and impossibly thick eyelashes giving her the air of a glamorous movie star.

With Hunter here, Sinclair felt an unexpected pang of self-consciousness at the contrast between her and Chantal. Quickly, though, she reminded herself that her two-piece taupe suit and matching pumps were appropriate and professional. She also reminded herself that she'd never aspired to be a squealing, air-kissing bombshell.

She tucked her straight, sensibly cut hair behind her ears.

"So what happened at the spa?" asked Hunter.

"Unfortunately, it was a no go."

"Really?" He frowned with concern. "What was the problem?"

"Some kind of conflict with their supplier."

"Did you—"

"Sorry. Can you hang on?" she asked him, noticing a disagreement brewing between the new cashier and a customer. She quickly left Hunter and moved to step in.

It turned out the customer had been quoted a wrong price

by her beautician. Sinclair quickly honored the quote and threw in an extra tube of lipstick.

When she looked back, Chantal had crossed the floor. She was laughing with Hunter, a long-fingered, sparkly-tipped hand lightly touching his shoulder for emphasis about something.

He didn't seem the least bit disturbed by the touch, and an unwelcome spike of annoyance hit Sinclair. It wasn't jealousy, she quickly assured herself. It was the fact that Chantal was ignoring the customers to flirt with the CEO.

Sinclair made her way along the counter.

"Chantal," she greeted, putting a note of censure in her voice and her expression.

"I was just talking to Hunter about the new mousse," Chantal trilled. Then she fluffed her hair. "It works miracles."

Sinclair compressed her lips.

In response, Chantal's gaze took in Sinclair's plain hairstyle. "You should…" She frowned. "Uh…have you *tried* it?"

Hunter inclined his head toward Sinclair. He seemed to be waiting for her answer.

"No," Sinclair admitted. She hadn't tried the new mousse. Like she had time for the Luscious Lavender treatment every morning. She started work at seven-thirty after a streamlined regime that rarely included a hairdryer.

"Oh." Chantal pouted prettily.

Sinclair nodded to a pair of customers lingering around Chantal's sample station. "I believe those two ladies need some help."

Chantal giggled and moved away.

"Nice," said Hunter after she left.

"That better have been sarcasm."

All men considered Chantal beautiful, but Sinclair would

have been disappointed in Hunter if he hadn't been able to see past her looks.

"Of course it was sarcasm." But his eyes lingered on the woman.

Sinclair elbowed him in the ribs.

"What?"

"I can tell what you're thinking."

"No, you can't."

"Yes, I can."

"What am I thinking?"

"That her breasts are large, her skirt is short, and her legs go all the way to the ground."

Hunter coughed out a laugh.

"See?" blurted Sinclair in triumph.

"You're out of your mind."

"The doors are closing," murmured Sinclair, more to herself than to Hunter, as she noticed the security guards stop incoming customers and open the doors for those who were exiting.

"You got a few minutes to talk?" he asked.

"Sure." Hunter was the CEO. She was ready to talk business at his convenience.

She nodded to two empty chairs across the room.

They moved to the quiet corner of the department, and Sinclair climbed into one of the high leather swivel chairs. She parked her clipboard on the glass counter.

Hunter eased up beside her. "So what's the plan now?"

She glanced around the big room. "The cleaning staff will be here at six. Amber will make sure the leftover samples are returned to the warehouse. And I'll write a report in the morning." Later tonight, she was going to start painting her new apartment, but she didn't think Hunter needed that kind of information.

His gray eyes sparkled with merriment. "I meant your plan about the spa."

"Oh, that." She waved a hand. "It's dead. We couldn't make a deal with the Millennium."

Her gaze unexpectedly caught Chantal. The woman was eyeing them up from across the room, tossing her glittering mane over one shoulder and licking her red lips.

Under the guise of more easily conversing, Sinclair scooted a little closer to Hunter. Let miss Barbie-doll chew on that.

Hunter slanted a look toward Chantal, then shot Sinclair a knowing grin.

"Shut up," she warned in an undertone.

"I never said a word."

"You were thinking it."

"Yeah. And I was right, too."

Yeah, he was. "It's something Pavlovian," she offered.

His grin widened.

"I didn't want her to think Luscious Lavender mousse trumps brains, that's all."

"It doesn't."

"I don't even use mousse. It's nothing against Luscious Lavender. It's a personal choice."

"Okay," said Hunter.

"Kristy has always been the glitter and glam twin. I'm—"

"Don't you dare say plain Jane."

"I was going to say professional Jane."

He snorted. "You don't need a label. And you shouldn't use Kristy as a frame of reference."

"What? You don't compare yourself to Jack?"

"I don't." But his expression revealed a sense of discomfort.

"What?" she prompted.

"Gramps does."

Sinclair could well imagine. "And who comes out on top?"

Hunter raised an eyebrow. "Who do you think?"

"I don't know," she replied honestly. Jack seemed like a great guy. But then so did Hunter. They were both smart, handsome, capable and hard-working.

"Jack's dependable," said Hunter. "He's patient and methodical. He doesn't make mistakes."

Sinclair found herself leaning even closer, the noise of the store dimming around them as the last of the customers made their way out the door. "And you are?"

"Reckless and impulsive."

"Why do I hear Cleveland's voice when you say that?"

Hunter chuckled. "It's usually accompanied by a cuff upside the head."

In the silence that followed, Sinclair resisted an urge to take his hand. "That's sad," she told him.

"That's Gramps. He's a hard-ass from way back." Then Hunter did a double take of her staring. "Don't look at me like that."

She swallowed. "I'm sorry."

"It makes me want to kiss you," he muttered.

"Don't you—"

"I'm not going to kiss you." He glanced back to Chantal. "*That* would definitely make the company newsletter." He focused on Sinclair again. "But you can't stop me from wanting to."

And she couldn't stop herself from wanting to kiss him back. And it didn't seem to matter what she did to try and get rid of the urge, it just grew worse.

"What can we do about this?" She was honestly looking for help. If the feelings didn't disappear, they were going to trip up sooner or later.

Hunter rose to his feet.

"For now, I'm walking out the door. Chantal is already wondering what we're talking about."

Sinclair shook herself and rose with him. "Check." If they weren't together, they couldn't give in to anything.

"But later, I need to talk to you."

She opened her mouth to protest. Later didn't sound like a smart move to her at all.

"About the spa," he clarified. "Business. I promise. What are you doing tonight?"

"Painting my apartment."

"Really?" He drew back. "That's what you do on Saturday night?"

Yeah, that was what she did on Saturday night. She rattled on, trying not to seem pathetic. "I just bought the place. A great little loft in Soho. But the colors are dark and the floor needs stripping, and the mortgage is so high I can't afford to pay someone to do it for me."

"You want a raise?"

"I want a guy with sandpaper and a paint roller."

"You got it."

"Hunter—"

"Give me your address. We can talk while we paint."

Her and Hunter alone in her apartment? "I don't think—"

"I'll be wearing a smock and a paper cap. Trust me, you'll be able to keep your hands off."

"Nothing wrong with your ego."

He grunted. "I know you can't resist me under normal circumstances."

"Ha!" The gauntlet thrown down, she'd resist him or die trying.

Now that she thought about it, maybe painting together

wasn't such a bad idea. Hunter's family had bought the company. He was a permanent part of Lush Beauty Products, and the sooner they got over this inconvenient hump, the better. In fact, it was probably easier if they smoothed out the rough spots away from Chantal's and other people's prying eyes.

"Seventy-seven Mercy Street," she told him with a nod. "Suite 702."

"I'll be there."

On his way to Sinclair's house, Hunter stopped in at the office. He was pretty sure Ethan Sloan would still be around. By all accounts, Ethan was a workaholic and a genius. He'd been with Lush Beauty Products for fifteen years, practically since the doors opened with a staff of twenty and a single store.

He had developed perfumes, hair products, skin products and makeup. The man had a knack for anticipating trends, moving from floral to fruit to organic. In his late thirties now, he'd wisely set his sights on fine quality, recognizing a growing segment of the population with a high disposable income and a penchant for self-indulgence.

Hunter was also willing to bet Ethan had a knack for management and the underlying politics of the company. And Hunter had some questions about that.

He found Ethan in his office, on the phone, but the man quickly motioned to Hunter to sit down.

"By Thursday?" Ethan was saying as Hunter took a seat and slipped open the button on his suit jacket.

Ethan was neatly trimmed. Hunter had noticed that he generally wore his shirtsleeves rolled up, although he'd wear a jacket on the executive floor. Smart man.

"Great," said Ethan, nodding. "Sign 'em up. Talk to you then."

He hung up the phone. "New supplier for lavender," he explained to Hunter. "Out of British Columbia."

"We're running short?"

"Critically. And it's our key ingredient." He rubbed his hands together. "But it's solved now. What can I do for you?"

Hunter settled back in his chair. "Not to put you on the spot. And way off the record."

Ethan smiled. He brought his palms down on the desktop, standing to walk around its end and close the office door. "Gotta say." He returned, taking the second guest chair instead of sitting behind his desk. "I love conversations that start out like this."

Hunter smiled in return. "Tell me if I'm out of line."

"We're off the record," said Ethan. "You can get out of line."

"What do you think of Chantal Charbonnet?"

Ethan sat back. "Sly, but not brilliant. Gorgeous, of course. Roger seems to have noticed her."

"She was at the Bergdorf's promotion this afternoon."

"Yeah?" asked Ethan. "That's a stretch for her job description."

"It got me wondering," confided Hunter. "Why was she there?"

"Eye candy?"

"Women were the target demographic." Hunter had been thinking about this all the way over.

"Maybe she asked Roger really, really nicely?"

Hunter had considered that, too. But he didn't have evidence to support favoritism. He was coming at this from another angle. "Could she have been a role model for the consumers?"

Ethan considered the idea. "There's no denying she knows how to wear our products."

"Lays it on a bit thick, wouldn't you say?"

Ethan grinned. "My kind of consumer. We want them all to apply it like Chantal."

Ethan's words validated the worry that was niggling at Hunter's brain. Chantal was dead center on the new target demographic. Hunter was worried that Roger had seen that in her, and it wasn't something he'd seen in Sinclair. Sinclair was a lot of things—a lot of very fabulous, fun, exciting things—but she wasn't a poster child for Lush Beauty Products.

He filed away the information and switched gears. "Did Sinclair mention her spa plan to you?"

Ethan nodded. "Had lots of potential. But I hear it went south with Millennium."

"I'm going to try to revive it."

"I hope you can. If you secure the outlet, we can provide the product."

"Including lavender."

"Got it covered."

"Do you have any thoughts on a spa release overall?"

Ethan stretched out his legs, obviously speculating how frank he could be with Hunter.

Hunter waited. He wanted frank, but there was no way to insist on it.

"If it was me," said Ethan. "I wouldn't target a single spa, I'd go for the whole chain. And I'd try for the Crystal. The Millennium is nice, but the Crystal has the best overseas locations."

Hunter didn't disagree with Ethan's assessment. The Crystal Spa chain was as top of the line as they came.

"You get into Rome and Paris," said Ethan. "At that level. You'll really have some momentum."

"Tall order."

Ethan brought his hands down on his thighs. "Osland International usually shy away from a challenge?"

"Nope," said Hunter. When he was involved, Osland International always stepped up to the plate.

He could already feel his competitive instincts kick in. Although he'd come into the job reluctantly, making Lush Beauty a runaway success had inched its way to the top of his priority list.

He also knew he wanted Sinclair as a partner in this. He liked the way she thought. He liked her energy and her outside-the-box thinking. And, well, okay, and he just plain liked her. But there was nothing wrong with that. Liking your business associates was important.

All his best business relationships were based on mutual respect. Sure, maybe he didn't want to sleep with his other business associates. But the principle was the same.

Sinclair hit the buzzer, letting Hunter into the building.

She didn't know whether she'd been brilliant or stupid to take him up on his offer to paint, but there was no turning back now.

She'd dressed in a pair of old torn blue jeans and a grainy gray T-shirt with "Stolen From the New York City Police Department" emblazoned across the front. Her hair was braided tight against her head, and she'd popped a white painter's cap on her head. She had no worries that the tone of the evening would be sexy in any way.

The bell rang, echoing through the high-ceilinged, empty room. Her living room furniture was in storage for another week. But she'd already finished the small bedroom, so it was back together.

She opened the front door and the hinges groaned loudly in the cavernous space as Hunter walked in.

"Nice," he said, looking around at the tarp-draped counters and breakfast bar, the plastic on the floors, and the dangling pieces of masking tape around the bay window.

"It has a lot of potential," she told him, closing and locking the oak door. There was no doubt it was smaller than he'd be used to, but she was excited about living here.

"I wasn't being sarcastic, honest." He held up a bottle of wine. "Housewarming."

"That might be a bit premature." She still had a lot of work to get done.

He glanced around the room for somewhere to set the bottle down. "In a cupboard?" he asked, heading for the alcove kitchen.

"Beside the fridge," she called.

He got rid of the wine and shrugged out of his windbreaker. Then he returned to the main room in a pair of khakis and a white T-shirt that were obviously brand-new.

She tried not to smile at the outfit.

It really was nice of him to come and help. Still, she wasn't about to pass up an opportunity to tease him.

"You don't do home maintenance often, do you?"

He glanced around the tarp-draped room. "I've seen it done on TV."

"It's not as easy as it looks," she warned.

He shot her an expression of mock disbelief. "I have an MBA from Harvard."

"And they covered house painting in graduate school?"

"They covered macroeconomics and global capitalism."

She fought a grin. "Oh sure, go ahead and get snooty on me."

"Dip the brush and stroke it on the wall. Am I close?"

"I guess you might as well give it a try."

"Give it a *try?*"

Her grin broadened at his insulted tone.

He bent over and pried open a paint can. "You might want to shift your attitude. I'm free labor, baby."

"Am I getting what I paid for?"

"Sassy," he said, and her heart tripped a beat.

"You need to shake it," she told him, battling the sensual memory. He'd called her sassy in Manchester. In a way that said he wanted her bad.

"Shake it?" he interrupted her thoughts.

She swallowed. "You need to shake the paint before you open the can."

He raised his brow as he crouched to tap the lid back down. "You're enjoying this, aren't you?"

"You bet. Nothing like keeping the billionaire humble."

"Don't stereotype. I'm always humble."

"Yeah. I noticed that right off, Mr. Macroeconomics and Global Capitalism."

"Well, what did you take in college?"

She hesitated for a second then admitted it. "MBA. Yale."

"So, *you* took macroeconomics and global capitalism?"

"Magna cum laude," she said with a hoity toss of her head.

"Yet you can still paint. Imagine that."

She glanced at him for a moment, trying to figure out why he hadn't escalated the joke by teasing her about the designation. Then it hit her. "You got summa, at least, didn't you?"

He didn't answer.

"Geek," she said.

He grinned as he shook the paint. Then he poured it into the tray.

She broke out the brushes, and he quickly caught on to

using the long-handled roller. Sinclair cut in the corners, and together they worked their way down the longest wall.

"What do you think of the Crystal Spa chain?" he asked as his roller swished up and down in long strokes.

"I've never been there," said Sinclair from the top of the step ladder. This close to the ceiling lights, she was starting to sweat. She finally gave in and peeled off her cap.

Wisps of strands had come loose from her braid. Probably she'd end up with cream-colored specks in her hair. Whatever. They were painting her walls, not dancing in a ballroom.

"You want to try it?"

She paused at the end of her stroke, glancing down at him. Was he talking about the Crystal Spa? "Try what?"

"I was thinking, we shouldn't let the Millennium's refusal stop us. We should consider other spas."

Was he serious? More importantly, why hadn't she thought of that?

She felt a shimmer of excitement. Maybe her spa idea wasn't dead, after all. And the New York-based Crystal Spa chain would be an even better choice than the Millennium.

She'd learned from the Millennium experience. She'd make sure she was even better prepared for a pitch to the Crystal.

"Can I try out the Crystal on my expense account?" she asked with a teasing lilt.

"Of course."

Scoffing her dismissal, she went back to painting. "Like Roger would ever go for that."

Besides, she didn't have to test out the Crystal Spa to know it was fantastic. Everyone always raved.

"Forget Roger, will you?" urged Hunter. "Here."

She glanced back down.

With the roller hooked under one arm, he pulled out his wallet. Then he tossed a credit card onto her tarp-covered breakfast bar. "Consider this your expense account."

She nearly fell off the ladder. "You can't—"

"I just did."

"But—"

"Shut up." He went back to the paint tray. "I know the spa idea's great. You know the spa idea's great. Let's streamline the research and make it happen."

"You can't pay for my spa treatments."

"Osland International can pay for them. It's my corporate card, and I consider it a perfectly legitimate R & D expense."

Sinclair didn't know what to say to that. Trying out the spa would be great research, but still…

He rolled the next section. "It's not like I can go in there and check out the wax room myself."

She cringed, involuntarily flinching. "Wax room?"

He chuckled at her expression. "Buck up, Sinclair. Take one for the team."

"You take one for the team."

"I've done my part. It's my credit card."

"They're my legs."

"Who said anything about legs?"

She stared at him. He didn't. He wouldn't.

"We were this close!" She made a tiny space with her thumb and index finger. "*This* close to having a totally professional conversation."

"I'm weak," he admitted.

"You're hopeless."

"Yeah. Well. Irrespective of what you get waxed, and whether or not you show me, it's still a good idea."

It was a good idea. And her gaze strayed to his platinum

card sitting on the canvas tarp. Even if he couldn't keep his mind on business, this was not an opportunity she was about to give up. "I'm thinking a facial."

"Whatever you want. I need to know if they can deliver the kind of opportunity we're looking for."

"What if they're locked into a supplier contract like the Millennium?"

Hunter shrugged. "Every business is different. We'll deal with that when and if it happens. Tomorrow good for you?"

She nodded.

With only twelve days until Valentine's Day. There was no time to lose.

Three

The next day, lying on her back in uptown Manhattan's Crystal Spa, a loose silky robe covering her naked body, Sinclair was feeling very relaxed after her facial massage. A smooth, cool mask was drying on her face. Damp pads protected her eyes, and she found herself nearly falling asleep.

"Sinclair?"

She was dreaming of Hunter's voice. That was fine. Dreaming never hurt anybody.

"Sinclair?" the voice came again.

No.

No way.

Hunter was *not* in this room.

Warm hands closed up the wide V of her robe. "No sense playing with fire," he said.

"What are you doing here?"

"I need permission to cancel your appointments for this afternoon."

She tried to form words, but they jumbled in her brain and turned into incomprehensive sputters.

"We need to fly to L.A.," Hunter told her matter-of-factly.

"This is a dream, right? You're not really here."

"Oh, I'm really here. But, hold on, are you saying you dream about me?"

"Nightmares. Trust me."

He chuckled. "The only appointment I could get with the president of Crystal Spas was in their head office in L.A. at three today. We have to get going."

She blinked. Why did they need to talk to the president?

"I want to pitch the idea of debuting the whole chain."

Sinclair gave her head a little shake. "Seriously?"

"Yes, seriously."

They were going to debut Luscious Lavender in the entire Crystal chain? That would be a phenomenal feat.

"I could kiss you," she breathed.

"Bad idea. For the obvious reasons." Then he looked her up and down. "Plus, you're kind of...goopy."

She just grinned.

"It's not a done deal yet," he warned.

"But we are going to try."

"We are going to try. Can I cancel your appointments?"

"You got a cell phone?"

He pulled it out of his suit pocket.

She dialed Amber's number.

The whole chain. She could barely believe it. The whole damn chain.

* * *

Hunter was sorry now that he'd even told Sinclair about Crystal Spas. The meeting hadn't gone well, and she was clearly disappointed as she climbed into the jet for the return trip to New York.

"We knew it was a long shot," she said bravely, buckling up across from him.

"I'm sorry."

"It's not your fault. Some people can't make quick decisions."

The whole thing had frustrated the hell out of Hunter.

"At his level, the man had better learn to make quick decisions. He had a chance to get in on the ground floor in this."

"His loss," said Sinclair with conviction.

"They're superior products," replied Hunter.

"Of *course* they're superior products," she agreed.

Hunter did up his own seat belt. "We say emphatically as two people who've never tried them."

She smiled at his joke.

"We should try them," he said.

"I'm not trying the wax."

He chuckled. "I'll try the wax."

"Yeah, right."

"Right here." He pointed to his chest. "I'll be a man about it. You can rip my hair out by the roots if I can massage your neck with the lavender oil."

She stared into his eyes as the jet engines whined to life. "You don't think we'd end up naked within five minutes?"

"I don't think your ripping the hair from my chest would make me want to get naked."

She obviously fought a grin. "Waxing your chest is probably the worst idea I've ever heard."

"But it cheered you up."

She sighed, and some of the humor went out of her eyes. "Crystal Spas would have been perfect."

He reached for her hand. "I know."

The jet jerked to rolling, and he experienced a strong sense of déjà vu. It took him a second to realize it was Kristy, Kristy and Jack on this same airplane. During their emergency landing in Vegas, Jack had held Kristy's hand to comfort her.

Right now, Sinclair's hand felt small in Hunter's, soft and smooth. The kind of hand a man wanted all over his body.

"You want to go see your sister?" he asked.

Sinclair looked startled. "What?"

"She's in Manchester. It's on the way."

"We'd be too late."

She had a point.

"Maybe not," he argued. A visit with Kristy might cheer Sinclair up.

"Thanks for the thought."

Hunter wished he had more to offer than just a thought. But then she smiled her gratitude. Hunter realized that was what mattered.

Business deals would come and go. He'd simply find another way to make Sinclair happy. Even as the thought formed in his mind, he realized it was dangerous. But he ignored the warning flash.

"You don't need to worry about me," she told him. "I'm a big girl. And I still have the ball to plan."

"The ball's going to be fantastic," he enthused. "It'll be the best Valentine's ball anybody ever put on anywhere."

"I hate it when people humor me."

"Then why are you still smiling?"

"Because sometimes you can be very sweet."

"Hold that thought," he teased, and he brought her hand to his lips.

"I'm not going to sleep with you." She retrieved her hand, but the smile grew wider. "But, maybe, if you're very, very good, I might dance with you at the Valentine's ball."

"And maybe if you're very, very good, I might bring you flowers and candy."

"Something to look forward to."

"Isn't it?"

They both stopped talking, and a soft silence settled around the hum of the engines as they taxied toward the runway.

"It's just that we've worked day and night on this product launch," she said, half to herself.

"I can imagine," he responded with a nod.

"All of us," she added. "The Luscious Lavender products are strong. The sales force is ready. And marketing showed me a fantastic television commercial last week. I really want to make sure I do my part."

"You are doing your part." He had no doubt of that. "There's still the ball."

She gave a shrug and tucked her hair behind her ears. "The ball's pretty much ready to go. I know it'll be fine. But I wanted that something extra, that something special from the PR department." Then she sighed. "Maybe it's just ego."

"Contributing to the team is not ego. Taking all the glory is ego."

"Wanting recognition is a form of ego," she countered.

"Wanting recognition for a job well done is human."

Her voice went soft. "Then I guess I don't want to be human."

He watched her for a silent minute, trying to gauge how

deep that admission went. For all her bravado, he sensed an underlying insecurity. What Sinclair presented and who she really was were two different things. She was far more sensitive than she showed.

In the privacy and intimacy of the plane, he voiced a question that had been nagging at him for a while. "Why did you sleep with me?"

She startled and retrieved her hand. Then her shell went back into place. "Why did *you* sleep with me?"

"Because you were funny and smart and beautiful," he said. Then he waited.

"And, because I said yes?" she asked.

He didn't respond to her irreverence. "And because when I held you in my arms, it was where you belonged."

She stayed silent, and he could almost see the war going on inside her head.

"You going to tell me?" he asked.

"It was Christmas," she finally began. "And you were fun, and sexy. And Kristy had just married Jack. And life at your amazing mansion is really very surreal."

She'd buried the truth. He was sure of it.

Kristy had married Jack, and for that brief moment in time, Sinclair had felt abandoned. And there had been Hunter. And she'd clung to him. And that's what it was. He was glad he knew.

Even though he shouldn't, he switched seats so he was beside her. He wanted to be the one she clung to.

She stiffened, watching him warily.

"The steward's only a few feet away," he assured her. "Nothing can happen."

His reassurance seemed to work.

She relaxed, and he took her hand once again.

The cabin lights dimmed, the engines wound out, and the plane accelerated along the runway, pushing them back against their seats. Hunter turned his head to watch her profile, rubbed his thumb against her soft palm and inhaled her perfume, as he captured and held a moment in time.

The next morning, for the first time in her life, Sinclair came late to the office.

Amber jumped up from her desk, looking worried. "What happened?"

"I got home really late," she said as she passed by.

"Roger was down here. He wanted your files on the Valentine's ball."

Sinclair crossed the threshold to her office, dropping her briefcase and purse on her credenza, and picked up a stack of mail on the way to her desk. "Why?"

"So *Chantal* could review them."

"What?" She stared at Amber. "Why would she do that?"

"Because she's queen of the freakin' universe? Is there something I should know, Sinclair? Something pertaining to PR?"

"No." Sinclair set down the mail. "There's nothing for you to worry about." She moved to the door. "Wait here."

"I'm not going anywhere."

"I assume you gave him the files?" Sinclair called over her shoulder.

"I didn't have a choice."

No. She didn't.

When the president asked for the files, you gave up the files. But there was nothing saying you didn't go get them back again. Roger's micromanaging was getting out of hand. So was Chantal's apparent carte blanche in the PR department. Sinclair took a tight breath, pressed the button, and waited as the elevator ascended.

This inserting of Chantal into Sinclair's projects had to stop. You didn't add a new voice ten days before the ball. And you sure didn't empower a neophyte like Chantal on a project of this size and importance.

What was the matter with Roger? Was he trying to sabotage Sinclair's efforts?

Maybe it was due to her frustration over the failure of the spa plan, but Sinclair was feeling exceedingly protective of the ball. It was her one chance for the PR department to shine, and she was determined to do it or die trying.

The doors slid open on twenty, revealing burgundy carpet, soft lighting and cherrywood paneling. Myra, Roger's secretary, looked surprised to see her.

"Did you have an appointment?"

"I need two minutes with Roger."

Myra glanced at Roger's door. "I'm afraid he's—"

The office door opened.

Chantal Charbonnet stepped out, a stack of files tucked under her arm. She was wearing a leather skirt today, with a glittering gold blouse. Her heels were high, her neckline low. She gave Sinclair a disdainful look and passed by with a sniff of her narrow pert nose

"Looks like he's free," said Sinclair.

Myra picked up the phone. "Let me just—"

"I'll only take a second." Sinclair didn't give the woman a chance to stop her.

Before Roger's door could swing shut, she blocked it. "Excuse me, Roger?"

He glanced up, lips compressing, and a furrow forming in the middle of his brow.

"I don't recall a meeting," he said.

"I believe you have my files?"

"Chantal's taking a look at them."

Sinclair struggled hard to keep her voice even. "May I ask why?"

"I've asked her to provide her opinion."

"On?"

"On the Valentine's ball preparation. She's taking a bigger role in the new product launch. I think we all recognize Chantal's talents."

Well, Sinclair sure didn't recognize Chantal's talents. And the ball preparations were all but done. She just needed to babysit it for the next week and a half. She sure didn't need somebody messing with the plans at this late date.

Roger took in her expression, and his tone suddenly turned syrupy. "I appreciate how hard you've been working, Sinclair. And I know you're busy. This will take some of the burden off your shoulders."

"There's no—"

"You'll get your files back in a couple of days. Thanks for stopping by."

Thanks for stopping by?

He'd pulled the most interesting and important project of her career out from under her, and *that's* all she got?

Short of a raid on Chantal's office, Sinclair didn't know what to do. If the woman started messing with things, the ball could be completely destroyed. What if she called Claude at the Roosevelt? The head chef was temperamental at the best of times, and Chantal might push him right over the edge.

The conductor also needed hand-holding. The music was cued to coincide with speeches and product giveaways. Entrances and exits of VIPs were specifically timed, and the media appointments had to come off like clockwork.

But Sinclair couldn't outright defy Roger.

She headed for the elevator, desperately cataloguing potential problems and possible solutions. By the time she punched the button, she realized there were too many variables. With a rising sense of panic, she knew she couldn't possibly save the ball from Chantal. That left her with Roger. How could she possibly make Roger understand the danger of Chantal?

She entered the elevator, then froze with her finger on the button.

Wait a minute. She had this all wrong. She shouldn't be fighting them. What better way to demonstrate the error in their thinking than to go along with it? Ms. Chantal wanted to take over the ball? She could bloody well take over the ball. It would take less than twenty-four hours for her to get into a mess. Sinclair wouldn't argue with the president. She'd graciously step aside. She'd take the day off and leave Chantal with just enough rope to hang herself.

When Sinclair came back tomorrow, hopefully they'd be ready to listen to reason. As the elevator dropped, Sinclair drew a deep, bracing breath.

It was all but suicidal. But it would be worth it.

Ha!

Roger wanted to give Chantal a chance to shine? Sinclair would graciously step aside. When she came back tomorrow, hopefully they'd be ready to listen to reason.

As the elevator dropped, Sinclair warmed to the idea. When she got back to her office, she informed Amber they'd have the files back in a couple of days, and that she was going home to paint.

* * *

A few hours later, with U2 blaring in the background, Sinclair's frustration had translated itself into a second coat on most of one wall. She was busy at one corner of the ceiling when there was a banging on the door.

She climbed down the ladder and set her brush on the edge of the paint tray.

The banging came again.

"I'm coming," she called. She wiped off her hands, then pulled open the door.

It was Hunter, and he was carrying a large shopping bag.

"I've been buzzing you downstairs for ten minutes." He marched across the room and turned down the music. "Thank goodness for the lady on the first floor walking her dog."

"I was busy," said Sinclair.

Hunter dropped the bag onto the plastic-covered floor. "What happened?"

"I decided I should spend the day painting my living room."

"I talked to Amber."

Sinclair shrugged, picking up her paintbrush, and mounting the ladder. "What did she tell you?"

"That you were painting your living room instead of working."

"See that?" she gestured to the brushes, paint cans and tarps. "All evidence points to exactly the same thing. I am, in fact, painting my living room."

"She also told me you haven't taken a day off in eight years."

Sinclair dipped the brush in the can on the ladder and stroked along the top of the wall. "Meaning I'm due."

"Meaning you're upset."

"A girl can't get upset?"

He crossed his arms over his chest. "What happened?"

"Nothing much." The important thing now was to get the painting done, then go in tomorrow and see if her plan had worked.

"Do I have to come up there and get you?"

She laughed, dabbing the brush hard against the masking tape in the corner. "Now that would be interesting."

"Quit messing around, Sinclair."

She sighed in defeat. Being micromanaged was embarrassing. "You want to know?" she asked.

"Yes," said Hunter. "I want to know."

"Roger gave Chantal my Valentine's Day ball files. She needed to review them because, apparently, we've *all* recognized her *talents*."

"We have?"

Sinclair dipped the brush again. "Therefore, she's ready to be the PR assistant. No. Wait. I think she's ready to be the PR manager."

"What exactly did Roger say?"

"Not much. He just gave her the files. He seems hell-bent on involving her in every aspect of my job."

"Oh."

There was something in Hunter's tone.

Sinclair stopped painting and looked down. "What?"

He took a breath then paused.

"What?" she repeated.

"There's something we should discuss."

"You know what's going on?"

"Maybe."

Sinclair took a step down the ladder. "Hunter?"

He dropped his arms to his sides. "I have a theory. It's only a theory."

She climbed the rest of the way down. "What is it?"

Hunter took the brush from her hand, setting it on the paint tray just before it dripped on the floor. "Chantal asked if you used the mousse."

He lifted the shopping bag. "I think that might be what Roger's picking up on. Chantal's, well, pizzazz."

A sick feeling slid into Sinclair's stomach.

Roger thought Chantal knew better than Sinclair?

Hunter thought Chantal knew better than Sinclair?

"You have to admit," Hunter continued. "She's the demographic Luscious Lavender is targeting."

"You sure you want to keep on talking?"

"We both know she's not you. We both know you're smart and talented and hard-working."

"Well, thank you for that."

He opened the bag to reveal the full gamut of Luscious Lavender products. "I think you should try these out. See what you think, maybe—"

"Right. Because all my problems will be solved by a good shampoo and mousse." Her problem wasn't a bad hair day. It was the fact that Roger, and maybe Hunter, too, preferred beauty over brains.

Hunter attempted a grin. "Don't forget waxing."

She reached down for the paintbrush. "I'm forgetting all of it."

"Will you at least hear me out?"

"No." Without thinking she waved the brush for emphasis, and paint splattered on the front of his suit.

Her eyes went wide in horror. "Oh, I'm so sorry," she quickly blurted out.

"Forget it."

"But I ruined your suit." She could only imagine how much it had cost.

"I said to forget it."

How was she supposed to hang on to her moral outrage when he was being a gentleman?

"It's more than just a good shampoo," he said. "It's about relating to your customers. Having your customers relate to you."

She started up the ladder.

"They relate to Chantal in a particular way," he said. "They see her look as an idealized version of themselves. These are people that put great stock in the value of beauty products to their lives, and they want to know that you put great stock in them, as well."

"You're suggesting I could replace an MBA and eight years of experience with a good makeover?"

What kind of a man would think that?

"Yes," he said.

She stopped. She couldn't believe he'd actually said it out loud.

"But," he continued. "I'm also suggesting you'll blow the competition out of the water when you have both."

"You think Chantal is my competition?"

"I think *Roger* thinks she's your competition. I think you could do a makeover with your eyes closed. And I think she's only a threat to you if you let her be a threat to you."

"So *I'm* choosing to have this happen?"

All she'd ever done was her job. She'd shown up early every day for eight years. She'd written speeches and press releases, planned events, supported her coworkers, solved problems and taken the message of Lush Beauty far and wide. If her performance evaluations were anything to go by, she'd been more than successful in her role as PR manager.

"You're choosing not to fight it," said Hunter.

"I shouldn't have to fight it." When had hard work and success stopped being enough?

"Too bad. So sad. Are you going to let her win?" He paused. "Do you *want* your career path to end?"

"Don't be ridiculous." She loved her job.

"I'm the one being ridiculous? Chantal's nipping at your heels, and *I'm* the one being ridiculous?"

"Why do you care?"

There were a few seconds of silence. "Why do you think I care?"

Sinclair didn't have an answer for that, so she finished climbing the ladder.

"I'm not saying it's right," he spoke below her. "I'm saying that's the business you're in. And you're the PR manager. And, yes, I'm sorry, but it matters. And, as for why I care."

He stopped talking, and she held her breath.

"I like you? I slept with you? You're an asset to Lush Beauty? You're family? Take your pick. But I'm about done fighting, Sinclair. If you don't want my help, I'm out of here."

She dipped her paintbrush, feeling hollow and exhausted. Hunter's words pulsed in her ears, while paint dribbles dried on her hands. She pretended to focus on the painting while she waited for the door to slam behind him.

Emotion stung her eyes.

She didn't mean to fight with him.

It wasn't his fault that Chantal was prancing around the city like a poster child for Luscious Lavender. It wasn't his fault that Roger was interfering in her management of the PR department. And what did Sinclair want from Hunter, anyway? For him to intervene with Roger?

Not.

She could take care of her own professional life.

Sort of. Maybe.

Because a tiny, little voice inside her told her some of what Hunter said made sense.

She focused on the paint, stroking it into the corner, listening for his footfalls, for the door slamming, for him walking out of her life.

"I'm sorry," his unexpected words came from behind and below her. "I should have approached that differently."

She stopped midstroke. Shocked, relieved and embarrassed all at the same time. She set down the brush.

"No," she spoke to the wall. "I'm the one who's sorry."

Silence.

"Will you come down then?"

She gave a shaky nod. She couldn't bring herself to look at him as she started down the ladder. Maybe all of what he said made sense. Maybe she'd been hasty in dismissing a makeover. After all, what could it hurt to try?

What exactly was the principle she was standing on? She'd always wanted the world to take her seriously. She hadn't wanted a free ride because of looks and glamour. But did she want to put herself at a disadvatange?

"I suppose," she said as her foot touched the floor and she turned toward him. "It wouldn't kill me to try the shampoo."

"That a girl." His voice was full of approval.

"It's just that I never wanted to cheat," she tried to explain. "I never wanted to wonder if a promotion or a pay raise, or even people's reactions to me were because of my looks."

"You're not cheating. You're leveling the playing field. Besides, being beautiful has nothing to do with makeup and mousse." He shrugged out of the ruined jacket and tossed it on the floor. He whipped off his tie. "You're beautiful, Sinclair. And there's not a damn thing you can do about it."

Her heartbeat thickened in her chest, wondering what would come off next.

But he rolled up his sleeves. "Okay, let's get to work."

That threw her. "We're going to the office?"

"We're painting your walls."

"You want to spend the afternoon here?"

"You bet."

By late afternoon, Sinclair's arms were about to fall off. Her shoulders ached, and she was getting a headache from the paint fumes. Her latest can was empty, so she climbed down the ladder to replace it.

Hunter appeared, taking the can from her hands.

"You're done," he said.

"There's another whole wall."

He pointed across the room. "See that bag over there? Full of bath oil, shampoo and gel?"

"Uh-huh."

"I want you to take it into the bathroom and run a very hot, very deep bath. In fact—" he set down the paint can and propped up his roller "—I'll do it for you."

Before she could protest, he picked up the shopping bag and marched into the bathroom.

She heard the fan go on and the water gush from the faucet. She knew any self-respecting woman would fight against his high-handed behavior. But, honestly, she was just too tired.

After a few minutes, he returned to the living room. He didn't talk, just unplugged her CD player and gathered up the two compact speakers. He popped out U2 and replaced it with Norah Jones.

Then he was back to the bathroom.

Curiosity finally got the better of her, and she wandered in to find her tub full of steaming, foamy water, and three cinnamon-scented candles flickering at the base of the tub. They'd been a Christmas gift from somebody at the office. But she'd never used them.

"I never have baths," she admitted.

"Why not?"

"Showers are more efficient."

"But baths are more fun."

"You have baths, do you?" she couldn't help but tease.

He faced her in the tiny room. "Guys don't take baths. They want girls to take them. It makes them all soft and warm, and in the mood to get beautiful."

She gave a mock sigh. "It's time-consuming being all girly."

He grinned. "Piece of cake being a guy."

"Double standard."

"You know it."

"Still." She glanced down at the steaming water. "It does look inviting."

"That's because it is." He reached across her shoulder and flicked off the light.

"Time to take off your clothes," he rumbled.

A sensual shiver ran through her, and she reflexively reached for the hem of her T-shirt.

But his large hands closed over hers to stop them. "I mean after I leave."

"You're leaving?"

He kissed her forehead. "I didn't come here to seduce you, Sinclair."

Suddenly, she wished he had.

"Don't look at me like that. I'm going to paint for a while, or we'll never finish."

"I can paint later."

His finger brushed over her lips to silence her. "The price of being a guy. Your mission is to get all glammed up and frou frou. My mission is to give you the time to do that."

Then he winked, and left the room, clicking the door shut behind him. And Sinclair shifted her attention to the deep, claw-footed tub.

It looked decadently wonderful. He'd set out the shampoo, bath gel and lotion. And he'd obviously poured some of the Luscious Lavender foaming oil into the water. She'd spent the last six months thinking about the artsy labels, the expensive magazine ads, the stuffed sample gift baskets for the ball, and the retail locations that needed some extra attention promotions-wise. Funny, that she'd never thought much about the products themselves.

The water steamed, and the lavender scent filled the room, and the anticipation of that luxurious heat on her aching shoulders was more than tempting.

She peeled off her T-shirt, unzipped her jeans, then slipped out of her underwear. She eased, toe-first, into the scorching bathwater, dipping in her foot, her calf, her knee. Then she slowly brought in her other foot, bracing her hands on the edges of the tub to lower her body into the hot water.

After her skin grew accustomed to the temperature, and her shoulders and neck began to sigh in pleasure, her thoughts made their way to Hunter. He was on the other side of that thin wall. And she was naked. And he knew she was naked.

She pictured him opening the door, wearing nothing but a smile, a glass of wine in each hand. He'd cross the black and white tiles, bend to kiss her, maybe on the neck, maybe on the lips. He'd set down their glasses. Then he'd draw her to her feet, dripping wet, the scented oil slick on her skin. His hands would roam over her stomach, her breasts, her buttocks, pulling her tight against his body, lifting her—

Something banged outside and Hunter swore in frustration. Clearly, he wasn't out there stripping off his clothes and popping the wine cork. She was naked, not twenty feet away, and he was dutifully painting.

She sucked in a breath and ducked her head under the water.

Four

By the time Sinclair emerged from her bathroom, wrapped in a thick, terry robe, her face glowing, her wet hair combed back from her face, Hunter had cleaned up the paint and ordered a pizza. The smell of tomatoes and cheese wafted up from the cardboard box on the breakfast bar while he popped the cork from his housewarming bottle of wine.

"How did you know sausage and mushroom is my favorite?" she asked as she padded across the paint splattered tarps.

"I'm psychic." He retrieved two stools from beneath the tarp, then opened the top of the pizza box.

"How'd it go in there?" he asked her, watching her climb up on one stool.

She arranged the robe so that it covered her from head to toe, and he tried not to think about what was under there.

She smiled in a way that did his heart good. "I'm a whole new woman."

"Not completely new, I hope," he teased as he took the stool facing her. The covered breakfast bar was at their elbows.

She grinned. "Don't worry. I saved the best parts."

"Oh, good." He poured them each a glass of the pinot. "So, are you ready to move on to makeup?"

She reached for a slice of pizza. "You planning to help me with that, too?"

He took in her straggled hair, squeaky clean face and oversized robe. If he had his way, he'd keep her exactly as she was. But this wasn't about him.

"I don't think you want to arm me with a mascara wand."

"But you've done such a good job so far." She blinked her thick lashes ingenuously.

"We could call one of the Bergdorf ladies."

She waved a dismissive hand. "I'll be fine."

"You sure?"

She hit him with an impatient stare. "It's not that I *can't* put on a lot of makeup. It's that I *don't* put on a lot of makeup."

"Oh."

She chewed on her slice of pizza, and he followed suit. After a while, she slipped her bare feet off the stool's crossbar and swung them in the air while they ate in companionable silence.

"What about clothes?" he asked.

"I'll call Kristy and get some suggestions."

He nodded his agreement. Having a sister in the fashion design business had to help. "Sounds like you've got everything handled," he observed.

She shifted on the stool, flexing her neck back and forth, wincing. "It's not going to be that big of a deal. I'm a pretty efficient project manager. The only difference is, this time the project is me."

Hunter wasn't convinced project management was the right approach. There was something in the art and spirit of beauty she seemed to be missing. But he was happy to have got her this far, and he wasn't about to mess with his success.

She lifted her wineglass and the small motion caused her to flinch in obvious pain.

He motioned for her to turn around.

She glanced behind her. "What?"

"Go ahead. Turn." He motioned again, and this time she complied.

"You painted too long," he told her as he loosened her robe on her neck and pressed his thumbs into the stiff muscles on her shoulders.

"I wanted to finish."

"You're going to be sore in the morning." He found a knot and began to work it.

"I'll live. Mmmmm."

"That's the spot?"

"Oh, yeah."

He'd promised himself he'd stick to business, and he would. But his body had reacted the instant he'd touched her. Her skin was warm from the bath, slick from the bath oil, and fragrant from the water and the candles. But he scooted his stool closer, persisting in the massage, determined to keep this all about her.

To distract himself, he glanced around at the freshly painted room. It was small, but the windows were large, and he could see that it had potential to be cozy and inviting. In fact, he preferred it to the big, Osland family house on Long Island.

He stayed there whenever he was in town, but with just him and a couple of staff members, it always seemed to echo with emptiness. Right now, he wished he could invite Sinclair over to fill it up with laughter. "Have you always lived in New York?" he asked her instead.

She nodded. "Kristy and I went to school in Brooklyn. You?"

"Mostly in California."

"Private school, I bet."

"You're right."

"Uniforms and everything?"

"Yes."

She tipped her head to glance up at him. "You must have looked cute in your little short pants and tie."

"I'm sure I was adorable." He dug his thumb into a stubborn knot in her shoulder.

"Ouch. Was that for calling you cute?"

"That was to make you feel better in the morning."

She flexed her shoulder under his hands. "Did you by any chance play football in high school?"

"Soccer and basketball. You?"

"I edited the school newspaper."

"Nerdy."

"Exciting. I once covered a murder."

He paused. "There was a murder at your high school?"

She gave a long, sad sigh of remembrance. "Mrs. Mitchell's goldfish. Its poor, lifeless body was found on the science table. Someone had cruelly removed it from its tank after hours. We suspected the janitor."

Hunter could picture an earnest, young Sinclair hot on the trail of a murder suspect, all serious and no-nonsense, methodically reviewing the evidence.

"Did he do it?" Hunter asked.

"We couldn't prove it. But it was the best headline we ever had. Broke the record for copy sales." She sounded extremely proud of the accomplishment.

"You were definitely a nerd," he said.

"I prefer the term intellectual."

"I bet you ran in the school election."

"True."

"There you go." He'd made his point.

"Billy Jones beat me out for class president in ninth grade." She put a small catch in her voice. "I was crushed. I never ran again."

"I'd have voted for you," said Hunter.

"No. Like everyone else, you'd have fallen for Billy's chocolate coconut snowballs—"

"His *what?*"

"Chocolate and coconut on the outside, marshmallow cream on the inside. He brought five boxes to school and handed them out during his speech. I didn't have a chance."

"Marshmallow cream, you say?"

Sinclair elbowed him in the chest. "Quit salivating back there."

"I'd still have voted for you."

"Liar."

He chuckled at her outrage and eased her back against his body. "Oh, I'd have eaten the snowball. But it's a secret ballot, right?"

"Traitor." But her muscles relaxed under his hands, and her body grew more pliant.

Finally, he stopped massaging and wrapped his arms around her waist. "I bet you were a cute little nerd."

She rested her head against his chest. He didn't dare move. He barely dared breathe. All it would take was one kiss, and he'd be dragging her off to the bedroom.

She tipped her head to look up at him, all sweetness and vulnerability.

"Hunter?" she breathed, lips dark and parted, eyes filled with passion and desire.

He closed his, fighting like hell to keep from kissing her lips. "I don't want to be that guy," he told her, discovering how true that was. Because he didn't want to screw up their budding friendship.

"That guy?"

"That guy with the bath and the candles and the shoulder massage."

"I liked that part."

He opened his eyes again. "It's Seduction 101 for losers."

"Are you calling yourself a loser?"

"I'm saying if I make love with you, I'll feel like I cheated."

"There's a way to cheat?"

He reflexively squeezed her tight. "I cheated, and you never had a chance."

"As in, I don't know my own mind?"

"Is there an answer for that that won't get me in trouble?"

"Not really."

He ruthlessly ignored the feel of her in his arms. He wasn't willing to risk that she might regret it in the morning.

"You're tired. You're vulnerable. And we haven't thought this through. We turn that corner," he continued, "we can't turn back."

"I know," she acknowledged in a soft voice.

He leaned around her, placing a lingering kiss on her temple. "I'll see you at the office?"

"Sure."

He forced himself to let go of her. Then, using every ounce of his strength and determination, he stood up and walked away.

* * *

By 7:00 a.m., Sinclair was in her office.

After Hunter left last night, she'd lain awake, remembering his soft voice, his easy conversation, and the massage that had all but melted her muscles. She would have willingly made love with him. But, he was right. They hadn't thought it through. It was hard enough ignoring what had happened six weeks ago, never mind rekindling all those memories.

Hunter was a thoughtful man. He was also an intelligent man, and she'd spent some time going over his professional advice. He saw Chantal as her competition. And he saw Roger in Chantal's corner. Sinclair realized she had to do this, and she had to do it right. It was time to stop fooling around.

So, she'd arrived this morning with a plan to do just that. She submitted an electronic leave form, rescheduled her meetings, plastered her active files with Post-its for Amber, and left out-of-office messages on both her voice mail and e-mail.

She was working her way through the mail in her in-basket when Roger walked in.

"What's this?" he asked, dropping the leave form printout on her desk.

"I'm going on vacation," she answered cheerfully, tossing another piece of junk mail in the wastepaper basket.

"Why? Where?"

"Because I haven't taken a vacation in eight years. Because I'm entitled to vacation time just like everybody else. And because I'm not currently needed on the Valentine's Day ball file."

"Of *course* you're needed on the file."

"To do what?"

Roger waved his arms. "To make plans. To order things."

"Plans are made. Things are ordered." She rose from her

chair and smiled at him. "You'll be fine, Roger. You've got Chantal on the case. She can oversee things."

"But, where are you going?"

"Chapter Three, Section Twelve of the employee manual. Employees shall not be required to disclose nor justify their vacation plans. All efforts will be made to ensure employees are able to take leave during the time period of their choosing. And leave shall not be unreasonably withheld."

"She's right," came Hunter's voice from the doorway.

Roger looked from Hunter to Sinclair and back again. "You knew about this?"

"Hadn't a clue." Hunter looked to Sinclair. "Taking a vacation?"

"I am."

"Good for you. A refreshed employee is a productive employee."

"I plan to be refreshed," she said.

Hunter smirked. "I'm looking forward to that."

"I've left notes for Amber," Sinclair said to Roger. "The meetings with the Roosevelt Hotel have been rescheduled. Unless Chantal wants to take them. You could ask her. The florist order is nailed down. The music…Well, there's a little problem with the band, but I'm sure Chantal or Amber can handle it."

She dropped the last piece of mail in the waste basket and glanced around the room. "I think that about covers it."

"This is unexpected," said Roger through clenched teeth.

"Can I talk to you for a minute?" asked Hunter.

"My office?" Roger responded.

"I meant Sinclair," said Hunter, stepping aside from the open door.

Roger frowned.

Sinclair should have cared about his annoyance, and she should have been bothered by the fact that the CEO had just dismissed the president in order to talk to her. But she truly didn't care. She had things to do, places to go, beauticians to meet.

Roger stalked out of the office, and Hunter closed the door behind him.

"Career-wise," said Sinclair. "And by that, I mean *my* career. I'm not sure that was the best move."

"You're taking some time for the makeover?" asked Hunter.

She straightened a stack of reports and lifted them from her desktop. "You're right that Lush Beauty Products is going through a huge transition. And you're right I should thwart Roger by getting a makeover. And, honestly, I believe Roger and Chantal need some time alone to get to know one another."

Hunter grinned, obviously understanding her Machiavellian motives.

"I'm a goal-oriented woman, Hunter. Give me a week, and I can accomplish this."

"I'm sure you can. Any interest in accomplishing it in Paris?"

She squinted. She didn't understand the question.

"I had an idea," he said. He paused, obviously for effect. "The Castlebay Spa chain. It's a very exclusive, European boutique spa chain, headquartered in Paris."

She got his point and excitement shimmered through her. "We're going to try again?"

"Oslands don't quit."

Enthusiasm gathered in her chest at the thought of another shot at a spa. She squared her shoulders. "Neither do Mahoneys."

"Good to hear. Because that platinum card I gave you works in Paris."

"Oh, no." She shook her head. "You don't need me to do

the spa deal, and I don't need to go to Paris. I've got things to do in New York."

He took her hand. "I want you in on the spa deal. And Paris is the makeover capital of the world."

"Paris is definitely overkill." She didn't need to cross an ocean to get a haircut and buy dresses. Plus, in Paris, she'd be with Hunter. And there was the ever present danger of sleeping together. Since they'd so logically decided against it last night, it seemed rather cavalier to take off to Paris together.

"Do I need reinforcements? I could call your sister. She'll back me up."

"Don't you dare call Kristy." Kristy would be over the moon at the thought of a Paris makeover for her sister. And Sinclair would have two people to argue with.

He pulled out his cell phone and waggled it in the air. "She's on speed dial."

"That's cheating."

"I've got nothing against cheating."

His words from last night came back to her, but she didn't mention it.

"I need you in Paris," he said.

She didn't believe that for a second. "No, you don't."

"I need your expertise on the Castlebay deal."

She rolled her eyes. "Like my track record on spa deals is any good."

"You know the Lush Beauty company and the products, and you can describe them a lot better than I can."

"There's a flaw in this plan," she told him. But deep down inside, she knew Hunter was winning. If she wanted to beat Chantal at her own game, a Paris makeover would give her the chance she needed.

"Only flaw I can think of," he said, shifting closer, "is that I desperately want to kiss you right now."

"That's a pretty big flaw," she whispered.

"We're handling it so far." But he moved closer still, and his gaze dropped to her lips.

"How long would we be in Paris?"

"A few days."

Her lips began to tingle in reaction to his look. "Separate rooms?"

"Of course."

"Lots of time in public places."

He returned his gaze to her eyes. "Chicken."

"I'm only trying to save you from yourself."

"Noble of you."

She couldn't help but smile. "If we do this—"

"The jet's waiting at the airport."

"Did I miss the part where I said yes?"

He reached for her hand. "I'm generally one step ahead of you, Sinclair."

She shook her head, but she also grabbed her purse. Because she realized he was right. He had an uncanny knack for anticipating her actions, along with her desires.

Five

They slept on the plane, and arrived in Paris a week before Valentine's Day. Then a limousine took them to the Ciel D'Or Hotel. And Hunter insisted they get right to the makeover.

So, before Sinclair could even get her bearings, they were gazing up at the arched facade of La Petite Fleur—a famous boutique in downtown Paris. A uniformed doorman opened the gold-gilded glass door.

"Monsieur Osland," he said and tipped his hat.

Sinclair slid Hunter a smirking gaze. "Just how many makeovers do you do around here?"

"At least a dozen a year," said Hunter as their footfalls clicked on the polished marble floor.

"And here I thought I was special." They passed between two ornate pillars and onto plush, burgundy carpeting.

"You are special."

"Then how come the doorman knew you by sight? And don't try to tell me you've been shopping for Kristy."

"Like good ol' cousin Jack wouldn't kill me if I did that. They don't know me by sight. They know me because I called ahead and asked them to stay open late."

Sinclair glanced around, realizing the place was empty. "They stayed open late? Don't you think you're getting carried away here?" She'd agreed to a makeover, not to star in some remake of Pygmalion.

He chuckled. "You ain't seen nothing yet."

"Hunter."

"Shhh."

A smartly dressed woman appeared in the wide aisle and glided toward them.

"Monsieur Osland, Mademoiselle," she smiled. *"Bienvenue."*

"Bienvenue," Hunter returned. "Thank you so much for staying open for us."

The woman waved a dismissive hand. "You are most welcome, of course. We are pleased to have you."

"Je vous présente Sinclair Manhoney," said Hunter with what sounded like a perfect accent.

Sinclair held out her hand, trying very hard not to feel as if she'd dropped through the looking glass. "A pleasure to meet you."

"And you," the woman returned. "I am Jeanette. Would you care to browse? Or shall I bring out a few things?"

"We're looking for something glamorous, sophisticated but young," Hunter put in.

Jeanette nodded. "Please, this way."

She led them along an aisle, skirting a six-story atrium, to a group of peach and gold armchairs. The furniture sat on a large dais, outside a semicircle of mirrored changing rooms.

"Would either of you care for a drink?" asked Jeanette. "Some champagne?"

"Champagne would be very nice," said Hunter. "Merci."

Jeanette turned to walk away, and Hunter gestured to one of the chairs.

Sinclair dropped into it. "Overkill. Did I mention this is overkill?"

"Come on, get into the spirit of things."

"This place is…" She gestured to the furnishings, the paintings, the clothing and the atrium. "Out of my league."

"It's exactly in your league."

"You should have warned me."

"Warned you about what? That we're getting clothes? That we're getting jewelry? What part of makeover didn't you understand?"

"The part where you go bankrupt."

"You couldn't bankrupt me if you tried."

"I'm not going to try."

"Oh, please. It would be so much more fun if you did."

Jeanette reappeared, and Sinclair's attention shifted to the half a dozen assistants who followed her, carrying a colorful array of clothes.

"Those are pink," whispered Sinclair, her stomach falling. "And fuzzy. And shiny." Okay, there was makeover, and then there was comic relief.

"Time for you to go to work," said Hunter.

"Pink," she hissed at him.

Hunter just smiled.

Jeanette hung two of the outfits inside a large, well-lit changing room. It had a chair, a small padded bench, a dozen hooks and a three-way mirror.

In the changing room, Sinclair stripped out of the gray skirt suit she'd worn on the plane, and realized her underwear was looking a bit shabby. The lace on her bra had faded to ivory from the bright white it was when she'd bought it. The elastic had stretched in the straps, and one of the underwires had a small bend.

She slipped into the first dress. It was a pale pink sheath of a thing. It clung all the way to her ankles, leaving absolutely nothing to the imagination. Making matters worse, it had an elaborate beading running over the cap sleeves and all the way down the sides. And it came with a ridiculous ivory lace hood thing that made her look like some kind of android bride.

There was a small rap at the door. "Mademoiselle?"

"Yes?"

"Is there anything you need?"

Cyanide? "Would you happen to have a phone?" Or maybe an escape hatch out the back? She could catch a plane to New York and start over again.

"*Oui*. Of course. *Un moment*."

Sinclair stared at the dress, having some very serious second thoughts. Maybe other women could pull this off, taller, thinner, crazier women. But it sure wasn't working for her.

Another knock.

"Yes?" If that was Hunter, she wasn't going out there. Not like this. Not with a gun to her head.

"Your phone," said Jeanette.

Sinclair pulled off the hood, cracked the door and accepted the wireless telephone.

She dialed her sister Kristy, the fashion expert.

Kristy answered after three rings. "Hello?"

"Hey, it's me."

"Hey, you," came Kristy's voice above some background

noise of music and voices. "What's going on? Everything all right?"

"It's fine. Well, not fine exactly. I'm having a few problems at work."

"Really? That's not like you. What kind of problems?"

"It's a long story. But, I'm in Paris right now, and we're trying to fix it."

"Hang on," said Kristy. "I'm at the Manchester Hospital Foundation lunch. I need to get out of the ballroom." The background noise disappeared. "Okay. There. Did you say you were in Paris?"

Sinclair's glance went to the three-way mirror. "Yes. I'm doing a makeover, but I think I many have taken a wrong turn here, and I need some advice."

"Happy to help. What kind of advice?"

"What do I ask for? Is there something that's stylish but not weird?"

"Define weird."

"At the moment, these crazy people are trying to dress me like an android bride, porn queen."

There was laughter in Kristy's tone. "Crazy people? What did you do to upset the French?"

"It's not the French. It's Hunter."

"Hunter's in Paris?"

"Yes."

Kristy was silent for a moment. "Are you sleeping with him again?"

"No."

More silence. "You sure?"

"Yes I'm sure. What? You think I wouldn't notice? We're shopping for clothes."

"I know things about Hunter that you don't."

"We're not having sex, we're shopping for clothes. And I'm all for that. Just not these clothes." Sinclair glanced in the mirror again and shuddered.

"Where are you shopping?"

"La Petite Fleur."

"Well, they're good. Is somebody assisting you?"

"Yes. A nice lady named Jeanette, who appears to have horrible taste in dresses."

"Put her on."

"Just a minute."

Sinclair cracked the door again. "Jeanette?"

"*Oui?*" The woman instantly appeared.

Sinclair held out the phone. "My sister wants to talk to you."

If Jeanette was surprised by the request, she didn't show it. She was gracious and classy as she took the phone, and Sinclair was grateful.

"*Allô?*" said Jeanette.

Sinclair closed the door. She didn't want to risk Hunter calling her to come out there.

She stripped out of the dress and tried the other. It was made of black netting, with shoulder-length matching gloves. A puffy neckline of feathers nearly made Sinclair sneeze, while rows of horizontal feather stripes camouflaged strategic parts of her body. The netting base was see-through, so underwear would be out of the question beneath it.

Another knock.

"Yes?"

"You going to show me something?" asked Hunter.

"Not a chance."

"Why? What's wrong?"

She took in her own image. Maybe she just didn't have the

body for high fashion. Other women looked good. Kristy always looked good.

"I really don't want to go into it," she said to Hunter.

"Keep an open mind. It can't be that bad."

"Trust me. It's that bad."

"Perhaps you'd care to try a different designer?" came Jeanette's voice.

"Is Kristy still on the phone?"

"She will ring you back. But she made some suggestions."

Sinclair flipped open the door latch. "No peeking," she warned Hunter.

Then his cell phone beeped and she heard him answer it. Good. Hopefully he'd be busy for a while.

She opened the door wide enough to take the new dresses from Jeanette. They were in blues and golds, and these ones didn't appear to be pornographic.

She closed the door, took a breath, and tried on another one.

It was much better, and she felt a surge of hope.

It clung to her body, but not in an indecent way, and the fabric was thick enough that she could wear underwear beneath it. The netting on this dress was brown, and it was only used for a stripe across the top as well as a flirty ruffle from midcalf to the floor. In between was a glittering puzzle pattern of gold, brown, purple and green material.

Sinclair turned. She liked the way the ruffle flowed around her ankles, and the dress molded nicely to her rear end and her thighs.

There was another rap on the door. "How are you, madame?" called Jeanette.

Sinclair opened the door.

Jeanette cocked her head to one side. "Not bad," she said

of the outfit. "You'll need some shoes with a little jazz to compete. And maybe a little more support in your bra."

Was Sinclair offended by that last remark? No way. She was starting to like her new image.

"One moment," said Jeanette.

She returned promptly with a bra, matching panties, a pair of stockings, and some spike-heeled, precarious-looking, rhinestone-studded sandals.

When Sinclair walked out of the change room, she nearly took Hunter's breath away. The dress was a dream. Well, mostly her body beneath it was a dream. She looked glamorous and stylish, and it only added to her innate class.

"Can you hang on a minute?" he asked Richard Franklin, one of the Osland International lawyers.

"Sure," Richard responded.

Hunter covered the phone. "Perfect," he stated to Sinclair.

She smiled and, as usual, it lifted his mood. He found himself thinking about the evening ahead, and tomorrow, and the next few days. What could he show her in Paris? How could he keep her smiling?

He forced himself to switch his attention to Jeanette. "Can you do two or three more like that? And a couple of ball gowns, and some daywear?"

"Absolument."

"You look fantastic," he said to Sinclair.

It was a rocky start. But then she reflexively glanced in the mirror beside her, and he could tell by the shine in her eyes that she liked the outfit, too.

"Try to have fun," he told her.

"I'm getting there."

He gave her a thumbs-up.

They'd need some jewelry to go with it, of course. But that could be tomorrow's mission.

It occurred to Hunter that he was probably having a little too much fun at this himself. But he shrugged it off. Dressing a beautiful woman ought to be fun. And if a man couldn't have fun spending his money, what was the point in making any of it?

Jeanette herded Sinclair back into the change room, and Hunter returned to his phone call.

"Thanks for waiting," he said to Richard.

"Do you have a contact name?" asked Richard.

"Seth Vanderkemp. The Castlebay Spa headquarters is on Rue de Seline. Do we have a contract lawyer on standby?"

"We do. In fact, I can get someone there overnight. When will you know?"

"Tomorrow. If it looks like we can get a contract, I'll give you a call." Hunter knew this was their last chance to get Luscious Lavender into a spa chain in time for the Valentine's launch. If Castlebay was open to making a deal, he didn't want to lose a single minute.

He ended the call.

Immediately, his phone rang again.

"Hunter Osland."

"What the hell?" came his cousin Jack's voice.

"What the hell what?" asked Hunter, reflexively cataloguing his actions over the past couple of weeks to see what could have upset his cousin.

"One, you've got Sinclair in Paris? Two, there's trouble with her job. Three, you're dressing her like an android hooker. And four, you're probably sleeping with her? Take your pick."

"Oh, that," said Hunter.

"*That's* your answer?"

"What do you want me to say?" Hunter could tell his cousin to shut up and mind his own business. It was hardly a crime to go shopping. And he was behaving responsibly, particularly considering the attraction that still simmered between them.

"That you're not sleeping with my sister-in-law."

"I stopped."

"Good. Stay stopped. She works for us. And you're you."

"What the hell is that supposed to mean?"

"You know what it means."

Hunter sighed in exasperation. His reputation as a womanizer was not deserved.

"Tell Kristy I am not having a fling with her sister. Sinclair's job is not in jeopardy. And she doesn't look the least bit like a hooker."

"And you're not going to break her heart?"

Hunter pulled the phone away from his ear and frowned at it for a second. Then he put it back.

"Obviously, that was Kristy's question," Jack went on.

"What exactly have you told her about me?"

"Anything she asks. Plus, Gramps gave her the lowdown on some of your previous relationships. And you and Sinclair did start out with a one-night stand."

"Thanks for the support there, cousin."

Hunter hadn't had that many relationships. All right, some of them may have been short-lived. But they simply hadn't worked out. It wasn't as if he went around breaking hearts on purpose.

"Personally," said Jack, with more than a trace of amusement in his tone. "I'm more concerned about you. She's got red hair."

Hunter didn't bothering answering. He hit the end button and shoved the phone back in his pocket.

His cousin's joke was lame.

When Hunter was sixteen years old, he'd accidentally burned down the tent of an old gypsy fortune-teller. The woman had predicted Jack would marry a woman he didn't trust. They'd lose the family fortune. They'd buy a golf course. And Hunter would marry a redhead and have twins.

So far, the only thing that had come close to happening was Jack marrying Kristy before he trusted her. But it was enough to get Jack fixated on redheads and the possibility of twins.

The door to the changing room opened again.

Sinclair emerged in a strapless, jewel-blue, satin evening gown that revealed creamy cleavage on top and silver-strapped, sexy ankles on the bottom. She'd pinned her hair up in an ad hoc knot. As she moved gracefully toward him, the fabric rustled over her smooth calves, while her deep, coral lips curved into a satisfied smile.

Hunter's body reacted with a lurch, but then his stomach went hollow when he realized he couldn't touch her.

Kristy had absolutely nothing to worry about. If anybody was getting their heart broken around here, it sure wasn't going to be Sinclair.

Sinclair knew she'd be disappointed if Castlebay didn't work out. There was her job, her future, Hunter's reputation at the company, the success of the Luscious Lavender product line all to consider. And she'd reminded herself, she'd lived through two letdowns already. Still, walking up the stone steps to the Castlebay Spas head office, she was determined to fight the butterflies in her stomach.

"What should I focus on first?" she asked Hunter, anxious to get her part right.

She was wearing a mini, tweed coat dress, with pushed up sleeves, large black buttons, black stockings and high-heeled ankle boots. She'd pulled her hair into a simple, tight bob, as Jeanette had advised, and put on a little extra makeup, especially around the eyes.

"Leave the financial details to me. Give out product information only. If I brush your hand, stop talking. And, mostly importantly, walk, talk and act like a winner."

She gave him a swift nod.

"Oh. And mention that you've tried the mousse."

She shot him a disgusted stare.

"That was just to lighten you up." He pulled open the heavy brass and glass door. "Relax."

She took a breath. "Right."

They didn't talk in the elevator. And while they crossed the marble floor of the Castlebay lobby, Sinclair concentrated on her new shoes. She did not want to stumble.

"We have an appointment with Seth Vanderkemp," Hunter said to the receptionist.

Sinclair caught the woman's admiring look at her outfit, and she couldn't help but smile. Wouldn't the woman be surprised to find out she was staring at plain, old Sinclair Mahoney from Soho?

"Mr. Vanderkemp is expecting you," said the woman. "Right this way."

She stood and led them down a long hallway to an opulent meeting room. It had round beech-wood table, with a geometric, inlaid cherry pattern. There were four high-backed, burgundy leather chairs surrounding it. And the bank of windows overlooked the Seine.

"Good morning, Mr. Osland. Sorry to keep you waiting."

"Not at all," said Hunter. "We just got here. And, please, call me Hunter." He turned to Sinclair. "This is my associate, Sinclair Mahoney."

"Seth," said the man, holding out his hand to Sinclair. "Pleasure to meet you."

Sinclair shook. "Sinclair," she confirmed.

Seth gestured to the round table. "Shall we sit down?"

Hunter pulled out a chair for Sinclair, then the men sat.

"Osland International's latest acquisition," Hunter began, getting right to the point, "is a boutique beauty-products company out of New York called Lush Beauty."

"I've heard of Lush," said Seth with a nod.

Sinclair thought that fact boded well for the discussions, but Hunter's expression remained neutral.

"We're in Paris for a few days," explained Hunter, "looking for partners in the upcoming launch of a promising new line called Luscious Lavender."

Sinclair mentally prepared herself to talk about the products. She'd start with skin care, move to cosmetics, then introduce some of the specialty personal care items.

"With Osland International's involvement," Hunter continued, "we're in a position to launch simultaneously in North America and Europe. A spa would naturally be an ideal outlet for us, and we believe Castlebay's clientele are dead center for our target market."

Seth continued nodding, which Sinclair took to be a great sign.

"Under normal circumstances," he said, "I would agree with you. And I've no doubt that Luscious Lavender would serve our client market well. But, there's a complication."

Sinclair's stomach sank.

Hunter waited.

"There's an offer on the table to purchase Castlebay Spas in its entirety."

"What kind of an offer?" asked Hunter.

"I'm sure you realize I'm not in a position to discuss the particulars."

Hunter sat back in his chair. "Let me put it another way."

This time Seth waited.

So did Sinclair.

"What would it take to get the offer off the table?"

Seth looked puzzled. "In terms of…"

"In terms of another offer to purchase."

Seth's eyes narrowed. "Are you empowered—"

"I'm empowered."

Seth stood up, crossing to a telephone on a side table, and picked it up.

Sinclair stared at Hunter.

Seth asked, "Do you mind if the head of my legal department joins us?"

"Not at all," replied Hunter. "I assume you have a prospectus and some financials I could review?"

"It's all in order. Plus a full set of appraisals."

"Thank you," said Hunter.

Then he turned to Sinclair, he penned a few words on a business card he'd pulled from his pocket and handed it to her. "Could you call Richard Franklin? Have him set up a meeting at our hotel this afternoon. I'll meet you there."

Sinclair palmed the card and quietly left the room.

On the way across the lobby, heart pounding, mouth dry, she flipped over the card. On the back was Richard's name, his number and the phrase NO ONE ELSE.

Six

When Hunter reached the ground floor of the office building that housed Castlebay Spas, Sinclair was waiting on a bench near the exit.

She jumped to her feet as he neared. "I couldn't wait," she said.

"Apparently."

"If you came down with anyone else, I was going to hide."

Hunter couldn't help but grin.

"What happened?"

"Looks like we may be buying ourselves some spas."

Richard would have to review the contract, but Hunter was satisfied with the price. And, the combination of Lush Beauty and Castlebay Spas was going to be dynamite. His grandfather insisted Hunter run Lush Beauty Products? He was damn well going to run Lush Beauty Products.

"Just like that?" asked Sinclair, with a snap of her fingers.

"Just like that," echoed Hunter.

"I can't believe it." She skipped a step to keep pace with him. "So we can use Luscious Lavender in the spas?"

"That would be the point."

"How much—" She stopped. "Never mind." She shook her head. "None of my business."

"Lots," said Hunter. He'd drained the available cash in the Osland investment account, and put up a manufacturing plant as collateral to secure low ratio interest.

"How many spas?" she asked.

"Twelve. I have a list if you want it."

They started down the steps.

"You bet." Her face nearly burst with a grin. "So, what do we do now?"

"Who is Richard sending to the hotel?"

"Miles something…"

"We drop the papers off with Miles something for review. Then we carry on with your makeover."

"Do we celebrate?"

"As soon as the deal is approved," Hunter answered as they turned onto the sidewalk. "The financing has to be put in place first. And we need to get the signatures on the contracts."

She nodded eagerly.

"And, until then, we carry on as normal." He hesitated over the wording of the next part. "And we don't tell anyone about it."

She squinted up at him. "Anyone being?"

"Anyone. Including Kristy and Jack."

"But, why—"

"Convention." Hunter shrugged with feigned unconcern. "We investigate things like this all the time. No point in cluttering up everyone's desk over it until there's something concrete."

It wasn't exactly a lie, but it wasn't the whole truth, either. The deal was somewhat larger than Hunter would normally undertake on his own. And he hadn't yet figured out exactly how to tell Jack and his grandfather. He knew they'd be worried, and they'd definitely come at him with accusations that he was being reckless and impulsive. But he didn't have time for his grandfather's plodding approach to due diligence, which had taken weeks, even when he'd "rushed" the Lush deal.

Still, Hunter was fully confident in his decision. And he was fully confident time would prove it to be an excellent investment. But, for the short term, he needed a few days to work up to an explanation.

In the meantime, all the reasons for Sinclair's makeover remained.

"Jewelry store?" he asked her.

She laughed and unexpectedly captured his hand. "You *are* in a spending mood."

"I am," he agreed, kissing her knuckles and pointing to a five-story, stone-arched jewelry store across the street.

They dashed across the traffic and entered to discover the building decorated for Valentine's Day. Golden hearts, red ribbons and bows hung from the ceiling. Massive bouquets of red roses covered every surface. And tiny, heart-shaped boxes of truffles were being handed out to the ladies as they exited.

Hunter scanned the glass cases and the stairway leading to the second floor. Then he looked down at their clasped hands.

"You with me on this?" he asked.

She nodded.

He rubbed a finger across her nose. "No complaints now."

She took in the festive scene. "I'm not complaining."

"I may buy you something expensive."

"Just so long as you take it back when we're finished."

He frowned. "Take it back?"

"Save the box," she said. "Or you can give it to a girlfriend in the future."

Hunter had no intention of taking anything back, or giving it to some future girlfriend. But he didn't see any point in sharing that with Sinclair.

"Sure," he agreed.

Sinclair smiled and turned her attention to the display cases.

Convinced she was buying for some other mythical girlfriend—who Hunter could not remotely picture at the moment—Sinclair plunged right into the game.

She selected a sapphire-and-diamond choker, a pair of emerald-and-gold hooped earrings, teardrop diamonds, delicate sapphire studs, a ruby pendant that Hunter was positive she thought was an imitation stone, and a whimsical little bracelet with one ruby- and one diamond-encrusted goldfish dangling from the platinum chain.

Hunter bought them all, clipping the bracelet on her wrist so she could wear it back to the hotel.

Then they walked to a nice restaurant, taking seats overlooking the river. The maître d' brought them a bottle of merlot and some warm French rolls.

Sinclair jangled her bracelet. "You're very good at this."

"I have a mom and a sister."

"Nice answer," she nodded approvingly, lifting her long-stemmed glass. "Never buy for girlfriends?"

"Why do you keep setting me up?" He didn't want to talk to Sinclair about his former girlfriends. "Tossing out questions I can't answer without being a jerk?"

"I know you've had girlfriends."

"But I don't want to tell you about them."

"Why not? Wouldn't I like them?"

"You're really going to push this?"

"No reason not to."

"Is that what you're telling yourself?" He didn't know what was going on between them, but he sure as hell didn't want to hear about any of her old boyfriends.

Then again, maybe her feelings were different than his. There was one way to find out.

"Melissa," he said, watching Sinclair's expression carefully, "was a weather girl in Los Angeles. We dated for three months, played a lot of squash and beach volleyball. She was a vegetarian and a social activist. She wouldn't let me buy anything from a very long list of countries with human or animal rights infractions."

Sinclair's expression remained impassive.

Hunter tore one of the rolls in two. "Sandra worked in a health club. She also played squash. We dated maybe two months. Deanne taught parasailing. We did a lot of mountain climbing, and some swimming, and she loved dancing at the clubs. But I introduced her to one too many movie stars, and she was gone."

Sinclair's expression faltered. "Did she break your heart?"

Hunter scoffed out a laugh. "It was at the six-month mark, normally my limit. Now, Jacqueline—"

"Is this going to take the entire dinner?"

"You did ask."

"I've had two boyfriends," she offered.

"I *didn't* ask," Hunter reminded her.

"Roberto decided his mother was right after all, and Zeke drove off on his Harley."

They left her? Now, that surprised Hunter.

"They break your heart?" he found himself asking, genuinely wanting to know.

"I thought so at the time. But, you know, neither of them even took me to Paris."

Hunter grunted. "It's a sad day when a man won't even take his girlfriend to Paris."

"Now that I've seen Paris—" Sinclair spread her hands palms up "—that's going to be the baseline."

"Smart girl."

"Thank you."

"You might want to add diamonds to that list."

"You think?"

Hunter nodded and pretended to give it serious thought. "Private jet, too."

Sinclair picked up the other half of his roll. "How else does one get to Paris?" She took a bite.

"A woman needs to be smart about these things."

"Thank you so much for the advice."

To his surprise, Hunter wasn't jealous of Roberto and Zeke. The men were morons.

He signaled the waiter for menus, and sat back to enjoy the company.

Sinclair awoke with a smile on her face in the river-view room at the Ciel D'or Hotel in downtown Paris. She felt different. The clothes Hunter had bought her were hanging in the closet and the jewelry package was sitting on the nightstand. Someone was tapping gently on her door.

She flipped back the comforter and slipped into the plush, white hotel robe, tying the sash around her waist. The fish bracelet dangled at her wrist. She knew it was silly, but she hadn't wanted to take it off.

Through the peephole, she could see a black-tuniced waiter carrying a silver tray. Coffee. Her entire body sighed in anticipation.

She opened the door, and the man set the tray down on a small table beside the window. She realized she didn't have any money for a tip, but he assured her it was taken care of.

Before she had a chance to pour a cup of coffee or tear into one of the buttery croissants, the phone on the bedside table began to ring.

"Hello?" She perched on the edge of the unmade bed.

"You awake?" came Hunter's voice.

"Barely."

"Did the coffee arrive?"

"It did."

His breath hissed in. "Call me when you're dressed."

Her gaze darted to their connecting door. "I'm covered from head to toe."

"You sure?"

She glanced down. "Well, maybe not my toes. But everything else. Come and have coffee."

"Toes are sexy," he said in a rumbling voice.

"My nails need trimming, and I haven't had a pedicure in months."

"In that case, I'll be right over."

She grinned as she hung up the phone and opened her panel of the connecting door. Then she settled into one of the richly upholstered chairs and poured a cup of extremely fragrant coffee and gazed at the sparkling blue sky against the winter skyline.

The door on Hunter's side opened. "Did I mention the Castlebay Spa offers pedicures?"

"Are you offended by my toes?"

He took the seat across from her, pouring his own coffee.

"I'm not even going to look at your toes. If you lied about their condition, they'll probably haunt my dreams."

She tore a croissant in two. "You got a fetish?"

"Only for gorgeous women." His gaze caught her bracelet. Their eyes met, and there was something excruciatingly intimate in his look.

And then it hit Sinclair. They were having an affair. They were having an affair in every possible way except sleeping together. The awareness brought a warm glow to her stomach. She deliberately moved her hand so the bracelet would tap against her wrist. The sensation sent a shot of desire through her body.

Hunter cleared his throat. "So, do you want to continue the makeover in Paris, or perhaps we should switch our base of operations to London...or Venice?"

"Is there a better place than Paris for a brand-new hairdo?" She had absolutely no desire to leave.

"Not that I know of."

"Then I vote we stay here."

She sipped her coffee from the fine china cup and bit into the most tender croissant she'd had in her life.

Hunter selected an apple pastry sprinkled in powered sugar, and Sinclair decided she'd try that one next.

"Are you at all worried I'll get spoiled and refuse to go home?" she asked, taking another bite.

He grinned. "Go ahead."

"You're not serious."

He paused for a moment, gazing at her in the streaming sunlight. "Actually, I am. But you're not."

Sinclair didn't believe it for a second. Although it was nice of him to say so. As fantasies went, Hunter sure knew how to put on a good one.

"Have you called for a special opening of a hair salon?"

He shook his head. "I don't know anything about hair salons in Paris. But I do know people who know people."

"And they'll do you favors."

"They will."

"Why is that?"

"Because I'm a nice guy."

"That you are."

Sinclair sat back, gazing around the room, at the ornate moldings, the carved ceiling, the marble bathroom, and the four-poster bed. "But the money must be frustrating. I mean, how can you tell if people like you or not?"

He shrugged. "How does anybody tell? They're friendly. They don't jeer at me. They laugh at my jokes."

"But how can you tell it's you and not the money?"

"You can tell."

"I bet you can't."

"Most people are terrible liars."

Sinclair pushed her hair behind her ears. "Not me. I'm a great liar." She and Kristy had pulled the wool over her parents' eyes on numerous occasions.

"Yeah?" asked Hunter, his disbelief showing.

"Yeah," she affirmed with a decisive nod.

He put down the pastry and dusted the sugar off his hands with a nearby linen napkin. "Okay. Go ahead. Tell me a good lie."

Like she'd fall for that. "You'd already know it's a lie."

"Then tell me something that may or may not be a lie, and I'll tell you if it's the truth."

"Oh…kay." Sinclair thought about it. After a minute, she sat forward, warming to the game. "That morning at the Manchester mansion, I stole something from your room."

Hunter sat back in apparent surprise. "What did you steal?"

"Is it a lie or not?"

He peered at her expression. "You're telling me you're a liar and a thief?"

She shook her head. "I'm either a liar *or* a thief. If I'm lying about being a thief, then I'm only a liar. But if I'm telling the truth about being a thief, I'm only a thief."

His eyes squinted down.

"Come on," she coaxed. "Which is it?"

"You're a liar," he said. "You didn't steal anything from my bedroom."

"You sure?"

"I'm positive."

"You got me," she admitted.

"Okay. Now it's my turn." He folded the napkin and set it aside. "I once wrestled an alligator."

"A real alligator?"

He nodded.

She was intrigued. Who wouldn't be? But she wasn't sold, yet. "Where?"

"A little town in Louisiana."

"Was it a trained alligator? Like in a zoo or something?"

"Nope. Out there in the bayou."

"It must have been pretty small."

"I didn't measure it or anything, but Jack guessed it was about six feet long."

"Jack was there, too?"

Hunter nodded.

Sinclair held out her hand. "Your phone."

"What?"

"I'm calling Jack."

"Oh, no, you're not."

"Oh, yes, I am." She wiggled her fingers.

Hunter shrugged and handed her the phone.

"You're *so* lying," she said. "Which speed dial?"

He grinned. "Four. And I'm not lying."

Sinclair hit number four, and waited while it rang. "You are busted," she said to Hunter.

"Jack Osland," came a sleepy voice. Too late, she remembered the time-zone difference.

"Hi, Jack," she offered guiltily. "It's Sinclair."

There was a pause. Jack's voice turned grave. "What did he do?"

She watched Hunter while she spoke. "He claims he wrestled a six-foot alligator in a Louisiana swamp."

"He told you that?"

"He did."

"Well, it's true."

Sinclair blinked. "Really?"

"Saved my life."

"Really?"

"Anything else?" asked Jack.

"Uh, no. Sorry. Bye." She shut off the phone. "You saved *his life.*"

Hunter shrugged. "He exaggerates."

Sinclair whooshed back in the chair. "I'd have bet money you were lying."

Hunter took a sip of his coffee. "I was."

She stilled. "What?"

He nodded "I was lying. I didn't wrestle a six-foot alligator. Are you kidding? I'd have been killed."

She looked down at the phone. "But…Jack…"

"Was lying, too."

"You couldn't possibly have set that up."

"We didn't have to." He lifted the phone from her hand. "You started the conversation by saying 'Hunter told me he wrestled an alligator.' Jack's my cousin; of course he's going to back me up."

"Tag-team lying?"

"It's the very best kind. Your turn."

"I'm not going to be able to top that."

"Give it a try."

Sinclair racked her brain. What could she possibly say that might throw him? Something believable, yet surprising.

Aha!

"I'm pregnant."

Hunter's face went white. "What?" he rasped.

Oh, no. No. She'd gone too far. "I'm lying, Hunter."

He worked his jaw, but no words came out.

"Hunter, seriously. I'm *lying*."

"You're not pregnant?"

"I am not pregnant."

"If you were, would you tell me?"

"I'm not."

"Because we'd get married."

"Hunter. It's a game."

"Will you take a pregnancy test?"

"*No.*"

"I let you phone Jack."

She stood up and rounded the table to him, bending over and putting all the sincerity she could muster into her eyes. "I'm sorry I said I was pregnant. I'm not."

He searched her expression. "You scared me half to death."

She smiled at that, reaching out to pat his cheek. "Not ready to be a daddy?"

He snagged her wrist and pulled her down into his lap. "Not ready for you to keep that big of a secret."

She shook her head. "I wouldn't. I'd tell you."

"Promise?"

"I promise."

He kissed the inside of her wrist. And then his gaze dipped down to her stomach.

She followed it and realized her movements had opened the robe. Her cleavage was showing, and the length of one thigh was visible nearly to her hip.

But Hunter wasn't looking at her thigh. His gaze was fixed on her stomach. His big, warm hand moved to press against the robe. It stayed there, and electricity vibrated between them. Then he slipped his hand beneath the robe to cup her soft stomach.

Arousal bloomed within her, radiating out to tingle her limbs. Her lips softened. Her eyelids went heavy. And she molded against his body.

He drew her head down, kissing her softly on the lips, trailing across her cheek, to the crook of her neck, to the tops of her breasts, burrowing down and inhaling deeply.

"I can't fight it anymore," he rasped, tipping to look up at her. "I can't."

"Then don't." She shook her head as she stared into the molten steel of his eyes. "Because it's killing us."

He bracketed her hips with his hands, lifting and turning her, so her legs went around his waist.

She ruffled her hands through his hair, kissing his hairline, his forehead, the tip of his nose.

He tugged the sash, and her robe fell away.

Then he smoothed his hands along her waist, wrapping around, splaying on her bare back, pulling her close over the rough fabric of his slacks. She bent her head and kissed his lips, slanting her mouth over his.

He met her tongue with his own, and she savored his taste,

content to let it last forever. But his hands slipped down, ratcheting up her arousal.

She whimpered.

"I know," he breathed, kissing her harder and deeper, letting his hands roam free, along her thighs, over her breasts, between her legs.

Her breathing turned labored, and she fought a war within herself. Part of her wanted him, right here, right now. Another part wanted to wait, to make it last. He felt good. He felt right.

She arched her back, pressing herself against his slacks.

He braced his forearms beneath her bottom, and came to his feet. She clung to his neck, anchoring her legs around his waist.

A few short steps, and they were there. The high four-poster. He set her down, then laid her back, pushing away the robe until she was completely naked.

She watched his hot gaze linger on her, not even considering adjusting her spread-legged pose. He traced a line between her breasts, down her belly, over her curls, into her center.

She closed her eyes, held on to the image of the unbridled arousal on his face.

She heard him stand.

Heard the rustle of his clothes.

The slide of his zipper.

The creak of his shoes.

"Sinclair?" he whispered, and she opened her eyes to see him standing naked above her.

She stretched out her hands, and he came down beside her, covering her with the weight of one thigh, smoothing her hair back from her face, kissing her gently on her cheek and on the tip of her shoulder.

"You are astonishingly, outrageously beautiful." His tone was reverent.

His words made her shiver.

He was beautiful, too. But more than that, he was Hunter. He was tender and funny, smart and determined—everything she could possibly dream of in a man.

"I want you so bad," he confessed.

Her throat closed up. She was beyond words, but she managed a nod of agreement.

"Do you remember?" he asked.

She nodded again, finding her voice. "Everything," she rasped. *"Everything."*

He inched a hand up her ribcage, finding the soft underside of her breast. He smoothed his thumb over the peak, drawing a lazy circle, pulling her nipple to a pebble. "I remember it, too."

Then he proved his knowledge, finding secrets and hollows, making her purr and moan.

She reached for him in return, running her fingertips over his chest and abdomen. He sucked in a breath as she brushed his erection. He let her test the length and texture, before trapping her wrist and calling a halt.

He pushed her arms over her head, where they had to behave. Then he kissed her mouth, and her neck, and her breasts. He released her hands, as his lips roamed free, testing and suckling. She tangled his hair, moaning his name, everything inside her tightening and heightening.

But he kissed his way back. And merged with her mouth. He moved atop her, linking his fingertips with hers, pressing them down against the softness of the comforter. Her knees moved apart, and their bodies met, slick and hot and impossibly sweet.

He eased inside her, slower than she could bear. She thrashed her head and squeezed his hands, her kisses growing deeper and more frantic. Then she instinctively flexed her hips, and he pushed the final inch to paradise.

He set a rhythm, speeding up and slowing down. She felt the fire of passion build within her. Her eyes squeezed shut, and her focus contracted to the spot where their bodies met.

The world turned to heat, and sensation and scent. She felt his muscles clench, and his desire take over. He sped up and stayed there, his thrusts intent and solid. A moan started low in her throat. It grew louder and more frantic, until she cried out his name, and the world fell apart, and his body pulsed within her.

They breathed in sync for long minutes after.

"You okay?" His voice seemed to come from a long way off. His body was a delicious weight on top of her, and she couldn't move a muscle, including her eyelids.

"Sinclair?" he pressed, sounding worried.

"I think we've cured the tension," she mumbled.

There was a chuckle low in his throat, and he eased his weight to the side, gathering her in his arms. "I do believe you're right."

Seven

Sinclair caught sight of her new haircut in the mirror at Club Seventy-Five. She'd second-guessed herself about getting it so short, but she had to admit, she loved it. Textured to spiky wisps around her ears and neck, it was light on top, and her new bangs swooped across her forehead, while the foil, blond highlights brought out the color in her cheeks.

Of course, the color could have come from the tote bag full of Luscious Lavender cosmetics that she'd had applied this afternoon. The beautician had painstakingly shown Sinclair how to apply the makeup herself, but she wasn't so sure she'd be successful—at least not without a lot of practice.

But, for tonight, she felt gorgeous.

She was wearing one of the jazzier dresses they'd bought at La Petite Fleur. A Diana Kamshak, it was a mint-green satin party dress. The short, full skirt sported blue horizontal stripes, and it was accented by a blue and silver border at the mid-thigh hem.

Above the wide silver belt, the top was tight and strapless, with a princess neckline that drew attention to her breasts. She wouldn't normally be comfortable in something so revealing. But every time she looked into Hunter's eyes, she felt beautiful.

She'd had dozens of covetous looks at her sapphire-and-diamond choker. Or perhaps it was because she was also wearing the Diana Kamshak dress. Or perhaps it was because she was with Hunter.

She'd decided on the teardrop diamond earrings, and she liked the way their weight bounced on her ears. She still hadn't taken off the goldfish bracelet, and it made a kicky addition to the outfit. She liked it. She liked it all.

The lights and the music pounded lifeblood through her bones. Or maybe it was Hunter that pounded through her bones. They were out on the floor, amidst the crowd, alternating between touching, smiling, and just moving independently to the beat.

He slipped an arm around her waist, tugging her close, spinning her to the rhythm of the house band. Sinclair smiled, then laughed out loud, she couldn't help it. The musicians launched into another lively and compelling tune.

"You thirsty?" he called in her ear as the song finished with a metallic flourish.

She nodded.

He put at hand at the small of her back, guiding her off the dance floor. "Water? Wine? Champagne?"

Sinclair did a little shimmy next to their table. "Champagne."

He gave her a kiss on the cheek. "My kind of girl."

Then he helped her into the high bar chair and disappeared into the crowd.

Sinclair liked being Hunter's kind of girl.

She liked the fashions. She liked the limos. She loved the sex. And she loved the way they arrived at a club and got escorted immediately through the side entrance. No waiting around on the curb for Hunter Osland.

But putting all that aside, what she liked most of all was Hunter—the person. Period.

Okay, the one thing she didn't like was the high shoes. She supposed she'd get used to them at some point, but right now, they just made one of her baby toes burn and both calves ache.

She slipped the heels off under the table.

Hunter returned with the drinks as the band announced a break. She sipped at the bubbles and grinned.

"Good?" asked Hunter, picking up his own glass.

"Great," said Sinclair.

Two men slid into the other chairs at the table. "Hey, Osland," one greeted.

"Bobby," said Hunter. "Nice to see you." Then he nodded to the other man. "Scooter."

Scooter nodded back.

Then both men smiled appreciatively at Sinclair.

"Sinclair Mahoney," Hunter introduced. "This is Bobby Bonnista and Scooter Hinze from Blast On Black."

"Sorry," said Sinclair, leaning into Hunter's shoulder. "I should have recognized you right away but I guess I was focused on Hunter."

Hunter's chest puffed out, and he put an arm around her. "What can I say?"

Both men guffawed at his posturing, but smiled at Sinclair and held out their hands.

She shook. "Loved the music."

"Thanks," Bobby nodded. "We're trying out some new stuff tonight. It's always a challenge."

"Well, it's great," she said sincerely.

"Got time for a drink?" asked Hunter.

Bobby shook his head. "We're on in ten minutes."

A server stopped at the table and topped up Sinclair's glass of champagne.

The two musicians rose from their chairs. "Coming to the party?" asked Bobby. "Suite 1202 at the Ivy."

"Not sure," said Hunter.

The men glanced at Sinclair with a sly, knowing grin. But, surprisingly, Sinclair found she didn't mind.

"Sorry about that," said Hunter after they'd left.

She shrugged. "Were they wrong?"

He leaned very close to her ear. "That," he rumbled, "is entirely up to you."

Blast On Black took the stage once more.

Sinclair wriggled her feet back into the strappy sandals. "Want to dance?"

Sinclair's shoes dangled from her fingertips as they made their way down the hotel hallway.

"Tired?" asked Hunter, slipping the key card into her room lock.

"A little tipsy," she admitted, crossing the threshold and tossing her shoes in the corner. The bed had been turned down and the adjoining door left open.

"Champagne in France will do that to you."

"It was delicious." She took a deep breath and blinked away the buzzing in her head.

Hunter locked the door, then reached into his pocket to retrieve his cell phone. He pressed the on button and sighed.

"Messages?" she asked, digging into her purse to check her own phone.

"Thirty-five," he said, hitting the scroll button with his thumb.

"I have six," she frowned. "Boy, do I feel unpopular." Two of them were from Kristy, the rest from the office. She'd been keeping in touch with Amber via e-mail, making sure the ball plans were under control, despite Chantal's meddling.

"Enjoy it," he advised. Then he pressed a couple of keys, putting the phone to his ear.

"Hey, Richard," he said.

Then he waited in silence.

Sinclair struggled to reach the zipper on her dress.

"They did?" said Hunter.

She gave up and crossed the room to Hunter, turning her back. She automatically reached to pull her hair out of the way, but it wasn't there. She touched the top of her head, raking her fingers through her new short hair, enjoying the light feel while Hunter tugged down her zipper.

She wandered into the bathroom to find fresh towels and robes. Stepping out of her dress, she shrugged into a robe. She scrubbed off her makeup and carried the dress to the closet. She'd have to send it for cleaning tomorrow, but she didn't have the heart to toss it on a chair overnight. It was a fabulous dress.

"Thanks, Richard," Hunter was saying. "That's great news."

The tone of his voice caught Sinclair's attention.

Hunter snapped his phone shut. "It's done."

"What's done?"

"You are looking at the new owner of Castlebay Spas. Everything should clear escrow tomorrow."

A huge grin burst out on Sinclair's face. "That's fantastic!" She skipped across the room to give him a hug.

He nodded against her shoulder, squeezing her tight.

"Sweetheart, the two of us are going to launch Lush Beauty to the stars."

"As long as I can keep up the glam charade so Roger is happy."

"I'll fire Chantal tomorrow if that's what it takes."

Sinclair sobered. "You wouldn't do that, would you?"

"I won't have to."

"But, even if you did. You'd never do that. I mean, I couldn't live with myself if I built a career based on your intervention."

He took both her hands in his and squeezed. "It'll never happen. Seriously. Stop borrowing trouble. We just had some amazingly good news, and we need to celebrate. And we need to plan a tour of the spas. Rome, London…"

She felt better. The makeover was moving along as planned, and the spa launch was more than she'd ever dreamed.

He loosened the knot in his tie. "I'm going next door to shower."

"Okay."

"While I'm gone, you get happy again. Okay?"

"I will."

"Good." He winked at her, stripping off the tie as he strode through the adjoining door.

Sinclair curled up in an armchair. She mentally did the math on time zones and realized she could safely return Kristy's calls.

"Hello," came Kristy's voice.

"Hey, it's me."

"*You.* Finally! What the heck's going on?"

"I'm still in Paris."

"Wonderful, dear sister. But tell me how you ended up in Paris in the first place?"

"We took the jet. That's one very cool jet, by the way."

"Funny. What on earth happened at work?"

"You remember my boss, Roger?"

"Short guy, big nose."

"That's him. Well, he's got this new protégée, Chantal, who's off the charts avante garde, giggly and girly and squealy. And he's decided she's the face Lush Beauty needs for PR."

"They fired you?"

"No. Nobody fired me. But I can easily see her at the podium and me in a dingy back file room if things keep going like this."

"You know Hunter's the CEO now, right?" asked Kristy.

"And, so?"

"Well, you are my sister…."

Sinclair was slightly insulted. "You're suggesting nepotism?" That was as bad as sleeping her way to the top.

"You don't need nepotism. But if Roger and this Chantal are out to lunch—"

"Actually, Hunter agrees with them."

Silence.

"He thinks my image could use some updating."

Kristy's voice took on an incredulous quality. "And you're okay with that? That doesn't sound like you."

Sinclair had to agree that it didn't sound like her. And she'd been avoiding delving too closely into her motivations for going along with him.

"True. But the new wardrobe is nice."

Concern grew in Kristy's voice. "Sinclair, you're not—"

"I'm not."

"—falling for Hunter. Because I've been talking to Jack, and to his grandfather, and he's not a good long-term prospect."

"You're getting ahead of yourself," said Sinclair, embarrassed that Kristy would have discussed the situation with the Osland family.

"You remember how you were after Zeke."

"I got over Zeke just fine." It hadn't taken that long, maybe a few weeks. "And I have Hunter completely in context."

"You sure?"

"I'm sure." Well, kind of sure. "It's all business," Sinclair insisted. "In fact, we're about to launch Lush Beauty in the biggest way." She thought about the spa deal and the time spent with Hunter. "Do you ever find your new life with Jack surreal?"

Kristy laughed. "All the time."

"Hunter and I went to a club tonight. First class all the way. The band even stopped by. And the weird thing? It seemed pretty normal."

"It does take some getting used to," Kristy agreed.

"Yeah, for the launch of the new Luscious Lavender line across Europe, Hunter bought a chain of spas!" She heard him moving around next door. "Sounds like he's out of the shower."

"Hunter is in your *shower?* What the—"

"He's next door. We have adjoining rooms." Then Sinclair realized she probably didn't want to have a detailed conversation on that, particularly when Hunter was about to waltz back into her room. "Better go."

"Wait—"

"Bye." Sinclair quickly disconnected.

"Hey, babe," said Hunter, padding inside in one of the white robes. "You're not going to shower?"

She stifled a yawn, dropping her phone on the little desk beside the armchair. "Tomorrow."

He crossed toward her. "Works for me." He smiled as he leaned down to kiss her. "Ready for bed?"

"Just let me find something to change into."

He burrowed into her neck, planting kisses along the way. "You're not going to need a nightgown."

She chuckled at his gravelly voice and the way his rough skin tickled hers.

His hands slipped beneath her robe. "What's this?"

"It's called underwear."

"You trying to slow me down?"

"Not worth the work, am I?"

"Always." He drew her to her feet.

Then his cell phone rang.

He swore, but picked it up and checked the number. "Richard."

"You need to take that?"

"Tomorrow," he said. "Tomorrow, we need to strategize."

"Over the spas?"

He nodded.

Sinclair squinted. "I thought the deal was done?"

"It is." His lips compressed. "Tomorrow I figure out how to explain to my family I spent several hundred million."

Everything inside Sinclair went still. "How do you mean?"

"I mean, I'm going to hear words like *reckless* and *impulsive*. They'll be ticked, so I need to figure out how to present this just right so Gramps doesn't go ballistic."

Her stomach turned to a lead weight. "But I thought…"

He waited.

"I thought you were ready to tell them."

He coughed out a cold laugh. "Not hardly." He tossed the phone down and moved toward her. "But it can wait until tomorrow; you're what's important tonight."

"I have to use the bathroom," Sinclair blurted.

"Sure," he said, obviously puzzled as to why she was

making a big deal about it. "You should go ahead and do that."

Hesitating only a second, she grabbed her phone.

He glanced at her hand. "Expecting a call?"

"Maybe. I don't know." She headed for the door. "Time zones, you know." Then she quickly shut herself in.

Her hands were shaking as she dialed Kristy.

"Come on. Come on," she muttered as the connection rang hollow. "Pick up."

She got her sister's voice mail and jiggled her foot as she waited for the beep.

"Kristy? It's me. I *really* need to talk to you. I'll try again in a few minutes. Make sure you pick up."

What to do now? She needed Hunter out of the way. She needed Hunter…asleep.

Okay, this was going to be tricky. He didn't seem like he was in the mood for anything remotely quick.

She exited the bathroom, and was pulled immediately into his arms, engulfed in a major hug, peppered with kisses that under any other circumstances would have been erotic and totally arousing.

"Uh, Hunter?"

"Yeah?"

"I'm…not…"

He pulled back. "Something wrong?"

"I'm still woozy from the drinks," she lied.

His eyes glowed pewter as he waggled his eyebrows. "You maybe need to lie down?"

She shook her head. "No. I mean yes. I mean." She hit him with the most contrite expression she could muster. "Can we wait until morning?"

His gaze grew concerned. "That bad?"

She nodded. It was worse, only not in the way he was imagining.

"Come on, then." He led her to the bed, pushing aside the comforter and tucking her in.

He slipped under the covers beside her and spooned their bodies together. He kissed the back of her neck, smoothing her hair. "Sleep," he muttered.

She nodded miserably, and pretended to do just that.

Half an hour later, his breathing was deep and even. Engulfed in his warmth, she was struggling to stay awake herself. She didn't dare wait any longer.

She cautiously slipped from the bed, snagged her phone, and tiptoed into the bathroom.

She tried Kristy again, still coming up with voice mail.

"Kristy?" she whispered harshly. "You have to call me. I'm sleeping with my phone on vibrate. Wake me up!"

Then she clicked it off, forced herself to swallow her panic, took a drink of water to combat her dry throat, and headed back to bed.

"You okay?" Hunter mumbled as she climbed back in.

"Thirsty," she responded guiltily as he drew her against him.

"You'll be better in the morning," he assured her with a kiss.

She'd be better when Kristy called and was sworn to temporary secrecy. That's when she'd be better.

Sinclair awoke to Hunter's broad hand on her breast. His lips were kissing her neck, and his hardened body was pressed against her backside.

"Morning, sweetheart," he murmured in her ear.

She smiled. "Morning."

He caressed her nipple, sending sparks of desire to her

brain. His free hand trailed along her belly. She gasped, the warmth of arousal swirling and gathering within her.

"I've been waiting," he rumbled. "You slept too long."

"Sorry."

"Make it up to me." His hand slipped to the moisture between her legs.

He flipped her onto her back.

"Right now," he growled.

In answer, she kissed him hard.

A pounding sounded on the door, and someone shouted his name.

Hunter jerked back. "What the—?"

It took her a second to realize the person was pounding outside Hunter's room.

"Don't move," he commanded, staring into her eyes. Then he jackknifed out of bed and stuffed his arms into the robe. He pushed the adjoining door shut behind him. Sinclair sat up, shaking out the cobwebs.

She felt a lump under her thigh, and realized it was her phone. Flipping it open, she quickly checked for a return call from Kristy.

Nothing.

The voices rose in the room next door, drawing Sinclair's attention.

"—be so freaking reckless and impulsive!"

It was Jack's voice, and Sinclair was afraid she might throw up.

"We have talked and *talked* about this," came another gravelly voice. It had to be Cleveland.

The family knew. They were here. And they were angry. And it was all her fault. Sinclair wrapped her arms around her stomach and scrunched her eyes shut tight.

* * *

At first, Hunter was too shocked to react.

He'd gone from Sinclair, soft and plaint in his arms, to his grandfather's harsh wrath in the space of thirty seconds. His brain and his hormones needed time to catch up.

"I can give you the prospectus," he told them. "The financials and the appraisals."

"You can bet your ass you'll be giving us the prospectus, the financials and the appraisals," shouted Gramps.

Then it was Jack's turn. "You can't make unilateral decisions!"

"I can. And so can you and Gramps."

"Not like this."

"Yes, like this. There's no advantage in three guys spending time on what one can do alone." Hunter was warming up now. He just wished he was wearing something other than a bathrobe. "This is a good deal. It's a *great* deal!"

"That's not the point," Jack said.

"The point being that you and Gramps are control freaks?"

"The point being you need to play with the team."

Hunter turned on his grandfather. "You thought it was funny to send me to Lush Beauty. You thought it was funny to send me to Sinclair. Well, guess what? You send me to run a company, I run the damn company."

"I have half a mind to take away your signing authority," Cleveland threatened.

"Because that wouldn't be an overreaction," Hunter countered, folding his arms across his chest.

"You, young man, spent hundreds of millions without so much as an e-mail."

"It's amortized over twenty years. The property values alone—"

"If it wasn't for Sinclair telling Kristy—"

"What?" Hunter roared, unable to believe what he'd heard.

Jack and Cleveland stopped dead.

Hunter stared hard at them. "You got information from your wife because my…Sinclair talked?"

"And thank God she did," said Cleveland.

But Hunter was past listening to Jack and his grandfather.

"We're done," he said to them, moving to open the door. "Richard has the details. You take a look at the deal. If you don't like it, I'll sell my Osland International stock and go it on my own."

Jack squinted. "Hunter?"

Hunter swung open the hotel room door. "Talk to you later."

"It wasn't Sinclair's—"

"Talk to you later."

Jack moved in front of him. "I can't let you—"

"What?" Hunter barked. "What do you think I'm going to do to her?"

"I don't know."

"Give me a break," he scoffed. He wasn't going to hurt Sinclair. He wouldn't let anybody hurt Sinclair. But the woman had one hell of a lot of explaining to do.

Eight

Hearing the latch click on the adjoining door, Sinclair broke out in a cold sweat. Her fingertips dug into the arms of the chair as she stared straight at the dove-gray painted panel.

The hinges glided silently and Hunter filled the doorway, his eyes simmering obsidian. But his voice was cool with control. "I thought we were a team."

She wished he'd shout at her, wished he'd rant. She could take his anger a lot more easily than his disappointment.

She'd let him down. She wanted to explain. She wanted to apologize. But her vocal cords were temporarily paralyzed.

"I trusted you," he continued. "I trusted your confidentiality. I trusted your discretion."

She fought to say something, to gather her thoughts. "I didn't know," she finally blurted out.

"Didn't know what? Was there something ambiguous about 'don't tell anyone, including Kristy and Jack'?"

"But that was before the deal went through."

"The deal went through at 3:00 a.m. this morning. Are you telling me in the five minutes I was in the shower—" He snapped his jaw. "You called Kristy." He gave a cold laugh. "You were so anxious to share gossip about my business dealings that you couldn't even wait until morning?"

"It wasn't gossip."

"Do you have any idea what you've done?"

She slowly shook her head. She could only imagine the implications of her behavior now that she had all the facts.

"Well, that makes two of us," he said. "Because I just offered to sell out of Osland International."

The contents of her stomach turned to a concrete mass.

She opened her mouth, but he waved a dismissive hand. "Much as I'd like to sit around and debate this with you, I've got a few problems to solve this morning. I'll have to talk to you later."

Then he turned back to his own room, shutting the door firmly behind him.

Sinclair's cell phone chimed.

She glanced reflexively down to see Kristy's number on the readout. She couldn't talk to her sister now. She didn't think she could talk to anyone.

There was every possibility she'd ruined Hunter's life. The worry that she might not get plum assignments or choice promotions at Lush Beauty faded to nothing in the face of that reality.

She stared at nothing for nearly an hour, then shoved herself into a standing position. She crossed to the closet and took out the clothes she'd been wearing when she arrived in Paris. They looked pale and boring compared to the new outfits, but she didn't have the heart to wear any of them.

She combed her hair, brushed her teeth, left the cosmetics on the counter and gathered up the suitcase with her old clothes inside. It seemed like a long walk to the elevator, longer still across the marble-floored atrium in the hotel lobby.

She figured Hunter would check out for her, so she wound her way past smiling tourists, bustling bellboys and intense businessmen. The men reminded her of Hunter and made her sadder by the moment.

Finally, she was out on the sidewalk, glancing up and down for a taxi. A hotel bellhop asked her a question in French. She tried to remember how to ask for a taxi, but it had slipped her mind.

In the sidewalk café next to her, propane heaters chugged out the only warmth in her world. People were eating breakfast, enjoying the sights of the busy street, their lives still intact.

The bellhop asked the question again.

She remembered. "Cabine de taxi?"

"Going somewhere?" came Hunter's voice from behind her.

"The airport," she answered without turning.

"I thought Mahoneys didn't run away."

"I'm not running away."

"You mad at me?"

The question surprised a cold laugh from her.

"Because I'm pretty mad at you," he said.

"No kidding."

A taxi pulled up, but Hunter let someone else take it. "So, what's your plan?"

She sighed. "Why'd you do that?"

"We're not finished talking."

"I thought you had problems to solve."

He snorted. "And how. But I want to know your plans first."

Sinclair looked pointedly down at her suitcase.

"You left the rest of your clothes in the closet," he said.

"Those are your clothes."

"So, you're going to pout? That's your plan?"

"I'm not pouting." She was making a strategic exit from an untenable situation before he had a chance to ask her to go himself.

Another taxi came to a stop, and Hunter sent it away.

"Do you think we could sit down?" he asked with a frustrated sigh, gesturing to the café.

Sinclair shrugged. If he wanted to ream her out some more, she supposed she owed him that much.

He picked up her suitcase, and she moved to one of the rattan chairs. She folded her hands on the round glass table and looked him straight in the eyes.

"Go ahead," she said, steeling herself.

"You think I'm here to yell at you?"

She didn't answer.

"Good grief, you're as bad as Jack." Hunter signaled the waitress for coffee, and Sinclair decided it might be a very long lecture.

"It seems to me..." said Hunter, as the uniformed woman filled their cups. He shook out a packet of sugar, tore off the corner and dumped it into the mug.

Sinclair just stared at the rising steam.

"You have two choices," Hunter continued. "You can slink back to New York with your makeover half done and take your chances with Roger. Or you can buck up and stay here a few more days to finish it."

"It seems to me," she offered, forcing him to get to the heart of the matter. "Those are your choices, not mine."

"How so?"

"Why would you want me to stay? Why would you want to help me? I ruined your life."

"We don't know that yet."

"Well, I might have."

"Possibly. Did you do it on purpose?"

"Of course not."

"So you weren't dishonest, you simply lacked certain details and a little good judgment."

She tightened her jaw. She normally had great judgment. "Right," she said.

A small glimmer flickered in his eyes. "You want to fight me, don't you?"

She wrapped her hands around the warm stoneware mug. "I'm in the wrong. I can take it."

"Very magnanimous of you."

"Are we done? Can I go now?"

"Do you want to go now?"

She didn't answer.

"Seriously, Sinclair. Do you want to walk out on Paris, the makeover and me just because things went off the rails?"

Things had done a lot more than go off the rails. She forced herself to ask him, "What do you want?"

"I want to turn the clock back a couple of hours to when you were sleeping in my arms."

"I want to turn it back nine."

He nodded, and they sat in silence for a few moments while dishes clattered and voices rose and fell at nearby tables. A gust of cool wind blew through, while the propane heaters chugged gamely on.

Hunter took a sip of his coffee. "Let me tell you why Jack and Gramps were so upset."

"Because you spent hundreds of millions of dollars without

telling them?" As soon as the flip answer was out, she regretted it. "Sorry."

But Hunter actually smiled. "Good guess. It's because they wanted me to call them first. They wanted to jump in and assess the deal before I made a decision. They wanted to research and analyze and contemplate. Do you have any idea how long Jack and Cleveland's brand of due diligence takes?"

Sinclair shook her head.

"The deal would have been lost before they even lined up the legal team."

"Did you explain that to them?"

He shot her a look. "That was my plan. Until you stepped in."

"Sorry," she said again, knowing it would never be enough.

"I know you are." But he didn't sound angry. He sounded resigned.

Cars whizzed by on the narrow street, while a contingent of Japanese businessmen amassed on the sidewalk nearby.

"What will you do now?" Sinclair asked.

"That's entirely up to you."

"You're seriously willing to keep this up?"

He nodded. "I am. There may be a lot of yelling from Jack and Gramps over the next few days, but I want to finish what we started."

"I can handle yelling."

"Good. You know anything about ballroom dancing?"

"Not much."

"Then that's next on our list." His expression softened. "You are going to take their breath away."

A knot let go in Sinclair's stomach.

"Flower for the pretty lady?" came an old woman's gravelly voice. She held a white rose toward Hunter, her bangles and hoop earrings sparkling against colorful clothing and a bright silk headscarf. "I will tell her fortune."

Hunter accepted the flower and nodded.

The old woman clasped Sinclair's hands, her jet-black eyes searching Sinclair's face. Then she smiled. "Ahhh. Fertility."

"I'm going to be a farmer?"

The woman revealed a snaggle-toothed smile, her gaze going to Sinclair's stomach.

Sinclair sure didn't like the implication of that.

"Trust your heart," said the old woman.

"I'm not pregnant," Sinclair pointed out.

The old woman released Sinclair's hands and touched her chin. "I see wealth and beauty."

"That's a whole lot better than fertility," Sinclair muttered.

Hunter laughed and reached for his wallet.

Sinclair caught the numbers on the bills he passed to the woman. Both hers and the old woman's eyes went wide.

The woman quickly hustled away.

"Did you know her or something?" Sinclair asked.

"I once knew somebody like her." Hunter tucked his wallet into his pocket and handed Sinclair the rose.

She held it to her nose and inhaled the sweet fragrance. Hunter wanted her to stay. The relief nearly brought tears to her eyes.

"Somebody like her?" she asked Hunter, inhaling one more time. "I once burned down a gypsy's tent." Then he smiled gently at Sinclair.

He swiveled his coffee mug so the handle was facing him. "When I was a teenager, a gypsy at the local circus told my fortune. She said I'd fall for a redheaded girl and have twins."

Sinclair reflexively touched her hair.

"The thought of twins freaked me out, too. I wanted to be a rock star."

"So, you burned down her tent?"

"She also said Jack would marry a woman he didn't trust, and we'd buy a golf course."

"But, you burned down her tent?" Sinclair repeated.

"It was an accident."

"You sure?"

He rocked back. "Hey, is there anything about me that strikes you as vindictive?"

"I guess not," she admitted, a small smile forming on her lips. Heck, he wasn't even kicking her out for ruining his life.

"It was an accident. And Gramps compensated her fairly. But, I guess I've always felt a little guilty."

"Have you been giving money to random gypsies ever since?"

"It's not like I come across a lot of them. Alhough…" He pretended to ponder. "I suppose a charitable foundation wouldn't be out of order."

"I'm sure they appreciate it."

Sinclair's cell phone chimed.

She opened her purse to check the lighted number. "Kristy." It chimed again under her hand.

"Better answer it," Hunter advised. "She's probably worried."

"So was I," Sinclair said over the sound.

His hand covered hers for a brief second. "We'll talk more."

Sinclair pressed a button and raised the phone to her ear. "Hey, Kristy."

"You okay?"

"Yeah. I'm fine."

"And Hunter?"

Sinclair looked at him. "He's had better mornings."

"What was he *thinking?*" There was a clear rebuke in

Kristy's tone. "Going out on his own. Jack says that Hunter was being dangerously cavalier with the family fortune."

Some protective instinct leapt to life within Sinclair. "He was thinking it was a good deal."

Hunter shook his head, mouthing the word, "Don't."

Sinclair ignored him. "And they might want to look closely at it before they decide it's a bad risk."

Hunter stood to lean over the table, but Sinclair turned away, protecting the phone. The least she could do was come down on his side.

"Are you *defending* him? Did he try to make this your fault? It wasn't your fault, you know. You were being honest. He was being underhanded."

"He was being smart."

There was a shocked silence on the line.

"Are you sleeping with him again?" Kristy demanded.

"None of your business."

"That's it. I'm coming to Paris."

Hunter lunged forward and grabbed the phone from Sinclair's hands.

"Goodbye," she quickly called as he snapped it shut.

"Have you lost your mind?" asked Hunter.

"She said you were being underhanded."

"You can't fight with your sister over me."

Sinclair folded her arms over her chest and blew out a breath. "Sure, I can."

Hunter handed back the phone. "No. You can't. She's your sister. Keep your eye on the long game."

Meaning Hunter was the short game?

"And she loves you," he said.

"She's coming to Paris."

"You want to go to London?"

Sinclair grinned. "We couldn't."

Hunter sighed. "You're right. We couldn't."

She caught a figure in her peripheral vision, turning to see Jack pulling up a chair at their table.

"You okay?" he asked Sinclair.

"You're as bad as Kristy," Sinclair responded. "What exactly do you think he'd do to me?"

"What *did* he do?"

"He invited me to go ballroom dancing. We're getting ready for the Valentine's Day ball on Thursday."

Jack shot his gaze to Hunter. "That true?"

"What if it is?"

"I just had a call from Kristy," said Jack.

"She's coming to Paris," announced Sinclair.

Jack nodded. "That's what she said." He was still eyeing up Hunter suspiciously. "You'd better sign us up, too."

After the day they'd had, Hunter wanted nothing more than to curl up in bed and hold Sinclair tight in his arms. He'd discovered he hated fighting with her. And he hated that her family and his had decided to protect her from him. Even now, across the floor in the Versailles Ballroom, Kristy was scoping them out, staring daggers at him.

A private jet had whisked her across the Atlantic in time for dinner.

Part of him wanted to thumb his nose at the lot and haul Sinclair away so they could be alone. Another part of him recognized they had legitimate concerns. His efforts to help her had gotten all mixed up with his desire for her.

He didn't want to hurt her, but he might in the end. The Lush Valentine's Day ball was only a few days away. He'd make sure she was a smash hit there, but then what?

She'd still work for him. Could they possibly keep sleeping together? Could they keep it a secret? And what did that say about them if they did?

As he guided her through a simple waltz, he considered the possibility that Kristy was right. After all, who would have Sinclair's best interests at heart more than her twin sister? A twin sister whose thinking wasn't clouded by passion?

God knew his was clouded by something.

Sinclair had dressed for the evening in a brilliant-red strapless satin gown. When he glanced at her creamy shoulders, the hint of cleavage, and her long, smooth neck, his thoughts were definitely on his own best interest. And that best interest was in peeling the gown off inch by glorious inch to reveal whatever it was she had, or didn't have, on underneath.

The bodice molded gently over her breasts, it nipped in at her waist, then molded over her bottom, while the full skirt whispered around her gorgeous legs.

"How am I doing?" she asked as the music's tempo changed.

"Fine," he told her, forcing his thoughts back to his job as dance instructor. "Ready to try something more?"

She nodded, blue eyes shining up at him, making him wish all over again that he could whisk her away.

He led her into a turn. She stumbled, but he held her up, tightening his hand in the small of her back, filing the sensation away in his brain.

"Sorry," she told him.

"No problem. Just pay attention to my hand," he reminded her, demonstrating the touches. "This means left. This means right. Back, and forward."

He tried the turn again.

She stumbled.

He tried one more time, and this time she succeeded.

But, while she grinned, she fumbled the next step.

He tried not to smile at her efforts. "I can see this is going to take practice."

"You're too sudden with your signals. And why do you get to call all the moves?"

"Because I'm the man."

"That's lame."

"And because I know how to dance."

"Okay, that's better."

Someone tapped Hunter on the shoulder. He turned to see Jack, looking to switch partners. Before he knew it, Kristy was in his arms.

"Hello, Hunter." She smiled, but he could see the glitter of determination behind her eyes.

"Hello, Kristy."

"I see you've spirited my sister away to Paris."

"I'm helping her out."

"That's one way to put it."

"What's another?" he challenged, keeping half an eye on Jack and Sinclair.

"Why don't you tell me what your intentions are?"

To have sex with Sinclair—the most amazing woman I've ever met—until we can't see straight. "I don't know what you mean?" he stalled.

"You know exactly what I mean."

He did. And that was the problem. His interests and Sinclair's did not coincide.

"I have no intention of hurting her," he told Kristy honestly.

"You think Jack intended to hurt me?"

"I think Jack was insane to marry you."

Kristy's eyes flashed.

"You know what I mean. He went into it for all the wrong reasons."

"Unlike you and Sinclair?" She didn't give him a chance to respond. "She's going to fall for you, Hunter. You're wining her and dining her and she's thinking she's become a fairy princess. How could she help but fall for you?"

"Point taken." Hunter tried a turn with Kristy, and she easily followed his lead. But it wasn't the same as dancing with Sinclair. It was nothing at all like dancing with Sinclair.

"So, what are you going to do?"

"For tonight—" Hunter took a deep breath and made up his mind "—I'm going to switch rooms with you and Jack."

Kristy and Jack were on a different floor of the hotel. And Hunter knew deep down in his heart that the adjoining door with Sinclair would prove too much of a temptation.

"You're a good man, Hunter," said Kristy, her eyes softening.

"Can I have that in writing? It might sway your husband."

"I'm talking about your moral code, not your business savvy."

"Nice."

"But that's none of my business."

"The push and pull has been going on a long time," said Hunter. "Jack, Gramps, the investors gripe and complain, but they take the dividends all the same."

"Your investments make dividends?"

"And capital gains, each and every one of them."

Kristy shook her head in obvious confusion. "Then why—"

"Because they think the odds are catching up with me, and they're sure I'm taking the entire flagship down one day."

"Will you?"

"Not planning on it." He danced her toward Jack and Sinclair. He might not be able to hold Sinclair in his bed tonight, but he could at least hold her on the dance floor until the clock struck midnight.

Nine

When Hunter had squeezed her hand in front of Kristy and Jack, down in the lobby and said, "See you in the morning," Sinclair knew it was all for show. So she brushed her hair, put on fresh perfume, and changed into the purple negligee from La Petite Fleur. She'd even touched up her face with a few of the Luscious Lavender cosmetics.

So, when the knock came from the adjoining hotel room, she was ready. Pulse pounding, skin tingling, anticipation humming along her nervous system, she opened the door.

"Hey, sis," sang Kristy. Then she tossed a command over her shoulder, "Avert your eyes, Jack."

Sinclair's jaw dropped open.

"I brought a nice Chardonnay." Kristy waved an open bottle in the air. "You got some glasses?"

Kristy breezed past her, and Sinclair met Jack's eyes.

"Jack," Kristy warned.

"Sorry," he called, lowering his gaze.

Sinclair turned to her sister. "What on earth—"

"You might want to shut the door," said Kristy.

"Where's Hunter?"

"We traded rooms."

Sinclair swung the door shut, battling her shock. "I can't believe you would—"

"It was his idea. He asked me to do it."

Why would Hunter ask to trade rooms? "Did you threaten him?" Sinclair asked suspiciously.

Kristy poured two glasses of wine. "Yeah. I did, so he backed off. Does that sound like Hunter?"

"No," Sinclair admitted. Hunter refused to back down from Jack and his grandfather. He sure wasn't going to back down from Kristy.

Kristy rounded the small coffee table and flopped down on one of the armchairs. "He traded rooms, because he doesn't want to hurt you. I admire that."

"He's not going to hurt me." Hurting was the furthest thing from what would happen between Hunter and Sinclair tonight.

Kristy took in Sinclair's outfit. "Well, he'd sure be doing something with you dressed like that."

Sinclair glanced down. "What? So we bought a few things at La Petite Fleur."

Dressed in a snazzy workout suit, Kristy curled her legs beneath her.

"And where do you see this thing going?"

"I haven't thought about it," Sinclair lied. She'd pictured everything from an "hasta la vista, baby" to a tear-stained goodbye, to a white dress and a cathedral.

"You work for him."

"I know. Don't you think I know?"

"Reality check," said Kristy. "Hunter's not a one-woman man."

"Reality check," Sinclair countered. "I'm not a one-man woman."

"Not before now."

"Do you honestly think I've fallen in love with him?" She hadn't.

"Not yet," said Kristy. "But you're taking an awfully big risk. You'll have to work with him afterward no matter what. With all the money he's invested in Castlebay, he's going to have to spend one heck of a lot of time at Lush Beauty. He *needs* this to work. And if your past becomes a problem, guess who's going to be gone?"

"You think Hunter would fire me?" Talk about extrapolating facts to the worst-case scenario.

"I think he might have to make a choice."

Sinclair took a long swallow of her wine, hating the fact that the scenario was possible.

She spun the stem of her glass around her fingertips. "What does Jack think?"

"Jack thinks Hunter's playing with fire. He's been reckless and impulsive before."

Sinclair tipped up the glass for another swallow. Reckless and impulsive, everybody seemed to agree on that, including Hunter.

"And it was his idea to switch rooms with you?" Sinclair confirmed.

Kristy nodded.

Sinclair played around with that little fact. Switching rooms meant Hunter thought it wouldn't last. Chivalrous of him to back off, really. Telling, but chivalrous.

"Did you get my message from last night?"

"I did."

Sinclair couldn't keep the hurt from her voice. "Why didn't you call me?" At least then she would have known to give Hunter a heads-up.

"I'd already told Jack what you said."

Sinclair watched her sister closely. "And Jack told you not to call me."

Kristy hesitated, then she gave a nod. It was her turn to drain her glass.

"Men coming between us," said Sinclair. "Who'd have thought?"

"He's my husband. And Hunter's his cousin. And this was family business."

"And I'm not family."

"Not the Osland family."

Sinclair nodded. "Not the Osland family."

Kristy tucked her blond hair behind her ears. "You sure you're not in love with him?"

She wasn't. Of all the things going on here, that, at least, wasn't an issue. "We've known each other a week. We've slept together exactly twice."

"I fell for Jack in a weekend."

"Are you *trying* to talk me into loving Hunter?"

"I'm wondering if you should come back to New York with me tomorrow."

"My makeover's not done yet."

She wouldn't run away. But she could keep it professional. They'd finish the dance lessons, take the planned tours of Castlebay locations, then she'd return to the U.S. and normal life. Her career would get back on track, and Hunter would go out and make more millions.

No big deal. No huge goodbye. They'd settle into their respective lives, and he'd forget all about her.

* * *

The next morning, as arranged, Sinclair entered the hotel dining room for a goodbye breakfast with Kristy. The maître d' recognized her and escorted her through the maze of diners, around the corner to a huge balcony overlooking the atrium.

There, the entire contingent of Oslands sat at a round table, heads bent together, talking rapidly and earnestly, frustration clear on Jack's and Cleveland's faces.

When Jack spotted Sinclair, he touched Cleveland's arm. The man looked up and stopped talking. Hunter and Kristy caught on, and all four shifted back. Forced smiles appeared on their faces.

She'd never felt so much like an outsider in her life.

Kristy stood. "Morning, sis." She came forward for a quick hug, gesturing to a chair between her and Cleveland.

Sinclair pointed to the way she'd come in. "I can…"

"Don't be silly," said Kristy. She shot a glance to the men.

They all came to their feet, talking overtop of one another as they insisted she stay.

She looked at Hunter, but his gaze was guarded. The intimacy was gone, and she couldn't find a clue as to whether she should be here or go.

Hunter moved around Cleveland to pull out her chair.

Sinclair sat down.

"Where were we?" asked Kristy. "Oh, yes. We were talking about the cruise."

Jack smoothly picked up on his wife's cue. "Can you be ready tomorrow afternoon?" he asked. "The captain could wait in port until Tuesday morning, but it's best if we keep the ship on schedule."

Cleveland sat in sullen silence.

"Do you think I should pick up a few sundresses before we go?" Kristy chirped. "Or maybe do a little—"

"This is ridiculous," said Sinclair.

Everyone looked at her.

She started to rise. "I'm going back to my—"

Reaching behind Cleveland, Hunter grabbed her arm. "You're not going anywhere."

She stared at him, then included everybody. "You have things to talk about. And it's not Kristy's sundresses."

Jack spoke up. "I happen to have a passionate interest in Kristy's sundresses. More so in her bikinis."

"Sinclair's right," barked Cleveland.

"Thank you," said Sinclair.

He swiveled in his chair to face her. "But she doesn't have to leave."

Sinclair didn't know what to say to that. The hollow buzz of voices from the atrium washed over her while his piercing eyes held her in place.

"I understand you were involved in the Castlebay acquisition."

"Gramps," warned Hunter.

"Well?" Cleveland pressed. "Were you or were you not?"

Sinclair struggled not to squirm under his probe, excruciatingly aware that this man held controlling interest in Osland International, which held controlling interest in Lush Beauty Products, and he could end her career with the snap of his fingers.

"Yes," she answered. "It was my idea."

"It was *my* idea," said Hunter.

"But—"

"Sinclair may have mentioned something about a single spa in New York. But I approached Castlebay. I did the research. I agreed to the price. And I signed the check. So, back off on Sinclair."

Cleveland turned to Hunter. "I'm interested in how much influence she has over you."

"None," said Hunter. "It was a business decision, and it was a good one. You read the reports."

Sinclair tried not to react to that statement. Of course it was a business decision. And she never assumed she had any influence over Hunter. But, somehow, his words hurt all the same.

Cleveland nodded. "I read the reports. The problem is cash flow."

"I just told you, borrow against the Paraguay mines."

"With currency fluctuations and the political instability? Do you want Osland International to fall down like a house of cards, boy?"

"Jack could give up the cruise ships he's just acquired," said Hunter.

"Jack cleared the cruise ship with the Board of Directors," Jack drawled.

Sinclair was afraid to move. She wanted to speak up, to explain. But couldn't summon the words.

Kristy leaned over and whispered in her ear. "Relax."

"We have options," Hunter spat.

"Are you kidding?" Sinclair hissed to her sister.

"They do this all the time," said Kristy.

"Castlebay is going to turn Lush Beauty into a gold mine," said Hunter with grim determination. "And *that's* what you sent me to do there."

"I sent you there to apologize to Sinclair."

Sinclair couldn't hold back. "He doesn't need—"

"You don't want a piece of this," Hunter warned her. Then

he set his sights back on his grandfather. "Next time you have a problem with my behavior, talk to me."

"Why? You never listen."

"And where the hell do you think I might have inherited that trait?"

"Insolent young pup," Cleveland muttered.

"Wait for it," Kristy whispered.

Cleveland squared his shoulders. "Don't you forget who built this company from an empty warehouse and a corner store."

"And you took exactly the same risks as me back then," Hunter practically shouted. "You didn't check with the Board of Directors, and you didn't convene a thirty-person legal panel with six months' lead time. You flew by the seat of your pants. *That's* how you built this company."

"Times have changed," said Cleveland.

"Maybe," Hunter allowed.

"And our current cash position is appalling."

"I'm not returning the cruise ships," said Jack, his arm going around his wife. "Kristy's buying a sundress."

"You're not returning the cruise ships," Cleveland agreed. "Hunter's going to fix this."

Hunter stared stonily at his coffee mug.

"I think we can join one of the ships in Fiji by the day after tomorrow," said Kristy in a perky voice that was completely at odds with the conversation.

Jack stroked her hair. "You'll look great on the beach," he cheerfully told her, clearly picking up on her lead.

Kristy elbowed Sinclair.

"Uh… What color bikini?" Sinclair tried, unable to take her eyes off Hunter.

"Purple," said Kristy. "And maybe a matching hat."

"Did you put any hats in the spring collection?" asked Cleveland. "I think we should start a new trend."

Hunter drew a deep breath. "Hats were up across the board at Sierra Sanchez last fall. Gramps may have a point."

Jack took a drink of his coffee and signaled for the waiter to bring refills, while Cleveland picked up his menu.

Sinclair glanced from person to person in complete astonishment. That was it? The blowup was over, and they were all having breakfast?

Hunter's family was insane.

Hunter could handle his family.

What he couldn't handle was his growing desire to be with Sinclair. When Gramps left and Jack and Kristy checked out of the Ciel D'Or Hotel yesterday, Hunter gave up the room adjoining Sinclair's, keeping the one on the top floor instead.

It didn't help.

Or maybe it did.

He still wanted to hold her, talk to her and laugh with her all night long. But being ten floors away made it harder for him to act on those impulses.

Before she left, Kristy had given him a lecture. Telling him in no uncertain terms to put Sinclair's interests first. Office affairs never ended well, and it was Sinclair who stood to get hurt. So, if Hunter cared for her at all, even just a little bit, he'd back off and let her get her career under control.

Then, just in case the lecture didn't take, Kristy had pointed out that things generally went bad for men whose cousins-in-law were gunning for them, as well. While Hunter was willing to take his chances with Cleveland and Jack's wrath, he didn't want to cross Kristy.

Plus, he cared for Sinclair. He cared for her more than just a little bit. Although he'd never admit it, she had influenced him in the Castlebay deal. Every time his instincts had twitched, or when Richard had pointed out a potential weakness in the deal, Hunter had seen Sinclair's smiling face, and he'd imagined the rush of telling her they owned the spas.

Castlebay wasn't a bad deal. But it wasn't a "pull out all the stops and get the papers signed in forty-eight hours" deal, either.

Yes, he cared about Sinclair. And he wanted her happy. And sleeping with her wasn't going to make her happy in the long run—even though it would make him ecstatic, short term.

Right now, he heard her heels tap on the hardwood floor. He glanced over to see her cross the dance studio in strappy black sandals and a bright, gauzy blue dress that flowed in points around her tanned calves. The skirt sections separated to give him glimpses of her thighs as she walked.

The dance instructor cued up the music, and Hunter braced himself.

"Ready?" Sinclair asked, her eyes sparkling sapphires that matched the brilliance of the dress.

He took a breath and held out his arms.

"You need to remember," he told her, watching them together in the big mirror. "From the minute you walk into the ball to the minute you leave, you're on stage. Roger will be watching what you do and how you do it."

"You're making me nervous again," she complained. But she glanced into the nearest mirror, then pulled back her shoulders and straightened her spine.

Hunter splayed his palm flat against her back. "Don't be nervous. Look into my eyes. Pay attention to my hand. We're in this together."

She met his gaze, and longing catapulted within him. Other

than a chaste peck on the cheek, he'd kept to himself since Kristy's lecture. But now Sinclair was fully in his arms. The back of her dress dipped to a low V, and his thumb brushed her bare skin.

He felt her shiver at the touch, and her reaction ratcheted up his own desire. Damn. He had to get his mind on the dancing.

Hunter led her through the opening steps.

"Go back, Sinclair," the instructor said. "Now left foot. Shoulders parallel. That's good. Get ready for the turn."

Hunter turned her, and Sinclair didn't stumble. Hunter smiled at her achievement.

"Promenade," said the instructor, and Hunter slipped his arm around Sinclair's waist, settling his hand above her hipbone.

"Good start," said the instructor. "Now, take it away, Hunter. Let's see what we've got to work with."

"Watch out," Hunter smiled at Sinclair, pulling her with his fingers, then pushing with the heel of his hand. She moved to the right, then the left, then backward, then into a turn. And she stumbled.

"Again," said the instructor, and Hunter started over.

She got it right. Then nailed it again.

After four times through the pattern, Hunter altered the ending and caught her by surprise.

"Hey," she protested.

"Stick with me. It's boring if we never do anything new."

"We never do anything at all, anymore," she muttered under her breath.

He didn't think he could have heard her right. "Excuse me?"

"Nothing."

He switched her to a cuddle position. He leaned down, intending to murmur in her ear. She wanted to flirt? He was there.

"Head high," the instructor called.

Hunter corrected his posture and caught her smirk.

He went back to the basic pattern, then changed it up, then whirled her through an underarm turn, her skirts flaring around her knees.

"You are absolutely gorgeous," he whispered.

"Thank you," she said on a sigh. "But I'm tired of being gorgeous."

The song faded to an end.

"What do you mean?" he asked.

She fingercombed her hair. "Restaurants and dances and fancy clothes are all well and good. But I want to kick back. Maybe hop into sweats, watch a sappy movie and cook something for myself." She pouted prettily. "I miss cooking."

"I don't miss cooking."

"That's because you're spoiled."

"I'm not spoiled."

She looked pointedly around the big, mirrored room. "We're having a private dance lesson."

The music started, and he took her into his arms once again, not fighting his feelings so much anymore.

"That," he said as he squared his shoulders and checked their lines, "is because *I'm* spoiling *you*."

She seemed to contemplate his words as the notes ascended. "That is also true."

Hours later, Sinclair glanced around at the huge arched windows, the kitchenette and the overstuffed leather furniture. "All this time you've had a kitchen?" she asked Hunter.

Hunter set two grocery bags down on the marble counter in the small kitchen alcove while Sinclair checked out the other rooms.

"Jack likes nice things for Kristy," Hunter called.

"Kristy doesn't need a four-person whirlpool," Sinclair called back. "I've been camping with that woman."

"The whirlpool's nice," said Hunter, meeting Sinclair in the main room.

She trailed her fingertips along the leather-accented bar. "So, you basically traded me in on a whirlpool and a veranda?"

She'd missed him.

She'd lain awake at night wishing he was there beside her. It would be nice to make love, sure. But she also wanted to feel his warmth, hear his breathing, even read the morning paper side by side.

"Don't forget the microwave," he said, and picked up one of the hotel phones, punching in a number.

"Well, then. No wonder. I can hardly compete with a microwave." She kicked off her high-heeled sandals and eased up onto a bar stool, arranging the gauzy skirt around her legs. She'd had fun dancing tonight. It seemed as if it was finally coming together. She was reading Hunter's signals, and she found herself looking forward to meeting him on the dance floor at the ball.

Of course, she'd have to dance with other people. But she'd savor the moments with Hunter, even though it would signal the end of their personal relationship. She couldn't see them spending much time together once they were back in New York.

She tried not to feel sad about that. Instead, she gazed at him across the room, taking a mental snapshot of his relaxed posture and smiling face.

He spoke into the telephone receiver. "I'm looking for some ladies' sportswear."

Sinclair turned her attention to the gilded mirror and the assortment of liquors behind the bar. In the meantime, she knew how to make a great mushroom sauce for their chicken breasts, if they had...there it was. Calvados brandy.

She slipped down and padded around the end of the bar. She doubted she could compete with the chefs who must cook for Hunter, but she'd give it her best try.

"Ladies' sweatpants," said Hunter. "Gray."

Sinclair grinned to herself, snagging the bottle of brandy. As he'd done so many times, he was giving her exactly what she'd asked for.

"Maybe a tank top?" He looked at her, and she nodded her agreement.

"Size small," he said while she headed for the kitchenette, scoping out the few cupboards for dishes. They were going to have a relaxing evening. Just the two of them. She hadn't felt this relaxed in weeks.

"Great," he said into the phone. "No, that should do it."

"A baking dish," Sinclair called, finding plates, silverware and glasses.

Hunter relayed the message.

"Oh, and a pot," she said. "With a lid."

"One pot and one lid," Hunter said into the phone. Then he looked to Sinclair. "That everything?"

She nodded, closing the cupboards and removing the groceries from the sacks.

"Thank you," Hunter said into the phone. Then he hit the off button.

"Wine?" he asked Sinclair.

"You bet." She'd worked hard today. In fact, she'd worked hard all week. Glamming up was no easy business.

"Red or white?"

"You pick."

"Mouton Rothschild," he decided, retrieving a bottle from the wine rack and snagging the corkscrew from the bar top.

"What's the occasion?"

"You," he said, slicing off the foil cover. "In gray sweatpants." Then he twisted the corkscrew.

"If that doesn't cry out for a fine beverage, I don't know what does."

"Me, neither." He popped the cork and poured the dark liquid into two wide-mouthed wineglasses. Then he carried them to the counter where she was working.

"Know how to make a salad?" she asked, setting out lettuce, tomatoes, peppers and cucumber.

"Nope," he answered, sipping the wine.

"Know how to eat a salad?"

"Of course."

She opened a drawer, pulled out a chopping knife and set it on the counter. "Then wing it."

"Hey, you were the one bent on giving up luxury."

"And you get to help."

"I bought the sweatpants," he grumbled.

"Don't forget to wash everything."

Hunter stared blankly at the assortment of vegetables. "Maybe I should call the chef."

"And how would that be a home-cooked meal?"

"He'd be in our home while he cooked it."

Sinclair pulled in her chin, peering at him through the tops of her eyes. "Shut up and start chopping."

"Okay," he agreed with a tortured sigh. "It's your funeral."

She removed the butcher's paper from the chicken breasts. "You can't kill me with a salad."

"I have never, I mean never, cooked anything in my life."

She stared at him in disbelief. "Don't you ever get hungry, like late at night?"

"Sure."

"And?"

"And I call the kitchen." He looked doubtful as he un-wrapped a yellow pepper.

"You seriously need a reality check."

"I seriously need a chef."

"Peel off the label, then wash the pepper, cut it vertically and take out the seeds."

Hunter blinked at her.

She rattled into one of the bags, looking for spices. "That's not going to work."

"What's not going to work?"

"That, oh-so-pathetic, lost-little-boy expression."

He gave up and peeled off the label, then turned to the sink. "It's tried and true on about a dozen nannies."

"You must have been incorrigible."

"I was delightful."

"I'm sure."

She spiced the chicken breasts, then chopped up the mush-rooms, while Hunter butchered a number of innocent veg-etables beyond recognition.

"Did you get cream?" she asked, peering into the bottom of the sack.

"Over here." He reached around her, and her face came up against his chest. His clean scent overwhelmed her, while her breasts brushed his stomach. Everything inside her contracted with desire.

"Here you go." He set the carton of cream on the counter in front of her. If he'd noticed the breast brush, he didn't let on. She, on the other hand, was still tingling from the contact.

She turned away and set the oven temperature. It was too early to make the sauce, so she put the cream in the half-sized fridge and moved to put some distance between her and Hunter.

"Can we get a movie?" she asked.

"There's a DVD library behind the couch. Or pay-per-view if you want something current."

"A classic?" she asked, skirting the couch.

"It's your night," he responded. "If it was mine, the fantasy would include waiters."

It was on the tip of her tongue to ask for details about his fantasy night, but she quickly realized that would take them down a dangerous road.

A knock sounded.

"The sweatpants," said Hunter from where he was running the cucumber under cold water.

Sinclair left the DVD library to go for the door.

She took the sweatpants and tank top into Hunter's bedroom, stripping off her dancing dress and hanging it in the closet. The V back of the dress hadn't allowed for a bra, so she wasn't wearing one. The sweats were loose and rode low on her hips. While the pale-purple-and-gray-striped tank top left a strip of bare skin on her abdomen. But the cotton fabric was soft and cool, and she felt more relaxed than she had in days.

"You should take off your tie," she said to Hunter as she reemerged into the living room.

He glanced up, and his gaze stopped on her outfit for a few seconds.

"Good idea." He dried his hands then worked open the knot. He unbuttoned his cuffs and rolled up the sleeves.

She crouched in front of the DVD rack. *"Notting Hill?"* she asked. "Or *While You Were Sleeping? Sweet Home Alabama?"*

"Is that the chick-flick shelf?"

"How about *Die Hard?*"

"Now *that's* a movie."

"Fine, but nobody ever got lucky watching *Die Hard.*"

"Am I getting lucky?"

She ignored him. "Here we go. *The Last of the Mohicans.*"

He nodded. "Good compromise."

She pulled it from the shelf. "Action, adventure, emotion and romance."

"Sounds like a winner to me."

"It's not very funny."

"Apparently, we can't have everything." He stepped back from the counter. "However, we have achieved salad."

She walked over to check it out. The lettuce pieces were too large, the peppers were practically pureed, and there was a puddle of water forming at the bottom of the bowl.

"Good job."

"Thank you. But I'm pretty sure it's going to be a once-in-a-lifetime experience."

She snagged a crooked slice of cucumber and popped it in her mouth. "Then I'll be sure to savor it."

He looked down into her eyes. "Excellent idea," he said, and her breath caught at the tone of his voice. "Savoring those experiences that are rare."

Ten

Dinner over, Hunter and Sinclair each found a comfortable spot on the leather couch. They had a box of chocolate truffles between them, and another bottle of Château Rothschild on the coffee table. He would have liked to draw her into his arms, or into his lap, or at least over beside him. But until she sent a signal, he didn't intend to make a move.

She curled up, her legs beneath her, and her pert breasts rounded out against the tight tank top. He could make out the outline of her nipples in the dim light, and he stared at them with a fatalistic longing. Her shoulders were tanned and smooth, her bare waist and cute belly button were nipped in above the low cut pants. And he could see the barest hint of her satin panties along the line of her hip.

She reached for a chocolate. "Did you try the Grande Marnier?" Her lips wrapped halfway around the dark globe, and she bit down with an appreciate groan.

He wasn't going to make it through the movie.

There was absolutely no way he was going to make it through the movie.

"Here." She held out the other half of the chocolate.

He leaned forward, and she popped it into his mouth. Then she licked the remaining chocolate cream from her fingertips.

"Good?" she asked.

He nodded, unable to form an actual word.

The American frontier bloomed up on the wide screen.

Sinclair reached for her wine. "Here we go."

He didn't even glance at the colorful screen. Instead, he stared at her profile, remembering what it felt like to kiss her lips, to taste the smooth skin of her shoulders and breasts, to stroke his fingers along the most intimate parts of her body.

She sipped her wine, and he watched her swallow. She smiled, then frowned, her eyes squinting down in reaction to the story.

"You done?" he asked, moving the chocolate box to the coffee table, clearing his path. If he had an opportunity to move closer, he'd take it in a split second.

She glanced at the box. Then she nodded.

Using the excuse of replacing the lid, he eased toward the middle of the couch, then he settled back to bide his time while the story unfolded.

As the heroine's party made their way through the bush and the music signaled the tension and danger, Sinclair pushed herself to the back of the couch.

Hunter moved a little closer, stretching his arm across the back. "You okay?" he asked.

She nodded, gaze not leaving the screen.

The first attack came, and she jerked in reaction. Hunter

covered her shoulder in comfort, and her hand came up to squeeze his. Her skin was soft and warm against his palm, and her fingers were delicate where they entwined with his own.

The story moved on until the hero and heroine were pinned down in the woods. They joined forces, and Sinclair sighed. Hunter had to admit this was a much better date movie than *Die Hard*.

He shifted closer still, so that their thighs brushed together. When, under gunfire, the hero and heroine finally came together to make love, Sinclair leaned her head on Hunter's shoulder.

Unable to resist, he kissed the top of her head, and wrapped an arm tight around her.

By the time the action got bloody, she was burying her face in his chest. And, at the resolution, she relaxed, molding against his body while she tipped her chin up to look him in the eyes.

"Hey," he said gruffly.

"Inspiring story," she returned.

Neither moved away, and they stared at each other in silence, her eyes reflecting the longing in his blood.

"Your sister's right," he finally offered in a last ditch attempt to be a gentleman.

Sinclair didn't answer, instead her hand crept up along his chest, finding the bare skin of his neck, and caressing it in a way that made him groan.

"My sister's sleeping with your cousin," she said.

Hunter didn't understand the point, but he couldn't formulate the right question.

Sinclair stretched up to kiss the corner of his mouth. "That means she can afford to be right." She gave him a swift kiss on the center of his lips.

He automatically puckered in response.

"I, on the other hand, am in the mood to be very, very wrong."

"So am I," he breathed, scooping his hand beneath her bottom and easing her into a reclining position beside him.

His lips came down on hers with all the purpose in the world.

Then he stripped off her tank top, wrapping his arms around her bare back and pulling her breasts flush against his body.

"I want you so bad," he rasped, kissing her collarbone, her breasts, the tight pebble of her nipple that he'd been watching for two long, painful hours.

"I've missed you," she confessed. "I don't care that we have to go back. I don't care that it has to end."

He slipped a hand beneath her sweatpants, beneath her satin panties, to her bare buttocks. "Nothing's going to end tonight. Not for a very, very long time."

She smiled up at him, her blue eyes turning to midnight sky as her fingers tugged his shirt from his waistband. "I want to touch every inch of your body."

"Good."

"I want you inside me for hours."

"Better."

"I want to make love so long and so hard…."

Hunter kissed her mouth, over and over, completely speechless with desire.

"What should I do?" she breathed.

"You're already doing it."

His hot gaze took in her bare breasts. He stripped off the sweat pants and stared at the satin panties he'd glimpsed earlier. He ran his hand down her thigh, along her calf, over the arch of her foot.

She managed to slip off his shirt.

Her hands went to his chest, stroking upward, pausing on his nipples. "I don't think we'll be waxing," she said, and he chuckled at her joke.

He ran his hand up her calf again. "Somebody's been waxing."

"It doesn't hurt that much."

"Glad you're tough." He ran the hand back down. "Really glad you're tough."

"Smooth, huh?"

"Smooth as silk." He trickled his fingers up her thigh, slipping them beneath her panties, teasing the smooth skin near the top.

Sinclair gasped at the sensation, arching her back, plastering her body against his, feeling the rough texture of his slacks against her thighs.

"You are amazing," he gasped.

"You are… You are…" She didn't even have words for it.

"Impatient," he supplied, pushing his way out of his slacks.

"Thank goodness." She smiled.

But he stopped, their naked bodies flush against each other. He rubbed a thumb across her sensitive lips, kissed them thoroughly, then rubbed it once more. "You sure you're ready?"

She nodded. Her entire body tingled in anticipation. Hunter. She was getting Hunter again. Finally.

He stroked her thighs, parting them, then slowly pushed his way inside.

A powerful, unfamiliar feeling surged through her body. She tunneled her fingers into his hair, she clutched his back, arching against him, delving into their kiss until the rest of the world disappeared.

"Damn," he muttered, pulling back ever so slightly, blinking his eyes. He glanced down to where their bodies met. "This has to last."

"Make it last," she whispered. Forever and ever and ever.

She kissed his forehead, his eyelids, his cheeks. Then she got serious again on his mouth.

His fingers moved to the small of her back. Then his hands cupped her bottom and he rocked her pelvis as his hard length moved in and out. The low buzz in her body ratcheted up to a roar. Shots of sparkling heat radiated out from her center. Her breath came in small gasps against his lips.

Her hands fisted on his back. Her thighs tightened, her eyes fluttered closed, and she rocked herself hard into his rhythm.

"I…can't…" she panted. "Oh…please…"

He lifted her ever so slightly, changing the angle, making her eyes pop open in wonder.

They both stilled, faces mere inches apart, staring at each other, gasping the same air. And then he moved, and she groaned, and her universe contracted to the place where their bodies were joined.

She wrapped her arms around his neck and held on tight, inhaling his scent as deep as she could manage, tasting the salt of his skin, feeling his taught muscles surround her and block out the world.

They both made it last, refusing to give in to the ultimate pleasure as the minutes ticked by and slick sweat gathered between their bodies.

Hunter's name began pounding in her brain. An exquisite pulse started low, becoming more insistent, forcing a moan from her lips and making her hips buck uncontrollably.

He whispered her name, and she was lost.

He followed her, her name on his lips over and over and over again.

* * *

They switched to the bed and made love again. Sinclair clung to him with all her might, wishing she could hold off the morning.

But when they finally separated, gasping and exhausted, the sun was an orange glow on the horizon.

"Now *that* was reckless and impulsive," said Hunter.

"Your family should really stop trying to beat those impulses out of you."

"You want to tell them that?"

"I do. Hand me your cell phone."

He did.

She pressed Jack's speed-dial button before Hunter whisked it out of her hand.

"I thought you were bluffing," he said.

She grinned. "And I thought you could wrestle a six-foot alligator."

"Okay," he groaned, dropping the phone on the bedside table. "All kidding aside. We've got trouble."

"We certainly do."

He propped himself up on his elbow and traced a line from her shoulder to her wrist. "Question is," he drawled softly, "what do we do about it?"

"You're still my boss," she said.

"I am."

"We still can't have an office fling."

"Agreed."

"Of course, we're not in the office now."

"I like the way you're thinking."

She popped up on her elbow, facing him, matching his posture. "We could keep it up until we get home."

Hunter watched her for a few minutes, concern flitting across his expression. "Kristy's afraid you'll fall for me."

"I know she is."

He took a breath as if he was steeling himself. "You gonna fall for me, Sinclair?"

"Don't flatter yourself," she quickly put in. "You're too reckless and impulsive to be a long-term bet."

"Plus, I lie."

"Plus," she agreed with a nod, "you lie."

He reached out to stroke her cheek with the pad of his thumb, brushing back her hair.

"I don't want to hurt you," he said.

She squelched her softer feelings. It was a fling or nothing, and that was the hard, cold truth of the matter. And she didn't want nothing, so she was taking the fling.

"What if I hurt you?" she suggested in return, just to keep things fair.

"I don't think Kristy cares so much about that." He paused. "We've got three whole days until the Valentine's ball."

"And two whole nights to go with them."

He kissed her nose. "So we're decided then?"

She nodded against him. "I think our only hope is to get it out of our system."

"Agreed."

Sinclair pushed to a sitting position. "We're going to see the spas today, right?"

"Paris, London and Brussels."

"Then we should get going."

Hunter groaned, tugging her back into place and pulling the covers over them. "First, we sleep."

"The sooner we get going, the sooner we get back."

He paused and opened one eye. "To this big, lovely bed."

"In this big, lovely suite."

"Can we get room service this time?"

"Poor baby," she cooed, drawing his fingertips to her lips and kissing them one by one. "Did you cut yourself chopping?"

"It's a time-saving ploy," he explained. "I have my sights set on the whirlpool."

Sinclair hopped up. "I'm in."

They laughed their way through the shower and into their clothes. Hunter had Simon pour on the power across the Channel and then back through Belgium. Sinclair gave the spa managers an orientation to the Luscious Lavender products, put them in touch with Ethan, and with Mary-Anne from distribution, then they hightailed it back to the heart of Paris.

By early evening, they were in the whirlpool.

Hunter pulled Sinclair back into the cradle of his thighs, handing her a flute of champagne and kissing her damp neck. She sighed in contentment, sipping the sweet, bubbly liquid while he lazily scrubbed a foamy loofah sponge over her back.

With his other hand, he touched the jeweled fish on her bracelet.

Sinclair had forgotten she still had it on. She jangled it in front of her eyes. "I think it's my favorite."

He drew her wrist forward to kiss the tender, inside skin. "*This* is my favorite."

"Really?" She pointed to her elbow. "I thought this was your favorite."

He kissed her there. "That, too."

"And this?" she pointed to her shoulder.

"Of course."

"This?" Her neck.

"All of it."

She laughed.

He sat back and his sponge strokes grew longer along her spine.

"Did you get a hold of Roger?" he asked.

"I did. He wasn't thrilled about me delaying my return even longer."

"You mean Chantal's not the wunderkind we all imagined?"

"He didn't complain about her. He said I was setting a bad example."

"By taking your holidays?"

"I guess."

"Want me to talk to him?"

"Oh, yeah. Great idea. Why don't you call him up?"

Sinclair's cell phone chimed.

"If that's Roger," said Hunter. "Tell him I say 'hey.'"

She elbowed Hunter in the ribs, drying one hand before reaching for her phone. "Hello?"

"Hey, you."

Sinclair guiltily pushed Hunter's sponge hand away. "Hi, Kristy."

He continued to rub her back.

"What's up?" asked Kristy.

"Not much. Where are you?"

"Off the coast of New Zealand. We just got cell service back."

"Great."

"So, what are you doing?"

Hunter's hand slipped around to her stomach. "Went to the spa in Brussels today, and the one in London. Met with the managers. Got them all set up for Friday's launch."

"Good for you." Kristy paused. "Hunter still in Paris?"

"He's here. But he was a little standoffish after you left." Hunter choked back a laugh.

"I guess he came to his senses," said Kristy.

"I guess he did," Sinclair agreed, as the sponge meandered toward her breast. She clutched it to her stomach to stop his progress.

"So, when are you coming home?"

"By the fourteenth, for sure. I need to be there for the ball."

Hunter wrenched his hand free.

Sinclair bit down on her lip to keep from gasping as the sponge brushed between her legs. "I better go," she blurted, grappling for Hunter's meandering hands.

"Anything wrong?"

"Uh, something's boiling on the stove."

"The *stove?*"

"I moved to a suite. Talk to you in a few days." She disconnected.

She turned on him. "Are you crazy?"

"No." He kissed her mouth.

"Do you know what would happen—"

He kissed her again.

"If they—"

He kissed her a third time.

She gave in and wrapped her arms around his neck, turning to press her body into his, the water slick and hot between them.

Hunter's phone rang.

"For the love of—"

"Give me the sponge," she said, holding out her hand.

"Forget it."

She snapped her fingers, then wiggled them in a *give it* motion. "Fair's fair."

He dried his hand, then lifted his phone, at the same time tossing the sponge to her.

She eased back on her heels and snagged it with both hands.

"Hunter Osland," he greeted.

There was a pause. "Hey, Jack." And he grinned at Sinclair, spreading his arms, giving her a wide-open target.

She couldn't decide whether to go for it or not.

Then Hunter's attention clearly shifted to the phone call. "I'd still use the mine as collateral."

He paused.

"Maybe in the short term, sure." He slicked his wet hair back from his forehead.

"Of course he'll be ticked off. Everything ticks him off."

Hunter absently smoothed the droplets of water down Sinclair's arm. She gave up goofing around and curled against him, leaning her head on his shoulder.

"Get in and out before the Paraguay election, and you won't have a problem." Hunter's hand worked its way across her stomach.

She glanced up to see if he was teasing her again, but he seemed absorbed in the call. He wasn't messing with her, just unconsciously caressing her body. She sighed and relaxed against him.

Hunter chuckled, jiggling his chest. "We'll check it out sometime." A pause. "I mean me, of course. *I'll* check it out sometime. None of your business." Hunter's hand squeezed Sinclair. "I'm going now," he said to Jack. "A nap, that's what. Time zone change. Okay by me. I'm turning off my phone. Uh-huh. Goodbye."

He hit the off button with his thumb and held it down until it chimed. Then he dropped it on the shelf beside them and hauled Sinclair up for a kiss.

"You are *so* distracting," he muttered.

"I was being good."

"You were being damn good."

She giggled as his mouth came down, hot and moist and demanding against her own.

The water splashed around the whirlpool in waves as they rediscovered each other's bodies.

Eleven

They were back in the U.S. by midmorning on the four-teenth, and Sinclair couldn't resist checking in at Lush Beauty in one of her new outfits.

Her hair and makeup perfect, she strolled into the office in a slim peacock-blue coat dress, with three-quarter sleeves, leather details on the collar, appliqué pockets, large contrasting silver buttons and high-heeled leather ankle boots. She carried a tiny purse, holding nothing but her cell phone, keys and a credit card.

Amber's jaw literally dropped open as Sinclair crossed through the outer office.

"I was going to check messages," Sinclair called over her shoulder. "You coming to the ball tonight?"

She pushed open her office door and stopped dead.

Chantal sat at her desk, computer open to e-mail, file folders scattered in front of her, and Sinclair's phone to her ear.

Neither woman spoke for a moment.

"Can I call you back?" Chantal said into the phone.

"You're at my desk," said Sinclair.

"You're back early," said Chantal.

Amber apparently recovered her wits and rushed into the office. "Roger asked—"

"I'll be needing it now," Sinclair informed Chantal. "Right now."

Chantal hit a few keys on the computer. "If you'll just give me a few minutes."

"I don't think so," Sinclair stated, walking around the desk. "Those the Valentine's ball files?"

"The Castlebay files," Chantal admitted.

"Oh, good. Just what I wanted." Sinclair dropped her small purse on the desk. She was vindictive enough to put it label up so that Chantal could see it was a Vermachinni.

She inched in closer, crowding the woman until Chantal finally stood up and clicked the close button on her e-mail program. Chantal started to pick up the files.

"You can leave them here," Sinclair told her. "I'll call you if I need anything."

Chantal glared at her.

"Did Roger mention the private party at the Castlebay Spa Manhattan tonight?"

Chantal didn't answer.

Sinclair pursed her lips, knowing full well Roger himself didn't even know about the after party yet.

The woman's eyes glittered black. "Amber said she e-mailed you the catering contracts yesterday?"

"She did. And we've substituted duck for the pheasant. We got rid of the peanut oil because of possible allergies. And the gift bags are now recycled paper, which will stave off any media grab by Earthlife."

Chantal scooped up her briefcase and stomped out of the office.

"Uh," Amber stammered in the wake of Chantal's departure. "Is there anything…you, uh, need?"

Sinclair turned. "Hi," she said to her assistant.

"Coffee?" asked Amber, quickly straightening a pile of magazines on the credenza. "Tea?"

"It's *me*," Sinclair pointed out.

Amber nodded. "Mineral water, maybe?"

"Amber."

"You look…"

Sinclair waved a dismissive hand. "I know. Did you see the ads for the Chastlebay locations? They're having special midnight openings tonight to coincide with the ball over here."

"Sinclair?" came Ethan's voice.

Amber quickly ducked out of the office.

"Good for you," Ethan said to Sinclair.

She assumed he was talking about her appearance and smiled.

"Somebody needs to stand up to Roger."

She realized Ethan was referring to her absence. "All I did was take a vacation."

"On the eve of the product launch."

"True."

"It took a lot of guts."

"I wasn't trying to make a statement." She was merely trying to keep her career path alive.

"I thought you were trying to prove we couldn't live without you."

Sinclair paused. "Can you?"

"It's tough. Not that Roger would ever admit it. Amber really stepped up to the plate."

"Good for her. What about Chantal?"

Ethan cocked his head. "I think she has a future as eye candy."

"That's it?"

"That's it."

Sinclair nodded, glad of Ethan's assessment.

"I really just wanted to give you a high five on the spa deal," said Ethan.

Sinclair grinned and held up her hand.

Ethan smacked his palm against hers. "Hunter's a smart man," he said.

Sinclair nodded her agreement.

"He told me the idea originated with you. So, you know, you probably have a supporter in that corner."

"That's good to know," said Sinclair, trying to keep the secretive glow out of her eyes. Earlier this morning, as the jet taxied to the terminal building at JFK, Hunter had kissed her goodbye and pledged admiration for her business savvy and his support for tonight.

Ethan made for the door. "See you tonight?"

"You will."

As Ethan left, Amber peeked through the doorway. "I hope you don't mind." She took in Sinclair's outfit one more time. "I gave your name and cell phone as an after-hours contact for the caterer tonight."

"Of course I don't mind." That was standard operating procedure.

"Oh, good." Amber disappeared.

Sinclair straightened the Castlebay files, hoping her makeover went a whole lot better tonight than it went today.

Ethan hadn't noticed, Amber was afraid of her, and who knows what Roger had thought? She'd hardly wowed them here on the home front.

* * *

Freshly shaved, in his dress shirt and tuxedo slacks, Hunter looped a silk bow tie around his neck. Sinclair would be wearing her most elegant dress tonight, and he wanted them to go well together. Although they were trying to keep their relationship under wraps—okay, their former relationship under wraps—he seriously wanted her to shine. And he was planning on at least a couple of dances.

He stepped in front of the hallway mirror in the Oslands' New York apartment and leveled the two ends of the tie.

Then his cell phone rang.

He retrieved it from the entry-room table and flipped it open. "This is Hunter."

"Two things," said Jack.

"Go," Hunter replied, squinting at a strand of lint on the crisp white shirt. He brushed it off.

"The incumbent president of Paraguay just dropped dead from a heart attack."

"No kidding?"

"No kidding."

Hunter sat down on the entryway bench. "Did you use the mine as collateral?"

"I did."

"Damn." That was a setback.

"And two," Jack continued. "Frontier Cruise Lines is filing for Chapter Eleven tomorrow morning. There are three ships up for sale in the next twelve hours."

"And our cash position sucks."

"It sucks."

Hunter paused. "You really want to get into the cruise-ship business?"

"Kristy loved it."

Hunter could relate. Sinclair loved the spa business.

Wait.

He shook the comparison out of his mind. He had to get used to thinking of himself and Sinclair as separate entities, not as the same thing.

"Where are you?" he asked Jack.

"Sydney."

Hunter glanced at his watch. "Banks open in London in four hours. You serious about this?"

"What does your gut say?" asked Jack. "You're the quick thinker."

"There's no denying the quality of Frontier ships. And it's an expanding market. We could dovetail Castlebay marketing with a new cruise-line marketing strategy, maybe even put Castlebays on each of the ships." Hunter clicked through a dozen other details in his mind. "You have a sense of the Frontier prices versus market?"

"Fire sale."

"We might be able to do something with the Lithuania electronics plant. Restructure the debt...."

"Gramps will kill us."

"Welcome to my world."

There was silence on the line.

"You know," said Jack. "I think I'm understanding the appeal of this. It's like Vegas."

"Higher stakes," Hunter quipped.

"No kidding," said Jack.

Hunter glanced at his watch. "I'd have to go to London." The Lithuania banking was done through Barclays, and they needed the time-zone jump start to pull it together.

"That a problem?" asked Jack.

Hunter's mind flashed to Sinclair. She'd be all right at

the ball. Truth was, he was merely window dressing tonight. She was *so* ready for this. And, anyway, he could make it up to her later.

"I need to make a couple calls," he said.

"You get the financing in place, and I'll nail down the contracts with Richard."

"Where is he?" asked Hunter.

"L.A."

"Too bad."

"Should I send him to New York?"

"It'd be better if you could get him to London." Hunter paused. "No. Wait. New York will work. Tell him I'll call him around 4:00 a.m."

"Perfect." It was Jack's turn to pause. "And, Hunter?"

"Yeah?"

"Thanks."

"All part of the game, cousin." Hunter disconnected.

He dragged off the bow tie and released the buttons to his shirt.

On the way to the bedroom, he dialed Simon and asked him to have the jet ready. Then he changed into a business suit, put another one into a garment bag and called down to his driver to let him know they'd be heading for the airport.

Sinclair stood in the lobby of the Roosevelt Hotel. She hadn't expected Hunter to pick her up and escort her every movement. It wasn't as if they were on a date. Still, she would have felt a little less self-conscious with somebody at her side.

Tuxedoed men accompanied glittering women dressed in traditional black or brilliant-red evening gowns. The couples were smiling and laughing as they made their way past the sweeping staircase and a central glass sculpture. Plush armchairs dotted the multi-story rotunda, while marble pillars supported sconce lights and settees along a lattice-decorated walkway to the main ballroom.

Flashbulbs popped and cameras rolled as the media vied for footage of the A-list event. The PR person in Sinclair was thrilled with the hoopla, the woman in her was disappointed to be there alone. She squelched the silly, emotional reaction and answered a few questions from a reporter for a popular magazine. But then the reporter spotted someone more exciting and quickly wrapped it up.

"Sinclair," came Sammy Simon's voice.

She turned to see one of the Lush Beauty Lavender suppliers decked out in a black tux and tie.

He took both of her hands in his. "Lovely," he drawled appreciatively, taking in her strapless white satin dress. It had a sweetheart neckline and tiny red hearts scattered over the bodice. The hearts gathered into a vertical, then cascaded down one side of the full skirt.

Sammy kissed her on the cheek. "I had no idea you were a fan of haute couture."

She gave him a laugh. "A little something I picked up in Paris."

He squeezed her hands. "Find me later for a dance." And he joined the throng headed for the party.

"Sinclair," came another voice, and an arm went around her shoulders.

"Mr. Davidson." She greeted the owner of a chain of specialty shops that had featured Lush Beauty Products for years.

"This is my wife, Cynthia."

Sinclair smiled and leaned forward to shake the woman's hand. As she did, Wes Davidson's hand dropped to an uncomfortable level near her hip.

"And one of my store managers, Reginald Pie."

"Nice to meet you, Mr. Pie." Sinclair shook the man's hand.

Wes Davidson spoke up. "It's such a pleasure to see you, Sinclair. I've been meaning to arrange a meeting to talk about the new product lines."

"Absolutely," she agreed.

"I'll call you," he said. "Great to see you looking… so…great."

Mrs. Davidson reddened.

Sinclair gently pulled away. "Oh, look. There's Ethan. I need to say hello. So good to see you Mr. Davidson. Mrs. Davidson."

Sinclair slipped away.

She made a beeline for Ethan. He was talking to two of their distributors.

"But if the price breaks don't work for the small retailers," one of the men was saying, "you're going to compromise your core business."

"Hello, Ethan," Sinclair broke in, grateful to find a safe conversation.

The men stopped talking and turned to stare at her.

"You remember Sinclair," said Ethan.

What a strange thing to say. Of course they remembered her.

"Sinclair," said Ron. "You look incredible."

"Fabulous to see you again," said David.

Then the conversation stopped dead.

Sinclair glanced from one man to the other. "You were talking about price breaks?" she prompted.

David chuckled. "Oh, not tonight," he said. "You look incredible," he repeated Ron's sentiment.

"Thank you." But that didn't mean her brain had stopped working.

There was another strained silence.

"I'll see you all inside?" Sinclair offered.

The men seemed to relax.

"Yes," said David.

"Looking forward to it," said Ron.

Ethan winked.

Sinclair walked away and immediately spotted Chantal.

She was surrounded by admirers, and she didn't seem to mind they were focused on her looks and not on her business savvy. She was a glittering jewel in low-cut bright red, and she seemed to revel in the role.

Sinclair, on the other hand, was having serious reservations about her makeover. Men used to take her seriously. She couldn't remember the last time she felt so awkward in a business conversation.

Her cell phone rang in her evening purse, and she welcomed the distraction. She picked up the call.

"Can you hang on?" she asked, not expecting to be able to hear the answer.

She sought out an alcove behind the concierge desk, next to a bank of phone booths.

"Hello?"

"It's Hunter," came a welcome and familiar voice.

"Hey, you," she responded, her voice softening, and the tension inside her dissipating to nothing. "Are you out front?" She glanced at the foyer, straining to see him coming through the main doors.

"I've had a complication."

"Oh?"

He was going to be late. Sinclair tried to take the news in stride. She really had no expectations of him. At least, she had no right to have any expectations of him. But in that split second, she realized she'd been counting the minutes until he'd arrive.

"I'm on my way to London."

"Now?" she couldn't help but ask.

"There's a couple of cruise ships, and a bankruptcy, and a complication in the Paraguay election."

"I understand," she quickly put in.

"I'm sorry—"

"No need. It's business." She'd been warned he'd hurt her. Hadn't she been warned?

She heard him draw a breath. Traffic sounds came through his end of the phone.

"We only have twelve hours," he told her.

She forced a laugh. "Another quick deal?"

"Jack's on board this time."

"That's good."

"We can get a really great price."

"Of course." She tried to ignore the crushing disappointment pressing down on her chest. She had no right to feel this way. He'd done so much for her already.

"You're great," he told her. "You'll do fine on your own."

"I know," she nodded, realizing how very much she'd been counting on their last dance tonight. There was something about their relationship that cried out for closure—a closure she hadn't yet experienced.

"I wouldn't do it, except—"

"Hunter, stop."

"What?"

"I knew this going in," she pointed out, proud of her even tone.

"Knew what?"

"You. You're reckless and impulsive. You have to fly to London. You have to buy ships. And you have to do it in less than twelve hours. That's you. That what I lo…like about you. Have a great time."

He was silent on the other end.

"You sure?" he finally asked.

"Do I sound sure?"

"Well, yeah."

Her lying skills had obviously improved. "There you go. I'll see you at the office. I gotta go now."

"But—"

"See you." Sinclair clicked off the phone.

She rounded the corner, taking in what now looked like a daunting mix of finely dressed people. And at the same time, she was beginning to fear her colleagues wouldn't take her seriously. While Chantal seemed to be managing the glam persona with aplomb. And now Hunter wasn't even going to show up.

Damn.

She had to stop caring about that.

Had she expected to be Cinderella tonight?

Had she expected he'd sweep the new her onto the dance floor, realize he'd fallen madly in love, and carry her off to happily ever after?

It was a ridiculous fantasy, and Sinclair was horrified to realize it was hers.

Her fingers went to the ruby-and-diamond goldfish bracelet—the one she hadn't taken off in a week.

She'd thought about him every moment while she'd primped tonight. She'd worn a white, whale-boned bustier. It gave body to the dress, but it was also shamelessly sexy. She told herself no one would see it. But, secretly, deep down inside her soul, she'd hoped he would. She'd hoped they'd find an excuse to make love one more time, or maybe a hundred more times.

Truth was, Kristy's fear had proven true. Sinclair had fallen hopelessly in love with Hunter. Hunter, on the other hand, skipped the ball to make a new business deal.

Her eyes burned while a knot of shame formed in her belly. Suddenly the designer clothes felt like zero protection for her broken heart.

She should have stuck with her regular wardrobe. Beneath her skirts and blazers and sensible blouses, she was in control of her world. People saw what she wanted them to see, and they respected what she represented. She was a fool to think she could beat Chantal at her own game. And she was a fool to think she could hold on to Hunter.

Reckless and impulsive. She'd heard those words so many times. There was nothing Sinclair could offer him that would compare to a high-risk, hundred-million-dollar deal in London at midnight.

She stepped away from the alcove, determined to get this horrible evening over with as soon as possible.

Twelve

The jets taking off from JFK squealed above Hunter's head as his driver circled his way through the terminals. He had his PDA set to calculator, running the numbers he knew he needed banking software to properly compute.

But the mini screen kept blurring in front of his eyes. He was seeing Sinclair in her white and red dress. The piping along the neckline. The teardrop diamonds. The ruby necklace. Her expression when she'd realized the massive ruby was real.

He chuckled at that, particularly the part where he realized she still liked the goldfish bracelet better.

He wondered if she'd worn it tonight.

He wondered if she'd got her makeup just right.

Had her hair behaved?

Were her feet getting tired?

She'd gamely practiced for hours in those high shoes, but he knew she didn't like them.

He wondered who she was dancing with right now, and quickly acknowledged that he cared. Something pulled tight inside him at the image of someone else holding her, their broad hand splayed across her back, another man's jacket nearly brushing her breasts, the jerk's lips whispering secrets into her ear.

If he was in the room, he'd probably rip her from the guy's arms.

His cell phone beeped.

"Hunter Osland," he greeted.

"Hey, Hunter."

"Sinclair?" His heart lifted.

"It's Kristy."

"Oh."

"Were you expecting Sinclair?"

"No."

"Because I think she's at that ball tonight."

"She is." He shifted in the backseat of the car. All alone at the ball.

"I just talked to Jack," said Kristy.

Sinclair was all alone, because Hunter had let her down.

"Jack's cell was running low on battery power," Kristy continued.

It wasn't like he'd had a choice. Osland International needed him, and his grandfather was always after him to be more dependable. That's what he was doing by helping Jack.

"Jack wants you to call Richard for him."

This was being dependable—and patient and methodical. Those were the other things his grandfather wanted.

Kristy's words rambled together on the other end of the

phone without making a whole lot of sense. "He said you'd know why."

Though he'd also been patient and methodical when he convinced Sinclair to get a makeover, then when he took her to Europe, then when he bought her clothes, then when he taught her to dance. He also made sure she was completely ready to face Roger and the rest of Lush Beauty.

"Hunter?" prompted Kristy.

And…then he'd abandoned her for the first exciting project that came along.

Oh no.

He pictured her in his mind, stunningly gorgeous and all alone, other men circling like wolves.

Was he out of his mind?

"No!"

"What?" came Kristy's worried voice.

The Sinclair project wasn't over. There were things left to do for her. A whole lot of things left to for her, patient and methodical things left to do for her, some of them involving the rest of their natural lives.

"Hunter? What's going on."

"Tell Jack I'm sorry."

"Huh?"

"Tell him I can't call Richard. I can't go to London. If he can't work it out himself, well, tell him there'll be other cruise ships."

"Other cruise ships?" Kristy parroted in confusion.

"For once in my life I'm not going to be reckless and impulsive. I'm going to be dependable." Why hadn't he thought about that before? He was such a fool.

"What are you talking about?" Kristy was obviously trying to be patient.

"I have to go see Sinclair."

"How'd Sinclair get into this?"

"Because," Hunter hesitated. Part of him didn't want to say it out loud, and part of him wanted to shout it from the rooftops. "I'm in love with your sister," he admitted to Kristy. "I'll have to call you back."

Then he disconnected and caught the driver's amused gaze in the rearview mirror.

"The Roosevelt Hotel," he hollered.

The driver's face broke into a full fledged grin.

"No, wait," said Hunter. "Make it the apartment. I have to change."

If he was going to do this, he was going to do it right.

It was Sinclair's job to stay for the entire ball, not to mention the after party at the Castlebay Spa. While the orchestra played on, she looked longingly at her watch, then over to the exit. Maybe she could lay low in the lobby for a while. At least then she wouldn't have to dance with men she'd rather be talking promotions and P and L statements with.

What was it about a pretty dress and bit of makeup that turned men into babbling idiots? And why didn't Chantal care? Her life must be exhausting.

Mind made up, Sinclair headed for the lobby exit. At the very least, she deserved a break.

"Going somewhere, Sinclair?"

She whirled toward the familiar voice, sure her mind must be playing tricks.

He was dressed in a classic black tux, with a black bow tie and a matching cummerbund. His hair was perfect, his face freshly shaven, and his smile was the most wonderful thing she'd seen all day.

"I thought you'd be on the jet," she blurted out.

"I changed my mind."

"About going to London?"

"About a lot of things." He held out his arm. "Dance?"

Her spirit lifted, but her heart ached. Still, there was no way she'd turn him down.

"You look stunning, by the way," he mumbled as they moved toward the dance floor. "Zeppetti should pay you to wear his dresses."

"You're good for me," she said.

"No, you're good for me."

They attracted a small amount of attention as they moved through the crowd, probably more Hunter than her. People recognized him, and knew his position in the company.

When they reached the other dancers, he drew her into his arms. It felt like the most natural thing in the world, and she had to caution herself against reading anything into his actions. He was probably off to London tomorrow morning. When you had your own plane, you could do things like that. And Hunter enjoyed every facet of his freewheeling, billionaire lifestyle.

But, for now, she couldn't seem to stop herself from melting into his arms and pretending, just for a moment, that things could be different. They were still drawing glances from the other dancers. She could only hope her expression wouldn't make her the office gossip topic tomorrow.

Hunter drew her tight against his chest.

She wasn't sure, but she thought she felt a kiss on the top of her head.

Risky move in this crowd.

"You leaving after the ball?" she asked, hoping to keep some semblance of professionalism between them.

"Here's the thing," Hunter muttered, leaning very close to her ear. "I've gotten rather used to seeing you naked."

She coughed out a startled laugh. Then she tipped her head back to play along. "Why, you sweet talker."

He smiled down at her. "I've also gotten used to waking up with you wrapped in my arms."

Sinclair sobered. That was the part she thought she'd miss most—Hunter first thing in the morning, unshaven, unguarded, and always ready for romance.

"An office affair still isn't going to work," he went on.

She nodded and sighed. "I know." They'd talked about all the reasons why. And they were right about them.

"It would make us crazy to keep the secret. Plus, we'd eventually get caught."

Sinclair followed the steps as Hunter led her through the dance. He wasn't telling her anything she didn't already know.

"So, I was thinking," he said. "We should get married."

Sinclair stopped dead.

He leaned down. "Sinclair?"

She didn't answer. Was that her fevered imagination, or did he just…

"Better start dancing," he advised. "People are beginning to stare."

She forced her feet to move. "Did you just…"

"Propose?"

She nodded.

"Yes," he growled low. "I'm proposing that you and I get married, so we can spend every minute together, and nobody in the office will be able to say a damn thing about it."

Her brain still hadn't made sense of what he was saying. "Is this one of those reckless, impulsive things of yours?"

He shook his head. "Absolutely not. I've been considering this for at least an hour."

Despite the serious conversation, his tone made her chuckle.

"Okay, probably twenty-four hours," he said. "Ever since leaving you became a reality."

Sinclair blinked back tears of emotion.

"Or maybe it's been ten days, ever since I walked into that boardroom. Or," he paused. "Maybe since the first second I laid eyes on you." He wrapped her in a hug that didn't resemble any of the waltz moves she'd learned.

"It feels like I've loved you forever," he said.

"I love you, too." Her voice was muffled against his chest.

He drew back. "Is that a yes?"

"If you're sure."

"I am one-hundred-percent positive. I blew off the London deal for this."

"You're not going to London later?"

"Actually, I'm never leaving you again." He kissed her mouth, and she caught Roger's astonished expression as he danced by.

"Uh oh," she said.

"Well, we can separate occasionally. You know, during the day. But not overnight. I'm not—"

"Roger just saw you kiss me."

"Who cares?"

"He thinks I'm your floozy now."

"Don't worry about Roger. I caught him kissing Chantal behind the pillar when I walked in."

Sinclair was shocked. "Roger and Chantal?"

Hunter nodded.

It actually made sense. It explained a whole lot of things. But, strangely, Sinclair didn't care.

She shrugged.

Hunter sobered, looking deeply into her eyes. "You, me,

us, your job. You know none of it has anything to do with the other, right?"

Sinclair glanced at Roger a few dance couples away, straining his neck for a view of her and Hunter. "Roger doesn't."

In response Hunter kissed her again, longer this time.

Roger's eyes nearly popped out of his head.

"Wait till he gets a look at the rock on your finger."

"You have a rock?"

"Actually, no. I have nothing at the moment."

"Reckless and impulsive."

"Not at all. This is good planning." He took her hand in his, rubbing the knuckle of her ring finger. "We can glam this up as much as you want. But I was thinking something custom-made, to match you bracelet."

Sinclair held up her wrist. "I do seem to have developed a fondness for the fish."

Hunter fingered the delicate gold and jewels. "I always assumed I was the diamond one, and you were the ruby."

"I never thought about it," said Sinclair.

"Liar."

"Takes one to know one."

"Well, whatever we do, it better be fast."

"Good idea. Since that last kiss totally trashed my reputation with my coworkers."

Hunter glanced Roger's way. "He looks at you like that one more time, I'm making him president of the Osland button factory in Siberia."

"You don't have a button factory in Siberia."

"I'll buy one. It'll be worth it."

Sinclair's phone buzzed in her little purse.

"That'll be Kristy," said Hunter, nodding toward the faint sound.

"How do you know that?"

"Because she knows I'm here. I bet it's killed her to wait this long."

"You told her…"

"That I loved you? Yeah. I'll be telling everybody soon."

Sinclair snapped the clasp on her purse and retrieved the phone, putting it to her ear.

"Is he there?" Kristy stage-whispered.

"Who?" asked Sinclair innocently.

"You know who. What's going on? Tell me everything?"

"We're dancing."

"And?"

"And, I think we're getting married."

"You *know* we're getting married," Hunter called into the phone.

Kristy squealed so loud Sinclair had to pull it away from her ear.

"When? Where?" asked Kristy.

"Hunter seems to be in a hurry. Could you maybe give us the name of that place you and Jack used in Las Vegas?"

Hunter scooped the phone. "Negative on Vegas," he told Kristy. "I've reformed my impulsive ways. We're doing some methodical planning on this one." He glanced softly down at Sinclair. "I want it to be perfect."

Then he handed the phone back.

"I'm designing the dress," said Kristy.

"You bet you are," Sinclair agreed, watching the heat build in Hunter's eyes. "I better go now."

"Okay. But I'm flying out there as soon as possible."

"Just as long as you don't come tonight," said Sinclair, hanging up the phone over Kristy's laughter.

"Good tip," said Hunter.

"Excuse me, Sinclair," Roger interrupted, his mouth in a frown and a determined look in his eyes. "Can I speak with you—"

Hunter jumped in. "You might want to know—"

"This will only take a moment," said Roger.

"Really?" asked Hunter, brow going up.

Roger nodded.

Hunter anchored Sinclair to his side. "Sinclair has just accepted my marriage proposal."

Roger blinked in confusion, clearly the words were not computing.

"And I'd like to talk to you about a job opportunity for you," said Hunter. "My office? Tomorrow? Sometime in the afternoon."

Roger's brow furrowed. "I don't... You're getting *married?*"

Hunter nodded slowly.

Roger took a step back. "Oh..." Another step. "Well..." A third. "In that case..." He disappeared into the crowd.

"Funny that he didn't congratulate us," said Sinclair.

"He can send a card from Siberia." Hunter smoothly drew her into his arms and picked up the dance.

"Is Chantal going with him?"

"It would only be fair. Who am I to stand in the way of true love?"

"Who, indeed?" asked Sinclair, snuggling close to his broad chest. "And now you and I get to live happily ever after." She sighed.

"Just me, you and the twins."

"You believe the gypsy?"

Hunter nodded. "It has to be true. Jack's probably out there right now losing the family fortune. I just found out the

Castlebay Spa in Hawaii has a golf course. And with your red hair, twins would make it a clean sweep."

She laughed with joy over everything.

"I love you very much," Hunter whispered.

"And I love you," she whispered in return. "Happy Valentine's Day."

He hugged her tightly. "Happy Valentine's Day, sweetheart."

* * * * *

HER ONE AND
ONLY VALENTINE

TRISH WYLIE

Trish Wylie tried various careers before eventually fulfilling her dream of writing. Years spent working in the music industry, in promotions and teaching little kids about ponies gave her plenty of opportunity to study life and the people around her. Which, in Trish's opinion, is a pretty good study course for writing! Living in Ireland, Trish balances her time between writing and horses. If you get to spend your days doing things you love, then she thinks that's not doing too badly. You can contact Trish at www.trishwylie.com.

To my readers—the dream-makers!

CHAPTER ONE

A TENNIS racquet was the first thing her hand settled on. Anything would have done, to be honest. The fact she had even heard the noise to begin with when it was so stormy outside was miracle enough. But, more than likely, her first night in the huge house alone with her daughter, combined with the thick walls holding the worst of the storm at bay, meant Rhiannon MacNally had more sensitive ears than normal.

And there was *definitely* someone there. She knew for sure as she stepped off the last stair and heard movement, a tremor of fear running up her spine. Going to see who it was probably wasn't the best idea she'd ever had, and she'd always detested heroines in horror movies who went where they were bound to be—well—*eaten*, but this was *her* house now, *damn it*! And she wasn't going to lie cowering in her bed.

So she crept along the hall, ignoring the goose-bumps on her skin and the chill of her bare feet on the slate floor, while her body hugged the wall and she held the tennis racquet in front of her, clasped firmly in both hands.

She froze, her pulse skipping. There it was again. This time a much more distinct rattle, followed by a muffled curse as someone bumped against furniture in the kitchen. So she swallowed hard, ran her tongue over her dry lips and crept closer to the door, fully prepared to scream her lungs out and frighten whoever it was more than they were currently frightening her…

It swung open as she reached out for the handle. And, with a stifled scream in the base of her throat, she raised the racquet to hit whatever might come through.

The shadow moved out towards her, but she sidestepped and swung hard at where she guessed the shadow's waist might be, fully prepared to swing lower than that if the need called, but making enough of a contact to double him up briefly. And she immediately knew it was a *him* from his deep grunt of pain.

He swore in response, moving remarkably fast, catching the end of the racquet, using the fact she didn't let go of it to twist her arm and pushing her much smaller body in tight against the wall so that she was trapped against the cold stone.

'What the hell—'

This had been a *big mistake*!

'Get *off* me!' She struggled for all she was worth, desperate to find a way to swing the racquet again. 'I phoned the police; they'll be here any minute! So you better just leave while you can!'

That was a fib, actually; she hadn't been able to find her mobile in the dark but he didn't need to *know* that!

'Rhiannon?'

The sound of her name in such a gruff, rumbling tone stilled her. And then his scent hit her, tingling against her nostrils and attaching to the back of her throat, with low tones of sweet cinnamon and a familiar something else that her memory immediately recognized.

Rhiannon *knew* that scent, even after ten years. She'd never forgotten it, no matter how hard she tried, and now *he* was in her house! He had her *trapped* against a wall! This was a *nightmare*!

'Kane!' There was no need to question; she already knew *exactly* who it was. What she didn't get was, 'What the hell are you doing here?'

His warm breath teased the strands of hair touching her forehead, his huge body still pressed along the length of hers. And Rhiannon hated that she was so aware of everywhere he touched, every breath he took, of how his scent opened the door to so many memories.

So she struggled again. 'Get *off* me!'

His large frame remained tight against hers, tension radiating from every pore. 'I'll only consider it if you promise not to hit me with *whatever* that is again.'

'You were lucky I didn't find anything larger or aim any lower, you frightened the life out of me! What in hell are you doing creeping around in the middle of the night? How did you even get in? You shouldn't *be* here! You have no right to just walk in here and—*and*—'

His voice held an amused edge to it. 'Let's cover the frightened part first, shall we? A lone female taking on what I assume she thought was a burglar was a stroke of genius, don't you think? And why *shouldn't* I be here? I've been a guest in this place just as many times as you have over the years. What makes you think I don't still have things here that might belong to me?'

The question flummoxed her for a second, a wave of panic forming in the pit of her stomach, so she took a moment to force it away with several deep breaths. Because he couldn't possibly have meant—

She stopped struggling, sighing a little in resignation when she realized that at least by staying still she didn't feel quite so sensually aware of him. That was a start. Then she took another deep breath and tried to form a coherent line of thought.

'Brookfield is *my house* now. You can't just pop in here when you fancy it now that Mattie is gone! If you have things here that belong to you then you could have got them in daylight, or better still they could have been couriered to you!'

And that way she wouldn't have had to see him or have him within twenty feet of her. 'How *did* you get in? Did you break in? Because if you *did*—'

'I have a key.'

He had a key—since when?

'I'll have that back—*now.*' She scowled up at the dark circle where his face was. 'And could you kindly get the hell off me?'

There was a long pause before he stepped back from her, cold air rushing in to replace the heat of his body. And Rhiannon shivered in response, lifting her empty hand to rub up and down against her arm.

'Now, why are you here, really? Because I sure as hell didn't invite you.'

There was a brief pause. 'We need to talk.'

Rhiannon gaped up at him as she stepped towards the door again. Talking to him in the dark was too disconcerting. 'We have nothing to talk about. And even if we did, which we don't, here's a newsflash for you: there's a new invention called the telephone. You could have tried using one instead of frightening the holy hell out of me in the middle of the night. This is breaking and entering, Mister.'

'Not with a key it's not. And I had a flat tyre or I'd have been here sooner,' his deep voice grumbled behind her as she set the tennis racquet against the wall and felt for the light-switch inside the kitchen door. 'I was reliably informed you wouldn't be here for another week.'

What business was it of his where she was at any given time? She frowned at the switch as she flicked it up and down and nothing happened. She'd assumed she'd blown a light bulb upstairs—apparently not. 'There didn't seem any point in waiting till next week.'

'I tried the lights; your power must be out.'

Great. She sidestepped, bumped her hip off the edge of the dresser and gasped at the pain, automatically flinching back, which brought her up against Kane again, his large hands lifting to grasp her arms.

She *really* needed some light in order to avoid all this accidental physical contact! So that she could look him in the eye and tell him to go *properly*.

His fingers brushed, almost absentmindedly, against the light silky material of her dressing gown, making her all too aware of how she was dressed even before a slight dampness seeped through to the skin on her back from his heavy jacket.

Wind rattled the rain against the kitchen windows as Kane's baritone voice rumbled closer to her ear, an edge of irritation to it. 'Aren't there candles anywhere?'

'*Yes.*' She shrugged her shoulders hard, freeing herself. There had damn well better be candles. Stepping away from him she felt her way along the dresser, hauling open a drawer to blindly search its contents in anger. Of all the things she had managed to unpack during what suddenly felt like the longest day ever, she couldn't recall there being candles or matches, but there had to be some *somewhere*. Had to be!

With Brookfield situated in the middle of nowhere for centuries, it was hardly likely that this was the first power cut it had ever experienced on a stormy New Year's night, right?

She heard Kane moving away, the sound of drawers being rattled open, and for a few minutes they worked in heavy silence, while Rhiannon's fingertips searched frantically until she eventually found what she was looking for. *Yes!*

'I found some.'

There was a rattle from across the large room. 'I've got matches. Stay where you are; I'll come to you.'

With her back against the counter, she waited with bated breath, her skin tingling, eyes wide, while she strained to see him in the darkness. But she didn't have to see; his scent preceded him, so she turned towards him, holding out the candle like a miniature shield.

'Here.'

She'd fully intended him to take it from her, but there was another rattle and the strike of a match that made her blink to adjust her eyes to the bright light as he touched the flame to the candle wick.

Rhiannon's lashes then rose as his face came into focus in the warm glow. He was older, yes, as was she, but he was no less ruggedly handsome than he'd been when she'd known him before. Avoiding him for as long as she had hadn't been an easy thing to do, but somehow she'd managed it, right up until Mattie's funeral.

And she'd had bigger things to deal with then, she hadn't had the time to see what he looked like. Not that she cared any more. But up close and personal, as she was now, she really had no choice but to look…

In the dim light his eyes were so dark they looked black, instead of the deep sapphire blue she remembered. And the fact that he towered over her, his chin dipped a little to study her face while she studied his, meant that she couldn't read any thoughts in those shadowed eyes. Not that she'd probably read much more on a bright summer's day these days. She didn't know him any better now than it had eventually proven she'd known him then.

'Are there more of those?'

The question gave her a reason to turn away, but it was too late to erase the picture of him now seared into her mind. She knew if the candle went out she would still be able to see him—the sheen of short, dark chocolate hair that hugged his head, shorter spikes of it brushing against the top of his forehead from his centre parting—the downward tilt of thick dark brows while he had studied her face—the dense lashes that framed his eyes—the straight line of his nose—the mocking quirk on the corners of his sensual mouth.

Yep, suffice to say, she had a fairly thorough mental image of him. More of one than she would have asked for; *thanks, anyway*.

Holding the candle above the drawer, she searched for more of the same, clearing her throat before she asked in a cool voice, 'Well, what *is* it you want, Kane? Because the sooner I know, the sooner you can leave.'

'I told you, we need to talk. Mattie's death has changed things.'

'*We* have *nothing* to talk about.' But, even as she said the words, she felt an old familiar sliver of fear run up her spine. He'd better not *think* they had anything to talk about! He was ten years too late for that!

'We need to talk about Brookfield.'

They what?

'Why?' Her hand halted halfway out of the drawer with another candle, her face turning to look up at Kane's in the shadows. 'Brookfield is nothing to do with you—Mattie left it *to me*.'

'He left the *house* to you.' His deep voice didn't hold as much as a hint of emotion as he laid the facts on the line for her. 'But I own the estate. And *that means* we need to talk.'

What did he mean—he *owned the estate*? The house and the estate went hand in hand, had done for generations! And, as daunting as the task of taking it on single-handed had been for Rhiannon, she had also been more excited by it than she had by anything else in years. She'd seen it as a challenge she could put her heart and soul into—building not just a home, but a future for herself and Lizzie.

Her gaze shot upwards. *Lizzie!* Rhiannon couldn't have Kane one second more under the same roof as Lizzie!

He read her upward gaze. 'Is she asleep?'

Damn him! She really didn't want to have a discussion about her child with *him*. She wouldn't even deign to answer the simple question when it was *him* asking it. 'What do you mean, you own the estate?'

He shrugged, raindrops on the dark material covering his broad shoulders glistening in the soft candlelight. 'It doesn't take much explaining; I own the estate. Mattie sold it to me a year ago.'

'Why?' She couldn't hold the incredulity from her voice. 'Mattie loved this place; he would never have parted with any of it while he was alive.'

'Under normal circumstances he wouldn't have.' Kane reached out a large hand to turn hers so that he could light the other candle, his dark gaze focused completely on the task, while he continued in a low, almost seductively male tone, 'But he'd overstretched himself on the estate and with all the treatments he tried to get well and he wouldn't accept a loan, so I bought back his shares in Micro-Tech and the estate, on the proviso that I would never sell it separately from the house.'

Oh, this really was a nightmare! Any second now she would wake up—she had to—because this just wasn't happening! And surely he didn't think she could afford to buy it back off him?

'I'm prepared to make you an offer on the house.'

Rhiannon gaped up at him, suddenly aware that his fingers were still curled around hers over the candle. She thrust the other candle at him and the movement dropped hot melted wax on to the back of her hand.

Kane scowled when she gasped. 'We need something to put these candles on.'

'While we have a business meeting in the middle of the night?' She shook her burnt hand to ease the sharp pain on her skin. It focused her mind, gave her a second to calm her thoughts into something resembling sense when all she could really concentrate on was one thing; she had been at Brookfield less than one full day, and already she was in trouble.

And, like all of the main troubles she'd been through in her life, it once again involved Kane damn Healey!

'I hadn't planned on talking to you in the middle of the night. You weren't supposed to be here yet. I've arranged for an estate agent to come value the place tomorrow morning so I had some figures.'

'Behind my back?'

He shrugged. 'If I had figures to show you, then you could make a more informed decision on a price.'

'I've just moved house; I have no intention of moving again.' And she'd given up her job, lifted Lizzie out of school—away from her friends and the only home she'd ever really known. She couldn't do that all over again. The only reason she'd been able to make the decision to uproot them both had been the fact that they would have a home of *their own.*

'You can't support a house this size.'

'You can't tell me what I can and can't do!'

Reaching over her shoulder for a saucer to balance the candle on, his darkened eyes noted how she snatched her shoulder back from him, one hand rising to draw the lapels of her silk dressing gown closer together. And he frowned in annoyance again.

This wasn't going the way he'd planned. Did it ever where Rhiannon MacNally was concerned?

Despite what she may think, he wasn't doing this just to make her life difficult. Because he knew that he was probably the last person she'd want to have dealings with, let alone be forced into any kind of a business partnership with. She'd made it more than plain over the years that she wanted nothing more to do with him.

But he was also pretty sure she couldn't afford to buy the estate off him, so that meant his buying the house made more sense. Then she could do what she wanted with the money. It wouldn't be anything to do with him any more. *Simple.*

Except that already it was more complicated than he'd thought it would be. Being hit in the stomach with what he now knew was a tennis racquet had led to her soft body being pressed against his. And *that* had brought back memories he'd had no intention of ever remembering again.

In the soft candlelight, she was simply stunning.

The intimate arc of light picked up the fine strands of red in her auburn hair, made her doe-brown eyes sparkle when she glanced up at him from beneath long lashes, surrounded her in a halo that made her seem even softer and more feminine than she already looked with her curves barely hidden beneath long, flowing rose-pink silk.

If they'd been two other people, in a different place and different time, then the temptation to be doing something other than talking in the candlelight would almost have been too much to resist.

She'd always been dangerous that way.

Leaning back from her, he dragged his gaze from her face and focused on dropping wax onto the saucer until there was a large enough pool to stand the candle upright while it cooled. Then, as the wind hailed rain against the windows again, he took a breath and glanced at her from beneath hooded eyes.

'It's late. We'll talk about this in the morning.'

Rhiannon's eyes widened. 'You're not *staying* here.'

Oh, for goodness' sake! 'It's a very large house, Rhiannon; you won't even know I'm here till you see me at breakfast.' He smirked. 'I promise not to come looking for you in the dark again.'

The innuendo didn't help. 'I don't want to see you at breakfast. If there's anything else to talk about, then you can come back when Lizzie has gone to school.' She looked away from his face, her gaze flickering upwards again while she frowned. 'Things are already unsettled enough without her asking a dozen questions about *you*.'

It was a feeble excuse, he felt. 'Then I'll wait until she's gone and, after the estate agent comes, we can talk. There isn't a hotel or a B&B for miles.'

'There's nothing to talk *about*!' Her chin rose as she punched the words out and for a moment she almost looked panicked, which didn't make sense to him.

He didn't see what the problem was himself.

'Yes, there is.' With another deep breath to maintain his patience, he leaned his face closer to try and make his point. 'Whether you like it or not, the estate and the house are a partnership and if you won't sell and you don't have the money to buy the land back, then that makes us partners, which means we have some negotiating to do.'

Her large eyes narrowed, her voice icy as she calmly informed him, 'I'd rather chew off my own leg than enter into any kind of a partnership with you.'

He quirked a dark brow. '*Again*, you mean?'

His gaze swept over the flush that immediately rose on her cheeks. Then he tilted his head to the side, his face hovering over hers. 'I thought we made quite a "partnership" last time, didn't you?'

'Oh, you are a complete and utter—'

'Now, that's hardly the right language for the new lady of the manor, is it?'

Her eyes blazed with anger and he smiled. She looked as if she would dearly love to hit him again.

But in a heartbeat she regained her control. Her breasts rose and fell as she took a deep steadying breath and then her lashes lowered before she focused on his chest and informed him through tight lips, 'I don't want to discuss this in the middle of the damn night.' She stepped back and around him. 'So how about you sleep wherever the hell you want? Just make absolutely sure that Lizzie doesn't set eyes on you before you leave. She has no idea who you are and I'd like to keep it that way.'

Kane turned on his heel and stared at her as she pushed the door open, unable to keep the bitterness from his tone. 'Why the hell would it matter to me whether she knows who I am? She's nothing to do with me.'

Rhiannon swore below her breath as she turned in the doorway, her eyes glittering in the candlelight. 'That's the first thing you've said in a *very* long time that I actually agree with. You stay away from her, Kane Healey. I mean it. She'll find out what kind of a low life you are over my dead body.'

Already irritated that an edge of bitterness had shown in his voice, he scowled at her. What in hell was she talking about?

But, before he could ask, she was gone, the door swinging on its hinges behind her. And he didn't follow, even if it left him clenching his teeth, feeling angrier than he had in a long, long time.

If he'd had any sense at all he would have done any 'talking' through a solicitor. But he had wanted—what?

Frankly, he was already too angry to look for an answer to that. What he *hadn't* wanted was to be made painfully aware of just how much of an effect her presence could have on his libido. And he'd just got that in spades, hadn't he?

The sooner he was out of this place the better.

CHAPTER TWO

'So, Mum, can I get a pony? And maybe a dog?'

Rhiannon smiled affectionately as they made their way out of the cavernous hallway and through the front door to scrunch across the gravel to her Jeep. Lizzie had hidden her first day at school nerves behind incessant chatter all the way through the breakfast that her mother had hurried in order to get them out before Kane appeared from wherever he had slept.

If she'd had her way they'd have eaten slices of toast in the Jeep. Just to be on the safe side.

'How about we get properly settled in first before we stock a zoo?' Though, after the adventure of the night before, a dog might not be a bad idea. They were two females alone in the middle of nowhere, after all. A dog would be a good idea. Something of a manageable size, with a nice deep, scary bark, that could live downstairs in the kitchen.

'Whose car is that?'

Rhiannon's heart sank, her hand on the Jeep's door. She'd so very nearly got away from the house without any questions. *So near and yet so far.*

Pinning a bright smile on her face, she glanced briefly at the sleek, low-slung sports car peeking from the edge of the house. He must have gone into the house at the back.

'It belongs to a friend of Uncle Mattie.' Well, it wasn't a lie. He *had* been a friend of Mattie's, more so the last few years than when she had first met them all.

Lizzie looked all the more intrigued. 'In the house? Why didn't he come down for breakfast? Will I get to meet him after school?'

Not if her Mother had anything to do with it, she wouldn't. 'No, he'll be gone by then. He didn't know we'd moved in yet.' A thought occurred to her. 'How did you know he was a "he"?'

Lizzie shrugged her narrow shoulders, her blue eyes still wide with curiosity. 'Guessed. What's he like? Can't he stay till I meet him? We can talk about Uncle Mattie. I'd like that.'

Rhiannon's heart twisted at the simple statement. Of course she'd want to meet people who'd known her favourite 'uncle'; talking about him was something that Rhiannon had been encouraging her to do. It was healthy. And, much as it killed her to have to deal with it when Lizzie hadn't even reached the grand age of ten yet, she didn't want her to bottle things up. But neither did she want her talking to Kane. *About anything.*

'He's very busy; I'm sure he'll be gone by the time you get back.' The look of disappointment on her daughter's face almost doubled her up with guilt. It was only natural for her to try and reach out for something comforting in the face of so much change. Talking about her Mattie with someone must have seemed an ideal security blanket, 'How about when you come back we go and see what pictures of Uncle Mattie we can find to put on that wall in the library?'

Lizzie brightened a little, her head bobbing up and down, which flicked her long, dark chocolate-brown pony-tail out behind her. 'Okay.'

'Right, well, let's get you to school, then.'

It was only once Lizzie was settled into her new classroom in the primary school, a universe smaller than the city one she was used to, that Rhiannon allowed her thoughts to return to what she had to face back at Brookfield. She wasn't looking forward to it.

And the night before she had tossed and turned, her ears straining to hear any sound of Kane moving around the house, while her thoughts had run riot, trying to cope with how her hatred of him burned like acid in the pit of her stomach as she searched frantically for a quick fix solution to the problem he had presented her with.

Maybe if she'd managed more sleep she might have found an option or two. To have what sleep she had managed uninterrupted by fitful dreams of the past would certainly have helped too…

Tugging angrily on the steering wheel, she made the final turn through the huge wrought iron gates that heralded the entrance to Brookfield.

Having Brookfield and its hundred and something acres to work on was supposed to help both her and Lizzie to focus their intense emotions from Mattie's passing, elsewhere. It was supposed to be a chance to look forwards, not back, and at the same time to allow them to never forget the one person who had helped them when they had needed it most.

They finally had a chance at a real future—the two of them together against the world.

Once through the gates, the Jeep was immediately surrounded by an avenue of tall skeletal trees that wouldn't see leaves for months yet, while Rhiannon thought about the bitterness in Kane's voice when he had asked her why it would matter to him whether or not Lizzie knew who he was.

He had to be out of the house before Lizzie came home; there was no question about *that*!

Even if a small, resentful part of Rhiannon thought for a brief moment that it might do him good to see how amazing and beautiful and bright and funny and audacious her child had turned out to be.

Low branches reached out to scrape against the high roof of the Jeep as she got closer to the one part of her past she had tried hardest to leave behind.

Designed for the coaches that would have driven to the large house when it was first built in the late nineteenth century, the original owners could never have envisaged the need for anything wider than a large coach to use the driveway, so they had simply built it to enter on one side of the lake and leave on the other in one large scenic circle that only ever widened in front of the house itself. It made for a beautiful drive, one that *normally* acted as a soothing balm for Rhiannon's soul.

The trees thinned and allowed a glimpse of the lake and the impressive house beyond. *Brookfield.*

All of her young life, growing up in a block of flats in a poorer part of Dublin, Rhiannon could only have dreamt that a place like Brookfield existed outside a fairy tale. And she still remembered the first weekend Mattie had brought her to his 'little country cottage'. That first turn on to the wide gravel in front of the three-storey country house, when the sun had come out from behind a cloud and glistened in every one of the dozens of small panes of leaded glass, had been like coming home. And it still did that to her, even if the place was now laced with loneliness, without her best friend to greet her at the door. And a rising resentment that Kane Healey was there when Mattie wasn't.

She wouldn't let him take it from her. She'd *find* a way to make it work without the estate.

With a sigh of resignation, she set the handbrake and unclipped her seat belt, but when she walked into the entrance hall there wasn't a sound except the echo of her footsteps on the smooth slate floor. *Nothing*. Not even a whisper.

And yet she could still *sense* Kane's presence.

She moved down the hallway and peeked through doors. Into the lounge, the dining room, the sitting room, the games room and lastly the gigantic kitchen—where she smoothed the palm of her hand over the well worn surface of the gigantic wooden table as she walked to the other end of the room.

Where in hell was he? She shouldn't have to go looking for him!

She raised a hand and kneaded the muscles on the back of her neck where her skin prickled with an awareness of his presence behind her before his deep voice sounded, close enough to make her jump a little, and softer than she remembered it being in a very long time.

'Still tired from the long drive yesterday?'

She lowered her hand. 'Yes.'

'You got your old place all packed up?'

'Yes.'

'And I'll bet you did that on your own too, right?'

'I needed to know where everything was packed so I could find it when it gets here.' She *really* didn't want to make small talk with him.

He nodded as he reached her side, glancing at her briefly from the corner of his eye on the way past. 'That makes sense. Though I'd have thought Stephen might have helped out.'

Rhiannon wasn't about to discuss her disastrous short-lived marriage with him either. So she took a breath and ploughed on in. 'Let's get this out of the way, shall we? I'm not selling you the house.'

'Yes, you mentioned that.' He smiled infuriatingly but, before she could react, he swung a hand towards the large Aga that heated the room. 'Coffee?'

Rhiannon silently groaned, then pinned a sweet smile on her face. 'Oh, please, do make yourself at home.'

'I will. Do you want a cup?'

Not unless he wanted to end up wearing it soon, no. 'I'm fine, thank you. I already *had* breakfast.'

'Yes, with Lizzie. It must be a big day for her, her first day at a new school.'

Even the sound of her name on his lips was enough to twist her gut. Lizzie was her one weakness and Kane had to know that. But having accompanied his words with a narrow-eyed, searching gaze that seemed to see right through her, it proved exactly what she needed to goad her into standing a little taller.

'That would be absolutely none of your business, now, would it?'

Kane blinked slowly, crossing his arms over his broad chest while he considered her. And, just when she was opening her mouth to add something more, he answered in a low drawl, 'You have a real problem with being overly defensive about her; you do know that, right?'

She folded her arms beneath her breasts in a mirror of his stance, frowning back at him. 'And I just wonder why that might be.'

'You tell me.'

Oh, he was a piece of work! In her eyes he was evil personified, even without the additional visual image of being dressed from head to toe in black—black thick-knit polo-neck sweater, black jeans, no doubt black shoes on his large feet. He was the bad guy.

And she'd already spent years honing her hatred.

Unable to look at him for a second more, she unfolded her arms and leaned forward, the palms of her hands flat on the table surface.

'I want you gone. Anything you need to discuss with me about access to *your* land or the use of *my* outbuildings, you can negotiate through a solicitor.'

He smiled a small smile that was far from warm. 'You're overreacting just a tad here, don't you think? There's no need to be immature about this. Just because I hit a nerve when I mentioned your over-protectiveness towards your daughter—'

Her mouth gaped open as he pushed the subject again. Oh, he could *not* be serious, could he? *Immature? Over-protective?*

She pushed her hands against the table, glowering at him as she ground out the words from between her clenched teeth. 'I'm only over-protective when it comes to keeping her away from *you*! And actually, for your information, I learnt to be mature fast. Motherhood will do that to you.'

'Bound to, when you have a baby so young.' He enunciated each word with a calm voice that Rhiannon dearly wanted to slap him for.

She would never have believed she had it in her to hate one person so much!

'Go away, Kane. Go away and don't ever come back. I won't let you hurt Lizzie. You even think for one second about playing daddy to her after all this time—'

He swore viciously, silencing her.

'Why the hell would I want to play daddy?' Unfolding his arms, his large hands bunched into fists at his sides, his blue eyes flaring with the same anger she could hear in his clipped voice. 'She *has* a father.'

'The hell she does! Her father wanted nothing to do with her from before she was even born!'

Kane scowled darkly. 'He married you, didn't he? I'd say that proved he wanted something to do with her.'

Rhiannon's breath caught, her chest cramping, and she even flinched back from him as if he'd slapped her with an invisible hand.

'Is that what you told yourself?' She shook her head in amazement, stunned not only by his words, but by the fact that hearing them still had the power to sting so badly. 'That she was someone else's child? Oh, you're really something, aren't you?'

For the first time, her words seemed to confuse him. 'What the hell are you talking about now?'

A tension-filled silence fell while Kane scowled darkly and Rhiannon shook with years of suppressed anger and resentment. So when the ancient doorbell jangled above the door behind her head she jumped at the sound, her eyes drawn to the small brass bell labelled 'Front'.

Kane was still scowling when she looked back at him. 'That has to be the estate agent.'

'Fine, then you can deal with that on your way out. There's no need for them to look at the house because it's *not for sale*.'

She was halfway across the hall towards the library when Kane blocked her way, his hand reaching out to catch hold of her arm. Long fingers circled and squeezed in silent warning— warning her to stay put because he wasn't done—while the heat of his touch seeped through her skin, radiating into her chilled blood.

'What do you mean, "*someone else's* child"?'

Rhiannon had to tilt her head up to look into his face, hissing the words up at him without trying to hide any of the venom held inside. 'I really don't care what you told yourself to ease your conscience. But the simple fact is you gave up the right to Lizzie a long time ago and popping in on some pretence to see how she's doing now won't fix that. I've made damn sure she has no idea who you really are. So keep your distance. Because if you hurt her, I'll kill you, I *swear* I will. She doesn't need to know what a disappointment her father is.'

The hold on her arm tightened when she tried to jerk free. 'Are you telling me that Lizzie is *mine*?'

Rhiannon swore under her breath as she tried again to tug her arm free. 'Let me go, Kane!'

'*Are you* telling me that she's *my child*?'

She tugged again, her focus drawn to where he was holding

her, while her mind sought frantically for a way she might possibly break free. How dared he use physical strength to subdue her? How dared he make her body burn from that touch when it was meant to do nothing but dominate her?

'*Rhiannon!*' The tone in his voice changed, with an edge of what could *almost* have sounded like hope to her disbelieving ears.

Which drew her gaze back to his face, and what she saw there shocked her to the core.

'Of course she's yours.' She shook her head in amazement, 'How can you not have known that? When I sent you that letter I made it more than plain—'

'*What letter?*'

CHAPTER THREE

THE front doorbell rang and rang until Kane had no choice but to release her and deal with it.

Rhiannon stood in the doorway of the library, her back against the wood frame, trying to make sense of what had just happened. He had genuinely looked as if he hadn't known, as if it had been a complete shock to him. He had even looked as if it mattered to him. But that couldn't be right. How could he *not* have known?

And yet the look on his face had been so raw, so unguarded, so—*real*—that it was hard to deny the truth of it. When Rhiannon had always *believed*—

No—had *known*. She shook her head. This had to be some kind of game. Something he'd convinced himself of so he could sleep better at night.

Turning away from the door, she jumped when his voice sounded from the hall behind her.

'Oh, no, you don't. You and I quite obviously need to have a *long* talk.'

When she looked over her shoulder he was walking her way with an expression of dark determination that sent her nerve-endings fluttering again.

'What about the estate agent?'

'I told them to reschedule. It'll wait. *This won't.*'

She didn't want to talk to him any more. It was too surreal, too much to take in or understand, and she was suddenly tired beyond the levels of normal exhaustion.

And it wasn't just a physical exhaustion either. Two of the most stressful things in life were supposed to be moving house and the loss of a loved one—and she'd suffered both in the last couple of months. So, on top of those things, to have to face *this* now... *Well*...

'We'll go into the sitting room. I'm not standing in a hallway while this is straightened out.'

Now he was directing her around her own home? Was there no end to his ability to rub her up the wrong way?

She lifted her chin and marched past his large body, careful not to brush against him on the way. 'We'll go into the stove room; it's more private in there if I'm going to argue with you again.'

Sound was less likely to carry anywhere from the room at the edge of the basement, with the sturdy stone walls that had belonged to the house when it started life as a fortified farm to act as a sound buffer. Lord alone knew there had been double the visitors she'd been expecting in the last twenty-four hours as it was! The last thing she needed was the part-time housekeeper or a visitor from the estate to pop in and hear all of the dirty laundry from her past aired!

But with the large stove in an archway at one side not having been lit for weeks there was a distinct chill in the room—a blessing on a hot day, few and far between as they could be—but not at a time when Rhiannon could have done with some welcoming warmth from *somewhere*.

In front of the empty stove she turned to face him, watching with cautious eyes as he closed the low door behind him before throwing an angry glare at her as he walked towards the high-set window that looked upwards on to the garden. He began to pace, anger radiating from every pore of his large body.

Rhiannon watched and waited, her breath held still in her chest as she contemplated what tactic he would try next, while still aware on a subliminal level of the way he moved—with a kind of harnessed inner strength, a presence that demanded attention without any words…

'Tell me about this supposed letter you sent.'

Her eyes widened. '*Supposed*? That's a joke, right?'

The pacing stopped and he cocked his head at a sarcastic angle. 'Do I *look* like I'm joking?'

Well, no, but… 'You know damn rightly what letter I'm talking about! The issue here, if there *is* one, is why you never had the basic courtesy to answer it—even if it was to tell me not to have her!'

Kane swore so viciously that Rhiannon baulked, even before she had time to be angry with herself for saying what she just had. She'd long since ceased to care why he'd done what he had and there was no way in hell she would let him think it still mattered.

'Is that what you honestly thought I'd do?'

'How did I know *what* you'd do? It was made plainly obvious to me that I didn't know you at all!'

And she'd made it sound as if she cared—*again*!

He looked as if he'd dearly love to hit something but threw another dark scowl at her before he leaned his large hands on the back of the sofa between them. Then he took a deep breath, looking around the room for a moment before he pushed back against his hands and began pacing up and down. And up and down.

One of those same large hands rose to rake long fingers through his thick hair, his head tilting back for a moment as he searched the low vaulted ceiling.

'And where exactly did you send this letter?'

Not that he deserved an answer, but, 'In your locker at the University. I pushed it through the top of the door. So the *it got lost in the post* excuse won't wash. You *had* to clear your locker out.'

She took another breath, shaking her head as her shoulders slumped, a bone-tired weariness settling on them like a dead weight. 'But it's history. Whatever reasons you had for not wanting to know Lizzie don't matter any more. What matters is that she doesn't get hurt in the here and now. That's all I care about.'

Kane stopped pacing, his brow creasing below the wisps of hair brushing against his forehead. Then, just like that, the frown momentarily disappeared, a far-off look in his eyes as his rumbling voice swiftly followed with an edge of realization.

'I had someone clear it out for me when I left. I told them there was nothing in there I needed, that they could keep the books they wanted and dump the rest.'

What was he talking about?

Rhiannon tried to focus her exhausted mind. Then her eyes widened in disbelief. 'You're seriously trying to tell me *now*, after *ten years*, that you *never got it*? Oh, surely you can do better than that?'

He glared again.

'That *is* what you're saying.' Full of incredulity, she repeated the words, as if somehow saying them again would make it real for her. Surely he couldn't be serious? But if he hadn't got it— no, that wasn't right. It couldn't be. She'd always believed—

The letter that she had spent days debating writing; the one that she had carried clenched in her hand while she'd stood in front of the locker, willing herself to put it in. The one he had completely ignored, which had laid the first foundation stones for the resentment and hatred she had carried for more than ten years…and he hadn't got it?

'Didn't it ever occur to you when I didn't reply that I might not have got it?'

She frowned at the question, the chill in the room seeping into her already tired bones, forcing her to shake inwardly. She sat down on the large stuffed chair closest to the wood-burning stove and tangled her cold fingers together on her lap.

Reluctantly she admitted the truth. 'Maybe for a very brief moment, but after the way you just disappeared off the face of the earth—'

'You figured that you'd made enough of an effort and to hell with me?'

'No!' She stared into his angry eyes, not prepared to even contemplate the notion that she might have been at fault during a time when she'd had so many important decisions to make— *alone*. '*You* were the one who had an overnight personality transplant and then left! Do you think that at eighteen, with no well paid career in my near future, that I was ready to face having a baby on my own? Get real.'

'But you still had her.'

She wasn't even going to grace that with a comeback. It had never occurred to her for a single second not to—no matter how terrified she had been at the time. And it wasn't because she'd wanted a part of Kane or to remain tied to him in some way. They hadn't been together long enough for her to form that kind of attachment, had they?

No, from the moment the test had turned blue Lizzie had been *hers*—a part of *her*. And she had done her best to forget where the other part of her beautiful child came from.

'You'd already made it plain that you didn't want to be tied down, by *anyone* or *anything*. When you didn't respond to the letter I assumed you wanted nothing to do with the responsibility of a baby. You can't be *that* surprised that I'd make that assumption. And I wasn't going to chase after you to beg for a handout either. I'd made the choice to have her, so caring for her needs was down to me too.'

It was the condensed version and Rhiannon knew it. But none of her explanation seemed to placate him any. In fact, if anything, he was looking at her with the same incredulity she'd felt only moments before, as if he couldn't possibly understand why she'd done what she had.

'As her father I had certain rights. I still do.'

Her shaking increased. Because she hadn't paid as much attention to the first part of what he'd said. 'What do you mean, you *still do*?'

'If she's my child, Rhiannon, then you've already had nearly ten years alone with her.'

She couldn't—he couldn't just—

When she managed to speak her voice came out smaller than she could ever remember it sounding before. She'd never allowed herself to feel like some helpless waif of a female before. Not once. No matter what life had thrown at her. But he couldn't—

'I won't let you take her from me.'

Because money could buy practically anything as far as some people were concerned, couldn't it? She'd fight with her dying breath to stop him.

Kane swore again. 'What the hell kind of man do you take me for? Of course I'm not bloody well going to take her from her mother! But I have a right to spend time with her, to be a part of her life. And you took that right from me. I can't believe that you thought for one second I *wouldn't* be angry about that!'

Rhiannon wrapped her arms around her body, pressing them in tight as if she could somehow force the inner shaking away while she continued to stare up at him. 'You knew I had a baby. Many things you may have been, but stupid wasn't one of them. Surely you were able to do the maths?'

His jaw clenched. 'You married Stephen.'

Rhiannon's jaw dropped—literally. 'And you assumed that meant that Lizzie was *his*?'

'Apparently I wasn't the only one making assumptions back then.'

Nice try. They might not have been head over heels in love, but he had automatically assumed she'd jumped straight into bed with someone else the second they had split up or, worse still, might even have been with him at the same time. That told her exactly what he thought of her, didn't it? He probably even thought that, coming from the background she had, any rich guy would do!

Rhiannon couldn't bear to be in the same room with him any more. She really couldn't.

Unfolding her arms, she stood up as tall as her five foot eight would allow. 'Well, if you're so certain that's the kind of person I am, then maybe I *am* mistaken about who her father is. I'll have to check through that long list of people I was sleeping with, won't I?'

He had her lower arm caught in yet another tight grip in the blink of an eye as she tried to leave the room. He tugged, just once, but with the shock of his hot hand on her cold skin it was enough to unbalance her and tip her in against his hard body.

Again.

No matter what she did, she seemed to end up being touched by him or trapped close to his body. Where his very male spiced scent invaded her nostrils so that she could almost taste the cinnamon undertones in the back of her throat and where the blazing heat of him immediately filtered through both layers of clothing to burn her chilled body—like being doused in boiling water after lying in ice.

Rhiannon gasped silently, her eyes focused on the column of his neck as she pushed against the wall of his broad chest with her free hand. But he already had his other hand pressed into the small of her back, his arm holding her still.

'I need to know if she's mine.'

Rhiannon swallowed hard while she tried to stay still, to ignore the building heat and the knot in her stomach because it was the way it had always been with them—physical aware-ness, in its purest form, on its most basic level—instant and powerfully overwhelming. It was exactly this—*chemistry*—that had drawn them together the first time. But she didn't want it to be there this time. She was mature enough now to know that there was more to any relationship worth having than just the physical. Even if the physical had given her the one person in her life she could love without reservation.

Slowly her gaze rose, following a ribbed line of dark wool upwards, over the fold of the polo-neck where it met his deeply tanned skin, over the tense line of his mouth, until she was looking into his blue eyes.

She searched, from one to the other, willing her heartbeat to settle at the sight of the fierce determination there, the need she could see to know the truth. It almost made him look vul-nerable. When he was the least vulnerable person she knew.

Whatever it was, it forced the truth from her lips. 'No matter what you think, there wasn't anyone else. There's no question of her not being yours.'

There had never been any question. And, even if there had, the evidence was staring her in the face when she looked at him. It had been the hardest thing about watching Lizzie growing up. Every day she would do something, say something, or simply smile a certain way—and Rhiannon would see Kane in her. And it was only the completely overwhelming love she'd felt from the moment she'd first held her in her arms that had stopped her from hating that those reminders were there.

Kane exhaled, his peppermint-scented breath washing over

her face as the hold on her arm loosened a little, his voice still strained. 'You should have told me.'

'I thought I had.'

'No, because if you had I'd have been there.'

'But you weren't there.' Her gaze lowered to his mouth, to the parting in his lips. 'You'd already gone.'

When he didn't reply she risked another upward glance to discover he was examining the top of her head with heavy-lidded eyes.

Then, just like that, he let go, stepped back a little, his hands shoving deep into the pockets of his dark jeans. 'I'm here now. And I'm not going anywhere until I get to know my child.'

She looked back at his neck and watched it convulse as he swallowed, unable to face up to the fact that a part of her—a minuscule part—ached at the possibility that she may have made a mistake by holding a grudge for so long. Had she let pain and confusion cloud her judgement? As an adult, shouldn't she have been able to see past those things? Had she hidden behind hating him?

No. How had he *not* known?

He tilted his head closer to warn her in dangerous tones, 'And there's not much point in trying to argue about it because I'm not going away this time.'

Rhiannon's heart thudded painfully against her breastbone, her breathing shallow. 'I can't just dump you on her like that—out of nowhere…'

His mouth twisted cruelly. 'Did you *ever* plan on telling *her*?'

'When she was old enough to decide whether or not she wanted to find you, I'd have told her. It would have been her decision.'

'But you wouldn't have encouraged her to ask…'

Maybe not, and it was a moot point now. But Lizzie was bright; already she was asking the odd question about her dad— Father's Day in particular guaranteeing a natural curiosity over the last few years. She'd even made a card for him when she was six. And it had broken Rhiannon's heart, for failing to give her the kind of father she deserved.

'It would have been her decision.'

'She has as much of a right to know as I did.'

He wasn't letting go, was he? Was this what he'd have been like if he'd known all that time ago? Was this the proof she needed to accept that he really hadn't known?

It was, wasn't it? No matter how much she still wanted to believe that he'd known all along, she couldn't deny the possibility that he hadn't any more. It was written all over him. And a very small part of her felt a hole form inside her chest—one that was swiftly beginning to fill with guilt.

Had she maybe known all along that he hadn't known? Had a part of her wanted to keep Lizzie from him? If that was the case, then why had she been so angry with him for so long?

Kane spread his feet a little wider apart as he stood tall to his full six foot two again, towering over her. 'It's like this, Rhiannon—if you don't tell her who I am, then I will. Or we go the legal route. Either way, now that I *do* know she's mine, I plan on being part of her life. And there's nothing you can do to stop that happening. Not this time.'

Even without holding her, with several *safer* inches separating them, Rhiannon knew he had her trapped. Now that he knew and was determined to be a part of Lizzie's life, he wouldn't change his mind, would he? She knew that from the various tales she'd heard over the years—of his determination and single-mindedness in business, his knack of always getting what he wanted in spite of the odds. And, after all, she had been one of those 'things' once, hadn't she?

It wouldn't matter where she ran to if she left Brookfield. Now that he knew…

What she needed was a way of making this work without causing any more damage. 'I need some time.'

'You've *had* ten years.'

'I'll *tell her*.' She glared up at him, making it crystal clear she wasn't happy about it. 'But I'm not going to collect her from school and just announce it. She's just had to adjust to losing her home, her friends at school, an uncle she adored... I can't just land a new father on her too.'

His jaw clenched; his large body even rocked forwards a little. And Rhiannon stood taller, prepared for whatever he would throw her way. But he corrected himself, rocking back as his rumbling voice resonated from deep inside his chest.

'I'll stay here until she's more comfortable with me.'

Rhiannon's eyes widened. 'You can't—'

'Can't I?' He quirked a brow again. 'There are two ways to play this: the easy way and the hard way. You tell me which way you think would be best for her. Because, frankly, right this minute, I don't give a damn what suits you best.'

Her mind swiftly filled in various versions of the 'hard way'. If he chose to fight for Lizzie she would put up one hell of a fight. But was that really what was best for Lizzie?

As if somehow seeing into her mind, he forced the point home for good measure. 'And if it comes down to a legal battle over this then we both know I can afford to fight it for as long as it takes.'

Rhiannon momentarily felt dizzy.

'I'll go and make arrangements to have equipment sent up from Dublin so I can work from here.'

Just like that? He was already making plans to move in?

'And I'll spend time with her when she gets home from school.'

He'd be right here, under the same roof, where she would have to stand by and watch as he tried to bond with Lizzie.

'And then you'll tell her who I am.'

From somewhere she finally found some words. 'You can't be like *this* with her. You'll have to try being *nice*.'

A sudden burst of sharp laughter caught her off guard. A laugh of disbelief, as if he didn't know how she'd just had the audacity to say what she had.

'Ah, but *she* didn't hold this back from me, did she? Why would I be angry at *her*?'

Rhiannon shook her head, a deathly sense of calm washing over her in the face of the inevitable. 'Fine. I obviously don't have a choice. And, to be honest, I'm done arguing with the people living under the same roof as me, even if they're only staying temporarily.'

'What the hell does that mean?'

And that just proved how vulnerable she was in her current state of emotional exhaustion, if 'secrets' were spilling out. 'It means that I have to tell her if you're determined to have access to her, because I won't put her through a battle. But she does need to spend some time with you and settle into her life here first. And that's a request for her sake, not for mine.'

'We're not talking months when it comes to telling her. I'm not even talking weeks. I'm talking days—within the week. Otherwise *I* tell her.'

Rhiannon closed her eyes for a moment. The temptation to run was so strong it was like a fishing line tugging at the back of her sweater. But she'd promised herself when they came to Brookfield that it would be the last time they moved.

When she opened her eyes Kane was studying her, a deep vertical frown line between his blue eyes—a sign that he frowned often, no doubt. But in the depths of his eyes there wasn't just anger, there was something else—a mixture of what looked like consideration of a puzzle yet to be solved, as if he was somehow trying to size her up.

And, for some reason, Rhiannon found herself fascinated by that, distracted even. For a heartbeat she forgot all the difficulties between them and was curious about the man who stood in front of her. Had he really been the person she'd once thought he was or had he lied to her all along? Why had he left the way he had? What had driven him to be so successful when he could simply have sat back and lived on the money his family already had?

Who *was* Kane Healey, *really*?

But all she really wanted to know was whether he could be the kind of father that Lizzie deserved. She prayed he could be. And now he was going to be a part of her life, and Rhiannon knew she was going to have to learn to live with that.

Because the sooner everything was sorted out, the sooner he would go.

She ran the tip of her tongue over her lips and fixed her gaze at a point past Kane's shoulder. 'I'll tell her as soon as she's comfortable with you. But we can't argue in front of her like this. If you have anything to say to me, you say it when she's not here. She shouldn't have to pay the price for our dislike of each other.'

Kane stepped sideways, his upper arm brushing briefly against her shoulder as he walked past, causing a sudden crackle of static to pass through the wool to her skin.

'She's lived her entire life without a father. I'd say she's already paid, wouldn't you?'

Rhiannon stood in the cold room for a long time after he left, her eyes dry and sore, while inside she felt—nothing, as if a part of her had just given up. It occurred to her that she should at least have wanted to cry, just a little, while she was alone.

But, with a resigned sigh, she knew a part of her *had* always known this day would come. All she had to do now was find the right words to explain it to Lizzie.

And a way to live under the same roof as the man she had spent a decade of her life hating.

CHAPTER FOUR

KANE looked out of his office's floor-to-ceiling windows, over the city and the River Liffey far below, swinging back and forth in his chair while he tapped one long finger against his chin.

It was the first time in years that he'd felt so completely floored, thrown by something he really hadn't been prepared for. To suddenly discover that Rhiannon had kept that big a secret from him for so long—

Well, suffice to say it had been a long time since he'd been so angry at anyone; usually he considered himself an even-tempered kind of a guy. After all, he was more aware than most of how life could be too short to get heated up over things.

But how could she have possibly thought he wouldn't have cared that he had a child? Hadn't she known him at all? Did she honestly think he'd have walked away from something like that? Damn her!

'So, basically the offer is on the table.' His corporate solicitor continued talking behind him. 'The shareholders—and you are, of course, a major one—stand to make a fortune.'

He forced his mind to follow the conversation. 'If they vote to accept it.'

'Well, obviously there are still months of negotiations but I'd say it's a safe bet they will.'

Kane continued swinging back and forth, his mind elsewhere. It was a bad time for him to be forced away from the office too… But for the first time in years he had something infinitely more important than his company and his work to think of. *Nothing* was more important than getting to know his child. Not even an attempt from an overseas company to make a takeover. Takeovers he could deal with, shareholders he could deal with, million dollar technological developments he was used to dealing with on an almost weekly basis. The time with his child that he'd had stolen from him was something he would never, *ever* deal with.

How in hell could Rhiannon live with herself? All right, maybe not so much when it came to how he would feel, but to have deprived her daughter of her father…?

'It's a once in a lifetime offer, Kane. How many men are self-made millionaires before they're thirty-two?'

Kane took a breath. 'How many men can stand by and watch something they put their soul into split up into tiny pieces and swallowed by a company seeking worldwide domination of the market?' He swung the chair around to look the older man in the eye. 'It'll mean a loss of creative control and some major job losses. And neither of those things sit well with me.'

Particularly the latter—because the value of family might not mean much to Rhiannon MacNally, but it meant something to Kane. As far as he was concerned, people came first.

'Well, yes.' The man looked vaguely confused at Kane's lack of enthusiasm. 'But this sort of thing happens all the time; it's the way of the world. Job losses happen every day.'

He studied his adviser for long silent minutes. He'd built Micro-Tech from virtually nothing with the help of a small group of investors and, of course, Mattie Blair's faith. But, regardless of what had driven him to succeed, Kane still found it difficult to let go, even for such a large financial reward. Yes, he could agree to it all—to the takeover and the job losses—but he would have a problem looking in the mirror in the mornings. And now that he had a daughter it seemed even more important to him that he was able to do that.

He swung his chair back towards the windows, not allowing his gaze to stray towards the vicinity of Trinity University, where he had first met Rhiannon, while he focused on more important thoughts.

It might not make much sense to want to be the sort of man a child would feel proud to have as a father when that child had lived almost a decade with an *absentee father*, but it was how Kane felt. If she was his then he had to step up and try to make up for the years Rhiannon had stolen from them both.

He frowned at the view in front of him. Maybe he should have figured it out, believed in what they had had at the time so that he hadn't been so quick to think she'd moved on to someone else the second he was gone. But he'd had so much to deal with, had been so eaten up with bitterness and anger and an inevitable sense of fear...

Whereas Rhiannon had thought a letter was enough to ease her damn conscience!

He had to focus on the here and now. What he needed was a plan. Maybe a plan would make him feel better, more in control, more proactive.

Step one was the knowledge that the loss of jobs involved in a takeover would have a devastating effect on a lot of people and their families—people who had gone out on a limb with him in the first place. And he couldn't allow that to happen if he wanted to be the kind of self-respecting father any child deserved.

Step two, as he sung his chair back round again, was to make sure everyone was clear where he stood—and quickly—so that he could get back to Brookfield to right a wrong that he may well have to admit to being part of, because he'd left when he had.

And that meant that part of step three would have to be to discover just how much of a difference his leaving had made to Rhiannon's decision. Because he needed to understand, not so that he could forgive her—he doubted that was even possible—but so he could at least find a way to deal with her.

After all, she was the mother of his child.

'Every kid should have a dog, don't you think, Kane?'

'Not every kid does, though.'

'Yeah, but they *should*.'

Kane smiled patiently at her. 'You don't give up easy, do you?'

Lizzie shrugged. 'Mum says I get my determine…detre…'

'Determination?'

She smiled. 'Yeah, that thing. I always get the word wrong. Anyway, she says I get it from my dad.' She shrugged. 'It's s'posed to be a good thing.'

He nodded in agreement. 'It can be; it helps you get the things you need to get.'

'And I *need* a dog and a pony.' She nodded curtly as she spoke, handing him another empty box to tear into flat pieces.

'And you think you'll get them if you pester her enough— is that the plan?'

'Mum? Yes.' Her nose wrinkled again. 'If it's not too expensive. We aren't rich.'

Kane smiled again at her matter-of-fact way of laying down the truth. But then he was enthralled by everything about her.

How could Rhiannon have kept all this from him for so long? She'd had no right to keep him from his child's first smile, first laugh, first step, first words—all of the things he would never get back or ever experience…

Even with only a few days of new-found knowledge, he couldn't ever remember resenting someone as much as he did Rhiannon. Hence he had chosen to stick closer to Lizzie since he'd moved in rather than allowing the tension that lay thick in the air when Rhiannon was around to *affect* Lizzie. At least on that one subject he could agree with her mother.

Clenching his jaw as a thought occurred to him, he forced nonchalance into his voice as he asked, 'Didn't your dad get you a pony or a dog before?'

'You mean Stephen?' She shook her head, a shadow briefly crossing her bright eyes. 'He wanted me to go to boarding school and said if I had a dog or a pony it couldn't go. But Mum didn't want me to go to boarding school. It's better when it's just me and Mum. And if we had a dog and a pony it would be *perfect*.'

Well, there was never going to be any problem getting information out of Lizzie, was there? That realization, along with the stunning sense of relief that washed over him that she had never called anyone else Daddy, brought a small smile back on to Kane's face. 'You always call him Stephen?'

'Yep,' She grinned as she lifted a pile of pony magazines out of a box. 'My mum called him Stephen.' She giggled and leaned closer to whisper, 'And some bad names too when she thought I couldn't hear her.'

Kane chuckled. Despite the fact that it was another subject he agreed with Rhiannon on he had called Stephen plenty of names over the years. There was just something about him that had always grated on Kane's nerves.

With a large bag of ripped up cardboard in one hand, he followed Lizzie on to the landing. His smile was still in place when she turned to check that he was following her, slowing down to allow him to catch up with her when in reality he could have managed it in two strides.

It was thoughtful of her. She was an amazing kid.

'Do you have any kids, Kane?'

His breath caught at the innocent question. How in hell was he supposed to answer that one? It wasn't as if he could say,

Not that I knew of. And Rhiannon had made it very clear that she had never even hinted at it to Lizzie before. Damn her.

'Are you married?'

'You're just full of questions, aren't you?' He swapped the bag to his other hand. 'Should I call my solicitor before we go any further?'

Lizzie stopped at the top of the stairs, turning and frowning up at him as one small hand brushed back a long strand of hair from her face—hair the same colour as his, the eyes that were looking up at him the same colour as his. It was surreal.

'Why would you need to call one of them? Are you getting a divorce too?'

'No, I've never been married. It's in case you ask me anything I might get into trouble with the police for.'

Her eyes rounded. 'Have you been in trouble with the police, like one of those guys on TV?'

A loud peal of male laughter escaped to echo up and around the cavernous entrance hall. 'That would make me much more interesting than I actually am.'

'Well, I think you're interesting.' She smiled up at him, then turned and headed down the wide staircase.

'Thank you.' The sense of pride that gave him as he followed her grew exponentially.

'Stephen thinks you're interesting, he used to ask Mum tons of things about you.'

I'll just bet he did. Kane frowned briefly at the back of her head, forcing his voice to stay light. 'Stephen and I know each other from a long time ago; he was probably just wondering how I've been getting along all these years since I last saw him.'

Lizzie turned her head slightly as she got near the bottom of the stairs. 'What *is* a control freak, anyway?'

Kane blinked innocently. 'A what?'

'It's what Stephen said you are.'

'Did he now?'

She bobbed her head before turning on her heel and grabbing hold of the banister as she jumped off the second last step. 'And something about being over a bear.'

He quirked a brow as she pushed the door to the kitchen. '*Overbearing*?'

She grinned. 'Yeah, that and another thing about—'

'*Lizzie*?'

Both sets of eyes turned in the general direction of Rhiannon's softly demanding voice.

But while Kane surrendered to a swift wave of pure unadulterated resentment again—for the simple reason that every time he saw her he had an immediate, uninvited visceral response—Lizzie was quick to bounce on regardless.

'Oh, hi, Mum. We unpacked all the stuff for my room and Kane helped me tear up the boxes.'

'That was good of him.' Rhiannon glanced at the anger in his eyes before refocusing on her daughter, as if she saw her as some kind of shield between them. 'So what were you just saying to Kane?'

Lizzie shrugged. 'We were talking about Stephen.'

Kane watched Rhiannon's throat convulse as she swallowed, her eyes flickering up to his face and then away before she answered with a tightlipped, 'I see.'

Yeah. He'd just bet she did. Because she'd known from the start how little he thought of Stephen and yet she'd still gone ahead and married him *and* allowed him to become some kind of a stand-in father figure to Lizzie too. It was hellish hard to swallow.

His eyes narrowed when she looked back at him.

'Kane says they were friends from way back.'

Rhiannon's finely arched eyebrows rose, her brown eyes full of disbelief. 'Friends?'

Kane rectified the misconception in a flat tone. 'I said we knew each other.'

Lizzie looked surprised. 'You weren't friends?'

Forcing a smile in the face of such innocent curiosity, he added, 'Not exactly, no.'

'How come?'

He took a breath. 'Because we don't always get on with everyone we know.'

'Just like *you* don't get on with everyone in school.'

Kane glanced at Rhiannon again as she spoke, understanding immediately what she was doing but ignoring any hint of a rapport between them that that might have indicated. He was way past the stage of appreciating anything nice she might try to do, even if she was currently trying to smooth over a difficult topic on his behalf.

Lizzie sighed. 'Mum's still mad at me 'cos I pushed Sarah McCracken and she fell down.'

'Little girls don't go around pushing other little girls over.' Rhiannon glanced at Lizzie, then briefly up at Kane before concentrating on unwrapping a few more of the plates on the table in front of her, stacking them into a rapidly growing pile. 'Even when the other little girl says something they don't agree with.'

Wasn't finding it easy to look at him for long, was she? Kane smiled a small smile as he glanced down again, trying to keep all of his attention on Lizzie. Maybe her mother was starting to feel a little guilty? Well, she damn well should!

'What did Sarah say?'

Lizzie shrugged again. 'She said I only played football so that the boys would like me.'

He bit back a larger smile. 'And *do* you?'

'You want to watch she doesn't push you too. She may look all sweetness and light, but she has a temper.'

Like her mother used to have. Kane remembered the sometimes heated debates they used to have; he remembered how defensive she'd been about where she'd come from and how single-minded she'd been about making something of her life. And she'd managed it through a marriage into one of the oldest families in Dublin in the end, hadn't she? She'd traded up.

At the time it had made him glad he'd broken up with her when he had, even if he *had* maybe handled it badly enough for her to make the decision that he wasn't worthy parent material. After all, if she was only interested in marriage to step her into a safe financial environment it wouldn't have been much of a marriage, would it?

Knowing that made it easy now to damp down the memory of how much fun he'd once had making up with her after one of their 'debates'—long, languid sessions of making up. Until there had been a time when they had debated less and 'made up' more. At one time he had thought the memories would haunt him. But then she had married Stephen and he'd known he'd had a lucky escape.

All it had cost him was his daughter. And there wasn't a single doubt in his mind that she was his, now that he had spent time with her.

Lizzie giggled, the sound dancing around the room and drawing his attention back to her face. And instantly he smiled in response. For no other reason than it was what he always felt like doing when he looked at her.

'I'd need to grow a bit first before I tried pushing Kane over. He's *humongous*!'

'Nah.' He moved towards the back door with his bag. 'We office types are real weaklings. I'll bet you could push me over in a snap.'

Rhiannon watched him from below long lashes as he made the journey across the kitchen. *A real weakling, my backside.*

Her gaze moved slowly over his body, making the most of

what had once been an everyday sight. The man had always had his own particular way of filling a woman's eyes and the years hadn't diminished that any.

Not that he was handsome in a conventional Prince Charming way, oh, no. He'd never been that simple to peg. He'd always been, well, *sexy*, truth be told. Ruggedly handsome, definitely all male, and there was a sexuality to that that had been hard to resist, for her anyway.

It had been the first time in her young life that she'd met someone who could affect her on such a basic sensual level with just a silent gaze or half a smile. And the kind of passion they had eventually shared had been inevitable from the first day he'd looked at her. Damn him.

'That has to go in the recycle bin.'

Rhiannon watched as he glanced over his shoulder and flashed a brilliant smile at Lizzie, one that was open and honest, almost affectionate. And it tore off another piece of her heart when he answered with a brief salute and a, 'Yes, ma'am.'

Already father and daughter had an ease with each other, a rapport of sorts. And Rhiannon felt unreasonably jealous about that. Not for the way Kane was with Lizzie, but more for the way Lizzie was with Kane. She was still so innocent, so unbiased, so damn open and trusting.

'It's 'cos of the planet.'

'*Naturally.*'

Rhiannon rolled her eyes at the pun while Lizzie giggled. But the second Kane closed the door behind him he looked straight at her with such a look of venom that she almost called him on it. *Almost.*

But in a small corner of her traitorous mind she immediately wondered what it would take to be on the receiving end of the look he wore on his face when looked at Lizzie. Not that she wanted him to look at her with that kind of open warmth. It was just that she was very aware of the vast difference in the way he treated them.

Surely he couldn't entirely blame her for all of this? She wasn't the one who'd disappeared without a trace. And if he'd thought anything of her, which she'd believed he did once upon a time, then surely he couldn't have been so dumb as to not work out her baby was his!

All right, so she hadn't known she was pregnant when he had broken up with her, and he had been gone for a while by the time she did know—but even so!

Whatever it was that had pulled him off the face of the earth so completely must have been damn compelling!

His deep voice broke into her thoughts. 'Is there anything else that needs to be carried out?'

'No. But thank you for asking.'

'Can we eat yet?' Lizzie kneeled on one of the long wooden benches at the side of the huge table. 'I'm starved.'

'You're always starved.' She smiled indulgently. At least with her daughter she was on safe ground.

'Kane's starved too.' Lizzie nodded her head in his direction, her eyebrows hinting that he should back her up. 'Right, Kane?'

'I'm not sure I would use the word "starved".'

Again Rhiannon's gaze strayed across his body, moving over his flat stomach and then upwards to where his ribcage tapered outwards to his wide chest and broad shoulders, upwards still, until her eyes met his.

Kane smiled a slow smile in response, one that didn't make it all the way up into his eyes, allowing her to silently know he'd witnessed her study of him—and almost hinting at it being a victory of some kind.

Rhiannon immediately frowned with annoyance and looked away. 'I'm sure Kane doesn't want to be stuck with us twenty-four hours a day.'

'Oh, I don't know.' He allowed the words to come out in a low drawl. 'I think we still have a *lot* of catching up to do, don't you?'

She gritted her teeth. Damn him, 'You must have things of your own to do, phone calls to make to corporate headquarters, that kind of thing.'

Anything that would give her time alone with her daughter— away from his constantly stifling presence.

'No, I'm all yours.'

God, she hated him. 'Well, dinner won't be ready for a while and there's still plenty of unpacking to do.'

Which wasn't a lie; the removers had barely been gone a couple of hours.

'I'll cook.'

Her eyes widened in disbelief as she stared up at him again. '*You'll* cook?'

His face remained impassive. 'I've been known to beat an egg.'

He did look as if he was ready to beat *something*.

'It's really not necessary.' She hadn't actually contemplated them all sitting down to eat together every night. Was that seriously what he expected would happen? That they would sit around and play happy families while he was there?

'While you're still settling in, it makes sense if I throw something together. Lizzie can give me a hand while you're busy with something else. And anyway—' he smiled at Lizzie '—we wouldn't want Lizzie to starve to death, would we?'

Lizzie rubbed her stomach and sighed dramatically in response. 'I might be having a growth spurt, Mum. What would happen if I didn't get all the stuff I need to get tall?'

'You'd stay short.' She frowned briefly at Kane in warning. If he thought she was that easily dismissed he had another think coming. 'Really, I don't think you should have to cook for us. We can all respect each other's space while you're visiting.'

'Or we could just spend the time to get to know each other

after all these missing years.' He let the innuendo hang in the air like poison. 'Don't make such a big deal out of the odd omelette.'

'I'm not.' Which was a lie. She was, because it *was* a big deal. 'It's just setting a precedent is all—'

He remained deathly calm, folding his arms across his broad chest. 'Is it?'

'Yes, it is. The last couple of nights have been thrown together but if you cook tonight you'll expect me to cook tomorrow night and then we'll end up in some silly routine.'

'And that would be silly, why?'

'You're always saying the more people that share the work the quicker it gets done, Mum.'

Rhiannon ignored her own words of wisdom. 'We don't need to eat together every single night.'

And the last couple of nights had been hell. Every mouthful of food had felt like swallowing broken glass.

'Because it makes much more sense for us all to fend for ourselves—cook at different times—that kind of thing? Next you'll want a rota for the cooker and the washing-up.'

She mumbled her response without looking at him. 'I don't happen to think that's unreasonable.'

'Well, I think you're being silly. Don't you, Lizzie?'

Rhiannon wondered how much time she'd get in prison for a spur of the moment murder...

'Yup, I think you're being silly too, Mum.'

Rhiannon glanced at Lizzie's face. She was smiling, but already her perceptive gaze was moving back and forth between the two adults.

'Are you okay with helping him?'

Lizzie shrugged nonchalantly. 'Yup. But then that means we don't have to do the dishes, right?'

Rhiannon smiled down at her, glanced sideways at the studious expression on Kane's face and then bowed her head to concentrate on unwrapping more plates, a curtain of her long hair hiding her from him.

'All right, then. Whatever you're happy with, baby.'

Lizzie paused for only the briefest of moments before she answered with, 'W-ell, what would make me *really* happy is *a dog* and *a pony*…'

Rhiannon couldn't help it, she laughed at the ridiculous situation she found herself in. Then suddenly realized she wasn't the only one laughing, the sound of her own laughter briefly mixing with deeper male laughter.

When she looked at Lizzie, the child's mischievous blue-eyed gaze moved again between the adults before she laughed too.

Rhiannon looked upwards in time to catch the tail-end of Kane's open smile before he tore his gaze from hers and ruffled Lizzie's hair, his voice gruff but laced with affection.

'That's it, kiddo, never give up.'

He hunched down beside her to discuss what they were going to make for dinner, the words fading into the distance as Rhiannon stood transfixed by the sight of them side by side. They were just so very alike—the shade of their hair, the colour of their eyes, the way that Lizzie would tilt her head in thought.

And there it was again, that instant ease between them. So natural, so uncomplicated—*already*!

Another bubble of guilt rose up inside her. She had kept them apart all this time. And why, really? Because of her pride, because she'd been so very quick to decide he wouldn't want anything to do with his own baby? She could justify it by looking back at how much of a mess she'd been back then, how young and naïve and alone and scared—but even so…

Seeing them together now made her look back on the judgement call she'd made and, no matter how she tried, she found the decisions she'd made coming up shorter than before.

It wasn't a good feeling.

When Kane glanced up at her again, it took a moment for his face to come into focus. She blinked back the moisture at the back of her eyes, avoided his gaze and cleared her throat with a soft cough as she lifted the last plates off the table.

'I'll leave you two to it, then. I'll be in the library.'

Still avoiding looking at him, she walked out of the room with her head held high, determined to get away before she let any of her inner doubts show.

She might have just been forced to realize she may have made a huge mistake. But she wouldn't show it in front of *him*. Watching him with Lizzie was punishment enough.

Because she already felt as if she was losing her daughter a little to him. And that hurt beyond words.

CHAPTER FIVE

INSIDE a week Rhiannon was starting to cherish the time she had with Lizzie on the short trips to and from school. It felt like the only time they were alone, as if somehow she'd suddenly been thrust into a kind of competition for quality time with her daughter.

And she *hated* that.

It had been just the two of them for a lot longer than it had ever been with someone else in their lives.

And Rhiannon was discovering she preferred it that way.

Even the time when Lizzie was at school was tense. Because, though she managed to avoid Kane by focusing all her energy on unpacking and cleaning and adding the little familiar touches that would turn Brookfield from Mattie's house into a home that Lizzie could be happy growing up in, she was constantly aware that he was still there, even if he wasn't.

He disappeared again briefly at the start of the second week to conduct business back in Dublin, but he still managed to be back before Lizzie went to bed. And while he'd been gone a van-load of high-tech equipment had arrived, specifically, it felt, to remind Rhiannon that he hadn't gone for good.

She wondered just how long he intended the charade to continue. Because it honestly felt as if a little of her was dying every day. She'd never felt so alone. There was no one she could talk to about how she was feeling, not really, and where would she begin? After all, she'd learnt early in her life to cope alone and, much as she loved the few close friends she had, she wasn't going to phone them every second to talk it through when there was no point. They couldn't fix it.

Under different circumstances she knew she'd have talked to Mattie. But all that thinking that way did was to magnify the grief she'd been burying at the loss of her best friend. The grief she had hoped to work through by keeping busy at Brookfield and focusing on Lizzie being happy.

The latter goal was something Kane seemed to have taken off her hands, which left her working on Brookfield alone and finding reminders of Mattie at every corner. Increasing the sense of isolation in her own home, and making her more miserable with each passing day.

As it was what she considered her 'turn' to make dinner, she laid the table and checked nothing was burning before she went to seek out Kane and Lizzie.

It was only as she walked up the sweeping stairway to the second floor that she heard laughter echoing in the distance. And once again, surreally, there was deep, distinctly male laughter as well as the familiar melodic giggle that Rhiannon knew so well, the sound floating down temptingly from the third floor where generations ago the house servants would have lived.

It felt as if he was deliberately taunting her as she got closer.

'No way.'

'Yes way.'

'Then how does the Warrior Princess get past the monster? Quick, before I get killed!'

'Ah, now, a smart kid like you should be able to work it out. That's the whole idea.'

Gently pushing open the low door, Rhiannon's eyes took

stock of the room with a quick glance. At one time it would have been a dormitory; it was long and low, with four small windows sunk into the low eaves.

Except now it had a high-tech office suite in varying stages of construction, with flat computer screens, telephone lines and sheets of bubble wrap hanging out of cardboard boxes.

Well, he hadn't wasted any time marking out his territory, had he? With a frown, she vowed to ask him outright just how long he planned on staying.

Sitting in front of one of the large screens, where an animated flame-haired woman seemed to be working her way through some kind of magical maze of roaring monsters, was her enthralled daughter. And by her side was someone Rhiannon hadn't seen in years.

With ruffled hair curling adoringly against the back of his broad neck, wearing a plain navy T-shirt, faded jeans and beaten up trainers. Looking like he had used to look when he had been so very infectiously enthusiastic about everything life had to offer.

His deep laughter sounded again as Lizzie huffed in frustration at the game they were playing—*together*.

While Rhiannon stood alone in the doorway and felt the knife twist again in her stomach. She really didn't know how much more of this she could take.

So she scowled hard at what she could see of his profile, at the deep crease in the cheek she could see while her mind filled in the one on the other cheek that she couldn't. And even as resentment swelled in her chest again, so consuming that it almost stole away her breath, she *remembered*. She remembered afternoons with him, doing exactly the same thing with much more antiquated equipment. She remembered his excitement for the technology, the ideas, so far beyond her realms of comprehension, to make it better. How he would talk for hours about things that didn't make any sense to her, but she would listen anyway, just to hear to deep rumble of his voice and to see the sparkle in his eyes.

'Why can't I get her to go through that gap?' Lizzie let go of her control pad long enough to point at the edge of the screen.

He examined her profile, his eyes still sparkling in a reflection of her enthusiasm even as his tone of voice changed. 'Why don't we ask your mum?'

They both turned their office chairs to look at her, Kane's expression cautious again.

'Kane has some *really* cool games.'

'I'd heard that.' Cool games that half the world's children played on various pieces of equipment these days. She'd been surrounded by Micro-Tech goods for years, had tripped over magazine articles and seen his face on TV more than once. He was considered a technological wizard.

Rhiannon frowned briefly at him as she remembered how it had felt as if he'd been deliberately rubbing her nose in it with his success back then.

Then she smiled at Lizzie. 'Dinner's almost ready. Don't you think you should go get cleaned up and change out of your school uniform? I'm sure Kane has stuff he wants to do too. He doesn't need you up here disturbing him all the time when—'

'I don't mind her keeping me company.'

Rhiannon ignored him. 'If you have your homework done after dinner you can maybe play again for a while before bedtime.'

The concessions weren't getting any easier to make, but with each passing day she was finding herself making more of them without stopping to think about it as much. Probably because she was becoming more and more aware of the fact that Lizzie was flourishing under her father's attention. He always had time for her, listening intently to the things she said, helping her with her homework when she asked him to, explaining things in a way she always seemed to 'get'.

And although Rhiannon knew that, for Lizzie, he still held an element of 'new friend' novelty, she also knew with the instincts of a parent that it went beyond that for Kane. He was making up for lost time.

And there was that inner pang of guilt again.

One dark brow quirked the tiniest amount at how easily she had given up some ground, then Kane winked at Lizzie conspiratorially. 'C'mon then, kiddo. I'll give you a hand with your homework so you can come back quicker, okay?'

Rhiannon had to damp down the sudden need to drag Lizzie from the room while telling Kane in no uncertain terms that she had just as much right to that time with Lizzie as he did. Because, yet again, he had made her feel as if he had formed some kind of 'team' with Lizzie that she wasn't a part of.

She was turning into a shrew, damn him.

If she knew what it was he expected to happen once Lizzie knew who he was, that might help, because there wasn't going to be much more time spent putting off telling her, was there? Not when they were getting on so damn well.

Rhiannon just *really* needed to know what would happen next. Maybe then she could settle her mind.

Lizzie bounced out of her chair, oblivious to any of the undercurrents surrounding her. 'Okay, we have maths tonight anyway and you're way better at that than Mum is.' Oblivious to any angst the words may have brought her mother, she grabbed hold of his large hand and tugged. 'But I'm not sure about playing more 'cos Mum said yesterday I could get a pony and a dog, so I'll have to make a list of things to get for them.'

'Mum didn't say anything was definite,' Rhiannon softly chided while she stared at the small hand still held in Kane's larger one, the need to step over and separate them so strong that she had to grit her teeth together to stop herself from saying something out loud. 'She said we would talk about it some more.'

It had been the first thing that had put that same light into Lizzie's eyes she had when Kane was around.

Lizzie frowned. 'But Mum—'

'Animals are a big responsibility. Go get changed.' She unconsciously stared again at their joined hands.

As if somehow sensing it was a bigger problem than it actually was, and maybe even as a slight reflection of the concessions she'd been making for the last couple of days, Kane let go of Lizzie's hand and used the same hand to ruffle her thick hair.

'Go on—do as your mum says.'

It was the first time he'd backed up Rhiannon, even briefly. And it was an unexpected move. Her gaze automatically rose to lock with his, her shoulders relaxing when he didn't scowl at her in response. But she couldn't think of anything to say, all she could do was study him while he studied her.

Lizzie wrinkled her nose, then, quick as a flash, threw a huge smile up at him. 'Okay.'

Okay? Just like that? No more argument—from the child who, over the last few months, Rhiannon had had to debate and reason with over every little thing, sometimes for days? What in hell had he done to her?

Rhiannon moved to one side as she ran past with a call of, 'I'll be really quick. And then we can talk more about my dog and my pony at dinner.'

With a blink and a shake of her head, Rhiannon turned to go back downstairs. Sometimes being a mother just completely exhausted her, the subject of children's levels of energy still a mystery to parents worldwide, no doubt. But this immediate affinity with the father she had never met before was proving draining on a whole new level.

As was the constant physical awareness of where Kane was and the never-ending attempts her mind was trying to make at deciphering him. To, in some small way, sort out the memories from her decade-old perceptions and the present evidence in front of her eyes.

Rhiannon had always liked everything laid out in black and white—no grey areas. Grey areas held the unexpected. And the unexpected inevitably led to heartache in her experience.

She was at the top of the stairs when the skin at the back of her neck tingled again, the way it did every time he got closer to her.

'I'll make sure she doesn't play the game for too long. She'll be in bed at the normal time.'

'Thank you.' It was another small vote of support from him, which didn't go unnoticed. When he appeared in her peripheral vision, she glanced briefly at him, then down at her feet as they descended the first flight, telling herself she was just making sure she didn't fall flat on her face. But knowing it was because she was uncomfortable constantly looking at him.

'She's very bright.'

'Yes, she is.'

'And she picked up the game very fast for someone of her age. The target market is a few years older than she is now.'

'Her last school couldn't keep up with her computer skills. They reckoned she was at least two years ahead of where she should be. Her teacher even said there were times when she was able to explain how things worked before she was told how.' She frowned as a thought crossed her mind, then swallowed hard before saying it aloud. 'I guess she gets that from you.'

There were several heartbeats of a pause before he responded. 'Knowing there are things she gets from me must kill you, when you've spent so long hating me.'

The lack of anger in his voice surprised her, so she risked another sideways glance at him to confirm it and, for the first time in days, she found him looking back at her with more open curiosity, less resentment, and the distinct lack of a scowl, which knocked her back.

What was he playing at now?

When she faltered on the next downward step, a hint of a smile briefly quirked the corners of his mouth. 'Yes, I'm aware of how much you dislike me. You have to, to have kept her from me for so long.'

Rhiannon sighed. *Here we go again.*

'I'd convinced myself you didn't want anything to do with her.'

'Because I didn't answer the letter.'

'Yes.' She shook her head and focused on the stairs again, long wisps of her hair working free from her braid to brush against her cheek. 'Because you didn't answer the letter. I had no other way of contacting you. No one was able to get you on the phone, your room-mate didn't know where you'd gone or how long you'd be gone. We didn't exactly have a long enough relationship for me to have known your home address to send a Christmas card to your family, so the letter in your locker was the only thing I could think of.'

There. She couldn't make it any plainer than that, could she? And, in reality, she'd been pregnant before she turned nineteen. She'd wanted a solution from *someone*—where to go, how to support a baby, somebody to talk to when she had moments of panic about her ability to cope. If she'd thought he wanted to be there she'd have wanted that too because she'd needed him. And she'd *hated* him for not being there when she'd needed him.

Kane went silent again. And after a few steps Rhiannon couldn't resist glancing across at his face to see if she could see what he was thinking.

Unlike her, he was apparently confident enough in his own ability to make it down a flight of stairs without looking at his feet. Instead his gaze was fixed forwards, thick lashes flickering while he looked at the various paintings and wall-hangings as they appeared in front of him. But Rhiannon knew he wasn't thinking about anything he was looking at. He was considering what she'd said. And more than likely coming up with answering reasons for why she shouldn't have let it go at a letter when it had been something so important.

Well, he wasn't going to find anything that she hadn't spent the last few days torturing herself over. The thing was, she'd ultimately admitted to herself, whether she should have kept trying to get a response from him, either then or in the years afterwards, it didn't really make any difference. It was already done. And now she had to deal with the repercussions.

She fixed her gaze on her feet again.

'Did you know when I spoke to you that last time?'

'When you did the *thanks for the good times* speech?' She resisted the urge to look at him again.

But she could hear the frown in his voice. 'I didn't say that.'

A wry half smile worked its way on to her lips. 'I read between the lines.'

'Well, it wasn't what I meant.' This time the words were firmer, his deep voice low and unnervingly intimate as they continued down each step side by side. 'If it counts for anything, I spent a lot of time rehearsing what I would say to you.'

For no reason, Rhiannon felt a lump form in her throat. When really there was no need for her to be upset by his words. The only thing he had hurt at the time had been her pride, and maybe a little of the romantic notion any eighteen-year-old female possessed for her first 'serious' relationship. And it had to have been serious for her to have slept with him, but emotionally? Well, emotionally she had been fond of him, had cared about him. But she hadn't been in love. He hadn't broken her heart.

That had come later, when she'd had her lack of judgement regarding his sense of honour and responsibility thrown back at her. When she'd had to realize that he wasn't as great a guy as she had thought he was, which made her a gullible fool for even getting involved with him in the first place. Now *that* had broken her heart.

But not for long; she'd turned heartbreak into hatred pretty damn quick. 'You handled it as well as it could have been handled. No break-up is ever easy.'

'We weren't together all that long.'

'I know.'

'It was intense.'

A lump demanded she clear her throat before she spoke again. 'Yes, I remember.'

They crossed the first landing between the flights of stairs before he stepped in front of her. And, even though he didn't reach out to stop her the way he had so cavalierly those first couple of days, it was enough to get her attention, to make her chin rise so that she lifted her gaze to his eyes in question.

And for a long moment he just looked at her, his intensely blue eyes studying her openly before his brows rose in question. 'How much *do you* remember?'

Rhiannon's breath caught. He couldn't just ask her that! Let alone expect her to reply. What was she supposed to do—set aside all those years of resentment and anger so that she could hold a conversation about what a great sex life they'd had?

Over her dead, cold body.

The thoughts must have crossed her eyes before she could hide them because, before her incredulous gaze, he smiled. A slow, toe-curling smile that said he remembered as much about the subject as she did.

His voice dropped. 'I didn't mean that part.'

Rhiannon pursed her lips together, hating the fact that she'd just given him yet another small victory. 'All right, where exactly are you going with this, then?'

Glancing briefly over her shoulder to check that Lizzie's bedroom door was still closed, he stepped closer, his large body looming over her so she had to tilt her head back further to keep holding his gaze.

'I've had a few days to think—'

Oh, great. Now what?

His eyes searched hers and then rose to examine her hair for a moment before he locked gazes with her again. And Rhiannon had to swallow hard to loosen her throat, had to run the tip of her tongue across her lips to ensure she would be able to answer when he threw whatever he was going to throw her way, which drew his gaze down to study the simple movement.

He frowned in response. 'I wondered how much you remembered about the way I was back then. You had to have liked me well enough at some point for us to have—'

Rhiannon blinked in confusion. It wasn't what she had expected him to say. 'Of course I *liked* you. What a stupid thing to say. I wouldn't have—'

'Yes.' He nodded slowly. 'That's what I thought.'

With his body close again, Rhiannon was aware of a faint scent of coffee on his breath. And it occurred to her that he always had a scent of something that hinted at taste— cinnamon, peppermint, coffee. As if he were subliminally inviting her to sample those flavours.

She took a steadying breath. This was *not* going to happen to her all over again.

Kane took a breath, his gaze fixed on hers, his voice still deep, low and intimate. 'And if you liked me enough to get intimate with me *that often*, then you mustn't have thought I was all that bad a guy.'

She laughed sarcastically in response. '*O-oh*, I see where you're going with this.'

When she stepped sideways to get past him, he blocked her

again. 'Well, if you didn't think I was all that bad, then why did you think I'd have ignored your letter? That I'd have let you have my baby on your own? I don't understand that part.'

Rhiannon glanced nervously over her shoulder, making quite sure that Lizzie wasn't within earshot, but dropping her voice to a stage whisper when she looked back at him anyway. 'I was *eighteen*! I was eighteen and I was pregnant and you were the bloody *Invisible Man*! When you didn't answer I was too busy trying to hold myself together to try and understand why such a great guy had turned into such an ass overnight!'

'So you only hated me later, then?' He had the gall to quirk an eyebrow at her.

'Damn you!'

Having spat the words at him, she made the first move and grabbed hold of his wrist, dragging him behind her as she headed down the second flight of stairs.

A hint of amusement sounded in his voice. 'Nice to see that motherhood has mellowed you over the years…'

Feeling vaguely safer on the landing above the last flight, she released his wrist, glancing upwards again before she looked into his sparkling eyes.

'What do you want me to say, Kane?' She swung an arm out to her side while continuing in a slightly louder stage whisper than before. 'Do you want me to say that, despite everything I thought at the time, I was wrong? Then *fine*!'

The admission of guilt widened his eyes a little.

Rhiannon continued, her eyes filling up with the frustrated tears she had held at bay since she'd been forced to watch him with Lizzie. 'I've watched her with you and she's crazy about you. And you're equally as enamoured with her! And if you honestly think that I can love her as completely as I do and not feel guilty about her not having had that sooner—'

She paused to control her voice, which had begun to crack

on the words, looking past him while she fought back the tears, only briefly glancing into his astonished face before she gulped out, 'Then *you* have no better idea of the kind of person *I am* than I do of the kind of person *you are*.'

'Rhiannon—'

The softer tone to his voice tore the last shred of control that she had left, so that when she looked up at him again she could barely see his face for the wash of tears in her eyes.

And she *hated* that he was seeing that! So her voice broke on the admission while she pointed an accusatory finger at his feet.

'I would *never* have denied her her father because I know what it's like to have a father reject his child! So you're right, okay? And I was wrong. *You win*.'

CHAPTER SIX

RHIANNON disappeared upstairs before Kane had time to react properly, which left him standing on the landing between flights. If nothing else she was right about one thing; he didn't know her any better than she knew him.

His gaze rose while he frowned, pondering whether or not to go after her, to ask all the questions she had left him silently asking. But somehow he didn't think she would appreciate it if he did, because, even without any actual confirmation of his gut feeling, he just knew that to push her again at this point would be too much.

No matter how much he hated what she'd done, he still had to respect the fact that she was Lizzie's mother. *His child's mother.*

And, no matter how much he resented having his child kept from him for so long, he still had to show some respect to the woman who'd raised her so beautifully, especially now she'd admitted some guilt for the choice she'd made.

The problem was, her admission, delivered with so much emotion, made him think some more about his part in the wrongs of the past. Yes, he'd had his own reasons for not being there, for not telling her why he couldn't—

Like she'd her reasons for not telling him? He allowed, reluctantly, that that could well be the case. There was more to both sides of the story. But the only way he would know for sure if he was right about that was to get her to trust him enough to tell him and that involved an open line of communication, didn't it? Parents were supposed to be able to have that. Well, *good parents* were. If it just didn't involve getting to know Rhiannon all over again…

Truthfully, what he needed was a little time to mull it all over. *Again.* In between rapidly falling in love with his daughter, he'd already been mulling over a lot of things about her mother, and not coming up with too many answers—a fact that bugged the hell out of someone who had built his business on varying degrees of problem solving.

It was why he had pushed Rhiannon again. He needed answers. Because, as easy as it was to just stay angry at her, a part of him still needed to equate the Rhiannon he'd known before with the one in front of him in the here and now. To have purposefully kept his daughter from him for so long had been cruel—crueller than she could possibly realize—she *had* to have hated him. And yet she had done such an amazing job with Lizzie—how could that be? How could she hate him so much and yet shower so much love onto his child?

Was that just a mother's instinct? She'd already hinted at how much of him there was in Lizzie and, having spent time with her, he could see a lot of those things himself. Surely that must have been hard to see over the years?

So he'd pushed her to try and make sense of it and instead had been presented with even more to confuse him. He hadn't expected the response he'd got, and that was before she even admitted she'd been *wrong*!

It was talking about their previous relationship that had confused him this time. Or rather, how she had immediately assumed they were talking about the sexual side of it and how he'd had an immediate, powerful physical response to that. Damn her.

In her large, soft brown eyes he could see that she remembered every bit as much as he did about their time together. Standing alone in the hallway now, he wondered if she *knew* that he could still see so much in her eyes. Oh, she was better at disguising her thoughts than she'd been at eighteen, there was no doubt about that, which meant he had to search a little harder now for answers than he maybe had back then. But when he caught her off guard he could still see more than she probably realized he could.

It had translated into another thing to resent about her. Because it meant he had another reason to study her, to spend time *looking* at her, seeking out those thoughts in her eyes and trying to decipher them.

And somewhere in the last few days, he'd remembered it was something he'd always liked about her before. That very 'visible' intelligence she had.

Lizzie had it too. Her skill in picking up things quickly didn't come just from him. Oh, no. Having spent so much time with her, he now knew that there was an equal amount of her mother in her—probably more, because she'd spent all of her life with Rhiannon.

His head was really beginning to hurt.

A door opened on the landing above him and he stood tall, every nerve-ending in his body tensing as he waited for Rhiannon to reappear. But, when he looked up, Lizzie appeared at the banister, a grin on her face.

'Are you waiting for me?'

Kane exhaled and smiled back at her, the tension in him disappearing in a heartbeat. 'Yep. C'mon. Let's go get something to eat.'

Being in Lizzie's company was the only time he felt completely at ease in the house. But he couldn't keep putting off spending time with Rhiannon and he knew it. The line of communication had to be opened. He wanted answers. More than that—he wanted to know *everything* so that he wouldn't have to keep studying her and *noticing things*.

Like her natural ability to move gracefully, the sensuous way she would tilt her neck to rub her long fingers against her shoulders, how everything from the soft fall of her hair to that way she had of running the tip of her tongue over her full lips when she was nervous constantly reminded him of how innately feminine she was. And how that femininity would tug at an invisible part of him, the part deep inside that he hadn't felt so keenly in a long, long time around another woman.

If familiarity really bred contempt then he wanted that familiarity.

'I lit a fire in the stove room.' He stood in the kitchen doorway, studying Rhiannon with cautious eyes while he attempted to keep a soft tone to his voice.

She looked tired—dark circles under her eyes, her pale skin lacking its normal creamy glow.

And he'd grudgingly admired her guts for coming down to sit through dinner. No matter how she felt about him being there, she never let it affect the way she was around Lizzie. And that couldn't be easy, he *knew*.

Running a cloth over the end of the table, she focused completely on her task, taking a breath before she answered him. And that had to be tiring too, the constant caution around him in the brief moments when they were alone together.

He pushed his hands into the pockets of his jeans, leaning a shoulder against the door jamb. 'This place is draughty as hell, isn't it?'

'Yes, it can be. Most old houses of this age and size are, I think.'

All right, that had worked. So maybe talking about Brookfield was a starting point.

'Mattie said you always loved this place.'

'Yes.' She nodded, turning to rinse the cloth out at the deep Belfast sink. 'Brookfield is special. It's the kind of place you dream about when you're a little girl. I once saw a doll's house with three storeys like this place in a shop window and it became a dream house in my mind. And Lizzie has always loved it here.'

Kane thought back to the little he could remember of Rhiannon's life from before. And discovered he didn't remember much beyond the fact that her family hadn't been well off. Had she told him more than that? She couldn't have; he'd have remembered.

She spoke again. 'Where is she?'

Ah, okay, she was looking for her shield again, was she? And, with a quick glance at the set of her narrow shoulders, he could see that she wasn't happy with being alone with him again minus that shield. Well, if he was going to have to do without it in order to open a line of communication then Rhiannon was going to have to deal with it too.

'She went up to take her shower.' He pushed off the door frame and walked across to the Aga. 'Do you want coffee?'

He sensed her hesitation so placed an air of nonchalance into his tone. 'I'm making one anyway.'

'All right, then.'

Lifting the kettle from the back of the Aga, he stepped closer to Rhiannon at the sink to fill it with water. The minute his arm brushed hers, she jumped back a couple of inches and Kane sighed impatiently, studying her from the corner of his eye as he poured the water.

'I don't bite.'

She didn't answer him.

But she did fold the cloth, set it over the edge of the sink and step away from him to gather mugs and coffee from a cupboard.

Kane lifted the plate on the Aga and set the kettle on the plate to boil, before moving to the fridge to get milk. And in the tense silence it occurred to him that it was the first task they had worked on together, albeit in silent communication, since he'd come to the house. She'd stayed on the periphery while he spent time getting to know Lizzie, hadn't she? Not that he would probably have appreciated it any if she hadn't. But, even so—

'I think you and I should spend some time together before we tell Lizzie who I am.'

Rhiannon's eyes filled with disbelief. 'Why on earth would we do that?'

'Because I happen to think two parents who can work together is a better combination than two parents who spend all their time arguing. And we need to know each other better than we do now for that to happen.'

He set the milk carton down beside the mugs and tilted his chin a little to keep looking at her, his eyes searching hers to see what she was thinking.

She wasn't too enamoured with his idea.

And he smiled a little at that. At least he knew he wasn't the only one experiencing difficulty with it. 'We both know she's a bright kid. She's bound to feel the tension there is when you and I are both in the same room. And eventually that's going to lead to questions.'

Brown eyes searched his in the same way he had been doing with hers and Kane smiled a little more as he realized she was trying just as hard to read him. He doubted she'd be as successful though; he'd spent years learning how to keep his thoughts hidden from those around him; in private as well as in business.

Her eyes narrowed. 'You're saying we should get on better for her sake?'

'Yes.'

'And how exactly are we going to manage that?'

He shrugged a shoulder as the kettle bubbled. 'We liked each other well enough to make her together in the first place.'

A rose-coloured flush spread on her cheeks as she looked away from his face, focusing on spooning coffee into mugs. Her voice lower, she said, 'That was a long time ago. We were barely adults ourselves.'

'That's true. But surely, as adults, we should be able to find a way of getting on well enough to put Lizzie before ourselves.'

Her hand faltered and some granules of coffee spilt over the edge of one mug so she had to set the spoon down and retrieve the cloth to wipe them up. 'I don't see how we can be friends— we never took the time to do that before. It's too late now.'

'I don't think it's ever too late to make the effort to ensure our daughter doesn't feel like she has to bounce from one of us to the other.' He lifted the boiling kettle and carefully poured the hot water into each mug. 'Do you?'

As he filled each mug, she followed up by stirring the contents until the granules dissolved. 'I don't want her to feel she has to do that.'

'Neither do I.' He set the kettle back on the rear of the Aga and replaced the cover over the hotplate. 'That would be something we agree on.'

He turned and watched as she poured milk into the mugs, her long lashes flickering while she thought. And then he watched as she ran the end of her tongue over her lips, as her throat convulsed when she swallowed, as her small breast rose and fell when she took a deep breath. Then her face turned and she looked up into his eyes, the tiniest hint of a smile on the edges of her mouth as she handed him one of the mugs.

'Yes, I suppose it is.'

His mouth curled into a more relaxed smile. 'It's a place to start.'

Rhiannon took a long time to answer him. 'Maybe.'

His fingers brushed against hers as he took the mug from her, the touch brief but the sensation of it lingering on his skin even as she withdrew her hand and turned away, taking her own mug with her.

Wrapping his hand tighter round the warm mug, he studied its contents for a second, before his gaze rose and he saw her curl her fingertips into the palm of her hand as she walked away.

At the doorway she looked over her shoulder, taking another breath before she spoke. 'If the fire is lit then maybe we could all watch TV for a while before Lizzie goes to bed.'

It would be the first evening they all spent together and they both knew it. And, even with his fingers still tingling against the edge of the mug, something he would have added to his long list of things to resent only a few hours ago, Kane was nodding in agreement.

This had been *his* idea after all, hadn't it?

CHAPTER SEVEN

RHIANNON felt brighter after a few nights' uninterrupted sleep. And the fact that the stormy weather had subdued enough to let the winter sunshine flood through Brookfield's many windows lifted her spirits.

She still wasn't entirely comfortable with spending so much time in Kane's company, even with Lizzie there to act as a catalyst between them. But at least they weren't arguing. And that had to be a good thing. Kane was right; it would be better if they parented with better communication. She couldn't argue that.

It had been his use of words like 'we' and 'us' and 'together' that she'd had the most difficulty swallowing. Those words hinted at a bond between them that just wasn't there.

And yet, reluctantly, she knew it was. Lizzie was a bond that held them together whether Rhiannon liked it or not. At least now she didn't feel like so much of an outsider any more.

So, in the spirit of *entente cordiale*, she made two cups of coffee and then, with a deep breath, she made her way up to Kane's territory. She did, however, have a moment of indecisiveness before she knocked lightly on the half open door.

'…and then e-mail them to me.'

He glanced up, his mobile held to his ear, brows rising in question while she hovered in the doorway. Then his gaze dropped and he caught sight of the mugs in her hand ushering her in with a wave of his large hand.

'Yeah, that's fine. But I want Colm to look at the new graphics first; he knows the issues I had with the last lot.'

He leaned forward in his chair and reached for the one Lizzie normally sat in beside him, turning it round to face Rhiannon and inviting her to sit down with another wave of his hand.

But Rhiannon shook her head. She hadn't meant to interrupt him, or to sit down and actually drink the coffee with him. All she'd intended was to leave him the cup she'd made before she went down to look for the laundry there was bound to be in Lizzie's room.

When she went to set the mug on the desk beside him, he tucked the phone between his ear and his shoulder and took it from her hand, his other hand closing around her wrist, tugging her towards the chair.

He could even be bossy silently.

'Absolutely not, that packaging sucked. The whole idea is to have it look like a more expensive game, even when it's not.' He pursed his lips slightly when she resisted his direction and tugged on her wrist again.

So, with a roll of her eyes, Rhiannon complied, sinking down into the chair with a sigh. She could spare him five minutes, *she supposed*.

'Not before I see it.'

Blue eyes glowed warmly at her, no doubt another indication that he knew he had 'won' yet again, even on something so simple. But rather than scowl at him, she rested her weight on her toes and rocked the chair around to look at the screens behind her—one filled with images of an animated forest and another with lines of code that may as well have been Swahili to her.

'Yes—' she could hear the smile in his deep voice '—I did ring them.'

His low rumble of laughter drew her gaze back to his face as he rocked his own chair back and forth. 'Well, it must have been another query. No, you just never believe me when I say I did unless *you* put the call through.'

He laughed again. And, by straining her ears a little, Rhiannon heard the tail-end of the voice on the other end of the phone—a female voice. Well, that explained why he was in such a good mood.

'Okay, then, the next time they ring you can check and when they tell you I *did* reply you can call me back to grovel.' He grinned at whatever reply his female friend made. 'No, but you should. Okay. That'll do.'

He withdrew the phone from his ear, flipping the cover back into place with one long forefinger while he reached for his mug with the other hand. 'Thanks.'

'I was making one anyway.' She didn't want him making it into a bigger deal than it was. 'I didn't mean to interrupt. It can't be easy running your business from so far away.'

'It's all right, Sara keeps me informed; it's her job to keep me in line.'

Rhiannon had to force an expression of disinterest on to her face. It was none of her concern what woman kept Kane 'in line' these days, though it would be interesting to meet the woman who could manage it...

As if he had read her thoughts, Kane added, 'She's been my PA for three years.'

Rhiannon nodded, avoiding his knowing look by focusing instead on the images that were moving on the screen—the trees giving way to an open valley where tiny men were working, building houses and chopping trees. 'Is this a new one?'

'Nah.' He set his mug down, tossed his phone beside it and then leaned past her to click on the mouse, moving the image out so that she could see there was a world beyond the busy valley. 'It's an updated version of one of our best-sellers. Having some peace and quiet here has let me tweak it some.'

'Then I'd better let you—'

But he had his other arm across the back of her chair and used it to stop her from leaving. 'Have a go. I'll take you back to the set-up menu.'

'I don't know how to play computer games.'

'Well, considering how much Lizzie loves them, maybe you should learn.'

Nursing her mug between both hands on her lap, Rhiannon tried hard not to be so aware of how close he was sitting to her, his body creating a frame for her smaller one in the chair. Instead she focused on his profile as he concentrated on the screen, on the way his eyes moved back and forth, making sense of everything in front of him as easily as he breathed in and out.

Her gaze swept upwards, to the short gleaming strands of dark hair touching his forehead, one strand sitting in a different direction to the rest, as if he had run his fingers through it at some point.

And her fingertips itched against the mug, begging that she reach up and smooth it back into place.

Rhiannon frowned in annoyance—annoyance that she knew came through in the tone of her voice. 'I'm the kiss of death to anything electronic.'

She watched the slow smile form on his lips, his voice low. 'Yes, I remember.'

He glanced at her from the corner of his eye and out of nowhere Rhiannon found herself smiling in response to the sparkle of amusement in the blue depths. 'Well, if you remember then you'll hardly want me killing this one. Whatever you design these days is worth a hell of a lot more than anything I killed back then.'

'Yes, but anything I design these days is more user-friendly and better protected. If you manage to kill it, then I've not done my job right.'

He focused his gaze back on the screen while Rhiannon felt her breath catch in her chest at the memories that rushed uninvited into the front of her mind—as they had the day she had walked in and found him playing games with Lizzie. Maybe even stronger because it was just the two of them. She remembered the last day she'd 'killed' one of his creations…

He had stared in amazement that day, his mouth gaping, while the now outdated graphics had got tangled up with lines of code and Rhiannon had laughed her way through her apology. Until he had pulled her away from the screen and coaxed more laughter from her as he'd tickled his revenge from her ribs, the laughter eventually fading as Rhiannon found a way to 'make it up to him'.

She lifted her mug to her lips and swallowed a large mouthful of coffee to dampen her dry mouth, hiding her thoughts behind the rim.

'Right.' The arm that had been on the back of her chair snaked forwards while he forced his chair closer to hers so he could reach the keyboard. 'The idea is that you're the ruler of a new kingdom—you're shipwrecked—and you have to build an entire civilization from scratch using the resources you have at hand.'

His long fingers tapped at the keys. And beside him Rhiannon tried to focus on what he was doing, rather than the fact that his knees were now pressed in against the side of her leg or the fact that somewhere in her clouded mind she'd recognized he wasn't wearing the aftershave he normally did. He just smelled of soap, and shampoo, and that purely male undertone that was all him. And the simplicity of it reached out to the very core of her femininity, where it tugged, hard, until a dull ache formed.

How in hell could she still be physically attracted to him when she had spent a decade of her life hating his guts?

She glanced at the screen as he typed in a user name. 'Is that the game name you're giving me?'

'It's *your* name.' He glanced at her with an amused glint in the depths of his eyes.

Hell. If she was going to play the silly thing she may as well enter into the spirit of it. Anything other than being so very aware of him or running screaming from the room—the latter of which was hard to resist...

'Well, if I'm the *ruler* of this kingdom I think I'd be called something more interesting, don't you?'

'There's nothing wrong with Rhiannon.'

'I doubt you really think that deep down,' she mumbled as she set her mug down, nudging her chair forwards, her voice louder. 'I'll pick my own name.'

The wheels on his chair creaked as he moved back. 'Okay. Just follow the instructions on the screen.' Turning back to his own screen, he grumbled in a vaguely amused tone, 'And try not to kill it.'

It took a while for her to ignore the fact that he was still beside her, or at least be less aware of it as he worked in silence, but eventually the game demanded her attention and after half an hour she chuckled in amusement.

Kane turned towards her. 'What?'

Rhiannon shook her head while her fingertips directed another set of characters across the screen. 'Now I get why kids end up in front of these things for hours on end.'

When she glanced sideways at him he smiled in response. 'Addictive isn't it?'

'It's clever is what it is. There's something vaguely omnipotent, having control over all these little lives.'

'I could argue that the game also teaches you about trade and commerce, how to delegate, the importance of all forms of a society working together for the greater good of the whole...'

Rhiannon leaned back in her chair and eyed him with a combination of open curiosity and silent amusement.

Until eventually Kane shook his head. 'What's that look for?'

'All of your games are for educational purposes, are they?'

His chin dropped an inch as he smiled again, his gaze darting away from hers to the screen and then back into her eyes. '*No-o*, I wouldn't say that.'

'Hmm, 'cos I'd guess they'd be a harder sell to the kids if they were solely for educational purposes.'

'They probably would. But that doesn't mean every game doesn't teach something—even if it's just better computer skills or mouse dexterity.' He fixed her with an intense gaze, but not in challenge, in more of a sincere faith in what he did type of way. 'Computers are a part of everyone's lives these days, not like it was in the days when you knew me before and I was considered a geek for being as interested as I was. So it makes sense that some of the kids' leisure pursuits should have a grain of computer education in there somewhere. It makes it easier for them to prepare for the bigger stuff when they start their working lives.'

Deep down he was an idealist? Rhiannon wasn't overly surprised by that, even though it was at odds with the opinion she'd held of him for so long. But with every passing day she had to face up to the fact that her perceptions of him may have clouded her judgement.

The truth was she maybe didn't want him to be the things she'd liked then, because she didn't want to like him the way she had before. Even if liking him would make it easier to get along with him, which would in turn make it easier for them to make any parenting decisions—*together*.

And there was that word *together* again.

She searched her mind for something to say, dragging her gaze from the intensity of his blue eyes and her focus fell on the screen again, where her little kingdom was rapidly growing.

'Well, I'm glad Lizzie has you around to help her with this; it was always beyond me—still is, to a certain extent. She's already flourishing under your influence. She got a glowing report for her maths test.'

There was a long moment of silence before Rhiannon heard the leather of Kane's chair creak. From her peripheral vision she saw him leaning towards her, his voice a huskier rumble than before. 'I know. But thanks for that.'

Rhiannon silently cleared her throat, chancing a short glance sideways and then regretting it when she found him closer than she had realized, resting his elbows on his knees so that his face was level with her shoulder.

She shrugged, feigning nonchalance. 'I'm just being honest.'

'And we both need a good dose of that if we're going to find a way to make this all work.'

It was a scary thought. And there was that damn 'we' again.

'So, in the spirit of honesty—'

She gasped when he reached out over her lap, grasping hold of the armrest to turn her chair to face his so that their knees pressed tight together. Then he tilted his chin and looked up into her eyes. '—you did one hell of a job raising her, Mac.'

The old abbreviation of her surname hit her in the chest with silent blunt force. Oh, that was just playing *dirty*! No one but Kane had ever called her that. And at the time it had been a term of endearment—similar to darling or sweetheart.

Her heart beat erratically. 'Thank you.'

He smiled a soft smile that made it all the way up into his eyes, turning them into a deeper shade of almost cobalt blue. 'I'm just being honest.'

She smiled shyly back at him, because in that moment she felt *ridiculously* shy. As if she had somehow been transported back in time to when she had been a shy eighteen-year-old, swept off her feet by the twenty-one-year old student with the roguish smile and the irresistible sensuality. If anything he was more dangerous now. Back then she hadn't known just how compatible they were physically. But she knew now. Oh, yes. And she also knew it would be very easy to be swayed again.

The knowledge made her reach out for a defence shield. 'Well—' she wrapped her hands round both armrests and pushed back with her feet '—now that you've wasted lots of my time with your silly game—'

He grabbed hold of both armrests, lower down where they met the chair, and tugged her back again, the smile gone from his face. 'Don't do that.'

'Do what?' She blinked innocently. 'Leave? I have just as much to do as you do, you know. A house this size doesn't run under its own steam.'

'That's not all you're doing, though.'

How could he know that? 'What *am* I doing, then?'

This time his smile had the same cool edge to it it'd had from his first few days in the house, even though he softened it by using the same edge of sincerity from before. 'You're running away.'

Her chin rose. 'To all the laundry I have downstairs? Oh, please, it's tough to keep the enthusiasm at bay. Hold me back, do.'

'And now you're using sarcasm in defence.'

She scowled at him.

But he astounded her by chuckling in response. 'I remember more about you from before than you might like to think I do. But it's okay; I get it. This honesty thing doesn't sit any more comfortably with me than it does with you. So, if it helps any, you're not alone.'

She knew she was staring at him, but she couldn't stop herself from doing it.

So she saw when his gaze rose to her hair, how it followed the waves down the side of her face, over her shoulder, to where the tips grazed her breast. Then it rose, slowly, pausing on her mouth for a moment longer than it had anywhere else, before his thick lashes rose and blue locked once again with brown.

He was frowning by then. 'We might not be happy about it. But we'll have to learn to be honest with each other, for Lizzie's sake.'

Rhiannon nodded dumbly, echoing his words in a monotone as he released her chair and swung back to his screen. 'Yes, for Lizzie's sake, I guess we do.'

There couldn't be any other reason. Not again.

CHAPTER EIGHT

IT WAS the largest dog she had ever seen.

Rhiannon's eyes widened as it stood with its huge head at her waist level, sad dark eyes staring up at her while long silvery threads dropped from its huge jowls all over the slate floor of the kitchen.

She swallowed hard, afraid to move in case it, well, *ate her*. She doubted it'd even need to chew.

'Isn't he gorgeous?' Lizzie grinned from the doorway. 'Kane let me pick and he had the bestest droopy eyes. His name is Winston.'

His name should have been Godzilla. 'This is *your* dog?'

'Uh-huh.' Lizzie skipped over to wrap her arms around the animal's thick neck. 'My very own dog. I'm gonna make him a bed to sleep on in my room.'

The hell she was. 'And *Kane* got him for you?'

Without consulting her? Oh, he was pushing his luck wasn't he? What had happened to *communication*? So much for letting the two of them loose for an afternoon on their own. 'Where *is* Kane?'

'He's taken John, you know, John who has ponies—round the back to look at the stables.'

Oh, had he, indeed?

Sidling gingerly past the largest dog on the planet, Rhiannon yanked open the kitchen door and walked out into the cobbled courtyard at the back of the house, taking a moment to listen for voices rumbling from the old stables that had once housed the carriage horses and hunters in days gone by. Yes, it was a sin to see them empty and unused, but that didn't mean that Kane could just hop out and fill them with a menagerie of animals at Lizzie's request.

Not without at least discussing it with Rhiannon first. Was she going to have to debate *every* tiny little detail with him?

Following the low sound of male voices, she then leaned inside one stone archway, her arms folded across her breasts while she eavesdropped on their conversation and allowed her disobedient eyes to rove over Kane from head to toe while she could do it unnoticed.

What she saw brought a smile out to twitch at the corners of her mouth. Because he was making quite an effort to fit in with country life—finely checked shirt, another pair of jeans and even heavy work boots on his large feet.

But she'd be damned if she found the fact he'd made any effort at all either endearing *or* sweet. He was Mister Corporate Big Shot now; he didn't belong in the middle of nowhere.

'A few thousand should pick you up something safe all right. But they do better in company.'

Kane was nodding. 'Well, there's plenty of room.'

And on that note she cleared her throat, making her presence known as she unfolded her arms and pushed her shoulder off the wall. 'Do I get to join in this conversation before you turn Brookfield into a zoo?'

Ignoring the all too familiar blue eyes that focused on her as she approached, her skin automatically tingling in awareness, she instead fixed her attention on the younger man at his side. 'Hello, John. It's nice to see you again.'

'And you, Rhiannon. You're looking grand as usual.'

She smiled a genuine smile at him, the sight of his openly friendly face a welcome break from the one she had to physically force herself not to look at. 'You're still the charmer, John. How's your dad?'

'Ah, sure, he's as much of a terror as always. He needs you to come up and soften him up. A visit from you and Lizzie always brightens him up.'

'We'll take a run up to see you soon, I promise.'

'Do now.' John winked at her. 'We can take the horses up into the forest this time.'

She laughed. 'Only if I get something half-dead.'

'Don't I always look after you?'

Kane's voice held a barely disguised tone of disapproval. 'You've obviously met before. John is here to check out the stabling for a pony or two.'

Or two? She quirked an eyebrow up at him, refusing to be put off by hooded eyes or the tight line of his mouth.

'We can have a talk about that—there's no hurry.'

'I told Lizzie I'd get her one.'

Rhiannon smiled sweetly, her voice coated with sugar as she practically purred back at him, 'I think the dog is a big enough gift for one day. And I do mean big. Weren't there any smaller breeds—Irish Wolfhound or maybe a baby elephant?'

John laughed while Kane managed a thinly disguised glare at him. 'Danes are known for their loyal and friendly nature. Winston's a big softie.'

Rhiannon nodded sagely. 'With emphasis on the big. Couldn't she at least have had a puppy?'

Kane eyes suddenly sparkled. 'He *is* a puppy.'

Her eyes widened. 'That thing is going to *grow*?'

John hid his second burst of laughter behind a cough, reaching a hand out to pat the iron bars that enclosed the top half of the stables. 'Well, it's certainly all still sound enough in here if you do decide to get a pony for Lizzie. Sure give me a call when you're ready and I'll keep an eye open for something that might do.'

'Thanks, John.' Rhiannon smiled again, reaching her hand out to shake his larger one as he stepped forwards. 'Send my best to your dad.'

'I'll tell him you'll be up to visit soon.'

'Do.' And she was still smiling after his tall, lean figure disappeared out through the same archway she had come through. Until, out of the corner of her eye, she saw Kane move to stand beside her, his arms folding across his broad chest, and she immediately felt the air change, every nerve-ending in her body coming to life.

She took a deep breath and waited, her gaze still fixed forwards while she listened for the steady sound of his breathing. And she didn't have to wait long for his deep voice to resonate.

'He's not your type.'

When she turned her head, she discovered he was tilting his head towards her, his eyes carefully studying her expression, waiting for her reaction. As if he would gauge his response by hers.

Lord, but he was tempting—physically speaking, of course. Up close, even when he was being all determined and forceful, there was just a delicious, very sexual intensity to him.

She damped her lips with the end of her tongue, taking her time to word her answer as the tingling awareness sparked like static electricity when his eyes focused briefly on her mouth. Maybe subliminally a part of her knew she would get that reaction when she did it?

Rhiannon sincerely hoped not; she didn't want to encourage him. But apparently she couldn't help herself. 'And what exactly *is* my type, then?'

His gaze rose swiftly, dangerously glinting eyes locking

with hers, narrowing briefly before he answered with a firm, 'Not him. You'd run rings round him.'

Not that she was actually planning on dating in the near future, but even so… 'You don't know that.'

The smile was slow, oozing with self-assurance. 'Actually, yes, I do.'

Rhiannon rose to the bait. 'So you're going to pick out my boyfriends as well as deciding how many million animals I'll have to care for after you leave?'

'Lizzie wants a pony, you know that as well as I do, so I'm getting her one, and I'm not going anywhere yet so the boyfriend thing isn't an issue.'

Meaning he would have a problem if she did date someone else under his nose? She wasn't sure she wanted to know the answer to *that* question.

So she tried to focus her mind on the pony issue instead, studying his eyes for a long time while a realization slowly grew inside her mind. 'Surely you're not planning on buying your way into her good books? You don't have to do that; she's already crazy about you.'

Seriously—was that what he thought being a father meant? Oh—he had a lot to learn, didn't he? And she couldn't believe he still felt he had to do that.

How could he not see how much Lizzie already cared for him? And frankly, having seen so much of them together of late, Rhiannon couldn't blame her. He had a gentleness about him when he was with her, looked at her without the smallest attempt at guarding his feelings—feelings that already ran deep. Certainly fathoms deeper than anything he had ever felt for her mother, which had hurt, in some strange way she'd chosen not to investigate further.

But he was still on a crash course in fatherhood, wasn't he? She hadn't known herself what parenting meant before she had

Lizzie, and she was still learning, every day. Even so, the reasoning astounded her. By buying her expensive gifts—granting Lizzie everything her heart desired—did he honestly believe he could get her to love him more?

'So everything she mentions she'd like, you're going to get for her? Just like that? Kane—' Her voice softened a little on his name, as if she was trying to convey that she understood why he was trying that method of inducement, even when it was the wrong way to go.

He frowned hard. 'So now I can't buy my own daughter presents?'

If it was at all possible, he stood a little taller, towering over her in a way that once again made his presence imposing and domineering. He fell back on that method a lot these days. And Rhiannon would bet that not too many people crossed him because of it.

But she didn't back down; instead, as usual, lifting her chin the extra inch to compensate. After all, they'd been making the effort to get on better of late, and if he remembered as much about her as he claimed to…

'That's not what I meant and you know it isn't. It's just better if she continues falling for you because of you rather than for what you can get for her, don't you think?'

Heaven alone knew it was why she'd ended up with him herself. And there were still the very odd moments when she was reminded of that while he was around.

The nod was very brief, his eyes warming a little as he studied her, before he glanced to one side and Rhiannon was momentarily distracted by the faintest breeze that lifted the finer hair against his forehead.

It was becoming an obsession, that hair of his. Again. She had used to love touching his hair, and it was probably why her fingers had itched that day in the office. Always, when they had sat in front of a computer screen or watching television, her hand had inevitably ended up at the nape of his neck, her fingertips absentmindedly moving from the shorter, coarser strands that touched his warm skin, to the slightly longer, smoother strands against the back of his head, where they would thread into the thickness.

It had been the simplest of physical contact really. But when he was tired, he would lean back into that touch, his lips would part as he sighed in relaxed contentment. Sometimes his head would turn and when his firm mouth moved across hers her fingers would thread deeper into his hair, willing him closer.

How had she forgotten that? Maybe, simply because she hadn't *wanted* to remember.

He took a deep breath. 'I still feel like I have ten years' worth of presents to make up for—Christmases, birthdays, all that. A pony and a dog don't seem to me to be that much in the great scheme of things. I'm not trying to buy her affection.'

When he turned away Rhiannon felt a bubble of disappointment grow in the pit of her stomach; it felt as if they had just taken a step backwards. And she really didn't want that to happen.

It left her floundering for a way back to where they had only just tentatively managed to get. And only one question came into her mind—the one that had been causing her the most headaches of late from trying to find an answer on her own.

Because there'd been a catalyst for her reactions all those years ago; that initial action that had driven her to make the choices she had, even though she now knew they hadn't been the right ones. And the guilt she now carried drove her to want to understand why he had disappeared when he had. The need to know growing exponentially, day by day, to almost consume her as she got to know him all over again.

And there was only one way to find an answer, wasn't there? So the question jumped out.

'Why did you disappear?'

Kane stopped suddenly. As if an invisible wall had appeared in front of him. Then his head turned and he looked over his shoulder, his eyes focused on a point on the ground in front of her feet. 'When?'

'You know when.'

'It doesn't really matter now. We're making an effort to fix things. Let's just let it go at that.'

She followed him when he stepped away again, her voice low. 'I don't think I can. I can't go back and change things. But every action has a reaction. Maybe I might have pushed harder to make sure you knew if you'd been remotely in the area of approachable.' She laughed a nervous laugh, fully aware that she was rambling. 'But you were some kind of ghost that was there one minute and gone the next. It was like you didn't even exist any more until you formed your company and made the announcement to the press with Mattie. Lizzie was almost three, then.'

She stopped when he stopped and then took a deep breath, forcing herself to stop rambling long enough to make sense of what she was trying to say.

'So now that I know I made a mistake not finding you to tell you, I need to know. Where did you go in those missing years? What made you drop out of Trinity early?'

Kane looked over his shoulder again. A muscle in his jaw flexed, his gaze shifted from her face to focus on a random point on the stone wall beside him. And in that instant, the minute movements told Rhiannon that, whatever it had been, it was something he still wasn't entirely comfortable with.

Thick, dark lashes flickered slightly as he searched the wall, taking the time to decide whether or not to answer her most likely. So Rhiannon tried again, feeling distinctly as if she were walking on eggshells as she braved another step closer to him, to where it would have taken very little effort to reach out and touch him.

Instead her arms hung redundantly at her sides, her cold fingers flexing in and out of her palms while she bit down on her bottom lip, willing him to give her a reason to understand, to complete the picture.

She really needed to know because, for her, it was the missing part of the puzzle. And it might only have been a moment or two longer while she waited for him to answer, but it felt like an eternity.

And still he seemed to be struggling inwardly. So Rhiannon tried to make it easier. 'I need to know.'

His gaze flickered briefly in her direction again, dark brow quirking, possibly in reaction to the somewhat breathless sincerity in her voice.

'It doesn't really matter any more, does it? We both made decisions then that we could have had no idea would stretch forward this far.'

The fact that he was trying to share the responsibility for the mistakes that'd been made softened a part of her she'd been protecting since he'd reappeared in her life. But it also made her need to know even stronger.

'It matters to me.' Rhiannon realized she had barely spoken the words aloud, so she cleared her throat. 'The reasons I had for doing the things I did then still matter to you, don't they? So why should your reasons be less important to me? It's all part and parcel of the same mess.'

'Maybe.' His voice was equally as soft, held a husky edge that drew her step closer to him. 'But I've been thinking some and what I think is that knowing doesn't change anything. And we're starting to make some progress, I think. Not arguing was a step in the right direction. And we agreed—this isn't about us—it's about Lizzie.'

'Yes, it is.' She knew he was right about that—there was too much water under the proverbial bridge. 'But I still need to know.'

He turned away, forcing Rhiannon to look at the back of his head. So she sighed and tried one last time, silently promising herself it *would* be the last time; she couldn't keep showing how much it still mattered. Because he was right about that too—it *shouldn't* matter any more.

'I've watched you with her, Kane, and the way you are reminds me of the way you used to be. You're right; I didn't hate you when we were together. And I don't want to carry around all the hatred I had for you afterwards any more either. But when you left and I found out I was pregnant, I was scared. And there was no one for me to talk to about that because the father of my baby was gone. I got through it on my own, but I don't think I ever forgave you for that.'

One last step and she was right behind him, her eyes focused on the short strands of hair against the column of his neck. 'I'd really like to understand it all so I can let it go. That's all.'

'Just like that? I tell you why I left and you put aside ten years of hating me? You have a tight control on your emotions, don't you, Rhiannon?'

She could hear the disbelieving edge of sarcastic humour to his deep voice. It was the last straw. She had tried. And, no matter what thoughtful, humorous, warm or even sensual roads he made into her psyche from here on in, she would burn in hell before she'd hold out an olive branch to their past again.

So she sidestepped around his massive frame and mumbled on her way past, 'Don't ever say I didn't try.'

She was almost through the arch when his voice sounded again, low, deep, rumbling, but with a flat matter-of-fact tone, so that she knew he still wasn't happy with telling her the truth. 'I was sick.'

Rhiannon froze. Without thinking about it, she found herself doing exactly what he had done only a matter of moments before—focusing on the stone wall, staring at the old cobwebs that had woven along the concrete lines within the irregular surface. While the words echoed inside her brain.

Like some kind of cruel cosmic echo of the day that Mattie had said, *'I'm sick.'*

'Sick—how?'

She forced her heavy feet to pivot round so that she could search his face for the same fatalistic expression Mattie had worn that day. And Kane's eyes rose to lock with hers, the blue so dark across the distance between them that they looked as black as they had that first night in the kitchen.

He shrugged his broad shoulders, his hands pushing deep down into his pockets again. 'Sick enough to have to go and make the time to deal with it.'

Tilting her head to one side, she tried searching his face for the information she couldn't get from his eyes. 'What kind of sick?'

'Not with anything you could have caught—if that's what you're worried about.'

Damn, but he could be cruel when he wanted to be!

'That wasn't what I meant.'

Maybe it was the way she choked the words out, maybe it was simply the fact that she was staring at him with such wide eyes. Whatever the reason, his shoulders relaxed a little.

But he still glanced away before clearing his throat and saying what she had prayed he wouldn't say. 'A form of cancer.'

No!

He must have read the anguish on her face because he immediately made an attempt to negate it. 'I've been in remission for a long time.'

Slowly, so very slowly, little snippets of memories rose inside her head to form a different picture.

'That's why you and Mattie suddenly became such good friends.'

They had been friends in university, but not in the same way they had been maybe four or five years after. It was the same way all over the world, she had reasoned—networks of friends forming because of their ties to one person and not necessarily because they got on with the whole ensemble. But, even though Rhiannon had always wondered why the relationship had changed, she'd never sat herself down to figure it out, until now.

'You had something in common.' Mattie had fought leukaemia for most of his short life.

'Yes.' A dark frown creased his forehead again. 'Except that I won and he lost.'

And he actually sounded as if he felt guilty about that!

Rhiannon felt as if her world had tilted beneath her feet. Everything she had thought she had known—everything she had judged him on—

'He knew that was why you left when you did.'

Kane stepped closer to her, while Rhiannon's gaze dropped, focusing on the smattering of dark hair she could see peeking above the V of his shirt.

'Not until he got sick again a few years back, no. He knew the truth about Lizzie too, didn't he?'

Rhiannon nodded. 'Yes.'

'I thought he had to have.' He shook his head, a wry smile on his mouth. 'I should have worked it out for myself. It's something that's been driving me crazy this last while. I *should* have worked it out.'

'No, I should have found you and told you. If I'd known—' She flung one of her redundant arms out to the side, then lifted both arms and wrapped them around her waist, squeezing in tight. 'Why didn't he tell me you were sick?'

When he didn't answer her gaze rose, and when she was finally looking into his eyes he smiled, his gaze softening in a way that reminded her again of the way he had been with her before.

She'd been so very wrong about him, hadn't she?

'If I had to take a guess I'd say that you weren't any more prepared to allow him to tell me than I was to let him tell *any-one* I'd been sick.'

He was right again—about her, anyway. The first time Mattie had asked her outright if Lizzie was Kane's, she'd made him promise never to bring it up with Kane. *Ever.* Or she would *never* forgive him. As her best friend, he had respected that— argued it, but respected it.

As far as she'd been concerned, she'd made the effort. She'd known *exactly* why she'd done the things she had, or rather, had convinced herself she had.

But *Kane*, wait a minute— Her eyes widened in question. 'You didn't tell *anyone*?'

He shrugged again, as if he was discussing the damn weather. 'My immediate family knew. But making it public knowledge wasn't exactly the best plan when setting up a new business and trying to attract investors. I wouldn't want share-holders to know now either.'

'But you said you were in remission.' Having hated him for so long, she was stunned to the core by the flash of excruciat-ing pain that cramped across her midriff. She wasn't sure she could go through that again with someone she cared about.

She frowned hard. 'Are you saying—'

Varying emotions crossed swiftly through the blue of his eyes, but were immediately hidden with the unreadable, hooded gaze that she was all too familiar with. 'No, I'm not. I've been clear for eight years. But the word cancer has a tendency to strike fear into the people who have money invested in you. That's all.'

Not to mention the fact that they looked at you differently. Mattie had made jokes in private about it, but Kane wasn't that type. Anything he felt ran deep. And the changes in him from when she had known him before made more sense with her new found knowledge. He'd shut himself off, had disappeared from the world, had dealt with it alone—had learnt how to hide his thoughts and emotions from the people around him.

And Rhiannon understood that, maybe better than most. The immediate rapport with Lizzie, the open affection, the complete honesty he had with her—the very things she had been so jealous of—had only made her feel so alone because she so badly needed to be all of those things with Lizzie too.

The realization must have shown in her eyes because Kane frowned in response. 'Thanks, anyway, but I don't need your pity, Rhiannon. I was sick; now I'm not. End of story.'

For all the times he had read her correctly, he was way, way off base with how she was feeling this time. 'I'm not—'

'Yes, you are.'

No, not in the way he thought she was. It wasn't pity; if anything, it was a new found understanding and respect. If she had known back then what she knew now…

Kane took a deep breath, his shoulders rising again as he dragged his large hands out of his pockets. Then he stepped closer and Rhiannon held her breath while she waited to see what he would do next.

She almost sighed as she breathed in the cinnamon scent of him up close. She almost closed her eyes as his closeness overwhelmed her.

He leaned his head in a little, his breath stirring the hair against her neck while he focused on a point past her ear. 'So now you know. As to the spoiling Lizzie issue that we started this with, you'll have to get used to it for a little while. But I'm not trying to buy her affection.'

Rhiannon turned her head slowly, tilting her chin upwards at the same time in one fluid motion so that she could look into his eyes up close. But when she did, she couldn't seem to find words, even ones to reason with him on the subject of spoiling

Lizzie. All she could do was stare, as if she was suddenly seeing him for the first time.

Kane's eyes studied her in a similar way, his gaze rising to sweep over the hair against her forehead, over each of her arched eyebrows, from one eye to the other.

And Rhiannon couldn't breathe. She couldn't remember ever wanting someone to kiss her so badly.

But his thick lashes merely brushed against his tanned skin a couple of times before he spoke in a husky whisper. 'I do want her to love me of her own free will. Of course I want that. What father wouldn't?'

'She already does.'

'I hope so. She's the only child I'm ever likely to have, thanks to the cancer.'

CHAPTER NINE

THEY slipped into a routine; one nowhere near as dreadful as Rhiannon had once thought it would be, but not completely comfortable either. Because fairly soon she was all too aware of the fact that she had gone back to relying on Lizzie as a shield.

And that just wasn't right. She should be able to have at least *some* kind of relationship with her child's father, shouldn't she? It had even seemed possible for a fleeting moment—tentative maybe, but a place to start. And true, she was discovering there was much more to like about him than hate, but she still couldn't let herself relax when he was around.

So each day became some kind of test, with a whole new set of thoughts and feelings for her to resolve. She would watch him when he couldn't see her doing it, she would listen carefully to his voice when he spoke, would try to put all the pieces of his personality together so that he made sense to her, all the while so very *aware* of him. Because her nerve-endings would tingle with anticipation when he walked into the room, her pulse would skip through her veins every time his body was close to hers, she would smile without stopping to think about it when he laughed, and most of all her heart would twist when he let his guard down with his child and his affection for her shone in his blue eyes.

Maybe because she now knew that this child he cared so

much for might be the only one he ever had and that broke her heart. Lizzie was so amazing—not that her mother was at all biased, of course—but the thought of her being the only one of her there would ever be…

It was almost too painful to think about. Not to mention being too *confusing* to think about, because it'd never occurred to Rhiannon to have another child after Lizzie, and she wasn't sure she wanted to know why she was suddenly so obsessed by the thought of another one.

But none of that was anywhere near as consuming as the ache she felt when she thought of Kane having to fight a battle with his illness alone. If she'd been given the choice, even without love to bind them together, she now accepted that she'd been attached enough to the young man he'd been to have wanted to be there. *Through all of it.*

So although only recently she'd been jealous of the time he spent with her daughter, she now found she was jealous of Lizzie's time with *him*. And that was unreasonable as hell from the woman who hadn't been able to stand in the same room as him until very recently.

But she hadn't known then what she knew now.

Meanwhile, *he* had slipped into his role as Lizzie's father as if he'd always been there. He liked taking turns doing the school run, he loved her chatter in the car when they were together and how she would run out through the gates to tell him about her day. He liked spending time doing homework with her, he loved being astounded by her intelligence and her ability to problem solve—the latter another reminder of something he was good at himself. And Rhiannon knew all those things from the chatter around the table at night, which was the time *she* loved the most.

She loved it because they would all sit together in the warm room as Lizzie bounced the conversation back and forth between them all, forcing Rhiannon to laugh out loud when she knew she would have felt awkward letting go that much if it was just Kane there. But even that special time was laced with a bitter sweetness—allowing her a small glimpse of what family life could be like if he was a permanent feature, if things were *different*…

So, in between sharing the daily tasks, Rhiannon launched herself wholeheartedly into learning about the intricacies of running a house the size of Brookfield. It kept her mind focused for a few hours each day when their 'buffer' was at school. It was important, she told herself. After all, Kane would be gone soon but Brookfield would remain, even if her owning Brookfield and Kane owning the estate tied them together all over again. Apparently there was no escaping him.

She grew restless after lunch, piles of papers all over the desk in the library testimony to the fact that she still had a long way to go to make sense of everything. And when her head started to ache, she knew she needed a break. It wasn't raining, so she took herself out for a walk to clear her head.

But she didn't get further than the courtyard at the back of the house before she heard a rustling from the stables, where she found Kane.

He had his shirtsleeves rolled up while he threw bales of straw down and then shook them loose. And, mesmerized, she watched the muscles in his forearms moving, watched as he bent down every so often to lift a section that wasn't quite loose enough for him to fork out, while her nerve endings tingled with the familiar sensual awareness.

It was the first time she'd been completely alone with him since she'd made herself so purposefully busy. And a part of her knew she'd be safer just walking away, but she couldn't seem to do it.

'Lizzie will kill you for doing that without her.'

He looked up in surprise, a broad grin immediately forming on his face. 'She'll forgive me when we go get the stupid beast.'

The stupid beast that had been his idea, but Rhiannon had eventually allowed—the one that he'd at least consulted with her on when it had come to the actual selection, which hadn't gone unappreciated. And honestly, if it settled into daily life as well as Winston had, then it would be fine. Though Rhiannon sincerely hoped she wouldn't end up with a pony trailing round the house after her in Lizzie's absence. Not that a pony could be that much larger, realistically.

'You do know she has you wrapped round her little finger, right?'

'Only because I let her think she does.'

The words drew forth an unguarded burst of disbelieving laughter. 'Liar.'

He grinned again. Oh, yes, now she remembered—*this* was when she liked him best, when they could just hold a conversation without there being an undercurrent. Why couldn't he be like this all of the time?

'Be nice now—especially since it just so happens I've been thinking about you.'

Rhiannon's eyes widened.

He continued. 'I was thinking that a computer system for the household accounts might make your life simpler. Lizzie said you had a ton of paperwork.'

And now he was being thoughtful on *her* behalf? *Wow*. What had brought that on? She dropped her gaze briefly to the toe she was using to absentmindedly push loose straw back into the stable. 'It would, actually—I'm going cross-eyed.'

'All right, good.' He grinned again. 'Not to the cross-eyed part, you understand. I'll find someone who can set something tailormade up for you.'

She couldn't help but tease him. 'Are you saying you're too expensive for Brookfield?'

'Well—' he cocked his head to one side, lifting his foot to

rest on the pitchfork '—that *is* true, as it happens. But I was thinking that someone closer by would be better, then they can help you with any problems when I'm not here.'

An unexpected cramp cut through her chest. 'Yes, I figured that might be coming. Lizzie will miss you.'

Actually, her mother might too, surprisingly.

'I'll miss her too. But I won't be so far away this time.'

Rhiannon felt the awkwardness returning when the conversation came to a halt. 'Well, I'll leave you to it. I'm just going to take a walk with Winston to clear my head before I go for Lizzie.'

She made a half turn before he stepped forward. 'Or you could give me a hand. That would be helpful.'

Turning back, she watched him make the two long strides it took to get to her, a flutter building in her stomach as he set the pitchfork against the wall and reached for a bottle of water resting between the bars.

'All that heavy straw-shaking getting to you?'

'It's taking more bales than I thought it would, but then making a bed for a pony is hardly an everyday occurrence for me.' He unscrewed the lid of the bottle and tilted it to take a long mouthful of water—right in front of her.

So that she really had no choice but to watch his throat convulse as he swallowed, or to notice how the moisture still rested on his bottom lip afterwards. It brought the term 'water torture' to a whole new level.

'You should have let Lizzie do it; she needs to realize that the pony is her responsibility.'

When he didn't reply, her gaze rose, until she was looking into the darkening blue of his eyes. He'd witnessed her study of him, hadn't he? He knew how aware of him she was, didn't he?

Heat rose on her cheeks. Damn.

'You're not the only one whose work was making them cross-eyed.'

Maybe because he was restless too? For the first time Rhiannon wondered if he was missing his life in Dublin. She knew he had a hugely successful business but she didn't know anything about his private life beyond the odd picture she'd seen of him in glossy mags at big social events with various stunning women at his side. But she was curious now.

Was he in a relationship of some kind? Was he between relationships? Did he just have casual affairs when the need was there? Not that his private affairs had anything to do with her, but she was *definitely* curious. After all, if he ever met someone he got serious with, then that woman would be a part of her daughter's life, wouldn't she?

Somehow that idea didn't sit well with Rhiannon.

Kane set the bottle back down. 'Come on; many hands make light work and all that.'

Without hesitation, he reached out and gently grasped her elbow, coaxing her further into the stable. 'You can shake straw over there and I'll shake straw over here and we'll meet in the middle.'

There was a metaphor in there somewhere.

Rhiannon gently extricated her elbow, looking around the floor for sections of straw to shake out. She could manage to spend a little time in his company one on one doing something simple. *Yes, she could.*

She heard rustling from Kane's side of the stable and, glancing over, saw that he had already gone back to work. He obviously hadn't an issue with her being there, and if he could make the effort then so could she.

So she rolled up the sleeves of her coat a little and bent down to lift a section of straw. 'I'll need to keep an eye on the time for Lizzie.'

'All right, I'll remind you. This shouldn't take long with both of us at it anyway.'

The sound of combined rustling filled the silence for a while as the depth of straw increased on the floor, each of them working from edge to edge on their side of the stable. But as they gradually worked their way closer together Rhiannon became increasing edgy, and the need for some inane chatter to fill the silence became too hard to ignore.

'You must be missing your life in Dublin by now.'

Oh, great. She could have raised a dozen topics, including the weather, but she had to go for one that demonstrated her curiosity. She was a genius.

'Parts of it. But the countryside isn't as boring as I remember it being.'

'That's right; your parents have a place in the country, don't they?' She'd forgotten that. Well, that explained why he'd made an effort with his country clothes, then. He already knew what he was supposed to wear—it was Rhiannon who was still trying to fit in. Just like always.

'Yep, that they do, not that I visit it as often these days, but it was a great place to grow up. Lizzie will love being here.'

And back on to the safe topic of Lizzie again. It suddenly occurred to Rhiannon that maybe she wasn't the only one falling back behind that particular shield.

Rustling filled the silence for a while again. 'I suppose it makes more sense living in the city when you have a hugely successful company to run, though.'

There was an amused edge to his voice. 'Yes, but that's just basic logistics. A company needs staff and there are more people in the city. When it comes to development of the games and new software, that can pretty much be done anywhere.'

Which was why he had been able to stay for so long, right? But that didn't mean his entire life centred on his work—there had to be other things to miss.

'More of a social life in the city, though.'

'Yes, there is. Why, are you missing the bright lights already?'

A glance across at him as he stood tall, shaking straw out in front of him, revealed a teasing light dancing in his eyes and Rhiannon rose to the bait, rolling her eyes. 'Oh, dreadfully. All that clubbing I normally do and the social whirl from one party to the next. You know how it is for we single mothers.'

The minute the last words had left her mouth her gaze locked with his again. Normally, that was exactly the opening he needed to make a caustic comment about how he wouldn't know anything about the life of a parent thanks to her. But instead he smiled wryly.

'Yes, it's exactly the same when you run a large company where hundreds of people rely on you.'

They both reached down for sections of straw while Rhiannon's loose tongue made the comment, 'Well, judging from the number of pictures of you at parties with various women over the years, you've managed to get out and about all right.'

From the corner of her eye she noticed him stop shaking out his section of straw. And she grimaced inwardly, all too aware that she'd just told him he hadn't been invisible to her over the years. It made it sound as if she'd been interested. When at the time she hadn't, not really. It had just been hard to miss all of the pictures was all…

But after a tense moment he started moving again. And she breathed out in relief.

They continued working until they were closer together in the centre of the stable. And, try as she might to concentrate on what she was doing, Rhiannon was only too aware of his every move, of how, even with a task so simple, he had a strength to him that was very palpably male. Just once she would like to spend time with him around and *not* be so aware of that.

She felt the need for chatter again, maybe on a safer topic this time. But before she could raise a topic his deep voice questioned, 'Do you think there's enough in here yet?'

Maybe she wasn't the only one who felt a need to fill the silence, then. She smiled at the thought of Kane Healey ever needing to make small talk, her eyes taking in the depth of the straw so that she could answer him. 'I think that pony is moving into the Ritz Carlton of stables, so yes. And anyway, why are you asking me? You're the one that grew up in the country— ponies were hardly a big part of my life, growing up.'

When she glanced up at him he smiled a slow, dangerous smile. 'Well, my brother and I did have a way of helping our sister check it was deep enough. It always worked for us back then.'

'Okay.' She felt a tingle run up her spine as the smile did things to her heart rate it really had no business doing. So she studied the straw instead and nodded. 'We'll use that method to check it, then.'

'We-ll, if you're sure.'

When she looked back at him there was something about the glint in his eyes that made her wary. 'What exactly *did* you do?'

He pursed his lips together in a way that suggested he was holding back another smile, then stepped towards her with a determined expression on his face. 'We rolled her in it and if she hit the concrete then we knew it needed more.'

Rhiannon gasped. He couldn't seriously—

She held up the armful of straw she still had in warning. 'You wouldn't dare.'

He hesitated very briefly, the glint in his eyes increasing. 'Is that a challenge?'

Automatically spreading her legs a little wider, she bent her knees and faked a dart towards the door, smiling when he went the same way. 'It's a warning.'

She lifted the straw higher.

'Now, Mac—' he tilted his head slightly and looked at her with an amused expression, his legs wider, knees bent in preparation '—I really don't think you want to do that.'

Actually, up until a second ago, she wouldn't have even considered it. But now that he'd warned her not to, a mischievous imp inside her was demanding she did. This was exactly the kind of dumb situation they would have got into back in the day. It was a reminder of lighter, less troublesome, happier times.

And it was maybe exactly what she needed to break through the tension.

So her eyebrows quirked at him. 'Do what?'

His forehead creased into a brief frown, as if he was confused by her reaction. And then, oh, so slowly, another smile started at the corners of his mouth while his voice rumbled out from his chest, low and deep.

'Put the straw down.'

'No-o.' Her mouth formed a circle on the 'o' as she swayed her weight from one leg to the other. 'Because I am *not* being used as a depth test.'

Kane took a deep breath and stood a little more upright, his lashes flickering down against his skin as he nodded. 'Well, I was teasing before.'

Rhiannon relaxed a little, her arms lowering. She'd known that after all, but it had still felt good to have a moment of fun. She'd forgotten what it had been like when they'd done stuff like this. 'Good.'

He nodded again, pursed his lips together again. 'I was— until you just did that.'

She squeaked in surprise as he lunged forward and swept her off her feet, the straw in her arms flying up in the air between them. Her empty arms then sought something to hold on to, her hands grasping hold of his shirt as he swung her backwards and forwards a couple of times.

'One—two—'

Rhiannon laughed uncontrollably, her hands moving up around his neck to hold on tighter. 'Stop it! I swear, Kane, if I go down, you're going with me!'

'You started this.'

'I did not.'

'Consider it an initiation to country life.'

With that, he swung her again and let go. But Rhiannon held on, so that when she fell her weight drew his upper body down with her. Then his feet slipped on the loose straw, dropping him on to his knees. Still laughing, Rhiannon moved quickly, loosening her arms from his neck to grab handfuls of straw and dump them on top of his head.

A battle commenced, with much scrambling and throwing of straw, but ultimately Rhiannon knew it was a battle she couldn't win and after Kane had used his size to his advantage and rolled her back and forth on the straw until she was spluttering, he let go and propped an elbow to lean his head on his hand and look down on her.

'I'd say it's deep enough myself.'

Rhiannon giggled breathlessly, revelling in the fact that she felt lighter than she had in years. And because of Kane, of all people. 'How often did you do this to your poor sister?'

'A lot over the years.' He reached over and pulled a long strand of straw out of her hair. 'It got to be a regular game of cat and mouse.'

'I bet you were a brat.'

'I kinda was.' He smiled down at her. 'I'm just a more grown up version now.'

Rhiannon smiled back. 'Yes, that you are.'

She watched as he focused on her hair, reaching out to remove another strand and toss it to the side. Then he looked into her eyes and in a moment the atmosphere changed, her heart immediately thundering in her chest in response.

He studied her for several long moments, his voice lower when he spoke again. 'This is more like how we used to be, isn't it?'

'Yes, it is.' Her voice was husky in reply, the lightness she'd been feeling replaced with the ache she normally felt when he showed any sign of softness towards her.

He nodded, studied her eyes again and then looked back at her hair, his fingers reaching for a strand close to her face. But this time, when he tossed the strand to the side, those same fingers came back to brush her hair from her neck, stroking briefly against her skin as she swallowed hard.

'Back in the days when you used to like me better.'

Rhiannon couldn't take it if they ended up in yet another debate, so she allowed the truth to slip free. 'I don't hate you so much any more.'

His fingers reached into the neck of her jacket to retrieve more straw, while his dark brows quirked. 'And what exactly did I do to deserve that when you've spent years hating me?'

Her breath hitched as he retrieved a strand of straw from the V of her sweater, the backs of his fingers brushing briefly against the top of her breast. 'I've watched you with Lizzie. And you couldn't be the way you are with her if you were as bad as I convinced myself you were.'

It was only half of the truth, but it was enough to bring his gaze back to lock with hers. And she held her breath as he studied her, her eyes wide as she tried to silently convey her sincerity to him.

When the backs of his fingers brushed gently along her jaw she breathed out, her eyes fluttering shut for a second as a wave of sensation consumed her. She should get up, move away—*far away*—because there was no point in succumbing to just the physical. Not again.

His hand turned, the tips of his fingers moving up along her cheek, across her forehead, where he smoothed out the frown that had formed before tracing the arch of each of her eyebrows in turn.

And, even though she was lying down, Rhiannon had the sensation that she was free falling into the unknown.

But it wasn't the unknown, was it? She knew every single step of this path, as did her body. The body that was awakening to a cornucopia of remembered sensation; her breasts feeling taut and confined, her stomach muscles tensing, an inner trembling forming low in her abdomen and spreading up and out. Because she'd never forgotten what he could do to her with his touch, with his hands and his mouth.

She sighed against the back of his hand when his fingertips traced her lower lip. 'This is a bad idea.'

'I know.'

His voice was so thick and husky that she opened her eyes to confirm what she could hear, her chest tight at the sight of his darkening eyes. She knew that look too.

'Because there's no point in letting this happen again.'

'No, there's not.' His thumb followed his fingertip along her lower lip, then back across her upper lip.

'The only thing we have in common now is our child.'

His eyelids seemed to grow heavier on her use of the word 'our', his head lowering towards hers as he mumbled back, 'Not the only thing, Mac. There's still this.'

The first touch of his mouth was heartbreakingly soft, almost reverent, as if he knew that anything more would have been too much too soon. But Rhiannon moaned low in her throat in protest at her need for more. In an automatic movement born of familiarity, her hand rose, smoothing her fingers into the hair at the back of his head.

Just like she remembered it—a slight coarseness to the touch that made it so very male and yet soft enough to add to the sensuality as her fingers moved.

He traced his mouth across hers from one edge to the other, slow, so slow, then he leaned his head a little closer to make the kiss firmer, deeper. While Rhiannon met each touch and mirrored it, her head spinning.

The fingers that had traced her features turned over, brushed over her cheek, turned again, trailed softly over her jaw and along the arch of her neck to rest on the beating pulse below her ear.

Her fingers tangled further into his hair, began a soft kneading at the back of his head that immediately relaxed his shoulders, and he sank his upper body tighter to hers. And somewhere in her mind she realized that she still knew what felt good for him every bit as much as he was showing her he still knew what felt good to her—because they had history.

But not a future.

She forced her hand out of his hair and went still. And Kane felt it the moment she did because he removed his mouth from hers and leaned back, looking down into her eyes with a silent intensity that tested her resolve to its limits. It would just be so very easy to give in to the temptation of him.

But she couldn't. Not again. Because unbridled passion may have been enough for a brief relationship when she was young and free, but it wasn't enough for her now.

'I should go get Lizzie from school.'

Kane nodded, leaning back to allow her to scramble to her feet before he pushed off his elbow and stood up, raising his hands to brush the straw off his clothes. 'You should get changed first.'

'Yes, I know.' She stepped through the straw and headed out of the stable, not looking back. Because she really needed to stop looking back, didn't she?

CHAPTER TEN

KANE had no idea why he'd let himself kiss her. Up until the very second he had, he most certainly hadn't intended to. And he wasn't best pleased with himself for it either.

They were too tangled up in the past—that was all it was. It was an echo of the way they had used to be and he'd succumbed to that, when really, as a fully grown male, he should have had more self-control.

That was just the thing, though, wasn't it? Ever since he'd walked into the house that first night, his control over things seemed to have been taken from him—piece by piece. It was no wonder he was having difficulty with it.

Being on such shaky ground might have explained why he'd told her the truth about his disappearance all those years ago. *Every action has a reaction.* That was what she'd said. Maybe that was part of the reason he'd told her too. Because she was right about that, wasn't she? If he hadn't got sick when he had, left when he had—

But he'd been twenty-one, for crying out loud! He'd thought he was invincible. Finding out he wasn't had been a lot to take in. And that was putting it mildly.

Actually, all in all, he'd felt he'd coped with it well, dealt with it, put it to the back of his mind and got on with his life.

Until he'd watched Mattie wage the same kind of war and lose…

And that loss had made him re-evaluate just what he had done with his life so far—a natural reaction, he supposed, when he was hit with a case of guilt over why he was still here and Mattie wasn't.

The sight of Lizzie trying to wrestle a stuffed monkey from the jaws of her new 'puppy' dragged a smile on to his mouth. Just watching her lifted his spirits in a way he couldn't remember them ever lifting before. And every day he spent with her—even if they talked complete nonsense or did nothing particularly exciting—had him more in love with her than he'd been the day before. She was a miracle after all, wasn't she? The child he'd resigned himself to never having.

And he knew he had Rhiannon to thank for that miracle and its associated joy. They had made this child together. And that bound him to Rhiannon for the rest of his life in a way that went beyond just the physical. The same physical he had given in to so damn quickly again after ten minutes rolling around in some straw.

She'd always had that effect on him. From the first day she'd flashed a smile at him across the counter of the coffee shop facing Trinity. A smile, a sparkle in her eyes, a mild flirtation that he'd soon looked forward to every day. That was all it had taken for him to be drawn in until he was almost addicted to her.

But he'd been a twenty-one-year-old typically hormone-driven male. He hadn't thought about things like the future or how miscommunication would have a long-term effect on both of them and the child they made. Life had been an adventure, a game, with days to be filled with nothing more complicated than fun and laughter.

It had taken the chance discovery of a lump for him to re-evaluate everything.

He leaned back, resting his weight on his elbows as he stretched his legs out, crossing them at the ankles. Then he tilted his head back, eyes closing, as he allowed the imagined warmth of the late January sun to put a red glow on the backs of his eyelids while he took a deep breath of the crisp air.

Knowing that Lizzie was a product of his time with Rhiannon was constantly pushing more and more of the memories into his mind from an earlier trouble-free time in his life. But there hadn't been any point in remembering, had there? That time had been gone. Breaking up with Rhiannon had been on a long 'to-do' list that he'd made to break contact with a world where people didn't have to face up to their own mortality.

But again he wondered: if he hadn't been sick, if he hadn't broken up with her—if he'd waited to see where that first flush of purely sexual attraction had taken them in the long term…

Kane hated 'ifs'. And now he had dozens of the damn things. In business he always researched variables—but in his personal life? Well, not so much. Because in his personal life he made quite sure there were no variables to begin with. He was always careful not to get involved with the kind of women who wanted long term—things like marriage and two-point-four of the kids he couldn't give them without the help of the medical profession.

But to add to all the variables he *now* had, he had to add another; whatever physical attraction there had been between Rhiannon and him before—was still there.

The kiss in the straw had proved that.

It had probably been creeping up on him a little more with each day he spent near her. And when he had witnessed that look of distress on her face after he'd told her the truth, he'd wanted to kiss the pity out of her eyes, to prove to her that he was still very much alive, still very much one hundred per cent male even if he couldn't ever make another Lizzie with her.

Which begged the question of whether that could be the

reason he'd kissed her this last time? Was there a part of him that felt it had to prove himself to her?

Opening his eyes, he dropped his chin, automatically turning his head towards the French windows at the back of the house, beyond which Rhiannon had been spending more and more of her time since the day in the stable. Most likely hiding—well, that was what he'd guessed she was doing—at first.

His gaze strayed back to Lizzie; her laughter echoed off the walls of the house, and he smiled again. But after a while he ended up looking back towards the windows, a breeze lifting the end of the long curtains out through a small gap that called to him.

Come on in—you know you want to.

He pursed his mouth in thought, because he *was* tempted. He wasn't so sure any more that Rhiannon was hiding, not judging by the dark shadows in her eyes at dinner the last couple of nights. And if there was a problem, then he needed to know about it. Forewarned was forearmed...

'Kane!' Lizzie stopped tugging the stuffed monkey, waiting until Kane looked at her before she grinned and asked, 'Can we take Winston up by the lake like we did yesterday? He loved it.'

'All right.' He uncrossed his ankles and pushed up on to his feet, lifting the jacket he had been sitting on and shaking it while his eyes strayed yet again to the open windows. 'Give me a minute and we'll see if your mum wants to come too. She might need some fresh air.'

'Okay.'

Rhiannon didn't hear him come in. He knew that the minute he stepped past the curtain and saw her resting her face in her hands. As if somehow sensing his presence, she glanced up, her soft brown eyes widening a little in surprise while she pushed long tendrils of auburn hair that had escaped her pony-tail off her flushed cheeks.

'Hello.' The greeting was soft, maybe a little cautious, and

Kane felt a momentary longing for the brief ease there had been between them before he'd kissed her. 'It can't be time for lunch already.'

He watched as she glanced at her watch, her finely arched brows then rising in question. 'Is something wrong?'

'Nope, we're fine. Lizzie wanted to know if you fancied going for a walk, so I said I'd ask.' He kept studying her, the changes in the tones of colour in her eyes as she thought, the way she moved her head, how her sweater rose and fell as she breathed.

Then her eyes softened, a smile curling her lips upwards. 'I could certainly do with a break.'

Kane smiled back at her, glanced away when it felt awkward, even momentarily considered just staying in the open doorway where he could make a swift withdrawal to the safety of Lizzie. But instead he found himself drawn into the room and perching on the edge of the huge old leather-topped desk Mattie had once sat behind when they'd talked business and life in general.

This had been the room where they could talk with ease and without boundaries—about the kinds of things Kane could never seem to talk to other people about—like being scared, which wasn't something any man ever liked to confess to...

He cleared his throat, then, with a quick glance down at the open books, paperwork and bills scattered over the surface of the desk, he risked looking back at Rhiannon's face. And, unbidden, his earlier thoughts about Lizzie being the child they had made together slammed into the front of his skull, vividly this time, with Technicolor detailed memories of 'how' it had happened.

Yep, and there it was again. That immediate physical aware-ness of her—even stronger now with the additional Technicolor details and the memory of their last kiss. Admittedly, Rhiannon may have been pretty when he had known her at eighteen, but she was an entirely different woman at twenty-nine. She'd blos-somed into adult womanhood, with more lush curves than she'd had when he'd known her so intimately, curves he'd been all too aware of when he'd been lying with her on a bed of straw.

That physical awareness had probably been there from the first night in the kitchen. And, before they had begun to communicate better, he'd been mad as hell at her for that, hadn't he? He hadn't wanted it to be there, hadn't sought it out. It was another example of the lack of control he seemed to have when she was around. And now that he'd given in to it once already…?

Well, now a part of him couldn't help but wonder what she'd do if he pursued it…

'You're still working on the house accounts?'

A shadow of doubt crossed her eyes, then she dismissed it with a sigh. And Kane knew how she felt. It wasn't as if either of them were the open book type. But this whole 'getting along for Lizzie's sake' had to be a two-way street, didn't it? One little kiss couldn't get in the way. And he was fully prepared to use that line of reasoning if he had to, especially having told her more than he ever intended to about himself already.

But, before he could decide what route to take, she took a breath, her gaze dropping to where her fingers were shuffling papers back and forth for no apparent reason. 'It's a lot to take in. I mean, I've worked on accounts before but these…'

He watched as she shook her head, loose strands of hair trailing over her shoulders. 'It's a large place.'

'Yes and a huge responsibility.'

'Mattie must have thought you were up to it.'

Rhiannon surprised him by laughing softly as she leaned back in the large chair. 'Well, he may possibly have got that one wrong.'

The words surprised him again. From what he'd understood over the years, Rhiannon had been the only one who had understood Mattie's passion for Brookfield. It wasn't as if huge country estates were all that common any more and it took a particular personality to enjoy the constant upkeep a place like this would take. It was a lifetime's work. At one time a legacy handed on from generation to generation—almost like a crown from one generation of royalty to another.

And for a long time in Ireland, the people who'd owned a legacy like this one had been universally hated, to the extent of being run off the land before their homes were burned to the ground. But Brookfield had somehow survived all that and was now in the hands of an Irishwoman. It was Rhiannon's legacy to hand on to Lizzie, wasn't it?

Which was another reason for Kane to be involved in any problem there might be, right? It had to do with Lizzie's future—his daughter's future—and *her* legacy. And that made it his business.

A sudden thought brought a frown to his face.

'What?' Rhiannon leaned forward in her chair, resting her elbows on top of the papers.

'I was right, wasn't I? This place can't look after itself without the income from the estate.' He didn't need an answer; he could see it on her face. 'How long did Mattie know about Lizzie?'

Rhiannon blinked in confusion. 'I don't see—'

'How long?' He leaned his upper body a little more in her direction and kept his voice calm. 'I'm not trying to start another argument; I just need to know.'

Recognition of the same words she'd used to coax his biggest secret from him seemed to persuade her to volunteer the information.

'I think he probably knew early on. He kept coming into the coffee shop long after you'd gone and it was only then that we really became friends.' She smiled at a memory. 'He brought Lizzie her first teddy bear at the hospital. But he didn't ask me outright until just before I married Stephen.'

Kane nodded again. Yeah, that was what he'd figured.

Rhiannon's eyes narrowed a little. 'Am I missing something?'

'There was always method in Mattie's madness. I should have known there was more to it.' Kane shook his head this time, a wry smile crossing his lips. 'He knew rightly what he was doing.'

'All right—you've lost me.'

He pushed up off the desk, glancing towards the open doors before he smiled and cocked his head in their direction. 'Come for a walk and I'll maybe tell you what I think.'

He hit her with a raised brows silent challenge, and smiled more when she rolled her eyes and chuckled. All right, so maybe getting along better with Rhiannon wasn't that bad a thing. And he felt a little more in control again, which felt good, if a little ironic considering he'd just realized that they'd both been manipulated to where they were.

'All right then.' She pushed back from the desk, still smiling as she walked past him. 'You've got me. I'll grab a coat. I'm a sucker for a mystery.'

'Well, this one's not my doing.' He stood up, teasing her in a low voice, 'You've already wheedled out all my darkest secrets.'

She turned around and walked backwards for a few steps, her head tilting flirtatiously. 'I doubt very much that I know them all.'

Kane studied her for a long moment. 'You know enough.'

'Yes.' The word was spoken softly, with a matching small smile and a light in her eyes that he couldn't quite read from across the room. 'Enough to know what I need to know, I guess.'

He stood in the empty room long after she'd left, not waiting for her but just *thinking*. What *was it* with him and this woman?

They were halfway around the lake, their exhaled breath forming puffs of steam in the cold air before Rhiannon couldn't take any more of the suspense.

Not that walking side by side talking about nothing more difficult than Lizzie's antics with Winston and pointing out wildlife as it appeared wasn't a moment of acquiescence that she subliminally recognized as a rare experience of camaraderie. But she was still curious as all hell about what he'd figured out in the library.

Just in case it was something that would lead them to awkwardness or harsh words again, she savoured the moment, tilting her head back to watch the breeze push the clouds by overhead before she closed her eyes and filled her lungs with a deep breath of cool winter air. And she smiled contentedly.

'You really do love it here, don't you?' Kane's deep voice sounded close by her shoulder.

When she opened her eyes and lifted her gaze to his, she smiled a smaller smile, suddenly feeling shy again, which wasn't really all that surprising, considering the last time she'd been 'alone' with him. And, even with Lizzie disappearing and reappearing out of the trees from time to time, they *were* still alone, weren't they?

The thought made her pulse skip. 'Yep.'

He nodded and stopped at the edge of the water, his gaze searching the ground while he spoke. 'Did you know Mattie planned on leaving you this place?'

'No.' She frowned as he bent over and selected a few round, flat stones, tossing them into the palm of his other hand. Surely he didn't think she'd done something to influence Mattie's decision? They'd been friends, better than friends—more like brother and sister. Mattie had been her family when she didn't have one any more. When her own family had turned her away—the 'good child' who had made a horrible mistake proving too difficult for them to even look at...

'I think he knew he was leaving it to you for a long time. In fact—' inhaling, he stood up again, glancing briefly at her before he started sorting through the stones in his hand '—I'm pretty sure he knew when he offered to sell me the estate.'

Rhiannon stepped closer, watching as he selected one of the

stones and stepped back on to one foot, swinging his arm out in an arc to throw the stone so that it skipped over the water's surface—once, twice, three times before it sank.

And he grinned across at her like a small boy. 'I was hoping I hadn't forgotten how to do that.'

Her heart caught.

'You have no idea how much you remind me of Lizzie when you smile like that.' Her eyes widened in surprise at the confession. They just seemed to constantly roll off the end of her tongue these days, didn't they?

But Kane merely continued grinning. 'Yeah.' He leaned back to toss another stone over the water. 'She's good-looking too.'

Rhiannon shook her head. Who *was* this man? Every day she was more and more enraptured by the different facets of his personality. And every day he would do or say something that knocked her off balance. She should have been mad about that, especially after the kiss that had still lingered on her lips hours after the event. But it was difficult to stay mad when he was like this—so charming, so good-looking, so damn irresistible.

'Well, thankfully she has me to keep her ego from growing to continental proportions.' She refocused on the topic of their conversation. 'What makes you so sure Mattie had planned that far ahead?'

Kane tossed the stones he had left in his hand up and down a couple of times, taking a breath of crisp air before he shrugged the shoulders beneath his heavy down-lined jacket. 'I think he knew for a long time that he was fighting a battle he'd lose. He fought for a lot longer than I had to with mine and I think he was resigned to just buying as much time as he could. But it gave him time to think about things and to make plans. It's the kind of guy he was. He thought about the people he cared about, and what would happen to them when he wasn't here any more.'

Rhiannon immediately wondered if Kane had had to make

those kinds of plans once—had thought about not being here any more—about his own death. How must that have felt at so young an age to someone so very alive?

And who had he talked to? For a man like him to confess any kind of weakness would have cost dearly, wouldn't it? When going away and facing his illness, fighting it, coming out the other side, had taken more bravery than she could even begin to respect him enough for having.

Her heart twisted painfully at another thought. How would she have felt if something had happened to him? No one would probably have thought she should know, except maybe Mattie. Yes, Mattie would have made sure she didn't read it in a paper somewhere. But it would have hurt. She knew that. It would have hurt so very much, maybe even worse than losing Mattie had.

But it wouldn't have hurt anywhere near as much as it would if anything happened to Kane now…

He glanced at her from the corner of his eye, a thoughtful expression on his ruggedly handsome face. 'Do you know how to skim stones?'

'What?' She shook her head, laughing a little to cover the dark thoughts that still hovered in her mind—troubled, confused thoughts that forced her to concentrate twice as hard to keep up with their conversation without giving anything away.

He leaned down and selected a larger handful of stones. 'They need to be fairly round, and as flat as possible or they don't bounce.'

'You're insane. I don't suppose you happen to know where Kane Healey went to? Big guy, pretty grumpy most of the time, prone to starting a topic of conversation and then gets easily sidetracked by children's games…'

She watched in amused amazement as he stepped closer, reaching out to tug at her elbow with his empty hand so that she was forced to pull her hand out of her pocket while he beckoned with his fingers.

'Give me your hand.'

'I can't do what you just did.'

'Don't be a girl.'

Even while his warm fingers curled beneath her hand so he could place a stone in her palm, she was looking up at his profile with raised eyebrows.

And he smiled again in response, his cheeks creasing into a hint of dimples as he glanced at her face and then down at her hand. 'All right then, try being *less* of a girl.'

The mischievous imp reappeared on her shoulder and forced her to bat her eyelashes frantically at him.

Still smiling, he moved round behind her, concentrating his focus on her hand as he moved her fingers into position. 'Curl your forefinger around the top, thumb round the bottom and then, when you throw, you flick your wrist back and, as you flick forwards, you let go. Try to keep it as flat as you can along the surface of the water and it'll skip.'

His hand still supporting hers, his gaze rose, and Rhiannon had to lean her head back further to lock eyes with him. It was disconcerting as all hell having him this close again, it really was. How was a girl supposed to do anything but stare?

The breeze caught his hair and ruffled it, his thick lashes brushed against the faint tinge of red the chilled air had created on his cheeks and his bluer than blue eyes warmed her as he continued softly smiling. And, just as it had done since the first day she had met him, Rhiannon's heart thundered against her breast and her nerve-endings tingled from head to toe in response. She even had to consciously stop herself from turning around and stepping in against him, tilting her head back in invitation, to…

She swallowed hard. 'All right, but just so you know, it'll

sink like…' she grinned as the words formed in her head '…well, it'll sink like a stone, *obviously*. But it'll sink. Trust me.'

'We'll practise a couple of times.' He blinked down at her, then lifted his gaze and looked out over the greyish blue of the water. 'And once you have it mastered, you can come down here and skim stones with Lizzie when I'm not here.'

Rhiannon swiftly turned her face away, her heart still thudding hard, but now accompanied by a dull ache in the pit of her stomach. She knew he would leave, had known all along—this time round. And at least this time when he left they'd be on friendly enough terms to be able to arrange visits for Lizzie and times when he could come back down to Brookfield. And she would be able to hold a conversation with him. It was all good, right?

Hand still on hers, he guided her arm out in an arc to her side. 'Put your weight back on to one foot and then, as you swing your arm, move your weight on to your front foot before you let go of the stone.'

She let him guide her movements in a couple of practice sways, his large body cushioning hers, aware that the simple act of throwing a stone across the water had somehow morphed into a seductive dance movement.

'Now have a go.' He stepped back before she threw and watched in silence as the stone sank without as much as a hint of a bounce.

With a brief glance over her shoulder, she blew her cheeks out and announced smugly, 'I told you so.'

With a chuckle and a shake of his head, he stepped round her again, lifting her hand to tip the remainder of the stones into her palm. 'Keep practising; you'll get it.'

Gathering more stones from the ground while she watched, he then stood beside her and tossed another one on to the water—skip, skip, sink.

'So, anyway…' he watched her make another failed attempt at skimming a stone '…I think Mattie knew when he sold me the estate that one day you would own the house. It was his way of forcing us into a locked room so we'd have to talk.'

Rhiannon stopped mid-swing. *'What?'*

'Yep.' His voice stayed calm as he swung again—skip, skip, skip, sink. 'He knew the estate and the house needed each other to survive, and he made quite sure I couldn't sell one without the other. I doubt he was even as badly off financially as he claimed to be. We were manipulated into dealing with all of this.'

Rhiannon couldn't believe what she was hearing, but in a heartbeat it suddenly made absolute sense. 'Why, that wily—'

'Exactly.' Kane stunned her by continuing to smile as he tossed another stone—skip, skip, skip, sink. 'He knew how stubborn we both were. And he knew we'd both built a firm set of misconceptions about each other—'

'So he decided to try and find a way to *fix it*?'

He stood still, his focus on the horizon as he nodded. 'Yes, I think so. I've only just figured it out now, but I'm pretty sure that's what he did. I remember he said a lot of things about the house and the estate having to work together, about partnerships and how a history like that can tie people together, grounding them. And I listened, but I don't think I really understood what he was saying, until now.'

Mesmerized by the familiar deep rumble of his voice, laced as it was in that moment with a warm edge of nostalgia, it took a moment for her to realize that he was looking at her again. When she did, her gaze rose slowly, locking with his as she felt a sense of inevitability sweeping over her.

'You see this place as your legacy for Lizzie, don't you— something that'll be here long after you're gone?'

Rhiannon nodded silently, deeply touched in a way she couldn't even begin to quantify.

'Well, I want my part of her legacy to be the estate. The way it should be—the two working together to survive in the future. Half of it yours to pass on and half of it mine.'

'You don't have to do that.' Somehow she managed to choke the words out through her thickening throat.

He shook his head, his gaze steady and determined. 'Yes, I do. And I want to.'

Rhiannon remained frozen to the same spot as he stepped closer, his voice huskier, filled with emotion as he told her in the same steady, determined tone, with his gaze locked on hers, 'I love her, Mac, I do. Whether it's too soon to feel something that strong or not, it's there. My world now revolves around her.'

Just as she had felt the very moment she had first held her baby in her arms. 'I know.'

'So it's what I want to do to provide for her future, and the rest of the stuff in between we can work out between us. I think we can do that now, can't we?'

'Yes.' She nodded to emphasize the word that came out on so low a tone that it was almost a whisper, her eyes filling as she looked at him. Because there was a huge bubble of emotion filling her chest while she did and she just couldn't stop it from spilling over. It had formed the moment he'd said he loved Lizzie. The only child he believed he might ever have.

'I want to tell her now, if that's all right with you. I don't think there's any need to wait any more.'

He nodded, still staring at her with his intense blue-eyed gaze as he moved another step closer, stopping a few inches away from her body.

'Yes, it's time—maybe after dinner? Then she can ask us both any questions she has and we can talk her through it together.'

Together. Rhiannon nodded, still frozen to the spot.

He cleared his throat. 'Do you know what you'll say yet?'

She laughed nervously, lifting a hand to swipe at the lone tear she felt streaking down her cheek. 'I haven't the faintest idea. I'm hoping I'll find the right ones when I sit her down. It's not easy explaining to your own child that you're not infallible when you've allowed them to believe you are.'

Without hesitation a large hand rose to her face, where he spread his fingers, snaking them back into the base of her ponytail while his thumb brushed along the fine line of her jaw until it rested at the edge of her mouth. Then he leaned his face down closer to hers, studying each of her eyes in turn.

'Mac, you've done everything to take care of her every step of the way. And you've done one hell of a job. Whatever you say will be just fine.'

The use of the old endearment hit her again. He'd used it in the stable that day too, hadn't he? How had she missed that? Accompanied by his softly spoken vote of confidence in her when she needed to hear it the most, it was almost too much. And she could feel the wall she'd erected around her heart so many years ago crumbling.

If she could go back in time, she would never have held this man from his child. Why would she? He was amazing. Any child would be lucky to have him as their father. Her own anger, pain, fear, confusion and eventual resentment had held them apart. How could he ever forgive her for that?

As if he could read her thoughts, a small frown appeared between his eyes, the blue deepened, his gaze dropped to her mouth. And, somewhere in the distance, Rhiannon heard stones dropping to the ground.

Then his other hand was on her face, fingers snaking into her hair, thumb moving to rest against her mouth; so that he held her head cradled in his palms with infinite tenderness.

Rhiannon sighed shakily, her eyelids growing heavy.

'Mum?'

Kane stepped back from her as if burned, and they both turned to look at Lizzie's curious expression.

'What are you doing?' She smiled impishly—she had a fairly vivid idea already of what they were doing.

'I'm teaching your mum to skim stones and she was having a crisis of confidence because she can't do it.' Kane cleared his throat. 'You want to learn?'

'*Oooh*, yes, I do!'

He retrieved the stones from the ground before she got there, glancing over her head at Rhiannon as he started to repeat the instructions.

And Rhiannon stared back at him, desperate to know if he regretted almost kissing her again—if it had merely been a reflection of the intense emotions they both felt talking about their daughter and her future, or if it had been because he knew how much her feelings for him had changed.

Instead she watched as Lizzie made her first attempt at skimming the stone, her small arm swinging back, the stone flying through the air—skip, sink.

First time.

CHAPTER ELEVEN

THE decision to tell Lizzie was taken out of their hands by an unexpected arrival when they returned to the house.

Rhiannon had never set eyes on her before, but the warmly smiling woman soon apologized for 'popping by' unannounced and introduced herself as the Chairperson of the annual Hunt Ball, which was normally held before Christmas at Brookfield, apparently. And over a pot of tea at the kitchen table she explained how they had postponed the Ball out of respect for Mattie's passing. Then she announced that they'd like to reschedule, with Rhiannon's permission, of course. At Brookfield, if it was all right with her.

In the space of an hour Rhiannon found herself agreeing to the event being held there for Valentine's Day, as it was a century-old tradition, and with Kane offering to step in and sponsor it, thankfully, while Lizzie bounced up and down at the prospect of a large party and a new dress to go with it, naturally.

Rhiannon was left feeling distinctly railroaded.

But it was outside on the gravel, as they all saw the nice lady to her car, that the damage was done.

'Thank you so much, dear. I know the committee will be over the moon with the news.' She beamed at Rhiannon, looked at Kane with an admiring glance and then patted Lizzie's head.

'And *you* are an absolute darling. I can't wait to see you in your new dress.'

'Me either!' Lizzie grinned up at her.

'She really is just beautiful.' The woman's eyes skimmed up to Kane's face again. 'And you look just like your daddy too, don't you?'

Rhiannon gasped. *Oh, no.* She *had not* just said that!

Lizzie looked over her shoulder and up at Kane, who stared down at her with the same stunned expression Rhiannon knew had to be written all over her own face.

The cheery voice continued. 'Oh, yes, she really is the image of you, there's no denying it. She has your eyes and your hair colour, doesn't she?'

Kane swallowed hard, his helpless gaze flickering to Rhiannon's before they both watched Lizzie turn round and start to slowly work it out.

'Well, I'll be in touch soon.' She pulled open her car door and ran the window down to wave. 'Lovely family. Super to meet you at last. Cheerio!'

Lizzie stood with her head tilted to one side, a frown creasing her forehead as she continued to study Kane's face. And it was only the edge to Kane's voice that drew Rhiannon out of her horrified silence.

'We need to go inside.'

'Yes, we do.' She stepped over to Lizzie and smoothed a hand over her hair. 'Come on, baby. We'll all go into the sitting room and we can have a talk.'

Lizzie silently studied Kane as she walked past him, while her mother grasped her father's hand, tangling their fingers together and squeezing.

He looked down at her as she whispered, 'I'm so sorry. It shouldn't have happened like this.'

His longer fingers wrapped tighter around hers. 'It's not your fault. We'll talk to her together, okay?'

Rhiannon nodded. Because there really wasn't much else to say, was there?

In the sitting room Kane released her hand and walked over to Lizzie, setting his large hand on her shoulder to guide her around the sofa, where he sat down and obviously assumed she'd sit with him.

But, before Rhiannon's wide eyes, she stood in front of Kane and reached her small hands up to frame his face, leaning in closer to stare at his eyes close up. She tilted her head, one chocolate-brown braid swinging over her shoulder.

'You have blue eyes, like me.'

Rhiannon pursed her lips tightly together, her heart twisting, tears filling her eyes as Kane nodded, his voice husky and filled with immeasurable gentleness.

'Yes, I do.'

Lizzie lifted a hand and caught a lock of his short hair between her fingers, studying it carefully before she looked down at the swinging braid, then back into his eyes. 'And brown hair, like me.'

'Yes.'

Rhiannon stepped closer, her hand smoothing over Lizzie's hair again as she bent down. 'Not quite, baby.'

Two sets of matching blue eyes stared at her. And she had to swallow hard to damp down a wave of emotion before she continued, 'You have blue eyes like *his*. And brown hair like *his*. Because, you see, he really *is* your dad.'

Lizzie's eyes widened before she looked back at Kane's face. '*Really?*'

He nodded again. 'Yes, really.'

The smile took a moment, but when it arrived her whole face seemed to light up from within, as if everything she had ever wanted with all of her young heart had just been set in front of her.

'I'm glad,' she announced with conviction.

Kane swallowed hard, his voice firmer. 'So am I.'

'Where were you?'

The question broke Rhiannon's heart in two. She opened her mouth to say something, but couldn't find the right words, instead listening with silent admiration as Kane answered the question with *exactly* the right words.

'Waiting for you.'

Lizzie threw herself forward, her small arms wrapping around his neck and holding on tight. And Rhiannon watched as Kane's eyes closed and he wrapped his arms around her waist, lifting her up off the ground, his face contorting briefly in what might have looked like agony to someone who didn't know better.

But Rhiannon knew what it was, even before his eyes opened and his gaze followed the path of the fat, heavy tears streaking down her cheeks, forcing her to raise a hand to her mouth to cover a sob.

Why had she ever kept them apart? She knew she would never forgive herself for that. Not after this. Because she'd never have found the perfect words he just had.

Had she ever really known this man? He was so different from the one she had known before and yet in so many ways just the same. She was certainly as attracted to him physically as she had been before, but this new version of him affected her on so many other levels. And the combination of his words by the lake and seeing him with his daughter now that she knew who he was was so heart-rending, so very precious to both of them, that Rhiannon couldn't have not loved him for being the father he was to her child.

She pushed herself upright, watching her child as she turned her cheek against her father's chest, nestling in with her eyes closed and a contented expression on her face. Then, just as Rhiannon turned to walk away, she felt her eyes drawn inexorably back to Kane's face.

He smiled up at her, his heart in his eyes. And that simple smile shattered her completely, tearing her heart from her chest and fading the rest of the world away so that the only thing she could see for a second was him. But she simply nodded, managed an answering smile and mouthed a, 'Thank you.'

It wasn't anywhere near enough, but she meant it, in so many more ways than just 'thank you for being everything Lizzie deserves'.

Fearful that anything more than that would show in her eyes, she stepped back, then turned and left the room, the tears flowing freely down her cheeks as she left them behind. Because what was happening in that room was nothing to do with her, was it? For the first time in her young child's life there was something that Rhiannon couldn't share, couldn't be a part of and never would. She couldn't stay there and watch as father and daughter bonded, became irretrievably bound to each other. But not because she was jealous or didn't want the bond to exist—not when they both needed each other as much as they did—but because Rhiannon wanted so badly to be able to share in what they had.

And it broke her heart that they were two halves of a family that just didn't fit together to make a whole. Maybe even to make *her* feel whole in a way she'd never felt before.

They eventually found Rhiannon in the kitchen, after a long time in the sitting room with Lizzie sitting across his lap, her arms around his neck while she brightly informed him how very pleased she was to have a dad of her own before she asked a dozen questions about her new family.

But even though Kane savoured every single second of a

time he knew he would never forget, he felt the lack of Rhiannon's presence in the room, almost as if there was something missing because she wasn't there.

Not that he didn't deeply appreciate the time she'd given them alone, because he did. But somehow, as Lizzie's line of questioning dwindled a little, it felt wrong not to have her mother there too. So he leaned his forehead in against Lizzie's to whisper, 'Let's go find your mum.'

She held on to his hand all the way to the kitchen, only releasing him to bounce up on to the long bench and announce in an excited voice, 'I have grandparents and an uncle and an auntie and cousins and everything!'

Rhiannon smiled at her from the Aga end of the room. 'That's amazing, isn't it?'

It suddenly occurred to Kane that Lizzie was more excited by that than he'd thought she'd be. Didn't Rhiannon have brothers or sisters? He vaguely remembered a brother somewhere. And, as to the grandparents…

'You already have a set of grandparents, don't you?' He moved further into the room, swinging a long leg over the bench opposite Lizzie.

Lizzie shook her head firmly. 'Nope. I had Stephen's mum and dad as kind of almost grandparents for a while, but they weren't really mine. And Mum's parents never knowed me.'

He scowled, his gaze immediately drawn to Rhiannon's face across the room. Why not? Had something happened to them? Surely he'd have heard that from Mattie, if no one else? Not, he guessed, that he'd ever been that open to hearing anything about Rhiannon when he'd shut all thought of her out of his mind and been determined to believe that she'd moved swiftly on from the brief relationship they'd had. And he'd been damn quick to make that assumption, hadn't he?

Maybe it had eased his conscience, because it'd been easier to believe he hadn't thrown away something that might have been important. How in hell would he have known if it was important at twenty-one? He'd been too wrapped up in other things…

Lizzie, as usual, continued to deliver reams of the kind of information it would have taken him weeks to get out of her mother. 'They didn't think Mum should have a baby 'cos she was too young and all. But Mum wanted me more than anything in the whole world so she left home and had me. And we made our own family.'

Rhiannon grimaced before she could hide it and Kane swore inwardly in response. That was what she'd meant when she'd said she knew what it was like to have a father reject her? They had turned her away?

They had turned their own daughter away?

No wonder she'd hated him for not being there. The father of her baby had disappeared off the face of the earth, her parents had disowned her and she didn't have a well-paid job or any kind of financial support. It all added together to form a mental picture that Kane found very difficult to see.

And the huge wave of anger that formed inside him must have shown because Rhiannon's soft voice sounded again from across the room, with a tone of reassurance.

'And we did just fine didn't we, baby?'

Lizzie nodded, oblivious to the undercurrents. 'Better now that Kane's here, though.'

Kane smiled at her, then glanced at Rhiannon, who smiled back at him but couldn't seem to look him in the eye. 'Yes, better now.'

He knew she meant better for Lizzie's sake. But he also discovered a part of him hoped she meant it a little from her point of view too. He'd like it if she thought his being there, being a part of their lives, was better for all of them. That was the way it was supposed to be, wasn't it? It was part of a father's remit, after all—to take care of his family.

The thought would have knocked him off his feet if he'd been upright. Instead he tried to complete the missing parts of the puzzle. 'Where did you live?'

Rhiannon didn't look overly surprised by the question. 'A friend of mine from the coffee shop let me rent a room at her place. And I worked full-time until I had Lizzie, and then went part-time until she was older.'

'Auntie Kerri.'

'That's right.' Rhiannon shrugged as if it weren't as big a deal as Kane knew it was. 'When Kerri worked at night in one of the bars near the campus I looked after her kids and she helped with Lizzie when I worked. It worked for both of us; we've been friends ever since.'

Kane frowned harder. She'd made sacrifices to bring his child into the world; had told that child that she'd been wanted more than anything else, had raised her to be bright, happy, well balanced. No small achievement in the world they lived in. While the father who could have provided everything they needed and more had dropped off the planet. Even when he'd been ill, even if he hadn't recovered, he'd still have provided for them both. Didn't she know that?

How could she *not* know that?

Rhiannon smiled again. 'We were fine.'

'What about the course you were doing at night?'

She looked surprised he remembered. Hadn't she got that part yet? They may not have been in love back then, but he remembered *everything*. He made an attempt to silently communicate that to her, almost testing her to see if she could read his thoughts as well as he'd started to read hers.

But, even though she faltered, she shrugged it off again, literally, in a way that was really starting to irritate the hell out of Kane. 'I kept going for as long as I could. When I had Lizzie I quit so I could look after her; young baby, part-time work and course work weren't a good combination. So something had to give.'

'But she finished it in the post when I was bigger. 'Cos school is important and she needed it for her work when I was big enough for school.'

Rhiannon clarified it for him. 'I switched to an Open University course. Took a bit longer but I still finished it. And then I did temp work as a PA, which paid better than the coffee shop career. It was fine.'

Fine. She kept using that word, didn't she? Well, it damn well wasn't fine with him. Fine wasn't anywhere near good enough.

'Motherhood matures you'—she'd thrown something like that at him right at the start of his stay at Brookfield, hadn't she? How much had she been trying to tell him between the lines that he'd missed? What else had he got wrong when he'd simply thought she'd held his child from him out of spite?

It hadn't been spite. He'd dumped her and left; she hadn't known why because he hadn't wanted to tell her—to show anyone for a single second that he was less of a man or might be less of a man by the end of his treatment. So, for all she knew, he didn't give a toss about her. She'd tried to get in contact with him and while he didn't answer her parents had disowned her and she'd been alone. Any wonder she'd believed he didn't give a damn. It had probably felt as if no one had, so she'd just knuckled down and got on with it.

All those years she'd worked hard to provide for Lizzie, just to keep their heads above water—she'd still managed to finish her education so that she could improve her career prospects—until—

'You didn't have to work when you married Stephen.' He clenched his teeth on the words.

It still bugged the hell out of him that that had happened. And knowing what he did now made it worse. Because Stephen hadn't just got to spend time with *his* child; he'd had Rhiannon.

He'd wanted everything of Kane's from their days in grammar school. She must have seemed like the ultimate prize to him and that was why it had been so easy for Kane to believe he'd moved in on her the second he was gone. Lord alone knew he had hung around the coffee shop enough when she'd been there—hell, even when Kane had been dating her. And Kane had had to warn him off often enough…

He'd thought when they got married it was just Stephen finally being a man and accepting his responsibilities. Had that just been another false belief for Kane to ease his conscience?

Whatever way he looked at it, he was finding himself falling desperately short of being much of a guy. And that just didn't sit well with him. Not just in the fatherhood department either. It mattered to him with Mac too.

'No, I still worked, not that Stephen liked it too much. And marrying him was a mistake; it didn't last long. We lived apart for most of it, and when we divorced I rented the house in Dublin from him.'

Kane's hands bunched into fists below the table.

'He wanted me to go to stupid boarding school.' Lizzie rolled her eyes.

'I didn't let that happen, did I?' Rhiannon added, more quietly this time, so that Kane's gaze immediately flew to lock with hers before she blinked and looked away. 'It's all history now.'

He watched as Rhiannon moved across the room to plant a kiss on the top of Lizzie's head. 'And that's probably enough information for one night. There's chicken for dinner.'

'Yay!'

'I'm going to have a bath; I take it I can trust you two to make sure nothing gets burnt to a crisp?' She glanced at him briefly again from the corner of her eye. And that one look told him he'd heard more than she would have ever volunteered. She still felt the need to hide things from him—but why? What else was she holding back?

If she really thought he was done with her, then she had another think coming. He was a member of this family now; the sense of protectiveness that filled him was overwhelming now, though not so much for feeling protective of Lizzie—that was a given—it was the sudden need to extend that protectiveness to Rhiannon that surprised him the most. When exactly *had that* happened?

He'd known all about the early resentment he felt when he'd been so aware of how she moved, how soft her hair looked, how her thoughts would cross over her expressive eyes. He was all too conscious of the physical attraction that flared every time he was near her—because he'd even come dangerously close to kissing her again by the lake before they'd been interrupted, hadn't he?

And he had spent the walk back wondering how she would have responded if he had. Would she have run away as she had last time? Would she have stayed? Would she have considered seeing where the physical attraction would lead them this time?

But the depth of emotion he had seen in her eyes, with tears streaking down her cheeks after they'd told Lizzie who he was—*that* had done the most damage to his original resolve not to get involved with her again, hadn't it? Maybe that was when it had happened.

'We never burn dinner,' Lizzie complained.

'Well, don't start now.' She glanced at him again as she left the room.

Oh, yes, she *knew* he wasn't done with her. So he winked at Lizzie. 'I'll be right back and you're in charge of the dinner.'

Rhiannon was almost on the first landing as he came out of the kitchen, her shoulders slumped, head bowed as she took each step.

He took the stairs two at a time. 'Wait a minute.'

Her shoulders rose before she turned, her eyes guarded. And Kane hated that. He'd thought they were getting past that stage.

'I thought you were going to watch dinner.'

'I didn't know your parents turned you away.'

'Why would you have; you weren't—'

'*There*? I know. It would have been better if I had been, I can promise you that.'

She frowned hard and glanced up the landing, almost as if she was wishing there was an escape route. 'It worked out fine in the end.'

He stepped closer, a part of him desperately wanting to take the dull tone from her voice. '"Fine". You use that word a lot, don't you?'

Confusion clouded her eyes for a moment. 'Yes, fine. I don't understand the problem with the word. It was—' she enunciated the word with a little more deliberation '—*fine*, as in not a problem. We got through. Just like now—everything is fine— it's working out, isn't it?'

He opened his mouth to answer that but, before he could say a word, she frowned and added, in a softer tone, 'Thank you for the way you were with Lizzie. I can't possibly feel any worse about keeping you both apart, especially after today. If it helps any knowing it, there's nothing you can do or say to punish me more than I'm already punishing myself for that mistake.'

'I don't want to punish you, Mac.' He reached out for her hand, his thumb grazing back and forth against the beating pulse below the soft skin of her wrist. 'And I don't think you should punish yourself any more either. I understand why you hated me when you did, and I think we can both look back on it all now and make more sense of the mistakes we both made. It's done. And now we're—'

'Fine?' She smiled a very small smile before her chin dropped and she studied his hand holding hers.

Kane smiled at the top of her head, his eyes following some of the deeper strands of red. And for the first time in a very long time he was at a loss for words.

But not managing to find what he wanted to say—in all likelihood because he didn't actually know *what* it was he wanted to say—gave Rhiannon cause to break the awkward silence by extricating her hand from his. And when her chin rose she had a brighter smile pinned on her face and a shield across her eyes that stopped him from reading her thoughts.

A wave of something resembling fear crossed his chest before she spoke. 'I'm glad this happened, I really am. I want you to know that, Kane.'

'I am too.'

She nodded. 'We've laid all the ghosts to rest now.'

His eyes narrowed at the statement, as if somehow by shutting a door on the past he sensed she was closing some kind of a door on the future too. When he wanted—

Hell. He didn't know what he wanted. She had an innate ability to pull the rug out from underneath his feet. And, just to add to his sense of frustration at that fact, she then reached out and patted his arm. *Patted his arm*—as of he was some kind of elderly relative or the damn dog!

'I'm glad we can be friends again.'

Kane frowned. 'And when exactly were we *friends*?'

Her long lashes flickered as she focused on a point past his shoulder. 'I think it's important we be friends now—for Lizzie's sake.'

For Lizzie's sake. It was a phrase he'd used all too often himself, but suddenly it didn't seem enough any more; there had to be…*more*…

'Well, yes, I agree b—'

She smiled the overly bright smile again. 'And the fact that we can communicate so well can only help with the decisions we'll probably have to make down the line, as parents.'

Kane pursed his lips, shoving his hands deep into his pockets in an attempt not to reach out and shake her. Because he *really* wanted to shake her! What was she doing? Not that everything she'd said didn't make a certain amount of sense, but—

She wasn't done. 'I know you'll need to go back to your own life soon, now that everything is sorted out. So maybe tomorrow we can talk about when you want to have Lizzie come to you or when you'd like to come visit here. Just so we both know where we're at.'

More practicalities and he agreed with all of that too, he did. It made perfect sense. It was pretty much the way he'd thought things would work out once everything was in the open. So why in hell did it feel like some kind of rejection?

Had he let himself get too comfortable at Brookfield? Was that all it was? It was true; they'd slipped into a kind of comfortable routine of late, despite the times when Rhiannon and he parted ways during the day to do their work. But then most couples spent some time apart during the day when they were working, didn't they?

Whoa. Now they were a couple in his mind?

He rocked back a little from her while he tried to quantify exactly what it was they were. They'd never at any stage been just friends. They weren't a couple. They most definitely weren't lovers any more, no matter how the memories of that time had been plaguing his thoughts of late—day and night. Especially since that one damn kiss he'd so very nearly repeated...

So what in hell were they?

Lizzie's parents—yes—but they were hardly two strangers who would work separately to raise her. At least, he didn't want them to be. That would make them two separate halves of one family. And, back in the days when he had actually allowed himself to think about a family in his future, that just wasn't the way he'd envisaged it being. But in order to be a family there had to be something more, didn't there?

He was still frowning when she spoke again, her gaze rising to look into his eyes. 'There's no need to feel guilty about leaving, you know—not when she'll know you're coming back. Your company is important to you; you've spent years building it up and you've been away from it for nearly a month now.'

It really would help him to sort his thoughts out if she'd just stop being so damn reasonable!

'I'm just going to come right out with this—bear with me, okay?'

All right—because if one of them maybe knew how they felt that would be helpful.

She took a breath. 'I know some people might have sat down and lived off the money their family left them, but you didn't do that.' She smiled a smaller, more genuine smile that made it all the way up into her eyes, softening them so that the warmth radiated across to him. 'And I think that's a wonderful example you've set our daughter.'

He shrugged off the words that should really have made him feel at least a certain amount of pride, because he had a sneaking suspicion he wasn't going to like where she was heading. 'I'm not the only guy in the world to have done that.'

'No, but you're maybe one of the few who felt they'd something to prove after being sick so early on, aren't you? I know you well enough now to know that some kind of control over *something* would have been important to you, wouldn't it?'

How in hell did she know that?

She stepped closer, her chin rising so that she could continue looking into his eyes. And Kane held his breath, his heart thundering loudly as he attempted to hold himself under control.

She may have a better idea of why he'd done some of the things he had back in the day but she really had no idea just how much she was testing him by being so close to him, did she?

It would take so little effort to unclench the fists currently held in his pockets, to reach for her, to haul her into his arms and kiss her senseless until she understood just how far they fell from the 'friends' description. But in doing that he would be moving them on to territory that would involve the 'more' that he hadn't quite got figured out yet. And if he couldn't figure that part out, then what in hell would he say to her? Because he doubted very much that a passionate affair like their last one would be enough this time round—not now that there were so many added complications—like their child and the fact that they were, technically speaking, business partners with the house and the estate.

Before he knew it, she laid one slender hand on his chest, right above his thundering heart, and the ache inside him was so powerful he almost groaned aloud. She really was pushing him to the limit.

'I just want you to know you don't have to prove anything to Lizzie. She loves you. You're an amazing father already. So you don't have to bury yourself in your work any more, thinking up games for all those millions of kids while convinced you'll never have any of your own. You have her. One day you'll have more—'

Right—enough was enough! He had one hand unclenched and out of his pocket in the blink of an eye, clasping her hand tightly as he pulled it off his chest. 'I don't need you to give me a pep talk.'

'I know you don't.'

He placed her hand back at her side and released it, a combination of frustration and confusion fuelling his rising anger. 'You're right, I do need to get back to work; I've been here longer than I planned. But it needed doing—' he clenched his jaw '—for Lizzie's sake.'

He leaned his head a little closer to add, 'But I won't have you feeling sorry for me, Rhiannon—just be quite clear on that.'

Her eyes widened, her mouth gaped open and then she completely stunned him by laughing, albeit a little nervously. 'You idiot. I don't feel sorry for you.'

Kane stared down at her in stark amazement. He'd thought he could read this woman's thoughts? He hadn't a clue how her mind worked!

'The irony is I don't think I've ever had so much respect for anyone. You're the strongest person I know. You faced and fought your illness, you built a business from the ground up when you really didn't have to go to all that effort, you've come down here and in the space of a single month shown what a terrific father you can be—not to mention turning every opinion I ever had of you right on its head—' She shook her head, focused again on the same point just past his shoulder. 'I don't feel the least bit sorry for you, Kane Healey. Not one little bit.'

She looked back into his eyes and again he was at a complete loss for words.

'All I was *trying* to say was that you have nothing to prove. Not to anyone. But you don't need to bury yourself in your work to compensate for anything either. You already have a family, even if you'd told yourself you'd never have one.' She smiled, her voice husky. 'Lizzie *is* your family.'

He ran his hand roughly over his hair and down his face as she turned and walked away, shaking his head as he tried to take in everything she'd just said and to untangle how he felt. And she was halfway up the second flight of stairs before he found some husky words of his own.

'Sometimes I think you don't know me at all—and then

sometimes I think you know me better than anyone else ever has. I don't know how I feel about that.'

'Well, when you do we can maybe have a talk about it. That's what being friends is all about.'

CHAPTER TWELVE

IF SOMEONE had told her just over a month ago that she'd miss Kane when he left she'd have laughed herself silly.

Thankfully she had the preparations for the Valentine Ball to occupy her between the brief times she got to hear his voice on the phone when he called Lizzie. Not that he didn't always take the time to enquire how she was, or how she was getting on with the combined running of the house and the estate, the latter of which he had been happy to let her look after when he was away—and she could consult with him if she needed to—that was all *fine*.

But *fine* really wasn't enough any more. In fact, fine would probably never be enough again. Not now that she'd had a glimpse into what might have been. And having Kane as a part of Lizzie's life, living under the same roof as them both so they looked like a happy family to the outside world, had left Rhiannon with a permanent sense of loss for that 'might have been'.

But it wasn't just that—it was *him*. She missed *him*. The sound of his voice, his deep laughter, the way her pulse would skip when he looked at her with his gorgeous blue eyes. And he was so much more than she'd ever thought anyone could be—strong in character as well as body, braver than probably even he thought he was and with an ability to care so very deeply, the way he did for Lizzie—all adding together to make him exactly the kind of man she'd once believed he might be.

So that having lost him back then, and not having him with her *that way* now, was just the most extreme form of agony she had ever felt. She might not have been in love before, but she was in love now, wasn't she?

For some reason it was the night of the Ball that she missed him most. And she couldn't just put it down to the fact that she was one of the very few there without a partner.

Everywhere she looked, the house was alive with people, laughter, soft lights, the scent of flowers and the sound of music. But she couldn't enjoy the fact that it felt as if Brookfield had finally come back to life because, even surrounded by so many people, she was still alone—because Kane wasn't there to share it.

She wasn't even thirty years old yet and it felt as if she were facing the rest of her life alone. There was still time to meet someone, she reasoned, but whoever it was wouldn't be *him*. He was going to take some getting over. And knowing that she'd have to see him, spend time with him, watch him with their daughter, all from the sidelines… Well, it was going to be complete torture, wasn't it?

Walking down the hall with her hostess smile firmly in place, she caught sight of herself in one of the huge gilt mirrors. She'd taken a lot of time and effort with how she looked, all too aware of the place she now had in the local community and the need to at least do *something* right. So she took a moment to smooth her hands down over the pale gold of her long empire-line dress, to check that all of her curls were still pinned up in the right places, that none of the curl in the longer strands brushing her shoulders had dropped out.

And then she glanced briefly at her make-up and was

stunned by the sadness she could see in her own eyes. Could everyone see how miserable she was? Damn him! It would be so much easier if she could still hate him.

She straightened the pearl choker at her neck and turned, to look straight up into familiar blue eyes.

'Lizzie told me there was a party somewhere.'

Oh, hell. He looked *amazing*! How was that fair?

She dragged her gaze from his eyes to make an inventory of what he was wearing, deciding in a heartbeat that he should spend every day of the rest of his life in a dinner jacket and a bow-tie. He just—filled it—better than any other man she'd seen in the same outfit that evening, even if he had the jacket unbuttoned and his hands deep in his pockets.

Actually, on reflection, there was something incredibly sexy about *that* too.

She bit her bottom lip, lifting her chin as he approached. 'I didn't know you were part of the local Hunt Club.'

'My daughter invited me. She said she had a new dress that I had to see "and everything".'

Rhiannon's gaze softened when he smiled a slow, ridiculously sexy smile. 'She's gorgeous in it.'

'I bet she is.'

But he didn't ask where Lizzie was or make an attempt to find her. And eventually Rhiannon couldn't take just standing there looking at him while that silent, almost *knowing* gleam shone in his eyes, even if she felt almost maniacally happy to see him.

'Can I get you a drink of something?'

Kane chuckled at her polite sweeping wave of one hand. 'Well, you're obviously very comfortable in the role of hostess.'

'As a matter of fact, I am.' She smiled more openly—couldn't seem to stop herself from smiling, as it happened. Then she looked up and around the huge hall. 'But you have to admit that Brookfield is an amazing setting. Just look at it, it was meant for this kind of thing. I don't think it's ever looked more beautiful.'

When she looked back into his eyes he smiled again, then looked slowly down over her dress and back up. 'Yes, beautiful is the right word.'

Rhiannon's breath caught. What was *that*?

She swallowed again. 'There's, um, there's still some food left from the buffet, I think, that is, if you're hungry. It's through here—'

She tore her gaze from his, aware that heat was rising on her cheeks as she stepped to one side to show him where the buffet was set up. But, without moving from the same place, he took a hand from his pocket and captured hers, his long, warm fingers immediately tangling with hers.

'Dance with me.'

His hand felt wonderful. And yes, she was fully aware that he'd just walked in unannounced, looking the way he did, and she'd pretty much reacted like a shy teenager with a crush, but she needed the physical contact. She needed to be with him like this, to let her guard down enough to prove to herself that she could still get along with him, spend time with him and not allow the fact that she was in love with him to get in the way.

So she turned her head and looked up at him with a challenging quirk of her eyebrows. 'How do I even know you can dance? You might have two left feet.'

Kane turned round, switching his hands as he leaned a little closer to her face, his deep voice low and deliciously seductive. 'Let's find out, shall we?'

Rhiannon let him guide her through the crowd to the sitting room, where all of the furniture had been cleared to turn it into a mini ballroom. And when they were surrounded by swaying couples he turned and drew her forward into his arms, waiting until her hands rose to clasp behind his neck before he drew her closer and began to sway them to the music.

Rhiannon let her thumbs brush against the short hair at the nape of his neck; she breathed in the hint of cinnamon, relaxed back on to the band of his arms and couldn't, for the life of her, tear her gaze from his.

She was officially smitten.

But it was perfect. And surely she couldn't be damned forever for wanting one perfect moment with him?

He smiled another slow, sensual smile with the kind of warmth she felt seep in to melt her bones.

'See, I don't have two left feet.'

She smiled back at him. 'Its early days.'

'Time will tell.' He leaned a little closer. 'How come we've never danced together before?'

Oh, they'd danced. They'd danced more than he probably realized. It felt as if she'd spent most of her life dancing *with* him and *around* him.

'We did that seventies disco night that one time.'

He laughed, his large hands flattening against her back, smoothing the material over her skin in small, slow, gentle sweeps. 'Ah, but back then, with us, that wasn't dancing. It was foreplay.'

With her hips swaying in time with his, Rhiannon wasn't entirely convinced that what they were currently doing wasn't exactly the same thing. Telling herself she'd blame the three glasses of wine she'd had when she looked back on it all in the morning, she didn't try to brush aside what he'd said or make a sarcastic comment in reply. Instead, she simply looked at him from beneath lowered lashes, damping her lips before she told him, 'You had a very one track mind back then.'

Kane grumbled his reply. 'Only because you were a bad influence on me.'

'I remember how much persuasion it took.'

He nodded, his hands continuing their slow smoothing over her back. 'I guess, considering the law of percentages, we were always likely to have a chance of making a Lizzie, weren't we?'

'Yes.' The word was almost a whisper. 'Nothing is ever a one hundred per cent guarantee.'

'No. But sometimes, even when we know that, we still take a chance. Maybe there's just no stopping something that's meant to be.' He drew her in closer as he spoke, so that the last words were said directly above her ear.

Rhiannon's eyelids grew heavy so she closed her eyes, surrendering to the waves of sensuality, while her heart ached all over again for what she couldn't have. It'd been like this last time, hadn't it? Maybe it had even been the start of what she felt now. Had she been falling in love back then and not realized? Was that why she'd fallen so quickly this time?

'Sometimes it's worth having a little faith that things will eventually work out the way they're supposed to, no matter what mistakes we make along the way.'

Rhiannon's eyes opened and she frowned. What did he mean by that? Was she starting to imagine that he was hinting at something he wasn't because she wanted him to want more? But, when she leaned back against his arms to try and read his expression, he was looking over her head.

'Aha, I see my daughter. And you're right, she does look gorgeous.' He flashed a smile over at Lizzie. 'I'd better go dance with her too.'

Rhiannon nodded, her brain still feeling fluffy. 'I think she'd love that.'

He leaned back, dropping his chin to look into her eyes. 'I'm glad we're friends now, Mac.'

Her own words. And he may as well have stabbed her in the chest. It certainly couldn't have hurt any less. But she managed to nod again, to smile a small smile, even if she had to look away from his eyes to do it. 'Me too.'

He released her, stepped sideways and then completely surprised her, twisting the knife at the same time, by placing a soft, fleeting kiss against her cheek before stage whispering into her ear, 'And, just in case I haven't already said it: you look very beautiful tonight. But then you were always beautiful.'

Rhiannon stood in the centre of the dance floor for a moment so she could blink back the tears that had formed at the back of her eyes, so that she could swallow hard and take a couple of deep breaths, to gain control before she pinned her hostess smile back on.

How in hell was she going to get through this?

She moved back into the crowd, shaking hands with people, listening to stories about Brookfield and Mattie's family. And then, halfway between two groups, she caught sight of Kane escorting Lizzie to the dance floor so she slipped back a little to watch.

He bowed, Lizzie giggled and Rhiannon smiled affectionately at them both. They were just so very alike—the two people she loved the most.

She swallowed hard, tears stinging her eyes again, while Kane lifted Lizzie up into his arms, her slender arms around his neck and legs swinging below his waist as they started to dance. It was the most beautiful thing Rhiannon had ever seen—heartbreakingly beautiful. And agonizing—because the need to walk over and join them, to dance with Kane with Lizzie held between them—was so strong it almost killed her.

This was the way her life was going to be from now on—standing on the outside looking in. And if it weren't for the seventy guests in her house she'd have disappeared upstairs so she didn't have to watch it.

Yet another deep breath, yet another lift of her chin, because she had to get on with it, didn't she? Standing and watching wasn't going to feel any better after ten minutes.

And she managed it, just. She got through the rest of the evening, even though she was constantly aware of where Kane was at any given time, of the people he was talking to—particularly the women—of the sound of his voice when he was close by or his scent as he walked past. And she even managed to smile across at him when he looked at her. But, as the night drew to a close and they stood side by side at the front doors waving goodbye to the last of the guests, watching their cars circle as they drove off the gravel, Rhiannon felt her mouth go dry, her heart beat a little louder, felt that no matter how many breaths she took she couldn't seem to get enough air into her lungs.

The door clicked shut and she rested her palm on its cool surface for a moment before turning round and flashing a small smile at him. 'I'll have to go check that Lizzie actually went to bed when I sent her an hour ago. Any clearing up can wait till the morning.'

'I checked; she's out for the count. You throw a hell of a party, Mac.'

Half of her really wished he would stop using the old nickname. It didn't help any. But then neither did his falling into step beside her as she walked to the staircase.

'Well, I did have some help from the Committee. They're an enthusiastic bunch.' She lifted her long skirt to negotiate the stairs, her focus on her feet so that she didn't notice him reaching out for her elbow until the searing heat of his touch burnt her skin.

When her breath caught his fingers tightened. 'Lizzie told me you arranged most of it, though, right down to the colours of the flowers and moving furniture under your own steam.'

She swallowed hard and tried to concentrate on not tripping. 'It all came together in the end.'

His warm fingers eased a little against her elbow, widened, smoothed over her skin in a caress she felt clean to the soles of her feet. Didn't he have *any* idea what he was doing to her?

But when they reached the landing and Rhiannon tried to gently pull her elbow free, he froze her to the spot with a flat toned, 'Did you love Stephen?'

'What?' Her head rose sharply. Where had that come from?

'Did you?'

'Why?' Rhiannon really didn't see what it had to do with anything. And she certainly didn't want to stand and confess to the man she'd made the biggest mistake of her life with, the details of the second biggest mistake she'd ever made.

He confused her even further by smiling wryly, his blue eyes studying her face intently. 'Because I think when I knew you'd married him was when I started hating you as much as you hated me.'

It was the very last thing she would ever have expected him to say and yet a part of her almost shouted with joy at the very idea of him being jealous. Which was ridiculous—it wasn't what he was saying, was it?

'It had nothing to do with you by then.'

'No, but it still bugged the hell out of me.'

Oh, she knew what he was saying now. And it was yet another twist of the damn knife! So she turned away as she spoke, determined she wouldn't show him how much he'd just hurt her. 'Because you thought Lizzie was his and that meant I had to have been with him right after I was with you, that's why. We already covered all that.'

He reached for her elbow again, tugged her round and then marched her backwards until she had her back against the wall. And when Rhiannon let go of her skirt, he took hold of both of her wrists, his thumbs moving back and forth against her erratic pulse. 'Yes, that was one element of it. But hell, Mac, it was

Stephen—it was a constant competition for him to have what was mine. I thought you knew that.'

Her heart caught on the 'what was mine'. Was that how he'd thought of her then? She searched his eyes for the answer and found him searching her eyes the same way, the air crackling between them.

'It had nothing to do with me marrying him.'

'Then make me understand.'

She was completely distracted by the movement of his thumbs on her wrists, so it took a moment for her to weigh up the pros and cons of telling him the truth.

His mouth curled into another devastating smile. 'And now you're trying to decide whether or not to be honest with me, aren't you?'

'Do you have any idea how annoying it is when you do that? I mean, *really*?'

'I seem to remember there were times when you liked that I knew what you were thinking.'

The words were pure seduction, especially when she knew *exactly* what he was talking about. 'That was different. That had to do with the whole physical thing we had going.'

His voice dropped an octave. 'Don't worry, we'll get to that subject in a minute.'

Rhiannon swallowed a moan. She really couldn't take much more of this. She couldn't! And why in hell was he putting her through it?

'Did you love him?'

'No!' She threw the answer at him. 'There—happy now?'

He tilted his head to one side, shrugging his broad shoulders. 'It's a start. So if you didn't love him, then why did you marry him?'

If she stood there much longer she was going to cry in front of him, she really was. So she tugged her wrists and scowled at him when he wouldn't set her free. All right, he wanted to know why, then she'd damn well tell him why!

'Fine, then. If you really want to know, it was because *he* wanted to marry *me*!'

The hold on her wrists tightened as he swore under his breath. And immediately Rhiannon pushed off the wall, standing on tiptoe to bring her face closer to his. 'And now you think he only wanted that to get at you in some way? Grow up, Kane! He was there and you weren't. He wanted to be with me and you didn't. It was nothing to do with you! And frankly, it still isn't, so let me go!'

'Did *he* love *you*?'

'Is that so very hard for you to believe?'

The steady tone of his answer did her in. 'No, that I could understand a lot better now that I actually know you. I wouldn't blame him for feeling that.'

What did he mean by that? Because there was no way in hell he meant... This was *insane*! She shook her head.

'You're unbelievable. And they say *women* twist things.'

Out of nowhere, he released her hands. But, as she looked down in surprise, both of his hands rose to her waist and he stepped forward, pinning her back against the wall again so that the entire length of his hard, heated body was pressed intimately against hers.

It was like setting a match to touch paper.

Her blood rushed faster through her veins. Her heart pumped harder to help the blood to move at the increased speed. She wanted him *so* badly!

'So you married him because he loved you, and because you were alone, and because you had a baby to support. You married him for security, right?'

'I didn't give a damn about his money, if that's what you mean.' Her words were breathless, her breasts rising and falling rapidly as she fought for air. And if the truth was the only escape route she had, then she had to take it. 'I could have supported Lizzie, I'd done it up until then. He wasn't as bad as you think he was. He was charming and funny and *uncomplicated*. And when he asked me to marry him, I told myself that it was better to go into marriage without love as the basis for it. Or, or—*this*—this thing *we* had.'

'No love and no—*this*?' His voice dropped. 'Because it was safer that way?'

'Maybe—partly—I don't know. But it doesn't matter now.'

His fingers spread wide against her waist, his thumbs brushing against the bottom of her ribcage as he tilted his face over hers, his eyes even more intense close up. 'No love so you couldn't get hurt—'

'Love doesn't guarantee a marriage will last.'

His gaze dropped to her parted lips as he moved his hands along her sides, drawing another gasp from her. 'And no *this*—because?'

'Because *this* doesn't last—when I'm ninety and grey-haired and round-shouldered, even *we* wouldn't still have this.'

His gaze rose, the pupils of his eyes large and dark, his voice huskier. 'Oh, I don't know. I think *we'd* still have *this*. It certainly hasn't gone away, has it? When I'm ninety-three, grey-haired and round-shouldered, I think I'd still give it my best shot.'

And talk like that just made her heart ache all the more. 'It's still not enough on its own.'

'All right, what more is there?'

'Like I'd know.' She laughed nervously, feeling herself on the edge of a mildly panicky hysteria. 'In case you hadn't noticed, my track record isn't very good. If you need tips for future reference you'd be better asking someone who hasn't discovered that they do much better on their own.'

'You married the wrong man, that's all.' When her eyes

widened at the statement, he leaned his head a little closer, his breath fanning out over her heated cheeks. 'And you *didn't* have *this* with *him*.'

There was nothing beyond the kiss; no sound barring their deep breathing, no light barring the ones that danced behind her eyelids, nothing that wasn't completely focused on his firm mouth moving against her soft lips.

She was drowning in him.

He traced his lips along hers, added a little pressure, tugged on her bottom lip until she opened her mouth on a low moan and he deepened the kiss, coaxing her tongue to dance with his.

It wasn't fair. She couldn't do this again—not the physical *alone*. This time she wanted more from him. And there was just too much history. Try as they might, the mistakes would always be there. The mistakes that would open up cracks in any relationship they tried and eventually drive them apart.

And Rhiannon knew she wouldn't survive it this time.

Kane tore his mouth from hers, his face still close as he searched her eyes. 'A lot of people don't even have this, you know. And we have more than this already. We have a child. Is that enough, do you think?'

What did he mean? He couldn't possibly mean…?

It took a split second for it to sink in. 'You can't be serious. You're suggesting some kind of a—what is it called—?' she stared up at him in disbelief '—marriage of convenience? You honestly think I'd ever consider that—with *you*?'

He scowled. 'Why not with me?'

'I can't believe you think I'd even consider it. With one failed marriage behind me, do you honestly think I'd enter into that kind of a *farce*? What the hell century do you think we live in?'

He stepped back from her. 'All along we've said for Liz—'

'*O-oh* no!' She waggled a finger at him when she had enough space, her eyes blazing with hurt, anger and a rapidly growing sense of humiliation. 'Don't you dare use the "for Lizzie's sake" line! I'm more than capable of looking after her on my own. I'll do whatever it takes for her to get to spend time with you, but that's only because you're a different person with her than you are with me.'

And that killed her above all else. He could love his child unconditionally and yet still think that a loveless marriage would be something her mother would consider! When there was just no way she could do it. And, even if she could, she couldn't with *him*. Not when she loved him like she did.

Tears glittered in her eyes as she laid it all on the line for him. 'The Kane Healey I saw dancing with his daughter tonight is a thousand times more of a man than the one who stood here right this minute! He's this amazing guy who doesn't have a problem with showing how much he loves her, even after so little time. If I ever married again it would be for a whole combination of things and part of that *would* be love—it would have to be, for me. And it's not here, so never in *a million years* would I ever marry you.'

He had the gall to look amused. 'A million years?'

'Yes! A million years.' She hiccupped on the words and stepped forward, lifting both hands to shove against his chest. 'Get the hell away from me. I take back every nice thought I've had about you since I got to know you this time round.'

'What kind of nice thoughts?'

She shoved him again. 'I was dumb enough to think you were much more than I'd realized first time around.' Another shove, and each one took him back a step until he had his back against the wooden banister, where she laughed in his face. 'I was even stupid enough to find it weird around here without you! But now I'm glad you left!'

His eyes turned a darker shade of blue, his mouth lifting into the softest smile she had ever seen, one that almost looked affectionate, but she knew was amusement again because she'd just given him yet another victory, hadn't she?

'Mac—' The nickname came out with a husky edge.

'And don't you dare call me that! I hate you!'

'No, you don't.'

She laughed again, sarcastically this time. 'Right this second I do! You might not have managed to completely break my heart the first time round, but you're close to managing it *this time*. If you gave a damn about me, even as Lizzie's mother, then you'd care about my chance at happiness!'

Grabbing her skirt in two fists, she turned on her heel and ran up the next flight of stairs, determined to get to her bedroom and lock the door before he could stop her. But he didn't follow her. He didn't make any attempt to stop her or to tell her she'd got him wrong. Or even to say that she deserved a chance to be happy.

And she *did* genuinely hate him for that.

CHAPTER THIRTEEN

KANE needed to find a way to get Rhiannon to talk to him again. And fast. Because the longer he let it fester, the harder she would be to persuade that he'd simply got his approach wrong the night before.

It was her damn fault, after all. If she didn't have him so sideways most of the time then he'd have made a better job of it! But oh, no, last night she had floored him the second he'd laid eyes on her. Ten years ago they'd have lasted five minutes at that party!

Then there'd been the dance and finally holding her in his arms when he'd done nothing but think about holding her again since he'd left. Damn her—even the five minutes he got to talk to her on the phone each time he called Lizzie had been proving the highlight of his day of late. He was obsessed by her. And that had made him look more closely at how he'd felt about her the first time around. Had he been in love and not known it? There was no way of knowing, but it would be a rational explanation for the fact that he'd felt so much so fast this time round. He'd felt every emotion going since meeting her again. And he hadn't known what it all meant, not really, not until he was away from her and from Lizzie—*his family*. He'd missed them—*both of them*—more than he would ever have thought it possible to miss anyone.

But it had taken Rhiannon to stand there in *that dress*, looking as beautiful as she did, with a frame of soft lights and flowers behind her, for him to have what he already knew confirmed. Yes, he knew what the elusive *something more* was now...

Now all he had to do was put it right.

After several hours tossing and turning in the wee small hours, while he fought the urge to storm down the hall and convince her the old-fashioned way that she'd misread what he was trying to say, a tiny seed of an idea came to him. By six-thirty it was a full-blown plan. Then all he had to do was hire an accomplice...

When Lizzie announced she was going to make dinner on her own, Rhiannon escaped to her room to take a break from the constant smiling she'd been forced to do all day long. She'd done everything to avoid spending time with Kane—everything. She'd put the furniture back, cleared up—and there was a lot to clear up!—and hoovered and dusted. She hadn't even stopped for lunch. The theory being that the busier she stayed then the sooner the day would be over and he'd be gone again.

Something she prayed would happen *very soon* when she caught glimpses of him with Lizzie during the day—laughing, smiling and hugging when the notion struck them. They were *both* torturing her and it *hurt*.

But after a long soak in the bath, when she felt capable of facing them both again, she found a picture pinned to the kitchen door with Lizzie's multicoloured handwriting telling her it was out of bounds.

A tingling on the back of her neck told her Kane was nearby.

'Apparently we're not allowed in the kitchen.'

He walked over to stand beside her, his arms folded across

his chest as he dropped his chin to read the note, frowning at it. 'I wonder what she's up to?'

Rhiannon sighed. 'I have no idea.'

They both stood there for another minute, until the ache in her chest started to demand her attention again. She was too emotionally drained to play games with Lizzie. 'I might just skip dinner. I'm still tired after last night.'

'You should eat something. You skipped lunch.' He knocked on the door, his voice rising, 'Can we come in?'

'*No!*'

Rhiannon sighed again. 'Have you any idea *when*?'

The door swung open and Lizzie stepped through, closing it behind her. Both of her parents stared at her before Kane asked, 'What's in your hair?'

She lifted a hand, swiped at it and then sucked it off her finger. 'Mayonnaise.'

Kane nodded. 'Of course it is.'

'You aren't having dinner in the kitchen; you're having it in the stove room. Come on.'

Oh, Rhiannon *so* didn't want to play, not today, but a glance at Kane, who quirked his dark brows in challenge, was enough to galvanize her. She'd be damned if he took anything more from her than he already had! So she followed Lizzie down the slope to the stove room, unprepared for what she found when she got there.

'What *is* this?'

The room was bedecked with various crêpe paper and cardboard hearts and pink paper chains. The hexagonal table underneath the window was set for two, with paper cups covered in yet more hearts and a single daffodil beside a candle.

Lizzie beamed up at them both after Kane ducked his head under the door frame. 'Happy Valentine's Day!'

Oh, no. Rhiannon could have curled up and died.

Kane leaned closer to ask her in a stage whisper, 'Did you know it was still Valentine's Day?'

Frowning hard, she shook her head, then stopped. 'Well, actually, yes, I suppose I did. The Ball was a day early because it couldn't be on a Sunday when most people have work on Monday and…'

Her words petered out as a thought occurred to her and she scowled up at him. 'I had nothing to do with this.'

He smiled. 'I know.'

'Mum, you sit over that side—' Lizzie pointed at the far chair '—and Dad, you sit here.'

It was the first time she'd called him Dad. They both turned to look at her, then back at each other with a shared smile of understanding at the importance of the one tiny word. It was a bittersweet moment for Rhiannon.

'Maybe we should just humour her?'

But it didn't feel any less dreadful to Rhiannon when they were sitting at the table and Lizzie handed matches to Kane. 'You have to light the candle. It's more romantic that way.'

Rhiannon moaned a low moan, resting her elbow on the table so she could hide her eyes behind her hand. She heard the door close and then a deep chuckle.

'This is nice.'

'I'm glad you think so.' She glared at him from behind her open fingers. 'You do know what she's doing?'

He grinned, resting his forearms on the table so he could lean forward, his voice still low. 'Yes, I know *exactly* what she's doing.'

Rhiannon moaned again and dropped her forehead on to the table. 'I really don't know how much more of these twenty-four hours I can take.' She continued in a muffled voice, feeling sick to her stomach, 'We can't let her think this will lead to anything. You'll have to talk to her.'

She heard him chuckle again.

'Why do *I* have to talk to her?'

Because her mother didn't think she could look her in the eyes and tell her that she didn't love her father that way, that was why, even when she currently hated his guts. Flip side of the same thing, she guessed... And, in fairness, it had always been that way—he'd always been able to make her as mad as a hatter with a few sentences. The only difference back then had been how he'd made it up to her afterwards.

She lifted her head and frowned at him. 'Well, *we're* not going to let her think—'

The door opened and Lizzie backed in, turning round to set a plate in front of each of them. 'Starters.'

Kane took one look at Rhiannon's face when Lizzie left and dissolved into raucous laughter, which she rewarded with another glare. 'Oh, I'm *so* glad *one of us* is enjoying this!'

'You'd be amused too if you could see the expression on your face.'

'It's not funny!'

'Oh, come on, it's a little bit funny. And romantic in an off the wall way, don't you think?'

He swallowed down his laughter when she aimed another glare his way, lifting a fork to play with the contents of his plate. 'What do you think it is?'

After a moment's debate on the merits of running away, Rhiannon lifted her fork and dug around, eventually rolling out an egg. 'Egg mayonnaise.'

'There's an egg in there?'

'Yes, a whole entire round boiled egg.' She glanced up at him and couldn't help but smile a small smile. He then smiled back, which helped some, but still... 'Seriously, we can't let her do this. She's trying to matchmake.'

Kane nodded. 'Well, you can't really blame her.'

'And what does *that* mean?'

He shrugged, his gaze dropping to focus on finding his egg. 'She's a smart kid; we both know that. And she's bound to have seen how we are together.'

'What do you mean, *how we are together*? We're not any *way* when we're together.'

His thick lashes rose, a glint of humour in his blue eyes. 'Now, that wouldn't be entirely true, would it?' He nodded at her plate. 'You'd better eat some of that or you'll hurt her feelings.'

Rhiannon honestly thought she'd choke on it. Whereas Kane had no difficulty whatsoever in tucking into his. 'You think she knows that we—?'

His brows quirked as he spoke with his mouth still half full. 'Kissed? Almost kissed? Which time do you want to discuss?'

She opened her mouth to say something cutting, but nothing came out. So she closed it again. Realistically, she was digging a bigger hole for herself every time, wasn't she?

'Eat something.'

She speared a piece of cucumber and popped it in her mouth, smirking sarcastically at him as she chewed.

'Now, Mac, don't go ruining a romantic evening by being petulant, it's Valentine's Day.' He reached across the table and stole her egg. 'The least you can do is make it look like you ate some of it; move it about on the plate or something.'

Lizzie reappeared. 'Lift your plates, please.'

She set two larger plates down and took the smaller ones from them. 'I put in more salad 'cos Mum always says it's good for you.'

Kane nodded, a better disguised smile on his face. 'It's lovely, sweetheart. You've done a great job.'

When Lizzie beamed at his praise, Rhiannon immediately felt guilty. 'It is, really. You've worked *very* hard on this.'

'But there's nothing green in the dessert, right?'

Even Rhiannon couldn't help chuckling at his question, but

she still kicked him under the table for it, his small flinch deeply satisfying, because she *really* wanted to stay mad with him. She didn't want to laugh with him again. Mad was easier. Mad had no hopes or dreams. Mad knew exactly where it stood.

'I'm only teasing. I'm sure it'll be lovely.'

'It's ice cream.'

'I love ice cream.'

'Me too.' Lizzie grinned and winked at him.

Kane winked back and Rhiannon had to shake her head to shift the ridiculous notion that in some way he approved of what she was doing.

'And you have to talk to each other.'

'We will.'

Right, she'd had about enough. So she called him on it when Lizzie left. 'We're *telling* her.'

She didn't look at him as she said it. Looking at him had a bad effect on her heart rate, even when she was mad. So she searched her plate for something to eat to make it look as if she'd made the effort.

Kane's voice rumbled across at her. 'Tell her what?'

'That this isn't going to happen.'

'It already happened.'

'No, it didn't. Not the *it* she's looking to happen.' She set her fork down and scowled at him again, because surely he had to know there was yet another argument looming. 'It's not fair, Kane.'

He stared across at her as he chewed, his blue eyes studying her with the intensity that she always found the most discon- certing. Then he smiled a small smile before he spoke. 'Maybe she just prefers it when we get along, did you think about that? And I happen to agree with that. You were the one who said you were glad we could be *friends*.'

Damn him! Her breath caught at the reminder, her heart

twisting again, and immediately she refocused on her plate, grumbling back between clenched teeth, 'Yes, I did say that.'

'Being friends is important, don't you think?'

She pursed her lips, lifting her fork to push her salad around. 'Of course it is, for Lizzie's sake.'

There was a long silence before he answered, his voice low. 'Not everything has to be for Lizzie's sake.'

Her heart missed several beats. 'Well, no, it doesn't, because we're business partners too, of course—technically speaking.'

'Being able to work together is important too.'

She risked an upward glance in time to see him slowly nodding his head, his gaze still locked on her. And her heart raced a little to make up for the missing beats. What was he *doing*? Hadn't she been clear enough last night?

'And communication is another one. We might need to work on that some.' He looked down at his plate, lifting his knife to slice some ham. 'Though, just for the record, you've always had really expressive eyes. It's why I'm able to guess what you're thinking as often as I do. I always liked that. It was one of my favourite things about you.'

Rhiannon couldn't believe he was saying these things to her *now*—sweet, almost romantic things. Didn't he know what it did to her poor heart? And she felt a shiver of fear run up her spine at the thought of him being able to see how she felt by looking in her eyes. Did he know how she felt about him? How she'd maybe always felt?

If he knew, then he had the advantage. If he chose to he could push her on the marriage of convenience issue. And she'd already learnt the hard way what happened when only one person loved the other.

When he looked up, she focused on her food, clearing her throat before she replied. 'Yes, those things *are* important. I agree with you.'

'That's a first.'

'Don't push it. I already don't like you much at this precise minute, if you remember correctly.'

'I don't think that's entirely true either, is it?'

That got her attention, while he continued in the same steady voice, 'I think you like me more than you're prepared to admit. At least that's what I'm banking on. If I'm wrong, then I'm about to make a real fool of myself here.'

Rhiannon's eye's widened. He *knew*, didn't he?

Lizzie reappeared and Rhiannon groaned, *'Oh, c'mon!'*

'I brought the ice cream.' She set them down. 'And I forgot to turn the music on.'

When she headed for the stereo Rhiannon tried to stop her. 'It's fine, baby; we don't need music.'

'Yes, you do.' She was already selecting a track. 'It's romantic music for you to dance to.'

'I don't want to dance.' The sharp tone drew attention from both of them so she was forced to pin yet another false smile on to her face. 'I'm really tired, Lizzie, that's all. I don't want to dance.'

'I don't have two left feet.'

She glared venomously at him. 'I don't want to dance with you.'

'Is it the wrong music?' Lizzie turned to Kane with a frown. 'You said that track three was the right one.'

He said?

'Yes, it's the right one, don't worry. And you did a great job with the food and decorations, thank you.'

'You did this?'

'For Valentine's Day.' Lizzie looked immensely pleased with her father's 'thoughtfulness'. 'It was Dad's idea, but I did all the food by myself.'

Rhiannon tilted her head towards one shoulder and closed her eyes in agony, suddenly breathless and dizzy. When she opened them again Kane was smiling a small smile at her, an incredible softness in his eyes.

Sympathy?

She shook her head in denial, her voice barely above an agonized whisper. 'I can't believe you did this.'

'Your mum and I need to have a talk now. Can you give us a while?'

'Yep.'

Lizzie gave him a hug, planted a smacking kiss on his clean-shaven cheek and then practically skipped out the door—leaving Rhiannon to face Kane alone for what she knew would be the most humiliating moment of her life.

She slumped back in her chair, watching as he pushed his back and stood up. 'I don't believe you did this to me. *Why* did you do this?'

'Take a minute to think about it and you'll figure out why.' He held his hand out to her, palm upward. 'Dance with me.'

'I don't want to dance with you.'

'Yes, you do; we can dance and talk at the same time. And *I* want to dance with *you*.' He lowered his voice. 'Please?'

She gaped at him. Kane never said please. At least she couldn't remember him ever saying it anywhere near *her*. And it was apparently all it took to get her to move. She found herself lifting her hand to slide it into his. She watched as his fingers curled around the back of her hand and at the same time she heard him exhale, as if he had been holding his breath, not quite sure of what she would do.

But that couldn't be right—Kane Healey didn't do unsure, did he?

Bracing on his hand, she pushed her chair back and stood up, allowing him to lead her around the sofa, watching in an almost hypnotic state as he stopped and drew her in against him, still holding on to her hand while his arm snaked around her waist.

Somewhere in the distance she could hear the soft tones of the music in the background but she couldn't have said who was singing. She couldn't focus on anything beyond the gentle swaying that began as her hips fitted in against his. And only then did she lift her chin and look up into his darkening eyes.

'Why are you doing this?'

'You know why.'

'I already told you I wouldn't marry you.'

'In a million years.' He nodded, his eyes sparkling. 'Yes, I remember.'

He continued swaying them, making small steps, beginning to move in a circle at the same time, turning her hand in his so that their fingers were locked together.

'Then why—'

He smiled a smile that curled her toes. 'Still not got it?'

She was afraid to hope, 'I told you I needed more than—'

'This?' He leaned down and brushed his mouth across hers fleetingly, in a whisper of a kiss that spoke of tenderness held within passion.

'Yes.' She closed her eyes as sensation washed over her, all too aware that she was letting him seduce her and unable to fight it as her loosely swinging arm rose to lay her palm on his chest—reaching for a firm anchor she could lean on while the world tilted around her. 'That.'

'You still think that's all there is between us?'

Her eyes fluttered open. 'Isn't it?'

'I plan on proving to you that there's more. And if I don't convince you this time, then I'll keep trying to prove it to you, for as long as it *does* take.'

Rhiannon could feel her heart swelling with hope and it must have shown in her eyes because he smiled again, the look in his eyes reminding her of the day they'd told Lizzie who he was, when he had held her in his arms and hadn't tried to hide how he felt.

Kane raised his brows. 'You're getting it now, aren't you?'

She stared in amazement. 'Keep going.'

They swayed back and forth, circling slowly.

'You said that this on its own wasn't enough.'

'*This.*' She smiled a very small smile at him and brazenly moved her hips across his in the opposite direction to their swaying, her smile growing when he sucked in a sharp breath. 'Yes, I did say that.'

He shook his head. '*Witch.*'

She smiled all the more, a bubble of happiness growing in the pit of her stomach.

'You also said that having a child together wasn't enough on its own.'

'An *amazing* child.'

'Yes.' His gaze changed, to a sincere intensity tinged with a hint of regret. 'And I need you to be very clear that she's the only one there might ever be with me. Though there are ways to try—'

Did he think that would make a difference to her? If he thought that then he couldn't possibly know how much she loved him, which meant he was taking a chance by doing this. He might not love her as much as she loved him. But she'd figured out that he was saying he wanted to try. There was no way she wasn't taking that chance.

So she lifted the hand she'd been resting on his chest, laying her palm against his cheek as she leaned up on her toes to place the same whisper of a kiss on his mouth, her nose close to his as she informed him in a steady voice, 'That doesn't matter. I already have one amazing child. Yes, a place like Brookfield was meant to be filled with children, and if this worked and we were lucky enough to have another one like Lizzie one day, then that would be more than *fine* with me…'

'For the record—I hate that word—*fine* isn't enough, for any of us.'

No, he was right. It wasn't—not any more. 'With a little work I reckon we could manage better than fine. But if we don't make another Lizzie then you should know I'd still want to fill this place with children for you to be a father to. There's adoption, fostering, we could run camps here in the summer—'

He kissed her into silence, not raising his head until she was breathless. 'Let me get used to being a father to just one for a while, shall we? I'm still trying to pick that up.'

'You're a great father.'

'Yes, but you have a head start on parenting—'

She took her hand off his face and gently smacked his shoulder. And he laughed, swaying her body a little deeper from side to side.

'That wasn't meant as a dig. I was just trying to say that you need to let me catch up some before you go shopping for a football team.'

'You can be horrible when you want to, you know.'

'I know. But you know that about me, just like I know that sometimes you can be stubborn and unreasonable. We learnt a lot of this stuff the first time round.'

'Yes, we did.'

'And that has to count in with the things to build on, doesn't it? Knowing those things and still wanting to be together means something.'

'Yes, it does.'

Rhiannon thought about the things he'd said at the table. 'You were counting friendship and working together in all this a minute ago too, weren't you?'

He squeezed her fingers. 'Yes, I thought you'd started to figure it out then, but you're obviously not as bright as I thought you were. If you were, then you'd have known that the *we're friends* line was complete nonsense—we were never *just friends*.'

For the first time since she'd met him all those years ago, she told him the absolute truth, without trying to hide anything.

'Well, what the hell else was I supposed to say? And maybe I was scared this time to hope you might want more, so I let myself assume that you were talking about the ingredients for working together as parents.'

'I was, but that wasn't the only reason.'

'And that was the part I was scared to look for.'

He smiled affectionately. 'Why?'

She smiled equally as affectionately, her gaze dropping to the top of his polo-neck—the same one he'd worn the first night she'd set eyes on him again. 'I think you did break my heart the first time you left me. I just refused to let myself believe I'd cared that much, so I made myself hate you instead. I was a kid back then. But I'm an adult now and I know exactly how I feel. If I got involved with you and you left again it would kill me. Or at least the part of me that might ever care that much again.' She glanced up at him from beneath long lashes. 'And then last night, when you suggested that ridiculous half a marriage—'

His arm tightened on her waist, holding her closer against his large frame, his words coming out on a rushed grumble. 'That didn't come across the way it was meant to. But, in fairness, you've had me on the run for a while and it took some time for me to get things straight in my head. I hadn't even thought about how I'd tell you.'

'And it's all straight in your head now?'

'Yes, crystal clear. I know what I want.' He leaned in for another long kiss. 'The only problem would have been what you wanted, especially after the mess I made last night—though it was the first real hint I'd got that you might actually feel something back. So I enrolled Lizzie's help to make a better attempt at it.'

'You two are always going to gang up on me, aren't you?' Not that it seemed like such a bad thing to her, considering where they were.

'Only for the good stuff.'

The music changed to a different beat in the background but Kane ignored it and kept the same slow swaying and circling as he took a breath and smiled a more confident smile. 'So by any chance did you miss me as much as I missed you this last while, even though we spend so much of our time arguing?'

'I missed you so much it hurt. Thanks. And we've always argued—we're both stubborn. All that was missing this time was the making up.'

He stopped swaying, removing his arm, releasing her fingers, so that he could frame her face with his hands and lean in to look into her eyes, as Lizzie had done when she'd examined his eyes and figured things out. 'I *really* want us to make up.'

Her palms flattened against the erratic beat of his heart, her smile broad. 'I love you, you idiot.'

A look of relief washed over his rugged features, removing any hint of the frowns he'd worn at the beginning from his face, so that he looked like a twenty-one-year-old again when he grinned at her. He let go of her face and crushed her to him, groaning by her ear as she hugged him back. 'Good!'

She laughed joyously against his chest, only just allowing herself to really believe that he cared as much as he did because he hadn't been sure of her feelings, had he? No matter what he said or did, what confidence he'd given the impression he had, until she'd said the words to his face, with her heart and soul in her eyes, he hadn't been completely sure.

They weren't so very different, not really. And maybe a sub-conscious part of her had recognized that matching need to let someone in coupled with an opposing defensive shield of anger and resentment to hold that very person away. Fear of letting go. They both had it, didn't they?

It was why, when he had let go with Lizzie, a part of Rhiannon's soul had known the man he was and had fallen in love with that man. Lizzie may have felt like the only thing holding them together, but she was simply the result of a bond that had already been there, if in a more fragile, youthful state.

'I love you too, Mac.' He whispered it huskily into her ear, pressing his lips into her hair before he rested his head against hers and held her tight.

She turned her head to tell him, 'Once you say that to me, you can't ever take it back. I won't ever let you go. You need to know that. So be sure, take some time if you need to.'

'I don't need time.' He stepped back a little to look down into her eyes, the familiar teasing light dancing in a blue clouded with a cornucopia of deep emotion, his baritone voice stronger, more confident. 'But if *you* want to take some time to get used to this, then that's okay, just so long as you know we'll need to discuss the *never in a million years* thing. I have a ring in my pocket that I can't give you for Valentine's Day next year if we can't negotiate the million years down to a more reasonable time frame.'

Her eyes widened in surprise again, even though she knew he'd probably surprise her on a daily basis for the rest of her life. 'You bought a ring?'

'I did, not that long ago, around about the time I figured out what it was I wanted. Didn't actually plan on it, but I saw it and it felt right buying it.' His sensuous mouth swung upwards into a smile. 'And I'd like the chance to prove my point about still having *this* when we're old and grey and round-shouldered. So, what do I have to do to change your mind about the time line?'

Her eyes shone. *'W-ell…'*

He stepped back and took her hand, dragging her towards the door. 'All right, if that's what it's going to take, I don't have a problem with that. We just need to tell our daughter she's having an early night.'

Rhiannon laughed loudly, neatly sidestepping him and then tugging him close, still laughing, so that they were pressed against the door. She drew his head down for the same heated kiss they had shared the night before and took it up a level, matching every slide of his lips, every stroke of his tongue, every small nip and intake of breath, while allowing her hands the freedom to roam up his arms, to hold on to his shoulders, to bury deep into the hair she'd always loved so much.

Until he mumbled against her mouth, 'Million years.'

She mumbled back, 'I might have lied about that.'

He lifted his head, shook it in disapproval. 'That was bad of you. Right, we'll spend time getting used to each other, then. Do this right this time. Though, just so you know, there's definitely marriage in our future.'

'I might need to see that ring.'

'No—you'll see it when I ask you to marry me.'

'I might not like the ring.' She batted her lashes at him. 'Go on—just a little look. Because I agree that there's definitely marriage in our future. And I happen to think it doesn't need to be all that far away. So I need to see the ring.'

He smiled, shaking his head as he looked at the upturned palm she was waving at his side. 'The ring comes with the question.'

Rhiannon let everything she felt for him shine in her eyes as she wiggled her fingers. 'Still want to see it. Weddings take ages to organize.'

Kane's beautiful blue eyes widened. 'Are you saying if I ask you now you'll say yes?'

'Why don't you ask me and see what happens?'

'Once this ring is on your finger, it stays on.'

'Yes, I know that.'

With a deep chuckle, joy lighting up his face, he reached into his pocket and produced the ring, holding it in front of her face for her to see, his brows lifting in question.

Rhiannon stared at it in wonder for a long silent moment, loving that he had chosen a stone the same colour as his eyes. 'It's beautiful.' She whispered the words. 'So ask me.'

'You're never going to do what I expect you to do, are you?'

'No, but you already knew that. Ask me.'

He twisted the ring back and forth between his thumb and forefinger, the light catching on the stone so it appeared almost hypnotic, especially when accompanied by a husky baritone voice filled with emotion.

'Marry me. Make us officially the family we already are. I love you; I probably always have. And life's too short to waste time; I know that better than most.'

She grinned like an idiot, her eyes filling with tears at the same time. How could she not want to live a lifetime with this man?

'I love you. So it's yes—a *million* times yes.'

Kane leaned in and kissed her again, for a very long time, taking a moment to smile down at her heavy eyes and swollen lips before she informed him with a sigh, 'You do know you've just ruined your chances of ever topping this Valentine's Day ever again?'

He reached for her hand, grinning wickedly as he slipped the ring into place. 'I think you'll find that I'm capable of more than a card and a box of chocolates every other year or so. You wait and see.'

Rhiannon pulled him close again, knowing that at some point they really should go and tell Lizzie that her romantic meal had done the trick. But when they bumped back against the door a voice yelled from the hallway, 'Are you two kissing?'

His mouth hovering over hers, Kane's gaze rose to fix on the door. 'Yes, we are! So shoo!'

A loud celebration commenced beyond the door, gradually dimming as Lizzie went further up the hall.

They laughed together before his mouth lowered to hers again.

'And we're going to be kissing for a long, long while to make up for lost time. We've ten years' worth of making up to do. Happy Valentine's Day.'

THE GIRL
NEXT DOOR

CAROLINE ANDERSON

Caroline Anderson's nursing career was brought to an abrupt halt by a back injury, but her interest in medical things led her to work first as a medical secretary and then, after completing her teacher training, as a lecturer in Medical Office Practice to trainee medical secretaries. She lives in rural Suffolk with her husband, two daughters and assorted animals.

CHAPTER ONE

IT WAS a gloriously sunny day at the end of January, ridiculously hot for the time of year, and Ronnie was cleaning her windows.

She hated cleaning windows, especially with that bright and beautiful sun pouring through the glass and highlighting every streak. She sighed and attacked a particularly stubborn mark again, then paused, her eyes focusing beyond the windows to the car pulling up on the drive next door.

'Next door' was the other half of her house—or the hospital's, to be exact. It had been empty for a couple of weeks, and she had been awaiting the new arrivals with interest and a certain amount of trepidation. Would they be civilised? Noisy? Teenagers with too much bass and too little discipline, like the last lot? Or perhaps a screaming baby to keep her awake all night, just for a change!

Abandoning her thankless task, she settled her hip more comfortably on the window-sill, tucked a stray strand of blonde hair out of the way and watched as the car came to rest and disgorged its occupants in a flurry of shrieks and wails.

A man—possibly late thirties to forty—tall and lean, with darkish close-cropped hair and sunglasses perched on a slightly battered nose, straightened and shut his door, just as the passenger door behind him flew open and a little girl leapt out.

'Quickly, Daddy! Hurry up!' she begged, hopping from foot to foot.

'I'm hurrying—damn, which key?' she heard him mutter as he fumbled with a keyring, and the child hopped and begged and danced and her eyes grew wider.

Ronnie stifled a smile. Unless she missed her guess, somebody needed the loo—urgently!

'Hang on, moppet,' he said encouragingly. 'Ben, this way.'

Young Ben had other ideas. He was out in the quiet little cul-de-sac, kicking his football and ignoring the man.

'Ben. Now!'

He went, with an impressive show of reluctance that brought a smile to Ronnie's lips, and they trooped up the path to the front door and out of sight, leaving the car doors hanging open in the quiet street.

Without leaning out of the open window, Ronnie couldn't see them any more, but she could hear them through the party wall. She heard footsteps drumming up the stairs, a sobbing wail and a deep groan.

Oh, dear. She didn't make it. Had they got any spare clothes with them in the car?

It wasn't her business. Still, at least there were no teenagers or screaming babies.

With a resigned sigh, Ronnie squirted more special non-streak-miracle-window-cleaner-with-vinegar onto the glass and made a few more random stripes in the grime.

Useless.

'You shouldn't do that in the sun,' her neighbour on the other side called up.

Ronnie laughed and hung out of the window, glad of an excuse to stop again. 'I noticed. Too depressing.'

'Makes them streaky.'

'Meg, they *are* streaky. It just makes it show worse.'

Meg shot a glance at the next-door house. 'You've got new neighbours.'

'I saw. Jimmy'll be pleased—someone to kick a ball about with.'

'Mmm.' Meg looked at the house again, then came up closer. 'I wonder where the mother is.'

Ronnie had been wondering the same thing, but rather more quietly. 'Why don't you ask?' she said mildly, tucking another strand of hair behind her ear, and Meg looked horrified.

'Don't be *silly*!' she almost squeaked. 'It wouldn't be polite!'

And this is? Ronnie thought, stifling a laugh.

'Anyway, I've got to go out and fetch Jimmy from school. I'll let you do it.'

She got into her car and drove off in a mass of grinding gears and protesting tyres. Ronnie sighed. Not a natural driver, she thought with a grimace—just as you aren't a natural window cleaner. Oh, well. Not everybody was good at everything.

She gave one particularly bad streak another half-hearted swipe, and gave up. She'd go downstairs, put the kettle on and offer her new neighbours a drink.

Just out of neighbourliness.

Of course.

She might even be able to find a pair of little knickers or some trousers for the youngster next door. She was sure her niece had left something behind last time she'd stayed...

The doorbell chimed—a ghastly tune that Nick hoped he wouldn't have to tolerate for long—and he abandoned his mopping-up operation in the bathroom and ran downstairs. No doubt it was his brother with the van—and clothes, furthermore, so Amy didn't have to run around naked.

'Thank God you're here,' he began distractedly, swinging the door open, and then his eyes dropped, down from the place he'd expected his brother to be, down about a foot or more to a dainty elf with curious, bright green eyes and a smear of dirt on one cheek. She had blonde hair, streaky and curly, scraped back into a pony-tail, and some of it had escaped and was tickling her cheek.

'Hi,' she said, her voice deeper than he'd expected, low and soft and somehow musical. 'I'm Ronnie—I live next door. I've brought you something to eat and drink. I thought you were bound to be thirsty, and I expect the kids are starving. I know what moving's like, and I just bet the kettle will be the last thing you can find—'

She came to an abrupt halt, as if she realised she was running on, and Nick had to fight down the smile that was threatening to engulf his face.

It must have shown in his eyes, though, because she flushed slightly and gave a nervous little laugh. 'Are you going to take it, or are you on a diet?'

He did smile then. The thought of him being on a diet was just a farce. It didn't seem to matter what he ate, the last few years the weight had just fallen off him.

'Hardly,' he murmured, and took the hugely over-laden tray in his left hand, supporting it easily. 'Thank you.' He stuck the other one out in greeting, and she took it, her cool, slim fingers somehow tantalising in his warmer, firm grasp.

'I'm Nick,' he managed inanely, groping for his mind, 'and somewhere about the place are Ben and Amy. Come on in and meet them. We were waiting for my brother—he's bringing our clothes and bits and pieces in his van. And you're right, the kettle isn't here yet.'

She smiled, her eyes crinkling at the corners as if she did it often, and heat shot through him, catching him by surprise. He stood dumbstruck for a second, then, clearing his throat, he turned away and led her into the kitchen, setting the tray down on the rather tired worktop.

'The fruit cake is my mother's, but I won't be offended if you don't like it,' she was saying. 'There's some shortbread and chocolate biscuits as well, which I thought the children might prefer—oh, and by the way, I found these, and I had a feeling your daughter might need to borrow them.'

'Do you read minds?' he asked, bemused, staring as she pulled little clothes out of a carrier bag.

She laughed. 'No, just body language.'

She held out the tracksuit bottoms, and he took them and held them up, eyeing her over the top.

'They either belong to someone else, or you had a crisis with the washing.'

She laughed. 'My niece's. Am I right? Do you need them?'

He gave a wry grin. 'Thank you. I don't know how you knew, but—thank you.'

He took them upstairs, gave them to Amy and told her to put them on and come down. She was still sitting on the loo, sniffing, but the sight of the trousers and thence dignity encouraged her. She wiped her nose on the back of her hand and slid off the seat.

'Wash your hands,' he reminded her, and went back down to his visitor.

'Thanks,' he murmured, and then the door flew open again behind him, crashing against the worktop.

'Dad, the bathroom's gross—oh. Who are you?' Ben asked, grinding to a halt in the doorway and cocking his head on one side. He looked resentful and unhappy, and Nick sighed to himself.

'Ben, I'd like you to meet our new neighbour— Miss…?'

'Matthews—but Ronnie will do.'

'Ronnie? That's a boy's name,' Ben said scornfully, and Nick wanted to curl up—or strangle him.

He opened his mouth to correct the boy, but Ronnie had got there first, laughing softly. 'Odd, isn't it? But it knocks spots off Veronica, which is the alternative.'

Personally Nick thought Veronica was a very pretty name, but he wasn't about to get involved in this argument. Anyway, it dissolved before it really got going, because Ben spotted the chocolate biscuits and had to be restrained from taking a handful.

'There's apple juice or tea…'

'Juice, please,' he mumbled through a mouthful of biscuit. Nick stuck his head round the door and called his little daughter.

She came trailing down the stairs in tears again, her teddy dragging and bumping down the stairs behind her, and he scooped her into his arms and held her close.

'*Now* what's wrong, sweetheart?' he asked a little desperately.

'Ben said I can't have the yellow bedroom, but I *want* the yellow bedroom. I don't *want* the blue bedroom!' she hiccuped, and buried her face in his neck.

'We'll sort it out in a minute,' he promised, feeling helpless for what felt like the millionth time in the last four years. 'Come and meet Ronnie. She lives next door and she's brought us a drink and a biscuit.'

Her head lifted. 'Chocolate biscuits?'

'Uh-huh—or fruit cake. And juice.'

'Orange?'

'No, apple.'

'I want orange—' she began, but Ronnie cut her off.

'Oh, look, you're just in time for the last two choc-olate biscuits—and there's some of my special juice for big girls—are you big enough, I wonder, or should I go home and get baby orange?'

Her head was tipped on one side, eyeing Amy as-sessingly, and Nick felt his daughter straighten in his arms. She slid to the floor.

'Apple,' she said round her thumb.

'Sorry, I didn't hear that?'

'Apple, please,' she said, taking her thumb out, and Nick wondered if women were born with the gift of communicating with children or if men were just par-ticularly slow to learn.

Either.

Both.

She handed him a mug of tea, hot and steaming, with just the right amount of milk, and a plate groaning with a huge slab of cake.

'Wow,' he murmured, and took them, propping him-self up against the worktop and sinking his teeth into the cake with enthusiasm. The cheese roll he'd had for lunch seemed a heck of a long time ago, he thought as the flavours burst on his tongue.

'Oh, wow,' he murmured again, his eyes thanking her over the top of the plate.

She smiled contentedly and leaned back against the cupboards, small, neat hands cradling her mug so that steam rose in front of her face, fogging it slightly.

'It's cold in here,' he said, suddenly realising, and turned to the boiler. 'I wonder how it works.'

She put her tea down, flipped dials, clicked switches

and the boiler roared into life. 'It's been on tickover, to protect the pipes. The hospital usually does that. It's the same system as mine.'

'You could be a useful person to know,' he said with a grin, 'between the boiler and the fruit cake.'

She chuckled. 'You'll need to know all sorts of things—dustbin day, where the supermarket is, how to get to the corner shop, where the nearest decent Chinese take-away is, which pizza place will deliver— oh, do you want the milkman to call?'

'Yes!' Nick gave a bemused laugh. 'You wouldn't like to stick it all down on a bit of paper, would you? I'll only forget otherwise.'

'Consider it done.'

She shrugged away from the worktop and headed for the door. 'I'll get back to cleaning my windows. Ben, there's a boy on the other side of me called Jimmy. He'd be about your age. He's always outside playing football. Perhaps you'd like me to introduce you later.'

He nodded without enthusiasm. 'Don't suppose he's much good.'

'Probably not, but he's in the under-ten town squad. I expect they were short of talent.'

Ben's eyes widened with interest, and Nick watched Ronnie hide a smile.

Damn, she was an expert.

'I'll see you later—I'll bring you more tea when your brother gets here. How many of them will there be?'

'Just him.'

She nodded, poorly concealed curiosity in her eyes, but he didn't feel up to talking about Anna just now. Maybe not ever.

'Thanks,' he said gruffly. 'You've been very kind.'

She smiled again, a quick, fleeting smile, and then she was gone, the door closing softly behind her.

'I want the yellow bedroom,' Amy said stubbornly.

'Well, tough, I'm having it, I saw it first.'

'Only because I had to go to the loo!'

'Too bad. I'm the oldest, I get to choose. Isn't that right, Dad?'

Seconds out, round two hundred and ninety-six, he thought, and dredged up a smile.

'Let's go and have a look. Maybe I can paint the blue one—it's only for a little while.'

'Have you *seen* that *guy*?'

Ronnie looked at Kate's dreamy eyes and laughed. 'Which guy is that?'

'The new consultant—Sarazin. You should have seen him in Theatre—poetry in motion, Ronnie, I tell you. We had an emergency—an RTA, had a fight with a tree. His guts were a real mess. I don't know how we didn't lose him. We nearly did twice, but somehow he managed to sort him out. I've never seen anyone find a leak and plug it so quick.'

'Not quick enough. We had a queue of pre-ops sitting, waiting, while he tied knots in your RTA,' Ronnie told her.

'Oh, believe me, he's worth waiting for! What a star! And then, when it was over, he pulled down his mask and grinned, and he was streaked with blood—I swear, he looked like Bruce Willis at the end of *Die Hard*. Bloody, sweaty, sexy—I thought I was going to melt, just looking at him.'

Ronnie laughed again. 'You're a sad case, do you know that? How many times have you fallen for eyes over a mask?'

'Oh, it works without fail,' she agreed cheerfully,

'but it usually falls apart when they take the mask off. The magic just vanishes.'

'But not this time,' Ronnie guessed.

Kate grinned. 'Absolutely not! Wow. I wonder if his wife realises how damn lucky she is?'

Poor Kate. 'Married?' Ronnie said sympathetically.

'Well, he wears a ring. Might not mean anything, though. Lots of them play away. I might get lucky yet.'

Ronnie felt a chill. And some other woman—some innocent woman who foolishly believed she was loved and cherished—would be unlucky, and probably not for the first time. Ronnie ignored the little twinge of pain. It was only hurt pride, she reminded herself. She hadn't really known David Baker, so how could she have loved him? Kate yawned and stretched, and stood up. 'I'll see you round. Let me know what you think of God's gift when you've seen him.'

Ronnie chuckled. 'I will.'

She watched her irrepressible friend go, then checked her watch. Three-thirty. Time she went back to the ward. The delayed post-ops were due to return from Recovery any time soon, and she ought to be there. One day, she promised herself, she'd have time for a proper lunch-break, instead of snatching a slice of toast in the ward kitchen and surviving till her tea-break—if she even got one.

She drained the last of her tea and headed back, still thinking about the new consultant. So he was good, according to Kate. Well, she ought to know, she'd worked with Ross Hamilton for years, and he was excellent—so excellent he'd been head-hunted to lead a team in pioneering bowel surgery. If Kate thought the new man, Sarazin, was good, he *was* good.

She palmed the door out of her way, automatically

scanning the ward for anything that needed her attention, and her eyes skidded to a halt.

Blue theatre pyjamas, white boots, shoulders to die for—and close-cropped, dark-tending-to-blond hair on a head she was sure she recognised.

She went over to him, smile at the ready, and as he turned his eyes widened in surprise.

'Ronnie?' he murmured.

'Hello, Nick. Are you our new superstar?'

He looked confused.

'I've just been listening to a flattering report of your surgical skills,' she told him. 'If your name's Sarazin, that is.'

He coloured slightly. 'Wildly exaggerated, no doubt—and, yes, that's my name. So, what am I supposed to have done?'

'Your RTA. I gather you're very good at finding and plugging leaks, according to Kate.'

'Ah, Kate,' he said, nodding in understanding. 'She's pretty hot herself. Useful member of the team, she knows her stuff. I'm looking forward to working with her. She's an excellent scrub nurse.'

Ronnie felt a sharp and totally irrational stab of disappointment. 'So, your RTA. How is he?'

'Andy Graham? In ITU. He'll live to drive too fast again, I have no doubt. So, what brings you here?'

She laughed softly. 'I work here—it's my ward.'

He blinked, then seemed to notice her uniform and the badge that said, VERONICA MATTHEWS—WARD SISTER.

'Ah. I didn't see you here yesterday.'

'No, I had a day off. I'm sorry I missed you—did you get a guided tour?'

He nodded. 'Thanks—yes. I've left my registrar

closing, and I thought I'd just check up on my post-ops. Do you know where they are?'

'They're not back yet from Recovery,' the staff nurse told them.

Ronnie nodded confirmation. 'They weren't when I went for tea. They were delayed, of course,' she said with a trace of a smile, and he gave a rueful laugh.

'Yes. I'm sorry about that. The RTA was a little time-consuming, more so than I'd thought or I would have warned you.'

'That's OK.' She let the smile widen. 'Want a cuppa while you wait? You can find your way round a coffee-machine, I take it?'

He shook his head. 'Not coffee. It messes up my mind. I try and avoid it when I'm operating. Tea, though?' He looked hopeful, and she gave in. There was little that needed her attention before the post-ops started to come back down, and until they did she might as well make herself useful, getting to know her neighbour and colleague.

'Come on. Tea it is. I'll put the kettle on.'

Nick wondered if it was to be his destiny, having this beautiful young woman making him tea at regular intervals throughout his life. He followed her into the kitchen, marvelling at how she could manage to look slender and sexy and so downright appealing in such a sexless little number as that royal blue dress, then he came to his senses.

What was he thinking about? She was a colleague—and his neighbour, for heaven's sake! He had to live with this relationship for the next however long, and there was no way this sudden, unheralded and unbidden flicker of interest could be allowed to fan itself into a flame.

Never mind the roaring conflagration he could feel threatening his sanity.

Think of Anna, he thought. Remember her. Remember all of it.

The little flame flickered once and died, extinguished under the weight of all those memories.

'White, no sugar, right?'

Ronnie turned, his mug in her hand, and slopped tea over her fingers. Dear God, what had happened to his eyes? Where had that emptiness come from?

She gave a little yelp and put the mug down.

'You've burned yourself—here, let me.'

He took her hand in his, engulfing her wrist and holding it so her fingers were under the cold tap. Her thigh was pressed against his, her shoulder jutting into his side, and suddenly there was nothing in the tiny room but the splashing of the tap and the sizzling awareness that threatened to set fire to her hip and shoulder and hand. She eased away from him, smiling distractedly and turning off the tap.

'It's fine now,' she assured him, and her voice sounded squeaky and unused. She grabbed her tea and propped her hips against the worktop, getting as far away from him as she could in the minuscule ward kitchen.

'So—how did your move go? All settled in?'

'Yes, thanks. I finally managed to stop the children fighting by promising to paint Amy's bedroom yellow.'

Ronnie remembered the damp, wounded eyes of his little girl, and the sulky recalcitrance of the boy, and wondered again about their mother. 'Did your wife arrive safely?' she asked, and then could have kicked herself because that bleak emptiness flashed again in his eyes, just for a second.

'I don't have a wife. She…died.'

So few words. Such a simple statement. So much grief.

Ronnie felt a huge pain in her chest, the ache of loss for those poor motherless children. 'I'm so sorry,' she whispered. She cleared her throat. 'I had no idea. I do apologise.'

He smiled awkwardly. 'I should have told you.'

'When? On Monday, when I brought you the tea? "I'm Nick and, by the way, my wife's dead"?'

The words hung in the air between them.

Ronnie closed her eyes and shook her head. 'Look, I'm sorry. I'm—I don't know what to say.'

'There's not much left to say, Ronnie. It was four years ago. We're pretty used to it. I imagine everyone's bound to be curious.' He looked around the room. 'I don't suppose there's anything to eat in here? I didn't get any breakfast, and we didn't have time for lunch.'

'Toast?' she offered.

'Please. Lots. I'm starving.'

She put four slices in the toaster, drank the tea that tasted like dishwater and left him to it, promising to call him if the patients arrived.

Nick didn't see Ronnie again to speak to. By the time his patients came back down she was busy with an emergency admission, and he was taken round by the staff nurse.

Odd, the sensation of disappointment.

Odd, and a little disconcerting. He couldn't allow himself to be interested. He had to concentrate on the kids, settling them in to school, painting the damn bedroom, finding a house—the list was endless, time-consuming and left no room for a liaison.

Not that he would remember where to start.

He glanced at the clock on the wall over the nursing

station, and frowned. Were the kids all right with the woman he'd arranged would pick them up and take them home? She was the mother of a boy in Ben's class. Would they like her? Would her kids be all right with them? He wished he'd had time to meet her, but the days had run away with him and they'd only managed to move on Monday instead of last weekend, and he'd picked them up himself yesterday.

Oh, Lord, so many new hazards. Please, God, let it all work out, he thought helplessly.

Then the phone rang, and someone looked up at him.

'Mr Sarazin?'

He nodded, a sick feeling in his stomach.

'Phone call—sounds like a child.'

He almost snatched the phone. 'Hello?'

'Dad, it's Ben. Come and get us *now*.'

He sighed inwardly and stabbed his fingers through his too-short hair. 'Ben, I can't.'

'You must. She's awful.'

'Where are you?'

'Mrs Livermore's. She's in the garden—she doesn't know I'm on the phone. Dad, she's horrid,' he hissed, and then played his ace. 'Amy's crying.'

He stabbed his fingers through his hair again, and rolled his eyes. 'Half an hour, Ben. I'll be there in half an hour. Hang on.'

Ronnie could hear the tears and pleading through the wall, but there was nothing she could do. She couldn't just interfere with every moment of their lives.

She had to leave them alone to sort themselves out. It was no good feeling sorry for them, they had to cope alone. They'd been doing it for four years—more than half of Amy's life, for heaven's sake. It was hardly new to them!

She couldn't interfere. She knew from her own experience that it didn't work.

But she could cook...

Humming contentedly under her breath, she got down her recipe books, flicked through them and stabbed her finger at the answer.

'Chocolate fudge brownies. Excellent.'

She beat and whipped and greased and spread, and by the time she'd finished the oven was hot and the tray of brownies went straight in. Now, a main course. Nothing too elaborate, but something kids would eat.

Toad in the hole. Tasty sausages, fluffy Yorkshire pudding, lots of gravy and bright, pretty vegetables—carrots and broccoli, perhaps?

She was just assembling the ingredients when the doorbell rang. Grabbing a tea towel, she scooped hair out of her eyes, scrubbed her hands and opened the door.

'Are you busy?'

She smiled up into Nick's distracted eyes, more than a little delighted to see him—them, she corrected, dropping her eyes and grinning at the children. 'Never too busy to see my friends. Come on in, I'll put the kettle on. I'm just going to cook supper. I don't suppose you'd care to join me? I get awfully sick of eating by myself.'

'We were going to have pizza,' Ben said sulkily, glaring at his father.

'I hate pizza,' Amy whined, obviously carrying on the same argument. 'I want chicken and mushroom pie and chips.'

'Yuck.'

'Kids, stop it.' Nick met Ronnie's eyes over their heads, and she saw a kind of longing in his face which she quite understood. 'We couldn't impose.'

She gave her most disarming grin. 'Yeah, you could. I'm having toad in the hole, but it's silly making it for one—and I've cooked chocolate fudge brownies so we could have them for pudding.'

Even Ben looked interested, despite his best efforts.

'It's cool with me, I suppose,' he said with a huge attempt at nonchalance, and Amy just grinned.

'I love toad in the hole—and chocolate brownies. Can I have lots?'

'Just enough to fill you up and not enough to make you sick,' Ronnie told her. It was obviously the right answer, because they nodded and headed for the sitting room at her suggestion.

A frown flickered in Nick's eyes as the kids disappeared. 'Ronnie, it isn't fair. You set this up,' he said accusingly.

She smiled innocently. 'How? You came to me, remember?'

He pulled a face, and without thinking she went up on tiptoe and kissed his cheek. 'Lighten up, soldier. No one's an island. It's only supper, for goodness' sake!'

He stood frozen for a moment, then a wry smile twisted his lips and he nodded. 'OK. Thanks. What can I do?'

'Peel carrots,' she said promptly, and he groaned.

'I knew there was a catch. They always say there's no such thing as a free lunch!'

Ronnie just smiled, handed him the potato peeler and a bag of carrots and wondered what it was about a perfectly ordinary man that made him so incredibly, irresistibly sexy. The feel of his cheek, roughened with stubble, faintly scented with something masculine and unravelling...

'So, was there a reason for the visit, or did you just need a referee for the pizza v. pie-and-chips argument?'

she asked, squashing out the lumps in the batter and trying not to think of the scent of his skin and the rasp of his end-of-day shadow against her lips.

He groaned. 'I'd almost forgotten. The child-minder I'd arranged for them after school turns out to be related to Godzilla. I don't suppose you know anyone else in the area who could bring them home from school and tolerate them until I get back?'

'Meg,' she said promptly, meeting his anguished eyes. 'My neighbour—Jimmy's mum. She's a registered child-minder. She looks after two little ones during the day for a teacher, and takes them back to Mum when she collects Jimmy. She could manage, I expect. What school are they at?'

'The local primary—Northgate Avenue.'

'Brilliant. So's Jimmy. I'll ask her.'

He shifted uncomfortably. 'I don't suppose you could ask her now? They refuse to go back there—I had a phone call at work from Ben. He'd sneaked into the hall to ring me while the woman was bringing in her washing. Thank God he didn't get caught. I was scared to death of her when I met her this evening. She probably would have skinned him alive.'

'Who recommended her?' Ronnie asked, amazed that he would leave his children with someone he'd never met.

'The school. I would have been here a couple of days earlier and met her and moved in sensibly, but Ben was in the school football team and wouldn't leave without playing in the match on Saturday, then on Sunday Amy was sick—hence the rush.' He cocked his head on one side and grinned appealingly. 'So—would you?'

Lord, what gorgeous eyes...

'Would I...?'

'Ask her? I need to sort something out for tomorrow.'

She threw more flour and another egg into the batter, beat them in and told him to peel more carrots. 'I'll ask them for supper,' she said and, without waiting for the argument, she slid past him, nipped out of the front door and stuck her head round the open door of Meg's house.

'Anybody home?'

'Yeah—the burglars. What do you want?'

She grinned and went in, propping up the kitchen doorway. 'I've got a job for you.'

Meg groaned. 'Another one? What is it this time? Don't tell me—cleaning your damn windows.'

Ronnie laughed. 'No. Actually, it's a real job, with money. Nick's looking for a child-minder after school to bring the kids home and sit on them till he finishes work.'

Meg brightened visibly at the prospect of a job. 'And the holidays?'

Ronnie shrugged. 'Probably. Don't say yes or no—just come for supper.'

'I've just put a shepherd's pie in the oven.'

'How long ago?'

Meg shrugged. 'Two minutes? Less, probably.'

'So sling it in the fridge and have it tomorrow. Go on. It's toad in the hole and chocolate brownies—and I thought it would be good to see how the kids interact before we said anything to them.'

Meg sighed and reached for her oven gloves. 'Anybody ever told you you're a manipulative little pest?'

Ronnie just grinned and headed back over the lawn, picking her way between Jimmy's abandoned bike and the remains of a broken skateboard.

'They're coming,' she told Nick economically.

His shoulders dropped about a foot, and he seemed to unravel before her eyes. She reached into the fridge.

'How about a glass of wine?' she said with a smile.

CHAPTER TWO

'So, HOW did the children get on with Meg?'

Nick's mouth kicked up in a grin. 'Brilliant. She's a star. They loved her to death, Ben and Jimmy got on like a house on fire and she spoiled Amy to bits. I had to bribe them to come home!'

Ronnie chuckled. 'Successful, then. That's good.'

'Excellent—and thank you. I owe you.'

She laughed. 'I'll bear it in mind, next time I want anything heavy moved.'

'Always a catch,' he said with a smile.

'Of course. There's no such thing—'

'—as a free lunch,' they chorused, and laughed together. Then the laughter died, leaving a lingering smile in their eyes, and Ronnie thought she'd drown in those stunning, smoky blue depths. Oh, Lord, she thought, he's gorgeous. I could love this man so easily...

'So, how are my post-ops?' he asked, his eyes still locked on hers, and she dragged her own eyes away and hauled in the first breath for what felt like several minutes.

'Fine, I believe. Let's go and see.'

She headed down the ward to the first bay, which contained yesterday's patients. 'Well, they're all still alive,' she said softly, scanning the beds, and he chuckled.

'I've started on the right foot, at least.'

'So it seems. How's your RTA?'

'He should be in here in the next few days—they're

25

short of beds in ITU so they'll kick him out soon, I expect. He's progressing.'

He picked up the notes from the end of the first bed and smiled at the patient. 'Mrs Dobbs. How are you feeling?'

'Oh, marvellous,' the elderly lady said, returning his smile with a twinkle that lit up her lined face. 'I thought I'd feel much worse than this.'

'That's the joy of keyhole surgery,' he told her. 'Just a couple of little snips instead of a great big hole. Much easier to get over.' He bent over his handiwork, nodded and straightened, covering her gently. Ronnie thought how, often, it was the big men who were the most gentle, as if they'd had to learn the hard way how to moderate their strength.

They moved on down the ward, chatting and laughing with the patients as Nick checked his handiwork and the chart at the end of each bed, then they moved on to the pre-ops, the patients who were in for surgery the following day.

One was Mrs Gray, a young woman, only thirty-two, who was in for surgery to remove gallstones.

Nick perched on the edge of the bed and explained to her how he was going to make just three incisions, one for the laparoscope, the camera which enabled them to see what they were doing, and the other two for the instruments which would remove the gall bladder and the cause of all her problems.

'And then you'll be right as rain,' he assured her.

'I hope I will,' she told him drily, 'because I don't know myself at the moment. I've never been this heavy, and I've tried every diet under the sun. I've done the chocolate diet, and the cabbage soup diet, and the banana diet—'

'Have you ever tried just eating normal, healthy food

in smaller quantities, with a lower fat content, and avoiding snacking? There's a lot of evidence building up that it's faddy diets and disrupted eating patterns that cause gallstones. All the fair, fat, fertile and forty nonsense is just coincidence, and women with the problem are getting younger and younger.'

She frowned. 'So you really think it's just my funny diets that have caused it?'

'Possibly. Anyway, I'll ask Sister Matthews to arrange for a dietician to come and have a chat with you, and we'll see you in Theatre tomorrow.'

They finished the ward round, and as they passed the little kitchen Nick looked at Ronnie hopefully. 'Don't suppose the kettle's on, is it? I haven't got time to get down to the canteen, and they only have vile coffee out of a machine down in Outpatients.'

'Poor boy,' Ronnie crooned sympathetically, and ducked as he swiped at her. 'Oh, if you must. We're quiet for once, and I could do with a cuppa.'

She felt him close behind her as they entered the tiny room, and the subtle, tingling awareness of him made the hair stand up on the back of her neck. He was so close, and yet not close enough—

What was she thinking about? She had to work with him! There was no way she could allow her mind to run off on such a track—especially as it was so one-sided. After all, he was still hung up on his wife, and she was just plain, ordinary little Veronica Matthews, the girl next door.

Then she turned round, and his eyes locked with hers, and the breath jammed in her chest and nearly choked her.

'Um—tea or coffee?' she asked after an endless silence that neither of them seemed able to break.

'Tea,' he murmured, and it sounded like a caress. He

cleared his throat and looked away. 'Um—tea, please,' he repeated, a bit more firmly, as if he was struggling to sound businesslike.

The kettle was half-full and hot—to Ronnie's huge relief. The thought of standing there in that minute room while the kettle boiled from scratch, with him inches away sending out shock waves, was too hideous to consider.

Well, not hideous. Perhaps too tantalising. Too inviting. Too tempting...

Anyway, she'd probably misread the signals. Either that or it was just sexual frustration. After all, when did a widower with two young children and a demanding career find time for a private life?

In the ward kitchen?

She choked down the hysterical laugh and yanked two mugs off the draining-board. She was being ridiculous. He wasn't really interested—and neither was she. Not if she had any sense. What did she have to offer him?

She almost laughed again. Nothing that he'd want. Nothing that would offer what he needed. Unless she'd drastically misread his eyes, all he was after was a sexual aspirin, and she wasn't in the market for that sort of affair.

Any sort.

Hell, she wouldn't know where to start—

'I don't take it that strong,' he said softly, making her jump, and she realised she'd put two tea bags in his mug and was mashing the living daylights out of them.

'Sorry,' she muttered, and started again, because she'd managed to mangle one so badly it had burst.

Fortunately a junior stuck her head round the door and gave her an apologetic grin. 'Vicky says can you

CAROLINE ANDERSON 29

come? We've got an emergency coming up for Mr Henderson and he's due here any second.'

'Sure.'

She slid the almost-respectable mug of tea across the worktop to Nick and threw him a distracted smile. 'Sorry, you'll have to drink it by yourself,' she said, and fled.

Nick felt down in a way he hadn't felt down for ages. The kids were finally in bed, and he opened the French door in the sitting room and stepped out into the dreary little garden. It was as cold as charity, but he didn't care. He didn't really notice, except for his feet, but the cold soaked up through his socks and his toes turned to ice.

Still he didn't go inside. It was too damned empty inside, empty and lonely and cold in a way the temperature itself couldn't compete with.

Go and talk to Ronnie.

He shook his head. It was a lousy idea. Most of his lousy ideas just popped into his head like that, but he never heard a voice telling him to get off his butt and go out and have fun. Just crazy things—like this job. He'd been idly flicking through a professional publication, scanning the jobs without interest, and this one had caught his eye.

Near Anna's parents, yet far enough away not to crowd any of them, a consultancy that had sounded exciting, although he hadn't been sure he'd been ready for such a big leap and huge commitment, with the children to consider—still, the advert had tantalised him.

No, he'd thought. Not yet. He'd dropped the magazine, and then this damn fool streak in him had interfered.

Apply for it.

I can't do it, he'd thought, but he had, and now he was here, away from all his old friends, alone. He hated it.

But he didn't need to go and see Ronnie. The way he felt about her, he'd get himself in all kinds of hot water if he went round there now. He liked to think it was Anna's voice he heard, but he knew better. There was no way Anna would send him round into another woman's arms!

Or would she? She'd been most insistent before she'd died that he shouldn't lock himself up like a monk. Maybe it was her, after all?

In which case, why was she never there when he really needed her? When the kids were sick and he didn't know what to do?

No, it was just his damn fool mind playing tricks and tormenting him. He felt tears sting his eyes. The voice wasn't Anna. She was gone, truly gone, for good.

'I miss you,' he murmured. 'Life's just too damned empty.'

Go and see Ronnie, his alter ego prodded. *She'll cheer you up.*

'No!'

He heard her door open on the other side of the fence, and the clatter of her dustbin, and the ache inside him seemed to ease. It was pathetic, he thought disgustedly, how pleased he was to have her near. Then she paused, invisible behind the fence panel. 'Nick?' she said softly.

'Hi.' Did his voice really sound that eager? Dear God.

'I thought you might be there. I can see your door open.' There was silence for a second, then she murmured, 'Are you OK?'

He nodded. 'Yeah, I'm fine. Just a little…'

'Lonely?'

He laughed, a soft, strangled sound without humour. 'Just for a change.'

He heard her settle herself against the fence, just beside him, and he stood on the step and leaned against his doorframe, just inches away from her, wishing he was nearer. 'Fancy a coffee?' she offered. 'I've just made myself one—you could have it over the fence, if you're worried about leaving the children.'

Or you could come round, he almost said, but he stopped himself in time. 'Thanks—that would be great.'

She disappeared, returning in a moment. 'Here.'

He looked up, and her slim, pale hand appeared over the top of the fence, a mug clutched precariously in it. He took it, their fingers brushing, and heat shot through him. He jerked, sloshing boiling coffee down the inside of his sleeve, and he swore under his breath and blew on his wrist.

'You all right?'

'Slopped it,' he told her economically.

'Whoops. Sorry.'

'I'm fine.' He settled down on the step, his feet curled against each other to keep warm, and looked up at the stars. 'It's a beautiful, clear night. I can see all the way up to heaven.'

Was it something in his voice? Or just the words, or perhaps the fact that he was sitting outside, freezing to death, for no good reason. Whatever, Ronnie seemed to tune in to him.

'You must miss her,' she said with unerring accuracy, after a moment's silence.

Nick swallowed, surprised that she'd read him so easily, wondering if he could talk about it. About Anna.

'Yes—yes, I do. I miss having someone to share things with, and it grieves me that she's missing so much of the children.'

'Tell me about her,' Ronnie asked, and he found he could. He told her things he'd never told anyone, things only Anna and he had known about. Maybe it was having the fence between them, almost like being in a confessional, so they could hear but not see, or perhaps it was because she was just the girl next door, or maybe it was something to do with the gentle caring in her voice and the echo of loneliness he heard there.

Whatever, he told her.

'We met when we were eighteen,' he started. 'We went to the same university. She was doing dentistry, I was doing medicine, and a lot of our lectures coincided. We spent more and more time together, and after a few months we became lovers.'

He paused, remembering the first time—the laughter, the wonder, the tears of joy, and then the beautiful voyage of discovery as they learned about each other. Amazingly, he found he could share it with Ronnie— not the intimate details, but the feelings, the love they'd felt grow.

'She was my best friend,' he went on, remembering, too, the times he'd come home and cried, after he'd started his clinical work and come face to face with the reality of death. He told Ronnie about that as well, and about the mistake he'd made which had nearly cost someone her life.

'She kept me sane. I don't know what I would have done without her. We were married at twenty-one, but we didn't think about children until we were twenty six and I was an SHO. She had Ben, and then two years later she had Amy—'

He broke off, remembering how happy they'd been.

Then, just a few short weeks later, it had all fallen apart. He heard the flatness in his voice, the detachment that always came when he talked about the end.

'She'd had mastitis with Ben. Then, after Amy, she felt a lump. Not really tender, but she put it down to mastitis again. By the time she realised it wasn't and said something, it was too late. She had a mastectomy, radiotherapy, chemo—they threw the lot at her, because she was only just thirty, and she went through hell, but it didn't work. She died a year later of secondaries—metastatic carcinoma of the lungs, liver and spine. Ben was four, Amy was two, I was thirty-one— and Anna was dead.'

He stopped, running out of words, feeling again the frustration of knowing that he could do nothing—he, a doctor, trained to save life, had missed the lump, missed the symptoms, missed everything until it had been too late.

'I'm sorry,' Ronnie said, her voice muffled behind the fence.

Nick blinked and stared up at the stars. Was she up there? She deserved to be. He didn't know. He didn't understand death. Even after he'd held Anna's lifeless body in his arms, he still hadn't been able to understand. Now he could hardly remember her, but the gap where she'd been still yawned in his life.

He was in danger of wallowing in self-pity, he thought disgustedly. It was Anna who'd lost everything, not him. He stood up and thrust the mug over the fence.

'Thanks for the coffee, Ronnie. I'll see you tomorrow.'

She took the mug, her fingers touching his again, warm and gentle. He took his hand away and went inside, closing the door softly. Ronnie didn't need him.

Ronnie went into the kitchen at the front of her house, with the hall between her and Nick, and shut the door firmly. She'd been a fool to go out there. She'd seen him from the upstairs window, standing alone in the garden, his shoulders slumped, his head hanging. She'd known it was asking for trouble, but she couldn't walk away from his loneliness any more than she could stop breathing.

Still, to hear him talk about Anna, to hear the love in his voice, and then the stark despair when he told of the end—what was it like to love so much, and to lose that love?

A ragged sob rose in her throat, then another. She turned on the taps, tuned the radio to a rock station and sagged into a chair, rested her head on her arms and howled.

Then she got up, washed her face, blew her nose hard and turned off the noise. Silly. She'd have to get a grip. There was no room for her in his life, and the last thing he'd want was her pity.

She changed into clean jeans and a jumper, grabbed her gym bag and headed for the door. It was late, but the gym didn't close till ten. She'd go and thrash herself around on the equipment for an hour and get him out of her system...

Nick could feel the heat of the lights getting to him. He rubbed his forehead against his shoulder and stretched, easing out the kinks in his back and neck. It was the last op of the morning, and he was tired and ready for lunch.

'Right, I'm going to give you a chance to see what you can do,' he said to Sue Warren, his SHO. 'We're going to make three incisions—here, here and here...'

He indicated. 'And then we'll look and see what we're dealing with.'

He stood back and let the young woman take his place, and over the top of his mask he saw Kate, the scrub nurse, wink slightly in approval.

At least, he hoped it was. He had a horrible feeling he was wrong. He cleared his throat and switched his attention to the operation. 'Right, a little bit farther over—that's it. Now, nice, light, firm strokes with the scalpel—remember we're going for keyholes here, not huge great incisions you can get your arm through.'

'There was a programme on TV about vets,' the anaesthetist mused, checking his instruments and readings with the lazy confidence of long practice. 'There were two vets, one each side of a conscious cow, trying to rearrange her stomach through a hole in each of her flanks. They were shaking hands through the cow's insides while she just stood there and ignored it all.'

'Oh, gross,' Kate said, and shuddered.

'You suggesting we should try it on the patients?' Nick said with a chuckle. 'Now, stand still, Mrs X, we're just going to see if we can find your stomach—'

'How do I do the next one?' the SHO asked, her voice a little tense. Nick forced himself to concentrate on her.

'Same, but different angle—like that. Excellent. Now, this lady's been suffering from intermittent colic. What do you suppose that would indicate?'

'Lots of small gallstones?'

'Yes, most likely. Some people have literally hundreds of tiny, gritty calculi, others have just one huge rock that totally blocks the gall bladder. I suspect this will be somewhere in between.'

Nick worked his shoulder round again. It was aching—no doubt from painting Amy's room last night. Still, at least it was yellow now instead of blue—even if she had had to camp on her brother's floor for the night while it dried.

He looked at the TV monitor, now showing a picture of the inside of their patient. 'Right, you see that dark red mass? That's the liver. Where do you need to go to look for the gall bladder?'

'Um—here?' the SHO suggested, moving the probe carefully towards the right area.

'Good. Let's find out what's inside.'

The operation proceeded without incident, to the SHO's relief, and Nick's prediction that there would be several small stones proved correct.

'We'll put them in a bottle for her—she can have them on the mantelpiece as a trophy,' Nick said with a chuckle. 'Right, would you like to close for me, please?' He watched her finish, then he stepped back, stripped off his gown and gloves and dropped them in the bin on the way through to the changing room.

He took time to shower and clean himself up, even though he was starving, but he had a clinic and they'd run over because his SHO had been naturally cautious. Damn. He probably wouldn't have time for lunch.

He palmed the door out of the way and almost fell over Kate.

'Sorry,' he apologised, catching her elbows to steady her.

'Don't apologise—actually, I was waiting for you, but I wasn't expecting you to be in such a hurry. I've got a favour to ask you.'

He resisted the urge to look at his watch, but his stomach growled loudly. 'Is it quick?'

'We could chat over lunch,' she suggested, and he felt a sinking feeling in his gut.

'No time, really,' he lied guiltily. 'Will it keep till Monday?'

She shook her head, her eyes assessing him. 'It's actually about next weekend—Saturday night. It's the hospital's League of Friends Valentine Ball. My escort can't come. I've got a spare ticket. I wondered if you'd care to come with me.'

He looked into her eyes again and recognised the look for what it was. Oh, hell. 'Um—well, I'm very flattered, Kate, but—ah—the thing is, I—um—I'm already taking someone,' he finished on a flash of inspiration.

Her face fell slightly in the brief millisecond before she slid a mask into place. Damn. He didn't want to hurt or alienate her, but he had very strict rules, and they precluded tangling with workmates.

'Not to worry. No doubt I'll see you there—save me a dance.'

He forced a smile. 'My pleasure. I'll see you on Monday.'

He fled, wondering how on earth he could get himself out of this mess, and then inspiration struck. 'Ronnie,' he said, and almost crumpled with relief.

'Help me.'

Ronnie looked up into Nick's laughing, frantic eyes and felt a bubble of happiness tickle her throat. 'Give me one good reason why I should.'

He closed his eyes and groaned. 'I mean it, Ronnie. I've got myself in a mess.' He looked round them at the crowded ward. 'Is there somewhere we can go?'

She was busy, but not too busy. Besides, her curiosity was piqued. 'The kitchen?'

'This is becoming a habit,' he said with a sexy, endearing grin that made her want to hurl herself at him and hug him. She grabbed the kettle instead.

'Tea?'

'No time. Listen—um.' He scratched his head, clearly at a loss, and Ronnie put the kettle down and waited. 'Ah, it's—uh—how well do you know Kate?'

'The scrub nurse?'

He nodded, his mouth twisting ruefully. Oh, dear.

'Fairly well. We aren't friends, exactly. I shared a flat with her when I first moved up here. Let's just say—we're different. Why?'

He heaved a sigh. 'It's the Valentine Ball next Saturday, apparently. She...' He scrubbed a hand round the back of his neck, looking uncomfortable. 'She told me her escort can't make it, so she's got a spare ticket and would I like to go with her.'

Ronnie shrugged, feeling a wash of something suspiciously like jealousy. 'So go.'

He rolled his eyes. 'Ronnie, she's a barracuda. I can't go with her. Anyway, I panicked. I told her I was already taking someone.'

'Well, that's all right, then.'

'No, Ronnie, it isn't all right. I'm not taking anyone—but I can't lie. I have to work with her every day.'

'So where do I come in?' she asked, wondering what he was getting round to, and rather afraid she already knew.

'Will you come with me?' he asked, confirming her fears. 'Just to rescue me? I have to go now that I've said I am.'

'So you want me to go with you just so you don't lose face?' she asked with a pang of regret.

'No! To hell with losing face. That's the last of my worries. No, it's Kate. Ronnie, I've got to put an end to her flirting. It's driving me nuts. If she thinks there's someone else, she'll leave me alone. It's one reason I still wear my ring—like garlic, to ward off evil spirits and predatory scrub nurses!'

Ronnie laughed in spite of herself. 'That's too subtle for Kate. She thought you were married and it didn't worry her. She was still keen to have a go. I can't think that you taking me to the ball will put her off.'

'But she's a friend—!' he began, and Ronnie laughed.

'And all's fair in love and war. She'd steal you from me without a flicker of emotion. She's only into one thing, and permanence doesn't feature. You'll have to tell her you're not interested.'

He stared at her in amazement. 'And that will work?'

She shrugged. 'Oh, yes. She won't waste energy on you if she knows it's futile. It's no good being subtle with Kate, she doesn't understand it. You have to be blunt.'

'Blunt.'

Ronnie nodded.

'Fine.' He heaved a sigh and scrubbed his hand through his hair, tousling the short strands and making it stick up. 'So, now we've got Kate out of the way, what do you suggest I do with these?' He pulled two bright red, heart-shaped tickets out of his pocket and held them up in front of her face.

She smiled wryly. 'Find someone to go with?'

He lowered the tickets and met her eyes searchingly. 'Do you already have an escort?'

Her heart thumped and pattered. 'I wasn't going.'

'Will you come with me? Since I've bought the tickets.'

'You may as well use them,' she agreed, wondering if her heart would go back to its normal rhythm in the end or if he'd have to resuscitate her. 'I gather it's quite a good do—the food's supposed to be excellent.'

'So you will come?'

She looked back into his eyes, and knew her heart was finished. 'Yes, I'll come,' she said, and wondered if her voice sounded husky and seductive to him, or if it was just her imagination. She hoped so, or he was going to think she was just as bad as Kate!

'You dark horse!'

Ronnie jumped guiltily and looked up at Kate. 'Oh—hi. What do you mean?'

Kate, grinning broadly and utterly unabashed, dropped into the chair opposite in the coffee-lounge, propped her feet on the low table and eyed Ronnie over her knees. 'Sarazin—the ball.'

She felt colour crawl up her throat. 'Oh. That.'

'Yes, that. Come on, don't play the innocent! When did you meet him?'

'Monday.'

'Monday! You didn't tell me you knew him on Wednesday!'

She smiled awkwardly. 'I didn't know I did. He moved in next door—I gave him a cup of tea, and then I had a day off yesterday.'

'And you've grabbed him for the ball before the rest of us got a look-in. Well, I must say, if it was anyone else I'd be irritated, but it's high time you had a fling.'

'It's only a ball…'

'Yeah, and I'm Santa Claus! It's the *Valentine* Ball, stupid! Do you know how romantic and sexy they are? The music is enough to get a eunuch interested—every last damn love song, every smoochy number they can lay their hands on—and you're going to be dancing with Nick Sarazin! Dear God. I could be *so-o-o* jealous!'

Ronnie laughed a little breathlessly. 'Smoochy?' she said, panic fluttering in her chest. Oh, lawks. Smoochy. Sexy. Romantic. She was already like an unravelled ball of string, without sexy music and Nick's warm, hard body to turn her into knots.

Damn. Oh, well, it was only a couple of hours. Even she could survive that.

Maybe…

'Daddy, I want *my* bed. I don't like this bed.'

Nick sighed and paused in the act of reinstating Amy's newly decorated bedroom. 'Sweets, it's only for a little while, till we find a house to buy.'

'Let's go and look,' she said firmly, turning round and running downstairs, her teddy clutched in her arms. He followed slowly, wondering how to deal with this. He didn't know anything about the town, where to look, where the estate agents were—anything.

'Amy, not this weekend, love. There isn't time.'

'There *is*,' she said, her chin jutting just like her mother's.

Go and ask Ronnie about estate agents.

He ignored the voice. He could do without throwing himself at Ronnie. Life was complicated enough since he'd rashly asked her to the ball. 'We have to pick up Ben from Jimmy's in a minute—'

'So get him. He can come.'

Nick sat down on the bottom stair and met Amy's determined little eyes. 'I was going to do all the legwork on my own, getting the details and that sort of thing. It's dreadfully boring.'

'I don't mind. I want a new house.'

He sighed again and stood up. 'OK, we'll go and

see if we can find any agents and get a few details, but I don't want you butting in when I'm talking to them, OK? No comments from the peanut gallery, or we'll come home. All right?'

She nodded. He wasn't fooled, but at least he'd laid down the ground rules. Now to find Ben and convince him.

'I don't *want* to go!'

Ronnie paused in her frantic scrubbing of the once-white resin sink and peered through the steamy window. Ben and Nick were standing on the path by her front lawn, hands on hips, nose to nose almost, Nick with his head ducked to Ben's height, Ben with his chin jutted and looking just like Amy in a strop.

She dropped the cloth, rinsed her hands and dried them, never taking her eyes off the scene for a moment. A slow, amused smile played over her face. Father and son facing off, she thought with a chuckle.

'I want to stay with Jimmy,' Ben was saying. 'I don't want to move to some crummy house in the middle of nowhere. I like it here. I'm not going!'

Move? *Move?* Ronnie felt a sick wave of disappointment wash over her. She didn't want them to move either. In a few short days she'd got very used to them next door—hearing their voices through the paper-thin walls, watching their comings and goings—looking out for Nick when he didn't know she was there.

He slept on the other side of her bedroom wall, the head of his bed against the head of hers. She heard him come to bed at night, and sometimes she heard him get up again during the night.

He didn't sleep well, and Amy sometimes seemed to wake.

Well, sometimes…! In the four nights they'd been

there it had happened twice. That was fifty per cent. A sample of four nights was a little small for solid statistics, but she had the definite feeling that Nick really didn't sleep very well, and the night before last she'd thought she'd heard him cry out in his sleep.

She wrapped her arms around her waist and hugged herself. Just thinking about him made her arms ache emptily. Crazy. She shoved a loose strand of hair out of her eyes, picked up the cloth and scrubbed the sink again with renewed vigour.

So what if they were going to move? Of course they were. Everyone always did, and if she wasn't such a sad, sad person it wouldn't matter a damn.

There was a scream from next door, and she flung the cloth down and ran out the front door. Amy was lying face down on the path, Nick heading for her at a run. He scooped her up into his arms and cradled her on his lap, kneeling awkwardly on the gritty path while Amy screamed and sobbed.

'I fell,' she hiccuped, and Nick crooned to her and smoothed her hair and made Ronnie wish it had been her who'd fallen over and torn her knees to pieces, just to experience that loving embrace.

'Come in and clean her up. I've got a first-aid kit,' she told him, and he nodded and stood up, the crying child cradled easily against his chest. He looked so protective and tender and caring, and Ronnie felt her eyes prickle.

'Stupid,' she muttered, shoving the front door out of the way and trying to sluice the cream cleaner off her hands.

'On second thoughts, you can do it—that stuff might not wash off,' she said almost to herself, and rummaged in the cupboard for a big mixing bowl. She filled it with tepid water from the kettle and found some sterile swabs courtesy of the hospital.

'Here.'

'My hands are dirty,' he said, and looked up at her helplessly, a mute appeal in her eyes.

So she tore open the packet of swabs, tipped them into the bowl of water then snapped on a pair of latex gloves, also from the hospital and bathed the poor, torn, skinny little knees while Amy whimpered and clung to her father.

He watched with an agonised expression as Ronnie carefully cleaned out every last tiny piece of grit as carefully as possible, only stopping when she was sure the skin was clean.

'Right, you'll do, little one. How about the hands?'

She held them out. They were grass-stained and a little pink, but unharmed. They must have hit the lawn on the other side of the path.

'Well, I think they'll do, and a little plaster on the knees should do the trick,' Ronnie said, and opened a box of cartoon plasters she kept for children. 'Mickey Mouse?'

'And Minnie,' she said, looking at the other knee. 'One each.'

She stuck them on upside down so that Amy could see them, and then the child slid off her father's lap and looked up at Ronnie. 'We're going to see the 'state agents,' she told her. 'I want a new house so I can have my bed back.'

'I don't want to go,' Ben said again, standing by the doorway with his arms folded and a mutinous expression on his face.

Nick's sigh was quiet but spoke volumes. 'Ben, nor do I, really, but we do need to find somewhere permanent. It won't take long.'

Ronnie stifled a snort of amusement. House-hunting was the most taxing and time-consuming and tedious thing in the world—so why was she suddenly volunteering to come with them and help them find their way round a strange town?

Didn't she have anything else to do with her precious Saturday morning?

Yeah, clean the sink, a little voice said, and she almost laughed. 'Come on, anything beats doing housework,' she said with a grin, and paused before Ben. 'I know a place in town that sells the best ice creams. I'll treat you.'

CHAPTER THREE

'THAT'S a good area.'

'Good?' Nick asked, interested in Ronnie's criteria.

'Decent local schools, mostly private housing, low crime, pleasant, leafy streets—that sort of thing.'

'Is it near our school?' Ben asked, peering at the agent's photo.

Ronnie shook her head. 'No, it's the other side of town—'

'Then it's no good,' he said firmly, and Nick shrugged.

'Is there a similar area near to where we are now?'

'Oh, yes. It's just that decent houses hardly ever come up. People tend to move in and stay forever because it's so nice.'

Great. Nick shook his head despairingly. 'Shall we give up?'

'We could try one more agent,' Ronnie said encouragingly. 'If anything ever does come up in our part of town, it's usually with them. It's a bit of a hike, but it might be worth it. Shall we give it a whirl?'

He almost said no, and then ten minutes later, as they stood outside the agent she'd mentioned, a house appeared in the window, a lovely old brick house, early Edwardian, with a little turret in one corner and lots of big windows to let in the light. The woman was just putting a photo of it in the window display as they arrived, and Ben looked at it and said, 'I want that one.'

'I want the tower,' Amy said.

'Well, you can't have it, you're a girl. Boys sleep in towers.'

'That's not true! Punzel hung her hair over the side of her tower and the prince climbed up and rescued her!'

'It's *Ra*punzel, thicko,' Ben said scornfully, 'and, anyway, it's only a stupid fairy tale!'

Nick felt like banging their heads together, but he restrained himself. He met Ronnie's eyes. 'Shall I go in and ask about it?'

'Why not? It's in the right area.'

He went in. The house was just three or four streets from where they were living, in the same school catchment area, and by chance was fresh on the market and the agent had a key.

'You could go and look at it,' she told them. 'No one else has seen it yet, and the owner has only just put it on the market. We've rushed a few photos for the press but we haven't got any details prepared at the moment. They won't be ready till Monday. It's a bit tatty here and there—it could do with a little love and attention, but it's got a nice garden. A bit overgrown, but it's west-facing—lovely after work in the summer.'

Nick signed in the key book, picked up the bunch of keys from the desk and then grinned at the others. For the first time in years, he felt a surge of enthusiasm and interest in something other than his children or his job. Maybe this house would be the new start that they needed.

He tossed the keys up in the air and caught them, his grin widening. 'Shall we go?'

It was gorgeous. Tatty, old-fashioned and in need of drastic TLC, but gorgeous. Ronnie watched Nick's face as he scanned the beautifully proportioned rooms, and for the first time she caught a glimpse of the man he really was—the man he could have been if the weight of the last few years hadn't been placed on his shoulders.

His eyes were alight and alive, dazzlingly blue, his mouth slightly parted as if he couldn't quite believe what he was seeing, the odd muttered 'Wow' coming from him as he entered another room or saw another lovely feature.

Ronnie felt a lump in her throat, and another pang of sadness for him that Anna wasn't here to share it with him. What a crying shame.

The children, quite untouched by the emotions of the adults, pelted through the rooms, yelling wildly in the echoing emptiness, their feet drumming on the bare boards. They skidded to a halt in the kitchen doorway, however, and Nick and Ronnie peered over their shoulders.

'Oh, yum,' Ronnie said, and started to laugh. 'Purple and orange, seventies-style. How tasteful.'

Nick chuckled, then eased past the children, something clearly catching his eye. He hunkered down and opened a cupboard door, his fingers running thoughtfully over the painted wood. 'These units are solid— they've been painted this ghastly colour, but I've got a feeling it's an original oak kitchen.'

Ronnie went and looked, and nodded. 'I think you're right. If you stripped it and colourwashed it, instead of having this inch-thick chipped gloss paint, it would be right up to the minute. My goodness, it must be worth a fortune!'

They drifted through the scullery behind, hesitated at the back door and then followed the noise of the children back through the house and up the stairs. They were getting a bit excited, and Nick was clearly unhappy to leave them alone.

'We'll do the garden together in a minute. I just want to keep an eye on them. There are signs of damp in one of the rooms, and the floor might be rotten if the damp's come from the roof. It might get worse as we go up.'

It did, but not drastically. They found Ben and Amy in the 'tower', an octagonal protrusion on one corner, not really a tower at all but more of a bay, with five sides projecting to take maximum advantage of the light.

Each side had a window, and like all the windows they were tall with sliding sashes. Some of the sash cords dangled here and there, and the occasional window wasn't quite shut, hanging at a crazy angle in the frame.

Still, it didn't seem to put Nick off. He went from room to room, marvelling at the size, the proportions, the number of rooms—everything seemed a plus point.

'There's a lot of work,' Ronnie murmured, flicking a peeling strip of wallpaper with her finger.

Nick shrugged. 'I'm glad it's as bad as it is, decor-wise, because I won't feel I have to preserve someone else's taste because it was freshly done—and I know they haven't papered over the cracks either!'

Ronnie laughed. 'Certainly not. What you see is what you get!' She went into the bathroom and stopped dead. 'Nick, look,' she called excitedly, and he arrived on her heels immediately.

'Wow,' he breathed for the hundredth time, but this time it really was a find.

The room was original, almost untouched, the vast bath sticking out into the centre with huge ball-and-claw feet, a great brass pipe for the plug and overflow and huge taps over the end sticking out of the wall. The basin and loo were beautiful, with lovely blue flowers all over the outside and inside of the bowls and down the pedestal and foot, and there was a huge wooden seat around the loo. The tiles had an original dado rail at waist height, and were in almost perfect condition.

'It's like a time warp,' Ronnie sighed.

'It's wonderful,' Nick said, running his finger over the surface of the bath. 'The enamel's a bit dodgy, but I'm sure it can be repaired.' He looked up and met her eyes, and his were bubbling with excitement. 'Ronnie, this place is one in a million. I love it. I want it.'

'It's got five bedrooms on this floor, and there's another floor above,' she pointed out, playing devil's advocate. 'Think of the heating bills.'

He shrugged. 'There's more to life than heating bills. We can be hardy. Very good for us. I could have a study in the tower and an *en suite* bathroom, and the children could share this one, and we'll need a guest room.'

'That takes care of this floor. What about the one above?'

He shrugged and grinned. 'TV room for the kids? Studies, when they get older? Maybe an au pair? That would make sense. Let's go and have a look.'

In fact, the upper floor was closed off by a door, and could quite easily be used as an attic for storage and left empty, if he wanted. Ronnie had to admit that the house was wonderful, but she wasn't sure if Nick had any idea how much it would cost to do up.

'It won't be cheap to get it right,' she warned, remembering her father doing up houses and running out of money in her childhood.

'There's no hurry. The roof, the central heating and rewiring, some plumbing—the rest I can do.' He grinned and ran downstairs again, following the sound of the children's excited voices. 'Ben, Amy, let's go and look at the garden.'

Ronnie followed them slowly down, and stepped out into the glorious sunshine of a lovely day. She eyed the brambles, the huge lilac bushes, the overgrown and unpruned roses—and saw instead a swing hanging from the branch of the old apple tree at the end, and a slide and climbing frame, and wooden garden furniture, and Nick sprawled out, a drink in his hand, smiling at her as she walked towards him.

She was holding a tray, and on it were drinks for the children, and some biscuits, and a bottle of juice for the baby—

This was getting ridiculous! She gulped and turned away, blinking away the mist that seemed determined to cloud her vision. If only it was as easy to clear her mind!

She propped her back against the wall and wrapped her arms around her waist, struggling to get her emotions back under control. He wasn't hers! He belonged to Anna, and it was clear he wasn't ready to let her go.

He invited you to the dance, that little voice said, but she ruthlessly ignored it.

'Only because of Kate,' she muttered.

'What's only because of Kate?' he asked, sneaking up on her.

She jumped guiltily and glared at him. 'Nothing. I was thinking about something totally different,' she said, making absolutely no sense.

He gave her a disbelieving look but said nothing more. What was there to say? He probably thought she was raving mad.

'I want to get back to the agent quickly and sign something, before someone else gets in. I've got cash sitting in the bank. Maybe that will buy me time.'

She shook her head and laughed softly. 'This is Suffolk, Nick, not London. There's no rush.'

'Whatever. Kids, come on. Let's go and buy a house.'

'What about a survey?'

He grinned. 'My brother's a surveyor. He can be here by three this afternoon—if I can catch him.'

He pulled a mobile phone out of his pocket, stabbed in the number and stood, tapping his foot, waiting for an answer.

'Richard? Did you have any plans for today? I've found a house.'

It was all tied up by nine o'clock on Monday. Nick was a few minutes late into work, grinning cheerfully, and told Ronnie that the house had passed its survey with flying colours, if you didn't count the wiring, plumbing and heating, all the windows needing repair and the hole in the roof!

'I've instructed my solicitor, and all we have to do now is sit back and wait for a couple of weeks, and it'll be mine!'

And you'll move, Ronnie thought, suppressing the surge of disappointment. She'd deliberately kept out of the way over the weekend, so as to not expose herself to any more heartache than was necessary, but it was a total waste of time.

She loved him. It was as simple and as complicated as that.

He hugged her, in the way one friend hugged another when something good was happening, and left for his outpatient clinic, totally oblivious of the turmoil of emotion he'd left behind.

She buried herself in her work, dealing with Oliver's operation list, soothing and reassuring and checking complicated equipment and administering drugs and generally running herself ragged, but it didn't make any difference.

Nick appeared at lunchtime, just as she was wondering if she should sneak down to the canteen quickly before he finished his clinic.

'Hi. Fancy a bite?'

'I'm busy,' she began, but Vicky, the staff nurse, came up at that moment and revealed her for the liar she was.

'No, you aren't. We're done for now. I was going to suggest you go early, if you could, because I'd like to meet David at one-thirty.'

Ronnie glanced at her watch, playing for time, but the face was unhelpful. Twelve-thirty, it said, and that gave her half an hour before the next shift came on. 'I can't be long, I have to give report to the new shift—'

'I'll do it,' Vicky said cheerfully.

And that was that. She shrugged feebly, gave a weak smile and trailed after him, cursing Vicky every step of the way.

Except after a few seconds she forgot to bother, because actually it was so good to be in his company that she couldn't remember why she shouldn't be enjoying it.

They settled down at a table in the corner once they'd picked up their meals, and she could see he was still excited about the house. 'I've got so much to do in the next couple of weeks. Still, the children are going to Anna's parents for the weekend, so that should give me some time to sort out a builder and plumber. Don't suppose you've got any idea who I should use?'

'Ask Meg,' she suggested. 'Meg knows everyone. If she can't sort you out, nobody can.' She lifted a forkful of rice and chicken to her lips, and caught Nick's eye.

'What's it like?' he asked.

'Lovely,' she mumbled. 'Have some.'

'My fork's got curry on it.'

So she scooped up some rice and chicken on her fork and held it out to him, then nearly dropped it as his firm, well-sculpted lips closed around the prongs. How could something so simple, so mundane, so *ordinary* as eating suddenly be so erotic?

She swallowed, choked on a grain of rice and nearly coughed herself to death.

'Ronnie?'

'Wrong way,' she wheezed, flapping him away and grabbing for her glass of water. Her eyes were streaming, her voice was up and down all over the place and he was watching her with a very strange look in his eye.

Probably debating sending for the little men in white coats to take her away, she thought, and gulped some more water.

'So, anything interesting in your clinic?' she asked when she could speak.

'Uh-huh. Aortic aneurysm—I'm going to try and graft it laparoscopically, because she's in her late seventies and I don't want to mess her about. She's coming in tomorrow, and I'm going to operate on Wednesday.'

'Have you done it before?' she croaked, still struggling with the grain of rice.

'Yes, a few times. Did Hamilton ever do it like that?'

'Ross? Yes, sometimes. He's coming in on Wednesday. I expect he'll come and annoy you in Theatre.'

Nick rolled his eyes. 'Something to look forward to—the outgoing maestro coming back to see what a carve-up I'm making of his firm! I can hardly wait!'

Ronnie laughed. 'Ross is lovely. He's not like that. You'll see.'

'Hmm,' he mumbled, and shovelled in another forkful of curry. 'I'll wait to be proved wrong!'

They talked about the house for a while, and then Ronnie, aching inside with hearing about a home that would never be her home, excused herself and almost ran back to the ward.

Vicky greeted her with a grin and a wave, and disappeared for her lunch with David, the boyfriend of the moment and clearly one that mattered.

Lucky girl, Ronnie thought, and threw herself back into her routine. She was tackling some of the paperwork that dogged her existence when Vicky came back and perched on the desk, her eyes bright.

'I don't suppose you want to do me a favour, do you? Only David's invited me to the ball on Saturday, and I'm on a long day, which means I won't have time to get ready. I wondered if you'd swap Sunday for me. I know it means I'll probably get to bed about three and have to be in for seven, but I'll cope. I just want to look my best.'

Ronnie sat back. Sunday off sounded tempting, and she didn't really need time to get ready. It took ten minutes to get home from the hospital, ten minutes in the shower—she'd be ready by eight-thirty at the latest, and it didn't matter if she didn't look stunning. She was realistic enough to know that, even if the thought did hurt.

'Yeah, sure, I'll do that. I don't need long to get ready.'

Vicky's face was puzzled. 'Oh—are you going out?'

'To the ball,' she said, and then realised that she hadn't told Vicky. The girl clapped her hand over her mouth.

'Oh—Ronnie, you can't swap, then. I'm sorry, I didn't realise.'

'It's fine, Vicky. Really. It's fine. Just make sure you're here, sober and ready to work at seven on Sunday, or it's the last favour you'll get.'

'You're a star!' To her amazement Vicky leaned over, dropped a kiss on her cheek and sailed out of the office on cloud nine, leaving Ronnie to consider the folly of working from seven-thirty in the morning to eight at night, and then going to a ball.

She groaned, just thinking about her feet, and then with a sigh she went back to her paperwork. At least she'd get Sunday to lie in bed—

The phone rang, cutting off her train of thought. It was ITU, asking if she could take Andy Graham, the man Nick had patched up the previous Wednesday on his first day. Good heavens, she thought, only five days ago! Was that all it was?

'Yes, we can take him—just. Anything special I need to do? How is he?'

'Stable but still pretty fragile. He's not critical, but he'll need some pretty intensive nursing. He can't do a lot for himself with his fractures.'

'So why isn't he going to Orthopaedics?'

The ITU sister laughed. 'Are you joking? They're bursting at the seams, and Mr Sarazin seems to think he might have further problems with his liver. He wants to keep a close eye with a view to opening him up again if necessary, so it makes sense if he's with you. The orthopods can't do anything but wait and see.'

Whereas we, Ronnie thought with a dry laugh, have nothing at all to do!

She went out into the ward and warned everyone that Andy Graham was coming down shortly, and they cleared a space for him in the single cubicle room beside the nursing station. He would need specialling and monitoring throughout the night, and it was easier to do it in a small room out of the way of the hubbub of the ward.

She put Vicky with him when he arrived, looking battered and anxious and very young. She saw from his notes that he was only twenty, and wondered how his parents felt about almost losing him. Gutted, probably. She bent over him.

'Hello, Andy, I'm Ronnie, the ward sister. How are you feeling?'

'Sore,' he murmured through closed lips. 'I hurt everywhere.'

'I expect you do. We'll give you a minute to settle down from your journey and then we'll make you more comfortable. You just rest for a bit. This is Vicky— she's going to stay with you.'

'Hi,' Vicky said cheerfully, and perched on the chair beside him with his clipboard. 'I'm just going to do your obs and then you can go to sleep, OK?'

He nodded painfully, and Ronnie left them. Vicky knew what she was doing, and there were still a million and one things to do—like that dratted paperwork. Still, today it was quite appealing. She'd just started a period, and she felt heavy and achy and was quite happy to sit down quietly in the corner and deal with the backlog.

'So, what are you going to wear?'

Ronnie looked at Meg as if she were mad. 'Wear? Well, I don't know. That green thing?'

Meg's lip curled eloquently. 'Ronnie, it was nice six years ago. Times change. You need a new dress. We'll have to go shopping. How does your week look?'

Ronnie laughed. 'Hectic. Why?'

'Because I don't have the boys on Thursday mornings so, if you could wangle a late, we could go then.'

She thought, and shrugged. 'I'm on a late. I don't have to wangle anything.'

'Brilliant. We'll have an early start—in town for nine, round all the right places, make a short list, then go and have coffee, decide and go and buy *the dress*!'

'The dress?' Ronnie said, laughing. 'You make it sound like a—I don't know—a real date.'

Meg smacked herself theatrically in the middle of her forehead. 'Silly me. And there I thought a handsome, eligible man asking you to a Valentine Ball *was* a date. How stupid can I get?'

Ronnie coloured and chased a bubble round the top of her coffee. 'Meg, it's not like that. It's only because Kate chased him—I told you that.'

'So you did. I must have misread the look in his eyes the other day when he dropped you at the door and watched you go in.'

Ronnie's head snapped up. 'What look?'

Her friend smiled victoriously. 'Oh, just a look. Just like a child saying goodbye to a favourite puppy.'

Ronnie threw a biscuit at her, and Meg ducked and grinned. 'Tut-tut. I won't give you biscuits if you're going to waste them. So, are we on for Thursday? Because, my dear, date or not, you *cannot* go out in that green thing *again*!'

Ross Hamilton strolled onto the ward on Wednesday morning, looking bright and chipper and very pleased with himself. 'Morning, Ronnie,' he said in his lovely, soft, Scottish burr, and Ronnie found herself smiling almost before she registered his presence.

'Ross,' she said, taking his hands and squeezing them. 'Good to see you. How are things?'

He nodded. 'Fine. Wonderful. The kids and Lizzi have settled well, the boys like the house, although they won't really be there that often now they're away at college—it's good.'

'And the job?'

'Excellent. I love it—well, so far. I still miss this place, though. How's the new man?'

Ronnie felt warmth climb her cheeks. 'Oh, he seems to have settled in well. Kate rather threw herself at him, but apart from that it's all going fine.'

Ross shook his head. 'I can't understand that. You know, people say that about her, but I never had any trouble. Maybe I just don't have what it takes.'

Ronnie laughed. 'Not much,' she said honestly, and it was his turn to colour.

'I'm serious,' he told her.

'Then you're blind, but Kate's not. If she didn't trouble you, perhaps it's because you never noticed anybody except Lizzi anyway, so why would your scrub nurse register?'

Ross laughed. 'Maybe you're right. So, anyway, how are you getting on with him?'

Ronnie shifted a little. 'Um—fine. He's a very reasonable human being. He seems to be an excellent surgeon—he's doing a keyhole aortic graft today.'

'Is he? What time?'

'About ten. She's all prepped and ready. Why don't you go up and see if you can put him off? I told him to expect you.'

Ross laughed. 'Good idea. I might well do that. It would be good to see the team in action again.'

He glanced at his watch. 'I'd better go—I'll need to change if I'm going to observe, and it might be diplomatic to ask the man's permission!'

Ronnie chuckled. 'I would just walk in and frown disapprovingly and see what he does.'

'Have me thrown out, if he's got any sense! No, Ronnie, I think I'll do it diplomatically.'

'You're so boring,' Ronnie told him with a smile. 'Shall I put the kettle on?'

'I thought you'd never ask!' he said with a chuckle, but then the smile faded from his face and he glanced over Ronnie's shoulder. 'Looks like trouble.'

She turned, just as Vicky came running up. 'It's Mrs Foster—her pressure's going through the floor. I don't know what's happened, but I reckon her aneurysm's probably burst.'

'Oh, Lord—Ross, I know you don't work here any more, but would you? I'll ring Theatre.'

She called, warned them there was a crisis coming up and ran to Mrs Foster's bedside. Ross was doing CPR with Vicky, another nurse was opening a giving set ready to insert it, and Ronnie took over from Ross so he could insert the needle and start giving the patient the fluids he'd ordered.

'Spoken to Theatre?' he snapped.

'Yes—they're just closing. There's another theatre empty—Nick's going to scrub and meet you in there. He wondered if you'd like to assist.'

Ross laughed humourlessly. 'I only came for a coffee. Damned Hippocratic oath. OK, let's get this Haemaccel in fast, while we take her up. I reckon we've got two minutes if we're lucky.'

He slapped a bit of tape onto the tube, grabbed the bag of Haemaccel and crushed it ruthlessly in his fist. They kicked the brakes off the bed, pushed the curtains aside and ran for the door.

'Vicky, you stay, I'll take over,' Ronnie said, and they left her at the doorway, heading down the corridor through the stream of pedestrian traffic with yelled warnings to everyone to clear the way, and Ross joking that they needed a flashing light on the end of the bed.

The theatre lift was there, waiting for them with the ODA standing by to help, and without delay Mrs Foster was wheeled into the anaesthetic room. The theatre team took over, leaving Ronnie with a massive surge of adrenaline and nothing to do.

Ross shot off to change, and she caught a glimpse of Nick in fresh theatre pyjamas, diving into a clean gown and heading towards the patient. 'Right, let's get her opened up and see what she's done. Where's that cross-matched blood? It should be here by now.'

'It's on its way—there's two units of O-neg. here.'

'Well, get them in her—what are we waiting for? Let's go.'

The door slapped shut behind them, and quiet descended over the anteroom.

Ronnie turned and smiled at Ross, now changed and scrubbing rapidly. 'Have fun,' she said with a slight smile, and he grinned and winked.

'Put the coffee-pot on. We'll be down shortly to let you know how it went.'

'Consider it done,' she said with another tired smile, and then she turned and went back down to the ward, wondering how they were doing and if either Nick or Ross were clever enough to snatch Mrs Foster back from the jaws of death.

There were always those times when being clever just wasn't enough, and it looked as if this might be one of them.

'You win some, you lose some,' she murmured to herself, and bumped into Vicky.

'Earth calling Ronnie, come in, please,' Vicky said with a smile.

Ronnie sighed and pushed a stray strand of hair out of her eyes, dredging up an answering smile. 'Sorry. I was wondering about her chances.'

Vicky shrugged. 'Pretty grim, I suspect. I've made you a cup of tea. You look as if you could do with one.'

Ronnie did smile then, a genuine smile that reached her eyes. 'You're a love. I can almost forgive you for Saturday!'

'Ah, but you get Sunday off,' Vicky reminded her, and she thought how lovely it would be to wake up on Sunday morning at some ridiculously decadent hour, and be able to enjoy the luxury of not having to get up.

'So I do,' she said with a laugh, 'and you'll be here at seven. Are you sure about this?'

Vicky nodded. 'Absolutely. I need that time to get ready. I'm going to knock his socks off.'

Ronnie didn't think it would be that hard. She'd seen the way David had been looking at Vicky in the last few days, and she had a feeling he was going to propose to her on Saturday night—in which case it seemed unfair that she would have to do Sunday instead of spending it with him.

She spoke without giving herself time to think. 'Look, I don't suppose we'll stay all that late at the ball, so why don't I do Sunday for you and you'll just owe me a massive favour?' she suggested, and the glow in Vicky's eyes more than compensated for the sinking feeling that she'd just thrown away a lovely lie-in!

Oh, well, so she was a regular little angel. How comforting. She'd have to remember that at six-thirty on Sunday morning when she was dragging herself blearily out of bed!

She drank her tea while she scanned the paperwork of the day, checked the list of pre- and post-ops and new admissions, and waited for Ross to come back down and tell her how Mrs Foster had got on.

She could hardly believe her eyes when Ross appeared with Nick, both laughing, and she knew it was all right. Even so, she had to ask.

Nick shrugged and pulled a 'how could you doubt me?' face, and Ross laughed.

'She's gone to ITU. It must have been seeping gently for some while,' Nick told her, and scrubbed his hand round the back of his neck. 'Any chance of a cup of tea?'

Ross looked at him. 'Tea?' he said in disgust, and Ronnie chuckled.

'Yes, tea. Unlike you, he doesn't believe in poisoning himself when he's under pressure. I could make you instant.'

Ross pulled a face and sighed. 'Tea it is, then—good and strong.'

'I've got chocolate biscuits, as you've been such clever boys,' she told them to compensate, and they seemed quite contented. They ate almost all the packet, in the few moments they were there, and then they left again, deep in conversation.

'They seem to be getting on well,' Vicky said, watching them walk up the ward together.

'Mmm. Similar, in a different sort of way. I think they'd make a good team. It's a shame they'll never work together.'

'Well, barring the occasional well-timed crisis,' Vicky said drily. 'It's a good job he was here to help. I don't suppose it was easy once they'd got her opened up.'

'I gather not,' Ronnie said, thinking back through

the snippets of conversation over the tea and biscuits. 'I don't think they had a lot of time to spare either.'

'Brilliant. Just brilliant, the pair of them,' Vicky said with a self-satisfied smile. 'Aren't we lucky they aren't stuffy and pompous?'

Ronnie chuckled. She'd worked with some stuffy and pompous surgeons in her time, and she couldn't have agreed more. 'Aren't we just?' she said softly. 'Aren't we just?'

'No, I don't like it, it's a rag on you. Try this.'

Ronnie looked at the scrap of cloth dangling from Meg's hand and rolled her eyes. 'You think *this* is a rag, and you want me to try *that* one?'

'Just humour me,' Meg said, shoving it at her. 'Go. Try it.'

She went, and realised instantly that she couldn't wear a bra with it. Nevertheless, she tried it, and came out, peering doubtfully over her shoulder at the low-cut and revealing back, the slit up the side of the thigh and the sinuous fit of the bias-cut silk.

'It's outrageous,' she said, laughing, and then noticed Meg's jaw hanging.

'My God,' her friend said slowly. 'I always thought that green thing didn't do you justice. Now I know. Buy it.'

Ronnie's eyes widened. 'Buy it? But we were going to short-list over coffee—'

'No need. Buy it. We can have more time over coffee—maybe wallow in a really sinful cake, oozing with cream…'

Ronnie snorted. 'You must be kidding. If I just lick your plate I won't fit into this dress!'

'Yeah, you will. It's bias-cut—it expands.'

'And lovingly outlines every little bulge.'

Meg rolled her eyes. 'You have no bulges. You're talking nonsense. Just pay the woman and let's go. I'm starving.'

She changed, paid and went, feeling hustled and a little uneasy, but with a bubble of happiness tickling her throat. She hadn't had a new dress—not one like that, at least—for years.

Too many years.

She tried not to think about how many years, or that buying it for Saturday and Nick was probably a waste of time.

'Stop it,' Meg said. 'You're wrong about him. If he can resist you in that, he's too cold-blooded to be worth bothering with. Incidentally, you know you can't wear knickers under it, I suppose?'

Ronnie slammed on the brakes and came to a halt in the middle of the pavement. 'What?' she squeaked.

'VPL—visible panty line. You'll have to wear those tights with a built-in gusset—or nothing, of course,' Meg said with a wicked wink. 'That should get him going.'

Ronnie laughed a little awkwardly. 'But what if it's just lust?'

'What of it?' Meg said with a shrug, heading into the little coffee-shop. 'Even lust would make a refreshing change, after all this time! Get real, Ronnie. You need a life. This is just a step in the right direction. Now, coffee and walnut, or double chocolate heaven?'

She stared at them, gave up trying to choose the low-calorie option and plumped for the double chocolate heaven with cappuccino. So what if she had a bulge by Saturday? It might be the only thing that kept her out of trouble!

CHAPTER FOUR

SATURDAY was a nightmare. There was only one thing Ronnie hated more than a 'long day'—seven-thirty in the morning to eight at night—and that was an overly busy one.

It should have been quiet, but Mrs Foster, with her extensive surgery following her ruptured aneurysm, came back from ITU because they were short of beds, and Andy Graham was still feeling pretty rough. One of Oliver's patients admitted overnight was still in need of close supervision, and there was another one in Theatre who would be coming down soon.

Thus, apart from the usual chaos of patients going home after minor surgery on Friday, patients going home after slightly more major surgery on Wednesday and the normal busy ward routine, she had to organise two nurses to special her more critical two—and she was two nurses short! Great!

Mrs Foster was particularly unhappy because, if all had gone well, she might have been going home either that day or the following Monday, and as it was she would be in hospital now for several more days. 'Still,' she said tiredly, 'I suppose it might have been worse.'

'It might indeed,' Ronnie agreed, checking her obs and wondering why it was that with the ward at full stretch she was two staff down. On quiet days they were all there without fail—not that they got many quiet days. Maybe she'd ring Vicky and ask her to come in till three. That would help.

She settled Mrs Foster, asked a health care assistant

to keep an eye on Oliver's post-op for a moment, and rang Vicky's number.

There was no reply. 'Typical,' she sighed, and was about to hang up when Vicky answered, a little breathlessly.

'Do you remember that favour?' Ronnie began, and Vicky groaned.

'What, now?' she said, guessing.

'I'm two qualified staff down, and the hospital's at full stretch. Just till three, Vicky—please?'

'Three? Promise?'

Ronnie looked round the ward and rolled her eyes. 'Promise.'

'OK.'

'You're a star.' She hung up and went back to the patient, and let the HCA carry on with her work. Vicky would be there soon, and she could go and deal with the discharges.

In the good old days, of course, she wouldn't have had to worry about discharges on a Saturday. They simply would have stayed in another three days. Now, patients went home as soon as possible, to cut waiting lists and keep staffing costs down. If that meant chaos on the weekend, well, they could deal with it, and there was a part of Ronnie that thought people recovered much quicker at home anyway.

Peace and quiet was in very short supply in a modern hospital, and everybody needed peace and quiet to heal.

She'd needed it after David Baker and his emotional blackmail and infidelity, and it had been impossible to find anywhere to go. In the end she'd had three weeks off and gone to a Scottish croft and cried her eyes out. Then she'd come back steaming mad, thrown anything of his she'd found out of the window of her flat, handed in her notice and moved here.

It was the best thing she'd ever done, but it had been six years now, and maybe it was time her personal peace and quiet came to an end.

It was a bit of a scary thought. She wondered if she had the guts to wear the dress—especially with no knickers—and almost panicked. She'd considered buying a thong so that she didn't get Meg's VPL, and decided it was better to wear tights with a nice opaque top, which were infinitely more comfortable and felt safer.

Slightly.

Oh, Lord.

She was so out of touch with clubs and pubs and parties and balls. It was ages since she'd been to anything other than the most informal get-together, and then she'd slipped off as soon as it had been decent.

What if she was bored? she thought, and then imagined being bored while she was in the same room as Nick, never mind in his arms, and almost laughed aloud.

OK, so she wouldn't be bored. Would he?

Ronnie's heart started to hammer. Oh, dear heaven, what if she sent him to sleep? David Baker had never found her riveting—

'Why are you scowling?'

Her head flew up and she met Nick's eyes, crinkled at the corners with a smile that made her heart thump even faster. 'Just thinking about tonight,' she said without thinking at all, and then hurried to explain as a frown creased his brow. 'I mean, I was considering what to wear with my dress,' she elaborated, in case he thought she was scowling about going out with him. 'You know—accessories.'

'Shoes, jewellery, tights—underwear?' he suggested softly, his eyes laughing again, and she thought better than to explain to him that there would *be* no underwear! He need never know, thank God. She looked quickly away.

'Shoes,' she lied. 'I was wondering which shoes. I want to be able to walk tomorrow—I'm on duty again at seven.'

Nick frowned again. 'Tomorrow? But I thought you had tomorrow off?'

'I did,' she explained ruefully, 'but I think Vicky's David is going to pop the question, and I thought they might like Sunday together to celebrate.'

'So you offered to do Sunday for her.'

'For my sins. Still, Vicky's coming in now to give me a hand just until three, so I'm getting my own back a bit.'

He nodded. 'How is Mrs Foster?' he asked.

'All right. Tired and fed up, and a bit tender. I think her bowel has started to work again, I could hear sounds a little while ago.'

He nodded again. 'Try her with a little water later. Just ten mils at a time at first, I think. She's been quite poorly after all that pulling about.'

'OK.' She jotted it down on a scrap of paper in her pocket and stood up, moving out of the room so they didn't disturb the patient. 'So what brings you in on a Saturday?'

'Can't stay away. It must be you.' He grinned. 'Actually I wanted to check on Mrs Foster and make sure my discharges were all OK to go home, which they seem to be. I couldn't find you.'

'I've been in here.'

'So I realise.' He pulled something out of his pocket and showed it to her. 'Just been choosing carpet for the house. I thought of having this cream in the drawing room. What do you think?'

Ronnie winced and took the little sample of pale, soft carpet, and imagined it with football boots and chocolate ground into it. 'Cream? Do you think that's wise?'

He laughed. 'Probably not, but we've got a snug which we'll use most of the time, and children and animals will be banned from the drawing room unless they're inspected and shoeless.'

She shook her head, laughing. 'You're nuts. What about the rest?'

'Green—soft jadey grey-green. I couldn't get a sample of that, he wouldn't cut it off the book, but it's a lovely colour and it'll go with the suite for the snug. We had something similar in the other house and it was brilliant for not showing dirt.'

Ronnie chuckled. 'Sounds like a good idea.'

He glanced at his watch and pulled a face. 'I'm meeting the electrician at the house in half an hour. What time will you be ready to go tonight?'

'About eight-thirty,' she told him, and hoped there weren't any complications.

'Sure?' he asked doubtfully, clearly not believing her.

'I don't take long to get dressed.' Especially when I'm wearing *so-o-o* little! she added to herself, and felt another flutter of panic.

'Just so long as we don't miss our dinner.'

She smiled and patted his cheek. 'You won't miss your dinner, don't worry. I'll be quick.' She dropped her hand, turned round and surprised by a look of fascinated curiosity on Vicky's face.

'Ah, Vicky, I'm glad you're here,' she said quickly to cover her confusion. 'Could you special Mrs Foster for me, please?'

And with that she waggled her fingers at Nick and

the fascinated Vicky, and disappeared down the ward
to see to her other patients.

'Oh, dear God, I can't wear it!' Ronnie wailed, studying her reflection with something akin to shock. 'I look
ridiculous! I'm going to wear the green—'

'Don't be absurd, you look gorgeous. Don't you
dare change. Here, let me do something with your hair.
It needs to be up.'

'It's always up, I thought it needed to be down...'

'It's always up *tidily*. It needs to be up *untidily*—
you know, bits sticking out and little tendrils.'

'You make it sound like a badly trained honey-
suckle,' she said with a laugh, and let Meg push her
into a chair and fiddle with the still slightly damp mess
on her head.

'Right, that should do. Got any pins?'

She reached for a box. 'Is the Pope Catholic? I wear
my hair up every day—of course I've got pins—ouch!'

'Sorry.' Meg tweaked and teased and combed, and
then stood back. 'Tiara. No peeking,' she said firmly,
and vanished. Ronnie, overruled and defeated, sat there
and waited for her to come back. She was only gone
for what seemed like a few seconds, then she was back,
a little crescent of sparkles clutched victoriously in her
hand. With a laugh of triumph she plonked it on
Ronnie's head and stood back.

'Excellent. Have a look.'

Ronnie hardly dared, but time was running out. She
stood up, turned round—and gasped. 'Good Lord,' she
breathed, and bent forward, studying the intricate
tweaks and loops Meg had ingeniously worked into her
hair.

'I used to be a hairdresser in a previous incarnation,'
Meg explained.

'You dark horse,' Ronnie murmured, examining the overall effect. 'Wow. You're a love. Thanks.' She kissed Meg's cheek, grabbed her coat and bag and headed for the door.

'Drop the catch behind you—I have to fly!' she said, and she ran downstairs, putting her shoes on as she went, hopping to the door. She tugged it open and found Nick standing there, stunning in a dress suit with a long white scarf and black coat. He looked good enough to eat, and Ronnie's mouth all but watered.

Nick seemed to be having trouble as well. He did a mild double take, collected up his jaw and grinned. 'You look—gorgeous, Ronnie,' he said gruffly, and, taking her elbow, he shot a grin at Meg over her shoulder and seated her in his car as if she were a princess.

Ronnie found her heart somewhere up round her tonsils, drumming away like a mad thing. She gulped to push it back down, and took slow, steadying breaths to calm herself.

Suddenly it began to feel very much like a real date!

Nick couldn't believe it. All these years he'd shut himself away, not looking for anything except peace, and now suddenly he felt as if the safe, secure, familiar ground had been snatched out from under his feet, tumbling him into a strange place filled with forgotten emotions and wild longings—and Ronnie.

She looked stunning. That dress—it fell softly from a demure, high neckline, draping across her bust very discreetly, and from the front it looked entirely proper. Then he'd caught sight of the back, dipping away towards the hollow of her waist, and he'd nearly had a stroke!

He'd only invited her to protect himself from Kate—and now it seemed she was proving to be much more dangerous than Kate could ever be. Ronnie, his nice, safe, cheerful little next-door neighbour, full of useful advice about the milkman and the boiler, and Sister Matthews, crisp, efficient, kindly—they were gone, and in their place was another woman he'd never seen before.

Warm, soft, a little shy, with feminine curves and an elegance he'd never even guessed at—she was stunning. He dragged in another breath—just now he seemed to be having to tell himself to breathe all the time—and tried not to ogle.

They were in conversation with Oliver Henderson and his wife, and a group of others he'd not met, and Ronnie was standing next to him, so close that the delicate fragrance surrounding her teased his senses still further. Somebody pushed past him and he stepped forward, bringing his body hard up against hers.

Heat shot through him, and he was only too relieved when the person moved out of the way and he could step back.

'Sorry,' he murmured, and she smiled up at him. His gut clenched, and he had a feeling he probably looked a little ridiculous, but he couldn't drag his eyes off her.

His life was saved by the announcement that dinner was to be served, and they were able to move through to the buffet and break the tension that was threatening to kill him.

Maybe Meg was right, Ronnie thought, catching Nick's eye for the umpteenth time and surprising what could only be called a 'look'. Dinner seemed to drag for ages, and all she wanted was for it to be over and the dancing to start.

And then it *was* over, and he stood up and held out

his hand. 'May I have the honour?' he said, and his voice sounded a little rusty.

'Thank you.' She tried to smile, but her face felt frozen with anticipation.

Lord, woman, it's just a dance! she told herself. He's not going to make love to you on the floor! Her heart hiccuped at the thought, and she had to stop herself from hyperventilating.

The first few dances were quite lively, and they warmed her up and relaxed her. She started to smile again, and Nick returned her smile and winked. He looked a little relieved, as if he'd been worried about her, and she couldn't work out why—unless she'd looked as if she hadn't been enjoying herself!

She let her smile widen, and then suddenly the music slowed, changing to a soft, romantic number, and her smile slipped.

Their eyes locked, he held out his arms and she stepped into them and felt as if she'd come home.

Even though he was so much taller than she was, her head still seemed to fit just right into the curve of his shoulder. His hand lay against her back, his finger-tips cool against her skin and yet burning her with awareness. She settled against him, and felt the solid brush of his thighs against her legs.

He held one of her hands in his, clasped between them so that the back of his hand was lying against her breasts through the soft silk of her dress. Her left hand lay on his shoulder, feeling the powerful ripple of muscle underneath through the fine wool of his jacket. She wanted to take the jacket off, to explore him, to get to know every hill and valley, every plane, every angle of his body.

She wanted him, and the wanting made heat pool in her and turned her legs to jelly. Someone bumped into them and pushed her harder against him, and she felt a sudden shock of awareness.

He wanted her, too! Dear God. Shivers ran over her skin, and she lifted her head and looked up into his eyes. They looked dazed, a little puzzled, and with a groan he cupped her head in his hand and tucked it back under his chin.

His arms slid round her, his hands hot against her spine, and she slipped her arms under his jacket and circled his waist. He was hard and lean and fit, firm columns of muscle bracketing his spine, and she could feel the heat coming off him in waves.

They swayed gently to the music, oblivious to their surroundings, and all Ronnie could feel was the hard warmth of his body and the beat of his heart slamming against her ear.

They danced like that for hours, through the fast numbers as well as the slow, only pausing every now and again for another drink of mineral water to cool them down.

It didn't really work. It would have taken bucketfuls to make a difference, Ronnie thought. And Kate had been right—it was *the* most romantic evening. She saw Vicky and David glide by on cloud nine, and caught the faint sparkle of a ring on Vicky's finger.

So he had proposed, she thought, as Nick drew her back into his arms, and then she forgot about Vicky and David—forgot about everyone and everything except Nick and how good it felt to be in his arms. As the emcee wound up at the end of the night, they stepped reluctantly apart. 'We'd better go before the car turns into a pumpkin,' he said gruffly, and she somehow managed to remember how to smile.

They retrieved their coats from the cloakroom, and went out into the bright, frosty night.

'Oh, it's cold!' Ronnie said, shivering involuntarily, and his arm came around her and held her against the shelter of his side.

'The car's not far,' he murmured, and then they were rounding the corner and he was putting her in the seat and sliding behind the wheel.

And now what? Ronnie thought on the drive home. She felt suddenly terrified that he would kiss her good-night politely at the door—and terrified that he wouldn't. Oh, help.

He pulled up outside, cut the engine and looked across at her. 'Come in for a while,' he said, and she realised she'd been much more terrified that he *wouldn't* ask her in!

'Just for a minute,' she agreed, and wondered if she'd be able to walk with her heart in her throat and her knees on strike. Apparently she could, because she found herself inside his house, kicking off her shoes and heading for the kettle without giving herself time to think.

'Ronnie?'

'Tea or coffee?'

'Veronica?'

That stopped her in her tracks. She put his kettle down and turned slowly round, and was stunned by the raw desire she saw in his eyes. 'Come here,' he commanded softly, holding out his arms, and she went into them as if he'd reeled her in.

'You are utterly gorgeous,' he murmured, and then her chin was cupped in his strong, clever hands and his lips settled on hers like a sigh.

It wasn't enough. She opened her mouth to him, desperate to be closer, to taste him, to know all of him, and he groaned deep in his throat and engulfed her mouth with his.

She made a little noise, a trembling sigh of surrender, and she felt his hand glide up her thigh and curl around the swell of her hip, drawing her nearer.

'Veronica,' he whispered unsteadily, and his mouth found hers again, wild and demanding. It found an answer in a ravaging need she'd never known she possessed.

She needed to touch him, needed to hold him, to be one with him, without any barriers between them. He must have read her mind, then, because somehow they were together, so she couldn't tell where she ended and he began, and as she gave herself to him she felt an incredible rightness, a wholeness, as if for the first time in her life she was truly complete...

Ronnie ran her hand gently down Nick's spine, feeling the damp satin of his skin against her palm, loving it. Loving him.

Her lover.

Emotion welled in her, and she opened her tear-filled eyes and found him staring down at her, his face stunned.

'Dear God,' he whispered raggedly, and then wrapped her in his arms and cradled her against his shoulder. 'Ronnie, I'm sorry, I never meant this to happen. I just wanted—I didn't want the evening to end. I never dreamt—' He broke off, dropping his head against her shoulder, and another shudder ran through him. 'It just caught me by surprise. You caught me by surprise.' He sounded shell-shocked. She could understand that. She felt pretty shell-shocked herself.

She threaded her fingers through his hair and kissed him. 'Nick, it's OK. It caught me by surprise, too, but that doesn't mean I mind.'

He raised his head and looked around. 'We didn't

even make it upstairs,' he groaned, and started to laugh softly.

'No, and this floor isn't exactly yielding,' she said with a shy smile.

'Oh, Ronnie, I'm sorry.'

He rolled away from her, kicked away his trousers and scooped her up into his arms. 'Let's do this properly,' he said with a lazy smile, and carried her up the stairs to his bedroom. Then he lowered her feet to the floor, sliding her down his body so that she felt every inch of it, and then he stood back and stripped off the rest of his clothes.

He was beautiful. Firm, lean, his body well muscled and yet not heavy, Ronnie thought she hadn't seen anything so beautiful in her life. She reached out to lay a hand on his chest, curious to test the texture of the light scatter of hair, but he stepped back out of reach.

'Undress for me,' he said gruffly, and with a racing heart she turned around, pulled the hem up over her head and let the dress fall to the floor, leaving her naked. Meg's creation was starting to fall down, so she pulled out the pins and shook her head, sending her hair tumbling over her shoulders.

She heard his breath catch and a second of shyness gripped her, then she told herself not to be silly. This was Nick. She loved him. Of course he could see her.

And then she turned, and caught a look of shock on his face.

'Nick?' she murmured.

'Oh, God,' he said rawly. 'I didn't think…' He stared at her body, his eyes anguished, and then he covered his face with his hands and turned away. 'Oh, my God. I'm sorry, Ronnie. Give me a minute.'

And then she remembered Anna—Anna, whom he'd

loved more that life itself, who'd died of breast cancer after a mastectomy.

Tears filled her eyes, and she picked up the dressing-gown lying on the end of his bed and slipped it on. It drowned her, but it didn't matter. Perhaps it was even better that way. She turned up the cuffs, tugged the belt tighter and went over to him.

'Nick? I'm sorry,' she said gently, struggling to control the sadness that was threatening to overwhelm her.

He dropped his hands and stared at her. 'Sorry? Why ever are you sorry? You've done nothing wrong—nothing.'

'It's Anna, isn't it?'

He shuddered and looked away. 'I haven't made love to anyone since her. We didn't get round to undressing downstairs, so it didn't hit me. It was only now, seeing you like that—so beautiful—so whole—'

He broke off and tears filled his eyes. He ignored them and went on, anger in his voice. 'I should have noticed, Ronnie. I'm a doctor, for heaven's sake! I should have noticed there was something wrong with her. God knows, I touched her enough. You'd think I would have felt something…'

He closed his eyes and the tears hovered on his lashes for a moment, then slid heavily down his cheeks. 'I'm sorry,' he whispered. 'I didn't realise it would get me like this.'

Ronnie's heart overflowed with sadness, not just for Nick but for herself. She needed him so much, now more than ever, and yet it suddenly seemed as if there was no place for her here with him. 'Do you want me to go?' she asked in a strained voice.

'No!' He reached out for her, drawing her into his arms. 'No, of course I don't want you to go. It was just the shock. It just hit me—the guilt, again.'

'You've got nothing to feel guilty about, Nick,' she told him, aching to reassure him, uncertain that she could get through this conversation without falling apart. 'It wasn't your fault. It was just a cruel twist of fate. Most breast cancers in young women are too aggressive to treat except in the very early stages. You know that.'

He nodded wearily. 'I know. I just—I know it's irrational, but I thought if I'd checked her, I would have made her do something sooner.'

'And it would probably still have been too late.'

'Yes.' He lifted his head and tipped her chin up to face him. 'Let's go to bed.'

'You want to?'

His hand cupped her cheek, his face so gentle, so loving, so vulnerable. 'Oh, yes. More than ever. I need you, Ronnie.'

She nodded, understanding, knowing he was using her and yet unable to walk away from his need. 'Yes,' she whispered, and he tugged the belt free and slipped the dressing gown off over her shoulders. It puddled on the floor at her feet, and he looked down at her, at the soft fullness of her breasts, pink-tipped and puckering with the cool air, and sucked in his breath.

'Touch me,' she said, wondering if he could or if Anna would get in the way, and his hands came up, trembling slightly, and cupped her breasts.

'You're lovely,' he murmured, and she felt his fingers close gently and squeeze, just slightly. 'So beautiful. I want you, Ronnie,' he whispered, his breath soft against her skin, and his mouth lowered and brushed over one straining nipple.

She cried out and arched against him, and he scooped her up and laid her on the bed, coming down beside her and drawing her nipple into his mouth greedily.

She cried out again, shocked by the sharp stab of desire that shot through her as he suckled deeply on her breast. He switched to the other one, unable to get enough of her, and then his hand was touching her, testing her readiness, stroking her to a wild frenzy.

'Nick,' she sobbed, and he moved over her, covering her with his body, entering her with one swift stroke that brought her to a wild, shuddering climax in his arms.

He followed her seconds later, and this time the tears wouldn't be held in check. He didn't know. He dropped his head into her shoulder, his breath rasping, his heart pounding against hers as she struggled not to cry out loud, and then he shifted so that his weight was off her chest but their bodies were still intimately entwined, neither of them able to let go, too exhausted to move any further.

I love you! she wanted to say, but she knew she couldn't. Not now, with the spectre of Anna looming over them, and maybe not ever. And so she lay in the dimly lit room, the tears drying on her cheeks, and wondered if it would get easier, or if she'd feel this terrible pain of loving Nick every time he touched her.

After a while they grew cold, and he turned out the light and drew the quilt over them. She shivered, and he pulled her into his arms and loved her again and again through the night.

And then the cold fingers of dawn crawled over the horizon, and Ronnie woke with a start to the unaccustomed tenderness of a body well loved, and the sound of her alarm clock on the other side of the wall.

'Oh, my God,' she muttered, and, dropping a feather-soft kiss on his hair, she slid out of bed, dived

into her dress and fled downstairs. She found her shoes
under his trousers in the middle of the hall floor, and
her coat and bag dropped just inside the door.

There was no time to leave him a note, but he would
know where she'd gone, and she daren't wake him
again or she'd never get to work!

She eased the door open, hoping there would be no
one about at six-thirty on a Sunday morning, and as
she stepped onto her path she noticed her car window
was open a crack and it was just starting to rain. She
opened the door, wound it up and shut the door, just
as a battered old car pulled up and the young lad from
over the way was dropped off on the corner.

He jogged up the path, did a mild double take at
Ronnie's evening dress and unbrushed hair, and
grinned.

'I won't tell if you don't,' he called softly, and,
flushing to the roots of her hair, she shot through her
front door and clicked it shut behind her. At least he
hadn't seen her come out of Nick's house!

Ten minutes later she was showered, her make-up
was off and replaced with masses of concealer to cover
the whisker burn and the dark shadows under her eyes.
A pale lipstick to cover the soft, rosy blush of much-
kissed lips, and she was in her uniform and out the
door.

The sound of a car woke Nick, and he stretched and
turned over—and remembered. His eyes flew open, but
she was gone, only the lingering scent of her skin left
to remind him of the night that had passed.

Dear God, she was lovely. Warm, soft, willing—his
body reacted to the memory, and he groaned and rolled
onto his front. How could he feel like this still, after—
what? Four, five times?

'You've got a lot of catching up to do,' he reminded himself, and jackknifed out of bed to see if she'd left him a note downstairs.

He found nothing except her tights, shredded by his eager hands, and his hastily shed shoes and trousers, lying on the hall floor. His briefs were on the bottom stair, and the kitchen lights were still on from last night.

He scooped up his clothes, leaned against the wall and laughed, just with the joy of being alive. It had been wonderful. Making love to Ronnie had been everything he could have hoped for and more.

Much more.

His smile faded, and he sat down on the bottom step with a bump. What was he supposed to tell the children? He couldn't have a discreet affair with her when she lived next door, for heaven's sake! And, anyway, he couldn't expose the kids to any more hurt.

Still, they'd be moving soon. It would be easier then to be discreet—except that Meg and Jimmy might see them creeping around.

He knew that being open and telling the children about him and Ronnie was out of the question. If he ever decided to get married again, and he couldn't believe he would, then he'd tell them. For now, though, this affair with Ronnie had to be kept from them, and from their friends and neighbours, because it would get back to them at school, he was sure.

A secret, he remembered, was something you only told one person at a time.

So, no secrets.

A dull ache in the region of his heart caught him by surprise. Odd. It felt curiously like grief.

Shaking his head to clear it, he ran upstairs, stripped his sheets and put them in the machine, remade the bed and had a shower. Then he tidied up all trace of

Ronnie's visit, hung the sheets out on the line and sat down.

It was hours before he was due to pick up the children, but suddenly he needed to see them, to connect with them, to remind himself of how much he loved them.

He glanced at his watch. Mid-morning. Peter would be in church already, about to take the family service, but Clare and the children might still be in the house. He reached for the phone.

'Hello, darling,' Anna's mother said, sounding friendly and welcoming and making him feel guilty. 'You've just caught us, we were on our way over to the church. I was saying to Peter, it's ages since you've come for lunch. I don't suppose you want to come over, do you? It would be lovely to hear all about your new job and the house.'

'I'll bring the details,' he said, and hung up, humming softly. He didn't need Ronnie—and she certainly didn't need him with all his problems and hang-ups.

He was in the car in less than two minutes.

CHAPTER FIVE

RONNIE didn't see Nick until Monday, and then it was in the usual chaos of the ward. She'd gone home on Sunday afternoon to find he was out, and he didn't come back with the children until nearly nine, after she'd crawled into bed, exhausted.

She'd half hoped he'd left her a note, but there was nothing. She even pulled up the mat in the hall to see if it had drifted underneath—highly unlikely, but she was clutching at straws. Then they came home, and she slipped on her dressing-gown and sat downstairs, hoping he'd ring the doorbell, but he didn't, and in the end she crept back upstairs and lay in her bed, so close to him, and longed for his touch.

And then on Monday, when she was prepping pre-ops, he came in during what she imagined was his coffee-break and tracked her down.

'Ronnie.'

Just the one word, saying nothing really. His eyes gave nothing away, nor did his tone. Her heart sank.

'Morning,' she said brightly. 'All well?'

'Yes—um, fine. Look, Ronnie, can we have a word?'

'What, now? I'm up to my eyes,' she said quietly. 'How about later?'

But later didn't happen. She didn't get a lunch-break because one of Oliver's post-ops started to haemorrhage and had to go back up to Theatre, which took any time she might have scraped up.

Nick came onto the ward later and caught her eye, but she shook her head. She was too busy—a patient's relatives needed to talk to her about taking their mother home and dealing with her colostomy, and she was setting up an appointment for them to talk to the stoma nurse and have the management of her condition explained.

And that evening, of course, the children were about.

He rang her doorbell later on, about nine-thirty, after the house had gone quiet, but he didn't come right in, instead just hovered in the doorway.

'I can't leave the kids,' he explained in a low voice. 'I just needed to talk to you about the other night.'

He seemed distant, a little reserved, and her sinking heart slid a little farther down into her boots. 'What about it?' she said, trying to muster a little calm.

'We didn't—um—it was a bit unexpected. I wasn't prepared for it. I wanted to know if there was any chance you might be pregnant, but I assume you're on the Pill?'

Ronnie laughed, a hollow, humourless little sound that rang in the empty hall. 'Why would I be on the Pill, Nick? It was the first time.'

His brow creased in puzzlement. 'The fir— You mean—' He broke off, looking stunned. 'Ronnie?'

She shrugged. 'It's no big deal. It had to happen some time. It's not exactly a major issue—well, not any more.'

He glanced around, then stepped inside, pushing her back into the hall and closing the door softly. 'You were a *virgin*?' he said incredulously, his eyes locked on hers. She nodded, and his face softened. 'My God, Ronnie—why didn't you say something?'

'Such as what? Like I said, it had to happen some

time, and it doesn't seem to be such a big deal any more.'

'I had no idea. Oh, Ronnie, I'm sorry…'

'Don't be sorry. Just be nice to me.'

That slipped out without her permission, but it seemed to do the trick. With a ragged groan he drew her into his arms and hugged her gently. 'Oh, sweetheart. I wish I'd known, I would have made it special for you.'

She laughed into his shoulder. 'It *was* special. It was a wonderful evening, and a natural conclusion.'

'And I didn't do anything to protect you. Damn.' He cupped her shoulders and held her back, looking down into her eyes. 'Ronnie, are you likely to conceive at this time?'

She shook her head. 'No. I've just had a period—literally just. I'm safe for a few days.'

His shoulders seemed to drop. 'Thank God, because the morning-after pill has a lousy success rate if you leave it too long.' He paused, shifting uncomfortably, then raised his head again and met her eyes. 'Look, Ronnie, we've got to talk about this. It's the kids— I don't want them knowing about us. They've been through so much, and if they think there's any chance we'll get together they'll just get hurt again, and I can't let that happen. They have to come before us.'

The words fell like stones on her heart. He seemed so sure they had no future—and on Saturday night he'd cried for Anna. Maybe he wasn't really over her. Maybe his grief and guilt and love wouldn't let him go, in which case there was no chance for them.

'They don't have to know,' she assured him, trying not to cry out loud.

'If it happens again, they'll find out. What if some-one sees us creeping around?'

Like the teenager on Sunday morning, Ronnie thought with a little flicker of dismay, and knew he was right. Nothing could happen as long as they were living next to each other and the children were around.

'So is this goodbye?' she whispered unsteadily.

His arms tightened around her convulsively. 'No,' he denied. 'I need you, Ronnie. I felt whole again on Saturday for the first time in years. I just don't see how we can work it—and I can't contemplate meeting you in a hotel or anything like that. It's too sordid.'

'But we can still see each other when the children are about. I work with you, I live next door—we can spend time together if we're careful to keep it casual.' Did she sound as desperate as she felt?

'You can help me with the house. Maybe there...'

Her heart, clutching at straws, soared with hope. 'Maybe. I'm sure we can work something out—'

'Daddy?'

He straightened, his head coming up and his arms dropping as he moved towards the door. 'Amy's call-ing. I have to go.'

She followed him, stopping him for a second and going up on tiptoe to press a quick kiss to his lips. 'Knock on the wall and I'll bring you coffee out to the garden,' she suggested, and he laughed a little sadly.

'At least the fence will keep us in order. And, Ronnie? Thanks for Saturday. You're right, it *was* spe-cial.'

And then he was gone, the door clicking softly shut behind him.

Ronnie wandered into the sitting room to wait for

his knock, and curled up in a chair, thinking about what
he'd said.

It was both better and worse than it might have been,
she supposed. Better, in that he hadn't said it had been
a mistake and mustn't happen again at all costs, and
worse, because he seemed so convinced their love was
doomed to failure.

If it *was* love on his part. It certainly was on hers,
at least. there was no doubt in her heart about that.

She sat there in the dark, listening to the murmured
voices and occasional footsteps next door, and finally,
at about ten-thirty, there was a quiet knock on the wall.

She opened the garden door and stepped out, hugging herself against the cold. 'Hi,' she said softly.

'Hi. Sorry to be so long. Amy wouldn't settle.'

'I heard. Is she OK now?'

'I think so.'

A little voice drifted out on the night. 'Daddy? Who
are you talking to?'

He sighed. 'It's Ronnie,' he called softly.

'Is she here?'

He sighed again, and she could picture his resignation on the other side of the fence. 'Forget the coffee,'
he said heavily. 'I'll see you tomorrow.'

''Night,' she murmured. 'Sleep well.'

There was a soft snort, and the click of his latch.
She looked up at the stars, and the crystals of ice along
the top of the fence, and realised it was a bitterly cold
night.

She went back inside, suddenly aware of how cold
her feet were in their thin socks. She made a coffee
and went up to bed, and lay there, her head inches from
Nick's headboard, and missed him.

*   *   *

'Mr Sarazin?'

Nick looked up, to see Sue Warren, his fledgling SHO, hurrying towards him. 'Sorry to call you out of Theatre. She's in cubicle three—she's been brought in by ambulance direct. Her neighbour found her lying in bed, looking very shocked. I think she might have a ruptured bowel.'

'Why?' he asked, forcing himself to concentrate on Sue and not on his thoughts of Ronnie.

'Her abdomen's rigid, she's in a lot of pain, she's got a history of constipation and rectal blood loss, her temperature's 40°C, there's free gas on her abdo film—'

Nick nodded and pushed the curtain aside, moving towards the frail, elderly woman on the bed. 'Do we have a name for her?'

'Winnie Eddison.'

'Winnie?' He bent over the semi-conscious patient, taking her hand and squeezing it gently. 'Winnie, can you hear me? My name's Nick Sarazin—I'm going to have a quick look at your tummy.'

He scanned her as he spoke, noticing the profuse sweating and obvious pain. 'How long have you been feeling sore, Winnie?' he asked her.

She moaned. 'Oh, ages. I was a bit worried about the blood—it seemed a bit much for piles.'

Nick frowned. 'I'm just going to have a listen.' He ran the stethoscope over her abdomen, but it was ominously silent. Glancing up, he saw the X-rays on the light-box and nodded. 'OK. Right, we need to take her up now. Winnie, I'm going to have to have a look inside your tummy and find out what's making you so ill, OK? Do you understand?'

She nodded weakly, clutching at him with thin, bird-like fingers. 'Am I going to be all right?' she asked.

'I hope so. I think you've got a little hole in your bowel, and we need to find out why and sort it out. Right, everybody, let's get her under way. I want two units of blood cross matched, FBC, U and E, blood sugar and amylase, and let's get some saline into her, stat. She'll need a nasogastric tube to empty her stomach, and we'll start her on ampicillin, gentamicin and metronidazole IV. Has she had any pain relief?'

'No,' Sue told him. 'I wanted you to see her first.'

'Right, I've seen her. Let's get 2.5 mg morphine into her IV with 12.5 mg stemetil intramuscularly—now, please. It's all right, Winnie, we'll soon have you feeling better. I'll see you upstairs in a minute.'

He left the bustle in Resus and headed towards Theatre, to warn them and to scrub again. She was frail, she was elderly, she was in a bad way and he didn't want his promise that she would soon be better to be in vain.

They had yet to divine the cause of her perforation, of course. It might be that there was something very simple, or he might have to take out a large section of bowel or give her a temporary colostomy to rest part of it until it recovered. Or it might be much, much worse.

Only time would tell. He rang Ronnie from the theatre and warned her to stand by, giving her all the details he could. 'I don't know about relatives. They said something about a daughter—she might get directed up to you. I'll keep in touch if there's any news.'

'OK. I'll speak to you later.'

'Fine.' He glanced round, but there was no one there.

'What are you doing for lunch?' he asked under his breath.

Ronnie laughed, a soft, musical sound that made his gut clench. 'What's that?' she said wryly. 'We're up to our eyeballs here.'

He was conscious of disappointment, but then Winnie Eddison pushed herself back into the forefront of his mind. 'I have to go. I may not be through here anyway. I'll ring you.'

He scrubbed, finishing just as Winnie was brought in and the anaesthetist took over.

'Right, she's all yours,' he said, and Nick looked at Sue.

'Ever done one of these?'

She shook her head.

'Right. If she was younger or you'd done it before, I'd let you tackle it. As it is, watch carefully and keep your hands clean. I might let you do a bit if you're good.'

He caught Kate's eye and grinned. He and Kate were all right now. He'd spoken to her, told her he wasn't her type and she'd settled down into an easy bantering relationship which he could live with.

He held out his hand and she slapped a scalpel precisely into his palm. He thought it was a good job she wasn't a vindictive shrew, or that might have been the end of his surgical career.

'Right, we want a nice big incision so we can see what's happening, but we don't have to go mad. Let's find out what her problem is.'

Ronnie picked up the phone to find Nick on the other end, and gave a sigh of relief. 'How is it? You've been ages. Her daughter's frantic.'

'Sorry. She's OK. She had a very messy threadbare bowel. She's obviously had diverticular disease for years, and she's been neglecting it. I've had to remove about half of her colon and give her a permanent colostomy, unfortunately, but I'd say she was lucky her neighbour found her. I don't think she would have lasted much longer.'

'Is she coming to us or going to ITU?'

He snorted. 'What do you think? She's only got raging peritonitis and massive blood loss.'

'Oh, a day case, then,' Ronnie joked, and Nick snorted at the other end of the line.

'I'll see you later—she'll be with you in about half an hour. I have to go back to my list. Anyone prepped and ready?'

'Only about four. I'll warn them you're under way again.'

And that was how Wednesday went on. Thursday wasn't much better, and then she finally had a day off.

A long weekend, in fact. She could always go down to Southampton and visit her father, but a tiny bit of her about a mile wide wanted to stay put in case Nick had time to notice she was alive.

Then, on Friday night, when she'd cleaned the house from top to bottom, done her shopping and was about to start on a pile of ironing, he knocked on her door, children in tow, and dangled some keys under her nose. 'I've got the house.'

'It's yours?' she asked, and then without thinking she hugged him, pulling back almost as soon as she touched him because she remembered she wasn't supposed to do it. Then she looked down at the children and grinned. 'How exciting! Are you going over there now?'

'We're going to have a pizza picnic on the floor,' Ben told her.

'I want chicken and mushroom pie,' Amy began, and Nick hugged her against his side.

'You can have chicken and mushroom pie, sweetheart,' he assured her, and then met Ronnie's eyes again. 'Um—we wondered, if you're not doing anything, if you wanted to join us. After all, we wouldn't have found it without you, so you ought to be there to celebrate.'

She tried to be practical and not allow herself to drown in the smoky depths of his eyes. 'Isn't the power off?' she said doubtfully, looking round at the gathering dusk.

He chuckled. 'Oh, yes, and it will be freezing in the house, but I'm taking a few candles and I thought we might light a fire.'

It sounded like fun—much more fun than her ironing. 'I'll grab my coat,' she said, and ran to fetch it, scooping up a packet of biscuits on the way. 'Anything else I should bring?'

'Just yourself,' he told her, and she wasn't sure if she imagined it or if there was real warmth in his voice.

The journey was very short—so short it was hardly worth getting in the car, but it was cold and dark and, anyway, they had to get the pizza—and the pie!

The children were fizzing with excitement, and so was Ronnie. She'd hardly had a moment to speak to Nick except on the ward, and it had always been hurried, always about patients and always frustrating! Now he'd invited her to join them, and she wondered how much coercion he'd had from the children, and how much of the invitation had come from him.

'I'm sitting on the window-seat!' Ben yelled, pelting

into the house past them and going straight to the bottom of the 'tower' rooms.

Amy ran after him, protesting, and Nick and Ronnie followed more slowly. 'There are five window-seats—I don't think we have to rush,' he said drily. He put the bags down on the middle seat, spread out a rug on the floor and set out all the picnic paraphernalia in the middle.

They were able to see reasonably well because of the streetlights outside, and so he didn't have to bother with the candles, to Ronnie's relief. She could just picture Ben charging past and knocking one over, starting a fire.

There was a big pizza box, a paper-wrapped pie for Amy, four glasses, a carton of juice and a bottle of wine.

'Alky-free, I'm afraid, but I'm driving,' Nick said with an apologetic grin.

'I'm quite happy with that,' Ronnie assured him. 'Can I do anything?'

'Eat,' he said, and the children slithered off the window-seats and dived into the pizza box.

'Hey, you've got a pie!' Ben yelled, and Amy started to cry.

'She can have a bit of pizza, too, if she wants,' Nick said, and Amy stuck her tongue out. Ronnie said nothing, but wondered how much Amy didn't like pizza and how much she wanted the extra attention of having to have a pie as well.

Hmm.

She caught Amy's eye just as she took a huge bite of pizza, and the girl looked uncomfortable for a second. Ronnie stifled a smile. So, she was just playing games with her dad. How like a little girl.

'Are you going to try the fire?' she asked Nick as they munched.

'It's cold,' Amy said, shivering and unwrapping her pie, her little legs sticking out from under the paper. She looked like a little doll, sitting bolt upright with her legs out straight as only children were flexible enough to do.

'Yeah, light the fire, Dad,' Ben urged. 'It'll be really cool to have a fire.'

Ronnie nearly laughed. Cool, to have a fire? Still, never mind the strange phraseology, it was lovely to see them both so excited. She tore up the pizza box and crumpled up Amy's pie paper, while Nick took a torch and brought in some coal from the coal bunker by the back door.

'Here we go—a fire.' Then he patted his pockets a little helplessly, and looked at Ronnie. 'I don't suppose you've got matches?'

Ronnie fished in her bag and brought out a cheap plastic cigarette lighter, one of those disposable gas ones. 'Here—this any good?'

Nick took it thoughtfully. 'I didn't know you smoked.'

'I don't. My car-door lock freezes up sometimes. I always carry it in the winter.'

'How resourceful.' He flicked the wheel, and held the flame to the crumpled paper in the grate. As it caught and started to blaze, Ronnie wondered belatedly when the chimney had last been swept. There were flecks of soot on the floor by the grate, and more in the grate itself.

If it was blocked, of course, it wouldn't draw…

The cardboard box caught, greasy from the cheese,

and within moments the room was filled with billowing smoke.

Oops!

They started to cough, and Nick took the carton of juice and threw it at the fire, dousing the flames in a great steaming sizzle.

'Chimney's blocked,' he wheezed, and caught Ronnie's eye. She was laughing—she couldn't help herself, and nor could the children, and then Nick joined in, sagging back against the marble surround and laughing till tears streamed down his face.

'I'll open the window,' he gasped after a moment, and pushed one of the casements up to slide the catch across. As he released it, it crashed down, the sash cords broken, and the glass shattered all over the garden outside.

There was a second of stunned silence, then he swore, quietly and very mildly but with considerable feeling.

Ben wagged his finger. 'Swear-box, Daddy,' he said virtuously, and Nick rolled his eyes.

'I'll go outside and push it up—Ronnie, could you push the catch across for me? And I'll have to find some board and seal it up. Blast.'

He stomped outside, and Ronnie and the children started to giggle.

'What?' he said, standing outside in the garden, his hands on his hips, glowering at them through the window. 'What now?'

Ronnie shook her head, biting the inside of her lip, and stood up. 'Nothing. Shut the window.'

He harrumphed and stepped up to the outside of the window, and glass crunched under his feet.

'You'll have to clear that up so cats don't cut them-

selves on it,' Ronnie advised, and earned herself another dirty look through the shattered pane as he
slammed the window up. Oops! Somebody was in a
grump! She slipped the catch across, pulled out a loose
piece of glass and handed it to him through the hole.

'Here—another bit for the pile.'

'So kind.'

He stomped back inside, grinding to a halt when
Ronnie yelled at him, 'Shoes!'

'What about them?'

'They'll be full of glass.'

He muttered something that Ben didn't hear, or there
would have been another contribution to the swear-box,
and marched into the room in socks.

'Anybody got any other ideas?' he asked drily, and
Ronnie handed him a glass of wine.

'Yes—drink this and relax. I know it's unleaded—
just pretend.'

He gave a weary gust of laughter and took the glass,
dropping down beside her on his haunches. 'Come
round the house with me while these two finish off the
pizza and the biscuits. I want to tell you what I've
planned—and then we'll see if there's a bit of board
in the garden we can use to block up the window.'

He helped her to her feet, picked up the torch and
told the children to stay where they were. Then he took
her upstairs, right to the top, closed the attic door and
drew her into his arms in the dim glow from the streetlights. 'I've been wanting to do this all week,' he
sighed, and just as his mouth came down on hers, they
heard Amy's voice.

'Daddy? Daddy, I need a wee and I can't see the
loo!'

He groaned and laughed. 'Tomorrow. They're going

to Anna's parents in the morning, and staying for half-term. We'll come back tomorrow—and I'll sweep the chimneys and we can have a fire and a real picnic.'

He went down, and Ronnie looked around the gloomy attic. One room was still full of junk, and rolled up at one side was an old rug.

They could unroll it in front of the fire, she thought, and remembered all the films she'd seen with couples entwined in front of a fireplace, their bodies gilded by the dancing flames, and she wondered if that was what Nick had in mind, and if he'd think she was brazen to suggest it.

Whatever, just to be on the safe side, she'd nip into a chemist in the morning. There was no harm in being prepared!

'Stay for lunch,' Anna's mother coaxed.

Nick shook his head, feeling a little guilty. 'I want to get on with the house. The first thing I've got to do is fix a window, and then sweep the chimneys.'

'We had a fire, and it smoked all in the room, and Daddy threw orange juice on it to put it out!' Amy told her grandmother excitedly.

'Oh, darling, is it safe?' Clare asked worriedly. He nodded, laughing. 'Oh, it's safe. Richard's checked it for me. It just needs…a little work, that's all. Well, probably more than just a little,' he confessed. 'There's masses to do before the builders start, and I want to do as much as I can this weekend.'

'Well, be careful. Don't overdo it. You're looking tired.'

'I'm fine,' he assured her. 'Don't worry about me.'

'Ronnie can help you, Daddy,' Amy suggested.

'Who's Ronnie?' Peter asked.

'Um—my neighbour,' Nick said, being what Anna would have called frugal with the truth.

'How kind of him,' Clare said.

'He's not a him, he's a her,' Amy explained, and Nick avoided everyone's eyes and chuckled at Amy's grammar.

'I must get on—I need to get to the builders' merchants before they shut,' he said a little wildly.

'Well, have fun and keep in touch,' Clare said, eyeing him speculatively. He kissed her, and wondered if she could read his mind and realised that he just wanted to get back to Ronnie. Probably. Oh, damn.

It was lust, he told himself, temporary insanity. He'd get over it. Familiarity breeds contempt, he reminded himself. Given time, he'd lose interest. Not that he'd lost interest in Anna in over ten years. Still, that was different.

Wasn't it?

CHAPTER SIX

RONNIE had arranged to meet Nick at the house at eleven-thirty, after he'd dropped the children off with their grandparents.

There had been a sort of suppressed, guilty longing in his eyes as he'd asked her to spend the day with him, and she wondered if he felt guilty because of Anna's parents babysitting while he dallied with her, or if it was because of Anna, or if she'd just misunderstood.

She didn't have a clue. It could have been any of them, or a bit of each. Whatever, she didn't feel guilty, and she was having a lot of trouble being suppressed. She was *aching* to be alone with him again, even just to talk, to smile, to laugh without an audience of interested bystanders.

She rang the doorbell, a sort of metal knob that you pulled which made a great clanging down the hall in the bowels of the house. It was like something out of a horror movie, and she almost laughed.

She would have if she'd been able to breathe, but Nick opened the door and her jaw dropped. He was wearing a scruffy old shirt and jeans with holes in the knees, his face was smeared with soot and he looked about ten years younger and good enough to eat.

He propped himself in the doorway and grinned, boyish and grubby and gorgeous, and her breath eased out in a ragged chuckle. 'You remind me of Dick Van Dyke in *Mary Poppins*,' she teased, eyeing the delicious scruffiness of him. 'Or one of Fagin's little monsters in *Oliver*.'

'Fagin's little monsters.' He pretended to glare at her, but there was no malice in it. 'You wait,' he threatened. 'You get to do the clean-up. I've saved it especially for you.'

'Clean up what—you, or the fireplace?' she asked, following him into the tower room. Chimney rods and brushes were scattered about the floor, there was a heap of soot in the grate and more tramped over the floor, and she could only imagine how well it would have stuck to that orange juice he'd thrown on the fire last night!

He grinned, his teeth startlingly white against the soot on his face. 'Both,' he said slowly, and she felt heat run through her. 'In fact, let's clean up the fireplace together, and then we can clean up each other.'

'Let's not. It'll take a deep bath and half a bar of soap to shift that lot,' she said, tilting her head at him and trying hard not to think about cleaning him up, 'and there's no hot water here.'

He snorted softly. 'Wrong. The old gas geyser over the sink works, after a fashion. I'll open the window while it runs, and we can carry the water upstairs to the bathroom.'

'Isn't that a lot of effort?' Ronnie asked, clamping down on her hyperactive imagination. 'We could just go home—or use cold.'

He raised an eyebrow. 'I'm sick of cold showers at the moment,' he said huskily. 'I'm looking forward to a nice, hot bath—and there's lots of room in that one.'

Their eyes met, and heat seared between them. For a second Ronnie stood there, motionless, and then she managed to drag her eyes away. 'Ah—um—we'd better get cleared up here, then,' she croaked, and wondered where the self-possessed, sensible, unruffled Sister Matthews had gone.

Legged it, at the first sign of trouble, she thought with a quiet chuckle of despair, and looked around for a dustpan and brush.

It took them two hours to sweep the main chimney in the drawing room that overlooked the cloistered and secluded garden, and another hour to clear up the soot even vaguely.

It seemed to get everywhere, into every nook and cranny, and, as Nick said, there was precious little point in worrying about it, because the electrician and plumber were about to descend on Monday and make far more mess.

'I'm starving,' Ronnie announced as they stood back grubbily and admired their handiwork.

'Me, too. I've brought a picnic. Let's get cleaned up and we can eat.'

They didn't bother with the bath, because they couldn't find a bucket that didn't leak. Instead, they washed in the kitchen sink, swilling off their arms and hands and faces as well as they could. Then Nick took the flannel from her and dabbed at her cheek.

'You've got a streak still,' he said softly, and his voice was tender and a little gruff and Ronnie could have stood there forever with his hands dabbing gently at her face. He'd taken off his shirt, and she was only too aware of the breadth of his shoulders and the smoothness of his skin, gliding tautly over firm muscle and strong bone. A drop of water was slithering down his neck, over the hollow of his throat and down into the fine, dark hair in the centre of his chest. She wanted to catch it on her tongue, to lick the droplet away...

Then he dropped the flannel in the sink, cradled her face in his hands and pressed a simple, innocent kiss to her lips.

'I'm going to light the fire in the drawing room,' he murmured, and released her. 'There's an old rug up in the attic—you might try to bring it down and put it in front of the fireplace, so we can sit on it to eat.'

He tugged on a jumper instead of the sooty shirt and went out of the back door to fetch coal and wood and whatever for the fire.

She stood rooted to the spot for what seemed like an age, and then remembered to breathe again. That rug she'd had fantasies about! And a fire—oh, heavens!

She ran up to the attic, pulled the heavy rug out of the room and down the stairs, and looked at it. It was dusty and grubby, and needed a good thump. She dragged it out of the back door, just as Nick was coming back up the path with an armful of kindling.

'Want to help me bang the dust out of this?' she asked, and he gave her a slightly strained smile.

'Sure. I'll just put this in the fireplace and get it lit.'

Had she imagined the tension on his face? She didn't think so. What had happened to the easy camaraderie of earlier? And the light-hearted flirtation? The shared bath, for heaven's sake! Her heart sank and she forced herself to concentrate on being sensible. 'Want my lighter?'

He shook his head. 'I've got matches. I'm a good boy scout today.'

So was she, Ronnie thought, remembering the condoms in her bag and forgetting all about being sensible. Well, that sort of sensible, anyway. Colour ran into her cheeks, and she reminded herself that they very likely wouldn't be needed anyway, with that look on his face. With a sigh she hoisted the rug over her shoulder and set off down the garden to find a suitable spot.

There was a washing line, sagging diagonally across the overgrown lawn, and Nick appeared just as she was struggling to flop the rug over it.

'Let me help,' he said, and took the other end, lifting it easily. He'd brought an old broom and, telling her to stand back, he thumped the broom into the middle of the rug. Dirt and dust flew, and she coughed and stepped back, happy to leave him to it.

After a few minutes he gave up, and tugged it off the line.

'That should do it,' he said, and draped it over his shoulder. 'Time for lunch.'

They ate in front of the fire which was now burning merrily in the drawing room, with a good view out over the tangled garden, and the February sun poured in and warmed them from the other side. Ronnie thought it would have been perfect if there hadn't been that strange tension between them which she couldn't quite fathom.

She hadn't imagined it earlier, when he'd passed her on the path, and it had got worse. She didn't know why it had suddenly sprung up, but it was almost as if he was nervous. She had a funny feeling he was going to tell her something she didn't want to hear.

Then Nick caught her eye, and everything seemed to tilt on its axis and slide quietly into another dimension. 'OK?' he asked softly, and she nodded.

'Time for dessert,' he said, and reached into the cool-box. He held up a strawberry, fat and ripe and hopelessly out of season but all the more delicious for it, and she bit into it and juice ran down over her lips.

He ate the other half, then leaned forward and caught the dribble of juice on her chin with his tongue just before she wiped it away. Her breath jammed in her throat, but he didn't kiss her. He just fed her another strawberry, and then another, each time catching the juice with an elusive sweep of his tongue, until she was ready to scream with frustration.

Finally, he swept the picnic aside and moved closer, kneeling in front of the fire and drawing her up into his arms so that they knelt face to face.

Then, and only then, did he kiss her, and she thought her bones would melt with the tender onslaught of his mouth and the relief of knowing that he still wanted her.

She could still taste strawberries on his lips, sweet and fresh and somehow wickedly exotic, and she closed her eyes and sighed against him. This was where she belonged, she thought vaguely. Here, with Nick, in his arms, making what was surely love.

Common sense resurrected itself, and she looked past him to the window. 'Isn't this a bit dangerous?' she asked, looking out into the garden. 'We might be seen.'

'The gate's locked, and there are no houses overlooking us.' He trailed a finger down her cheek, under her chin and down to the buttons of her shirt, slipping the first one free. 'No one's going to see us.'

He was right. She stopped worrying and concentrated on Nick.

And Nick, being the good boy scout he'd promised, remembered what she'd forgotten yet again so there would be no unforeseen consequences.

She felt sad, with that tiny scrap of her brain that still had independent function, but she knew he was right. There were already too many complications, even if her body did cry out to bear his child.

Not now, she told herself, and maybe not ever, but for now at least she had him, and the flickering flames of a real fire, and the fading warmth of the afternoon sun sinking behind the lilac at the end of the overgrown garden.

And then she stopped thinking about anything except the power of his body locked with hers, and the feel of his skin, and the sensation welling in her until it fractured into a thousand fragments and sent her tumbling into heaven.

Ronnie ached from end to end. Two days of clearing up soot, ripping off wallpaper and scrubbing out the insides of the kitchen cupboards while Nick stripped the paint on the doors had left her tired, stiff and yet curiously exhilarated.

Or was that because of the little sorties to the drawing room, to picnic and make love on the ancient rug, surrounded by the secrecy of the garden and cocooned in the warmth of the fire?

Either. Both. Whatever the cause, she was finding Monday morning back at work a little hard to cope with. They'd settled into an easy camaraderie over the weekend, and Ronnie wondered how Nick would behave towards her in front of their colleagues.

They'd been seen at the ball plastered all over each other on the dance floor, so there surely wouldn't be any surprises to anyone if they were seen together. Of course they'd be professional, and there'd be no stolen kisses in the sluice or quick cuddles in the kitchen, she thought regretfully, but maybe he'd smile that special smile, or say something quietly to make her pulse race and her cheeks heat.

Heaven knows, just seeing him, it would probably be enough to do that!

And yet when she did there was no time to worry about what they'd done at the weekend or how they would react to each other in public, because he had just come onto the ward when he was bleeped.

'May I?' Nick asked, heading for her office.

'Be my guest.'

Ronnie followed him, hoping for a quiet word, but his manner alerted her professional instincts, and she eavesdropped shamelessly. He straightened, looked at her with growing dismay in his eyes and snapped out a few questions.

'Send him up now—just get him stabilised enough to move and send him straight to Theatre. I'll go and scrub—yeah, I'm on the ward now. I'll tell them.'

He put the phone down and ran his hand over his hair. 'That was A and E. Ryan O'Connor's been stabbed by a patient.'

Ronnie felt her blood run cold. 'Oh, my God. I'll get a room ready.'

'Don't hurry. It sounds as if he might not make it. I've changed my mind, I'm going down there—I might have to open him up in Resus. I don't know if we've got time to move him. Ring and tell them, would you? I'll be in touch.'

And he left, his long stride eating up the floor, and once through the doors she heard him break into a run. It must be serious, she thought numbly. Poor Ryan. She'd only met the gentle Canadian A and E consultant a few times, but he'd impressed her with his kindness and warmth, and he was very highly thought of professionally.

What a great loss it would be if some random act of violence wiped him out just like that, without warning.

She thought of Ginny, his wife of two years, and wondered if she knew, and how they would tell her.

And then she wondered how she'd feel if it was Nick, and she felt cold all the way to her heart. It was then, at that moment, that she realised how much she loved him.

'Chest saw,' Nick rapped out, and it was in his hand before he'd finished speaking. My God, he thought moments later, looking at the blood pouring into the cavity in front of him. 'Suction!'

Again they were there almost before he asked, a well-orchestrated team, working without thought, without hesitation, on one of their number, fighting for him as they would for anyone, but with that extra edge of commitment and determination. Nobody was going to give up on this man—nobody!

'Pressure's dropping,' the anaesthetist warned, and the nurse who was bagging in the blood as fast as she could squeezed even faster.

'We need another vein—someone do a cutdown on his ankle and get another line in fast, please. I can't see where this leak is.'

He took the sucker from the nurse and swept the area, watching like a hawk for any hint of where the blood might be coming from.

'Got it,' he said finally and, reaching into Ryan's chest, he grabbed the offending vessel. 'Right, let's sew this one up and look for the others.'

It took hours, tackling the main leaks in A and E

and then transferring him to Theatre for some slow, thorough searching to make sure all the leaks had been found and every vessel repaired. Amazingly, Ryan's heart had been missed, but his lungs and pulmonary vessels had been badly damaged, and Nick was still very concerned.

'He'll need to go to ITU,' he said, and was greeted with a wry snort from the anaesthetist.

'Not a chance. They're chock-a-block. Didn't you hear the news last night? There was a bad accident on the A14—some went to Addenbrookes, others to Ipswich, some here. ITU is already overstretched.'

Nick wiped his face on his shoulder and sighed. 'I can't just send him to the ward—unless Ronnie can get extra staff. He'll need qualified specialling for at least twenty-four hours.'

'Ring her.'

Nick nodded, his head still bent over Ryan's chest, scanning the surgical field for leaks and any other cuts he might have missed. Finally satisfied that there were none, he closed the chest wall and straightened. It was four-thirty—six and a half hours, give or take, since they'd started.

His stomach rumbled, and he stretched his neck and rolled his head on his shoulders. 'OK, let's take him through to Recovery and look after him there for a little while—I'll ring Ronnie and talk to her about a bed, and I suppose I ought to speak to his wife.'

'She's waiting outside.'

That comment was from Matt Jordan, the other A and E consultant, who had stood quietly at the back for the past hour without interruption. Nick turned to look at him, tugging down his mask and snapping off the blood-streaked gloves. 'I'll talk to her.'

'I'll come with you, if you like. I know her pretty well.'

'How is she?'

Matt raised an eyebrow. 'How would you be?'

Nick grinned. 'About that good, I suspect.'

Actually, she was holding up very well—until they went out there and told her that Ryan had come through the operation and had a chance. Then she seemed to crumple, first her face, then the rest of her body, and Matt caught her against his chest and hugged her, cradling her gently.

'That's right, you let go. You're a brave girl. Well done,' he murmured, and Nick left them alone. She was in good hands. He could speak to her in a minute. Just for now, he wanted to talk to Ronnie—and not only about their patient.

He just needed to connect with her, and it was a need he didn't like to examine too closely. He rang ITU first just to confirm the anaesthetist's prediction that they were full, then stabbed in the number of the ward extension. Ronnie picked up on the second ring.

'Surgical, Sister Matthews speaking.'

'Ronnie, it's Nick. We've just sent him through to Recovery.'

He could almost feel her sigh of relief. 'Well done,' she said, and she sounded a little choked. 'How is he?'

'Not good. I've plugged all the leaks but I had to open his chest in Resus. He's a mess, but I'm hoping he'll pull through. ITU, though, are over-full and can't take him. I'll keep him up here for a while, but then he'll have to come down to you. Is there anyone who can special him?'

'I'll do it,' she said without hesitation.

'But you've been on duty all day.'

'That's all right. There's no one else available at such short notice that I'd trust with him. I'll go home now, sleep till midnight and then come in. He can stay there till then, can't he?'

'Yes. I'll hang around here, just in case he springs another leak.'

'There's a duty room off the ward—it may not be in use. You could sleep there,' she suggested.

It sounded ideal. At least that way he could be within reach and still be fit to do his job tomorrow. 'I'll give you my keys and you can bring some stuff back with you so I don't have to look like a street bum in the morning.'

She laughed, a warm, sexy chuckle. 'I think you'd make a lovely street bum,' she teased, and he laughed.

'Thanks, Ronnie. I'll see you in a minute. I'll just check up on him and I'll come down and go over his notes with you. I imagine you'll have company most of the night—I expect his wife will stay beside him.'

'That's fine,' Ronnie assured him. 'She's a doctor, anyway. She won't be a problem.'

He hung up, curiously reluctant to break the connection, and cradled the phone tiredly. He still had hours of work to get through before he could even think about lying down, but right now he needed a short break. He checked that Ryan was stable and looking good, and then, without bothering to change, he headed down to the surgical ward—and Ronnie.

'Long day?' she commiserated, searching Nick's face with eyes all the sharper for loving him.

He grinned, a wry, tip-tilted grin with little humour and a lot of exhaustion, and nodded. 'I thought we were going to lose him,' he confessed. 'We couldn't find the leak, and every time we found one, he was leaking from somewhere else. It was a nightmare.'

'How's he looking now?' she asked, heading automatically for the kitchen and the kettle.

'Rough, but alive. Better than he did six hours ago.'

'I'll bet.' He was jiggling something in his pocket, and she held out her hand. 'Got your house keys?'

He dropped them in her palm. 'I forgot.'

He looked exhausted with the strain, and she tried to imagine what it must be like to come in new to an organisation and have everyone watch you struggle to save the life of a colleague. Talk about stress! 'What do you want—pyjamas? Wash stuff? Clean underwear?'

He grinned. 'Yeah—and a shirt, if you can find a clean one that doesn't need ironing.'

'I'll do my best.' She slid a cup of tea across the worktop to him and cradled her own mug thoughtfully. 'So, how long do you expect him to remain critical?'

'Hopefully, not long. The first twenty-four hours will be the worst. After that he should start to improve, but the greatest danger is clotting. His chest is like a colander—if we give him too much anticoagulant, he'll just leak all over again. If we don't, he'll clot. Catch-22.'

'So you'll juggle.'

He nodded. 'And let's just hope I don't drop the balls.'

He drained his tea, hot as it was, and put the mug down. 'I'm going back up. I'll see you later. Want me to give you a wake-up call?'

She smiled with relief. 'Would you? I might sleep through the alarm—or else not go to sleep in case I do!'

He chuckled. 'I know the feeling. You go to bed and sleep, princess,' he said softly. 'I'll wake you at eleven-thirty.'

And then he leaned over, pressed a quick, firm kiss to her lips and went.

CHAPTER SEVEN

'WAKEY-WAKEY, rise and shine!'

Ronnie groaned and rolled over, burying her face in the pillow. Nick was too darned chirpy for that time of night.

'Ronnie? Ronnie, wake up.'

''Mawake,' she mumbled into the receiver, and forced herself to sit up, pushing the hair back off her face and blinking in the dim light from the streetlamps. 'How is he?'

'Hanging on. Doesn't look wonderful. I keep bullying ITU, but they haven't got anything imminent. How soon can you get here?'

'I'm on my way,' she promised, sliding out of bed and standing up, just to make sure she didn't succumb to the urge to snuggle back down in the warm covers and slither off to oblivion again. 'Give me fifteen minutes and I'll be with you.'

She washed hastily, in tepid water to wake her up a little more, threw on a clean uniform and headed for the door. She was hungry, but she could make some toast on the ward. It wasn't a problem. She was on the ward in fourteen minutes, and rang Recovery to tell them she was in.

Five minutes later the rumble of wheels on the corridor warned her their patient was arriving, and Ryan was wheeled in and reattached to the waiting monitors. The night sister on duty came in and chatted for a moment, and then, once they were happy everything was working properly and he was stable after his transfer, she went.

'You made it, well done,' Nick said softly as she left.

'Of course. I said I'd be here.'

He grinned. 'So you did.'

'Where's Ginny?' Ronnie asked. 'Did she have to go home?'

He shook his head. 'No, I've sent her for something to eat—she hasn't had anything all day. The kids are with Matt and Sarah Jordan. They're at the same school or something and live just round the corner, so it's easy. I think Sarah's going to bring them in to see her in the morning. Where is she going to sleep?'

Ronnie thought how she'd feel, and knew the answer. 'Beside him—if she sleeps at all. I could bring in a little cot, but if he arrests or haemorrhages we could waste precious seconds moving it out of the way, so I think she'd better stay in the chair. They're pretty comfortable. She won't be the first person to have done it.'

'Or the last,' he said softly, looking down at Ryan. 'Tell me about him.'

Nick handed her the slim volume of notes off the end of the bed. 'Here are the details. I'm really more worried about things we might have missed than things we found, but as time goes by I think he might be lucky. Just watch his pressure and respirations like a hawk. Any sign of a pneumothorax, haemothorax, cardiac tamponade or any little gems like that, shout.'

Ronnie gave him a slight smile. 'Oh, don't you worry, I will. I put your stuff in the duty room,' she added, remembering how she'd felt, going through his drawers looking for clothes. She hadn't known where to find anything, and it was an odd feeling. It made her feel even more excluded in a way—after all, if she was a proper part of his life she'd know where he kept his pants and socks and shirts, and what type of toothpaste he used.

And there hadn't been an ironed shirt, so she'd taken one home and done it herself, quickly. It had felt frighteningly domestic, and she was well aware that she was only doing it to counteract the feeling of exclusion she'd had in his bedroom.

She forced herself to concentrate on Ryan O'Connor, but she was hungry and thirsty and Nick was just too close.

'How about some tea and toast?' she suggested.

He grinned. 'Sounds good. Who's going to make it?'

'Can I trust you with my patient?' she teased softly, and he chuckled.

'I think so, just about.'

So she left him with Ryan, went into the little kitchen and put the kettle on. The toaster swallowed four slices of bread with ease, and she leaned back against the worktop and wondered how she would cope with Nick just up the corridor, and if she'd be able to resist the urge to go in to him.

Thank God she was going to have to watch Ryan so closely! It might be the only thing to keep her sane.

The toast popped up and she buttered it generously. Never mind cholestrol, she thought. Tonight she needed comfort food, and hot buttered toast and tea would just hit the spot.

She took the tray back and found Nick making notes on the clipboard at the end of the bed.

'Problems?' she asked, setting the tray down on the locker.

'No. Just adjusting the dose of painkiller. He's got an automatic cylinder driver to deliver it, but he's bigger than I'd thought so I've upped the dose a touch. Can you adjust the pump?'

'Sure. Here, have some toast.' She altered the delivery rate on the infusion pump, and then sat down with her mug and a slice of dripping toast.

'Are you trying to kill me with heart disease?' he asked quizzically, and she grinned.

'Comfort food. There have to be some compensations for working all night and, let's face it, neither of us need to watch our weight.'

He chuckled softly, and took another slice. He didn't seem to mind, she thought, despite his words. There was something very companionable about sitting there in the dimly lit room, with nothing but the blip of the monitors and the soft, regular sound of Ryan's breathing to disturb them.

The nurses were going quietly about their duties, their feet almost silent on the shiny plastic floor, and, apart from the occasional groan from a patient in distress, there was nothing to distract her thoughts from Nick sitting there just across the bed, looking more tempting than he had any right to look after such a long day.

His jaw was heavily shadowed, his eyes red-rimmed and a little bloodshot, and he should have inspired her sympathy. Instead, she wanted nothing more than to drag him up the corridor to the privacy of the duty doctor's room and make love to him.

Apparently, it was mutual, she realised, catching his eye and surprising a look of longing there. 'Hello, foxy lady,' he said under his breath, and she felt her heart pick up and her skin colour softly.

Her lips parted slightly, and she closed her eyes and bent her head so she didn't have to look into those searing eyes and see what she couldn't have. At least, not now.

Ryan moaned softly, and instantly her head snapped up and she scanned the monitors automatically. His heart rate had picked up a little, but his blood pressure, measured by the central venous pressure line, was steady and constant.

'He's waking up,' Nick murmured. 'Damn, Ginny wanted to be here. Ryan? It's Nick Sarazin. How are you feeling?'

Ryan's eyes flickered open and he groaned again. 'Hurt,' he said, and tried to lick his lips. Ronnie tore open a pack of swabs and moistened his mouth with cool water. His eyes opened again and he tried to focus on her.

'Where am I?'

'Surgical ward—you had a fight in A and E.'

'Oh, Lord, yes,' he mumbled, and his eyes slid shut. 'So, what happened?' he slurred. 'My chest feels sawn in half.'

'It is,' Nick told him drily. 'I'm now intimately acquainted with the contents. He got your lungs and pulmonary vessels, but missed your heart. You're one lucky honcho.'

'I am?' he said with a weak smile. 'That's tough. Does that mean I'm going to live?'

'I'm afraid so.'

He said something rude under his breath, and Nick chuckled. 'I think you're definitely going to live. Ginny's just getting something to eat, she'll be back in a minute.'

He looked around, trying to focus, and frowned. 'Is this ITU?'

'No,' Ronnie told him. 'They didn't want you—too much trouble, they said. Staff are always difficult patients. They ask stupid questions and won't do as they're told, so they sent you to us.'

He chuckled, and then a spasm of pain crossed his features. 'Hell, you really did saw it up, didn't you?' he muttered after a moment. 'I always wondered what it felt like. Now I know, and I wish I didn't.' He said something else that would have had Ben reaching for the swear-box, and Ronnie wiped away the beads of sweat that formed on his brow.

He was propped up in the bed, his pillows carefully arranged to support his ribcage, and there was a long strip of gauze over the centre of his chest, covering the incision. The wound was sealed with plastic skin to prevent infection, but covered to prevent the sutures from catching on bedclothes. He was naked, of course, as were all post-operative patients of his severity, just covered with a light sheet for modesty and warmth. She checked the urinary catheter, the nasogastric tube, the wound drain, the intravenous line—and wondered how Ginny would feel about all the tubes going in and out of his battered body.

Awful, probably. It was a horrible shock, although, as a doctor, of course, she'd have seen it often enough. It must be different when it was your own partner, though. Ryan moved restlessly, and Ronnie shifted one of the pillows a fraction to prop his head better. He relaxed against it, his eyes fluttering shut, and he seemed to drift off again.

Then Ginny came into the room, looking taut as a

bowstring and worried sick, and as if he knew she was there his eyes instantly opened.

'Hi, honey,' he murmured, and Ginny swallowed hard and blinked away tears.

'Hi, yourself. What the hell are you trying to do to me, O'Connor?'

He gave a lopsided grin. 'Who, me? You mean you care?'

She gave up trying to be brave then, and sat down in the big comfy chair beside him, laid her head on the edge of the bed and sobbed. His hand, the one without the drip, came out and rested on her head, and she grabbed it like a lifeline and hung on until she had herself under control again.

Then she lifted her head and glared at him. 'What were you doing? I gather you tried to get the knife off him! You must be mad!'

Nick put a restraining hand on her shoulder. 'Can you tell him off when he's better?' he said with gentle humour. 'I think she's glad you're still alive, Ryan,' he added to their patient, and Ryan's mouth twitched in what could have been a smile.

'He needs to rest, Ginny, and so do you,' Ronnie told her. 'Can I get you a blanket and a pillow, so you can make yourself comfortable beside him?'

Ginny nodded, scrubbing the tears from her cheeks and looking embarrassed. 'I'm sorry. It's just been a hell of a day. I'll be good now.'

Ryan drifted off to sleep again, and for a while Ginny sat and watched the monitors with Ronnie. Then the strain of the day was too much for her, and her eyelids drooped. Ronnie stayed awake and alert, watching, checking, reading the notes and marvelling that he was so well and fit after his ordeal.

At four Ginny woke with a start and sat up. 'Is he all right?' she asked softly, her voice panicky with dread.

'He's fine—nice and steady.'

Ginny sagged back against the chair. 'I thought—I had a dream...' She couldn't finish, but it didn't take much imagination to know what was in the dream.

'Want some tea?' Ronnie asked Ginny.

'Please. I won't sleep again now. Do you want me to make it?'

She shook her head. 'No, it's all right. I'll do it. Holler if he has a problem.'

'I will,' Ginny promised fervently. 'Don't worry.'

Ronnie slipped out of the room and went into the kitchen. A staff nurse followed her in. 'All right?' she asked.

'Yes, he's fine. Can you keep an ear open? I'm just going to report to Mr Sarazin—he's in the duty doctor's room.'

'OK. Will do. If he's about, you couldn't ask him to have a look at Winnie Eddison, could you? She seems to be in a lot of pain—she might have a paralytic ileus.'

'Sure. I'll do it now.'

She left the kettle to boil, and went up the corridor to the duty room and slipped inside. 'Nick?'

'How is he?'

'Fine.' She shut the door and gave herself a moment to adjust to the darkness, then sat on the bed. 'Beth says can you have a look at Mrs Eddison? She thinks she's got a paralytic ileus.'

'Sure.'

She felt his hand curve round her hip and slide up, cupping the back of her neck and drawing her down.

Their lips met in the darkness, tender and regretful. 'I want you,' he murmured.

'Mmm,' she agreed, resting her head against his shoulder. 'Not a good idea. I can't leave Ryan that long and it might cause a bit of a stir amongst the gossips.'

He chuckled and patted her leg. 'Very likely. Go on, then, you temptress. Go back to your patient and let me get up. I'll go and see Mrs Eddison and come and find you. Any chance of a cup of tea?'

'The kettle's on,' she told him, and dropped a kiss on his rough, scratchy jaw. 'You might want to shave before you come out—you feel like a pirate.'

'I thought women found that very sexy,' he murmured in a gravelly voice.

'They do,' she assured him, and stood up before she did something stupid, like tear off her clothes and jump in beside him. 'I'll make your tea. Don't be long.'

She tugged her uniform straight, ran a hand over her hair and went back to the kitchen. The kettle had boiled, so she made three cups of tea, took them into Ryan's room and caught Ginny in tears.

'What's wrong?' she asked urgently, scanning the monitors. Surely nothing had happened in the few minutes she'd been gone?

'Oh, I'm just being silly,' Ginny assured her with a watery, apologetic smile. 'He seems fine. I can't believe it. I thought he was dying.'

'*Everybody* thought he was dying,' Ronnie told her gently. 'I think they just wouldn't let him.'

Ginny nodded. 'You don't always have a choice,' she pointed out. 'No matter how hard you fight, sometimes the injury's just too severe. I know that. I've been there. They say it never happens to you, but this time I really thought it had.'

'Well, he's made it through the surgery, anyway,' Ronnie said guardedly. She didn't want to overdo the optimism, because there was still a long way to go and there was many a slip 'twixt the cup and the lip, and all that. She passed Ginny a mug of tea.

'I woke Nick. He'll be here in a minute. He's going to have a look at one of the other patients, and then come and have his tea.'

Ginny nodded. 'It was kind of him to stay the night here.'

'I think he just didn't want to take any risks—not after spending so long yesterday struggling with leaks. If anything else crops up, he wants to be in reach.'

'He's very kind.'

'I'm sure Ryan would do the same for him.'

'Probably.'

They shared a smile, then Ginny turned her attention back to the monitors. 'We just have to watch and wait now, I suppose,' she said quietly.

Ronnie nodded. In truth there was little else that they could do. Ryan was on a special bed designed for immobile patients so he wouldn't get problems with pressure areas in the few days before he could move again, and in the meantime all Ronnie had to do was keep a constant eye on all his systems and let him rest.

Nick came and had his tea, chatting quietly with Ginny while Ronnie stretched her legs down the corridor and spent a few minutes staring into space.

Nick looked much tidier and more conventional now, she thought absently—clean-shaven, bright-eyed and dressed in clean, pressed clothes, he was a far cry from the exhausted surgeon of last night or the filthy, scruffy and yet sexy man she'd spent the weekend with.

So many people all rolled into one, she mused. Would the real Nicholas Sarazin please stand up?

'Penny for them.'

She jumped, startled by his silent approach, and turned and smiled at him. 'You sneaked up on me,' she chastised softly.

'What are you doing?'

'Just taking five. I was looking at the stars.' And remembering the weekend, she thought to herself. It seemed a lifetime since he'd held her in his arms.

He rested a hand on her shoulder and looked up into the night sky. 'Beautiful, isn't it? There'll be a frost.'

'It was icy last night when I came in.'

She turned and leaned against the wall. 'Is Ryan all right?'

'I've left Ginny in charge for a moment. I thought I might go back to bed—try and catch another couple of hours before morning. Want to wake me at seven with a cup of tea?' His lazy, beguiling smile was her undoing.

'You'll get spoilt,' she warned.

'Mmm. I could learn to enjoy it.'

And I could spend a lifetime doing it, given half a chance, she thought. She pushed herself away from the wall. 'Go on, then, go back to bed and I'll go and watch Ryan. I'll wake you if there's any change.'

He walked back with her, telling her about Mrs Eddison's paralytic ileus, and then paused at the door of the duty room. He seemed almost tempted to ask her in, but that was just wishful thinking. There was no way he would ask, and no way she could go.

She dredged up a smile. 'I'll see you at seven. Sleep tight, you lucky thing.'

'Won't you have tomorrow off?'

'Do you mean today? Probably not. Depends if they can get cover. I'll work till midday in any case. I can't remember who's on this afternoon. If it's Trish, I can hand over to her. If it's Vicky, I shouldn't, really. She's a bit young to have so much responsibility and since she's been engaged she's been a bit elsewhere on the concentration front.'

He chuckled softly. 'Elsewhere—I like that. I know the feeling.'

So did Ronnie, but she wasn't admitting it to him in a lifetime. She left him at the door and went back to Ryan and Ginny.

'How are you?'

'Sore as heck.'

Ronnie smiled and sat down beside Ryan on the comfy chair. 'So use the pump.'

He gave the infusion pump with its ready supply of pain relief a jaundiced glare. 'I have. It's the bone. It just scrapes every time I move—and the physio's just gone.'

'Ah. Torture time.'

'Tell me about it,' he snorted. 'She keeps making me cough.'

'You need to.' Ronnie ran a practised eye over the monitors.

'I'm fine. I'm watching myself. Don't worry, I'll holler if I start to go downhill.'

Ronnie chuckled. 'I doubt if you will now. It's been three days—it's time you got up.'

'Very funny,' he growled.

She rolled her eyes. 'Why is it,' she mused out loud, 'that doctors are so good at dishing it out and so bad at taking it?'

'Because they know how much it's going to hurt?' he offered drily.

'Could be.' She flashed him a smile. 'Nevertheless, I think you could sit out for a while this morning.'

'I quite agree—time we got you back down to A and E and working again, instead of lying about.'

Ronnie threw Nick a grin over her shoulder. 'Hi, there. Come and help me bully him. He doesn't want to get up.'

'Oh, he wants to get up,' Ryan corrected her. 'He just doesn't want to hurt like the blazes while he does it!'

'I'll let you get over your physio, then we'll help you out. Have another squirt from the pump in the meantime, help it wear off.'

'I've squeezed the thing dry. It won't deliver.'

'So yell when you've had the next dose.'

He gave a careful snort of disgust.

'Promise,' Ronnie threatened gently.

'I promise,' he sighed, and dropped his head back. He looked better, she thought, but not much. She supposed he'd come about as close to death as one would wish to, and not unnaturally it showed. However, thanks to Nick and his team, it looked as though all the injuries had been found and dealt with, so it was just simply a question of sitting out the healing time.

Not easy, when you were a busy, active man with a restless mind and a hatred of being dependent—and Ryan hated it.

Nick examined his handiwork, praised himself for his brilliance and followed Ronnie out, grinning. 'Don't you think I'm stunning?' he said with a chuckle.

'I don't need to—you're already sufficiently vain without my help. Come on, you've got a ward full of pre-ops to reassure and check over, and some post-ops, needing your attention.'

'How's Mrs Eddison's paralytic ileus?'

'Better.'

'Good.' He paused, well away from any ears that might be listening to their conversation. 'What are you doing tonight?'

'Nothing. Why?'

'The electricians have finished the rewiring and the plumber's making progress—I thought we could have a look at the house. Maybe pick up a take-away and eat it there by the fire.'

The message in his eyes was unmistakable, and Ronnie was tempted—too tempted to refuse. She smiled. 'Sounds good. What time?'

'Meet me there at seven?' he suggested.

'OK.'

'Good.' His eyes tracked over her, then returned to her face. 'Let's go and see these patients before I forget I'm supposed to be behaving and drag you into the linen cupboard.'

The evening was frustrating. The house was a mess from end to end, of course, but progress had certainly been made. There was no drawing-room floor to have a picnic on, though, because the boards were up, and the other rooms were at the front of the house or else it wasn't possible to have a fire in them—and it was too darned cold without one for what they had in mind!

In the end they sat in the bottom tower room with its newly reglazed window and panoramic view of the street, and ate their Chinese take-away in front of a properly drawing fire and with a safe foot of space between them.

Frustrating, but possibly a good idea, Ronnie reluctantly acknowledged—and it didn't stop Nick from spreading out a blanket on the floor under the window-seat and lying down with her and kissing her senseless, which was even more frustrating but probably very good for their self-control.

Of course, if they hadn't had to be so obsessive about keeping it all a secret, then they could have been in her bed or his, doing what their bodies and minds craved to do, without any feelings of guilt or shame.

Ronnie slept badly that night, with Nick just on the other side of the wall, and in the morning it was hard to find a smile at work.

'What's wrong?' Ryan asked softly as she tended to his drip.

'Nothing,' she said, pulling out the cannula and taping the little hole in his arm. 'Press that for me.'

Obediently he put a finger over the plaster and pressed. 'Funny-looking nothing. Is it Nick?'

Her head snapped up. 'What about him?'

Ryan shrugged, then winced. 'Just a thought. He was all over you like a rash at the ball. You couldn't have fitted a credit card between you, you were so close.'

She felt herself colour. 'You're imagining it.'

'And am I imagining the looks he gives you? Or the look you get when he's around? Come on, Ronnie. I know how it is. I've been married twice, head over heels in love both times. I can recognise the symptoms.'

'You should be resting,' she told him stiffly, avoiding his eye.

His hand caught her wrist, and she couldn't pull away for fear of hurting him. 'Look at me,' he ordered.

'No.'

'Yes. Ronnie, you can talk to me. It won't go any further. Sometimes it helps to have a shoulder to lean on.'

She gulped, blinking back the sudden tears that took her by surprise, and sank down onto the chair.

'That's better. Now, tell Uncle Ry all about it.'

She sniffed and gave him a watery grin. 'Oh, Ryan, there's nothing to tell. We're having an affair, but he's got kids—his wife died four years ago.'

'Sounds all very familiar to me,' Ryan said gently. 'Don't tell me—he's worried about hurting the kids and he's keeping you a deep, dark secret.'

Ronnie's head snapped up. 'How did you know?'

He gave a wry laugh. 'Been there, done that, worn out the T-shirt. Ginny had a word for it—she used to say she was Category Three. Not wife, not colleague, but sex slave. I thought she was mad, but afterwards I realised just how much it had hurt her. I never meant to, Ronnie, just as I'm sure Nick doesn't mean to hurt you, but at least you're an adult and you've got choices. The children in these relationships have no choices.'

'No. I know that. I'm just being self-pitying and be-having like a spoilt brat.'

He reached out his hand and patted her fist, clenched round a handful of blanket on the edge of the bed. 'No. You're in love, and you want to shout it from the roof-tops, and you can't. If it helps, he probably feels the same.'

Ronnie hadn't thought of that. Not that it changed anything, of course, but maybe it would help her to be more accepting of the situation. She nodded. 'Thanks, Ryan—and, please, don't say anything to Nick. He'd hate it if he knew I'd talked about us.'

Ryan smiled tiredly. 'Don't worry, I won't.' His eyes slipped shut, and she straightened his bedclothes and left him to sleep. He was still very weak and needed time to heal.

She wondered how much time Nick would take before he was healed enough to love again—if at all.

Patience wasn't her strong suit.

'So, what's this I hear about you sneaking out of Nick's house after the ball?' Meg said, leaning forward and scanning Ronnie's face eagerly.

'Oh, Meg, how did you hear about that?' she wailed, blushing furiously and burying her face in her mug.

'Sam's mother told me. She was looking out for him because she knew he hadn't come home, and she saw you through the window, just as he got back.'

Ronnie groaned. 'Hell. And I thought no one knew!'

Meg laughed. 'You can't do anything in this town without people finding out, far less this road! So, tell me all about it!' she continued, leaning forward again with that eager look still on her face. 'That new dress obviously did the trick.'

Ronnie sighed. 'There's nothing much to tell, really. We went to the ball, came back and I stayed the night with him.'

'And since?'

She thought of the weekend of decorating, and the frustration of the previous night, and closed her eyes. 'It's…difficult.'

'Because of the kids,' Meg said, understanding without having to have it spelled out. 'But they're on half-term at the moment—they're away. Why aren't you round there all night, taking advantage of that gorgeous man—or are you shinnying over the fence, you sly thing?'

Ronnie shook her head. 'Unfortunately not,' she said wryly.

'You need your bumps felt,' Meg snorted, getting up and putting the kettle on again. 'If a man like that showed the slightest interest in me, I'd be in there like a shot.'

'That's the trouble, of course,' Ronnie said softly. 'He only does show the slightest interest. Oh, he's keen enough if we get a chance, but he's obsessive about the kids finding out.'

'But surely they will?' Meg said. 'Children aren't stupid. They'll notice, no matter how careful you are.'

'That's why I said there's nothing going on. There really isn't, and I don't think there ever will be, unfortunately.'

'So no wedding bells?' Meg said sympathetically.

Ronnie sighed. 'No. No wedding bells—not as long as he's got the children, anyway. While they're around there's no danger of us getting married—not even close.' There was a thud, and the front door slammed back against the hall wall. Meg lifted her head. 'Jimmy?' she said, and he appeared in the doorway. 'Hello, love. Had fun?' she asked.

He nodded. 'I've been playing football with Mickey,' he said. 'Hi, Ronnie. What's for supper, Mum?'

'Shepherd's pie. You staying, Ronnie?'

She shook her head. 'I must go,' she said. 'I'll raid the freezer and then do my ironing. I'll see you. Thanks for the coffee.'

'My pleasure. Keep me posted.'

Ronnie went home, closed her front door and leaned

against it with a sigh. Nick was away for the weekend, and she wouldn't see him again until Sunday night when he came back with the children.

Funny, she'd never really felt lonely until they'd moved in. She'd been tempted to have supper with Meg, but that was silly. She had to deal with this. After all, it seemed very likely she was going to be alone for a long, long time, because Nick Sarazin and his children were going to be a hard act to follow.

She decided to go and visit her father and stepmother for the weekend. Perhaps that would take her mind off him—and she wouldn't have to deal with her ironing!

CHAPTER EIGHT

'GOOD weekend?'

'Sort of. I've been to Southampton to see my father.'
Ronnie perched on the edge of Ryan's bed and checked
his pulse.

'So that's why Nick's looking grumpy,' Ryan
mused.

'Nonsense. Shut up, I'm counting.'

Ryan grinned and she ignored him, losing count yet
again and having to start from scratch for the third
time. 'You're a nuisance—but you'll live. That's nice
and steady. How are you feeling?'

'Better than I was, but still a long way off.'

'I'm sure.' She eyed his colour thoughtfully. 'You
don't look anaemic.'

'I can't be. They pumped gallons of blood into me,
by all accounts.'

'And you promptly squandered it. You, of all people,
should know better,' she teased, and stood up. 'Time
to sit out?'

He groaned, but obediently swung his legs over the
side of the bed and sat himself up. 'Ow, ow-ow-ow,'
he muttered under his breath.

'Coward.'

'Yeah, right. Just give me a hand and shut up.'

She helped him into the chair, settled him down and
tucked a blanket round his knees. 'I feel about a hundred,' he grumbled. 'All I need is a nightcap on my
head—you know, one of those pointy ones with a little
bobble on the end?'

She chuckled and left him to it, wading through a stack of professional journals he hadn't had time to read. She'd take him for a walk later, and maybe get one of the porters to take him down to A and E to see his friends. Ginny came in when she could with the children, but they couldn't spend all day with him and he was feeling a little isolated.

Not for long. She was halfway down the corridor with him in a very sedate and steady walk when a crowd of doctors and nurses came round the corner and cheered.

'Hey, it's the boss!' one of them yelled, and his face cracked into a grin.

'Hello, guys and girls,' he said with a laugh. 'Come to brighten up my life?'

'We've brought you a present—us.'

'How are you?'

'You don't look too bad—isn't it time you were back?'

'Yeah, we miss you. Nobody to nag us.'

Ronnie waved at them all to quieten them down, and then carefully helped Ryan back to bed. 'Now, not too much noise, you lot, or I'll throw you out—savvy? I can't have you disturbing my post-ops.'

'Yes, ma'am!' one of them said, and she recognised Matt Jordan, the other Canadian A and E consultant.

'You—keep them in order,' she told him firmly, and he grinned and winked.

'I'll do my best.'

It wasn't good enough. After half an hour of steadily escalating racket, she went back into the room and good-naturedly threw them all out. Ryan had had enough anyway, she could tell, and he was only being polite.

She shut the door behind them and turned to him. 'You OK?'

'Yes—I will be. I think I could use some sleep.'

She laughed softly. 'I expect so. That lot are enough to try anyone's patience.'

'I can forgive them—they saved my life,' he reminded her, and she smiled and tucked the bedclothes round him.

'So they did. You rest now. I expect Ginny will be in later, won't she?'

He nodded tiredly, and she left him to it. He would probably sleep for ages, and it would do him good. For most of the first week he hadn't been able to sleep very well because of the pain and the unnatural position. Now at least he could lie down. She closed the door softly behind her, and went to check that Oliver Henderson's post-ops were all stable and comfortable.

'So will you be done by Thursday?'

The plumber scratched his jaw and stared into space, while Nick hung onto his temper with difficulty. 'Probably,' he replied at last.

'Is that very probably, or probably not?'

The man grinned. 'Depends.'

'On?'

He heaved a sigh. 'Well, that water tank in the loft, for one. And, of course, if the pipes in the bathroom all have to be concealed, then I've got to box them in on the wall behind—that's going to take longer.'

Nick nodded. 'But could you be out of the rest of the house by then so the decorators can start? I just want the hall and drawing room clear initially, and the kids' bedrooms, so we can slap on a quick coat of paint and tart it up to start with.'

'Hmm. Pushing it.'

'But?'

'Reckon we might manage that,' the plumber conceded.

Nick felt he'd gone ten rounds with a world heavyweight, but he had agreement—albeit reluctant—that he could bring the decorators in to start at the end of the week, and for now that would have to do.

He looked around the house in tired disbelief. So much to do. Just looking at it made him feel exhausted. If only he could afford to have it all done by someone else. Well, he probably could, but only by dipping into Anna's life assurance, and he'd got that invested for the children.

He leaned on the doorpost in the drawing room and looked at the floor in front of the fireplace where he and Ronnie had made love that weekend. It seemed ages ago. Too long.

He glanced at his watch, and sighed. He had to go home and fetch the children from Meg, then fight with them about homework and bathing and bedtime.

And then, once they were in bed, there was nothing to do but sit and think about Ronnie, about the softness of her skin, and the warmth of her smile, and the feel of her arms around him—

He shoved himself away from the doorframe with a growl of frustration, and headed for the door. 'I'm off, Steve,' he called to the plumber.

There was a grunt from under the kitchen sink, and he let himself out of the front door. He should be feeling good about the progress the house was making and the way the kids were settling down.

Instead, he wanted more.

He wanted Ronnie, and he couldn't have her.

He slammed the car door, gunned it out of the drive into the traffic and vented his spleen on the throttle.

*　　*　　*

'Are you sure it means that?'

Ben screwed up his nose thoughtfully, and Ronnie sat back and waited for him to see what he was doing wrong.

'Oh—you have to take it away,' he said eventually, and Ronnie tousled his hair and grinned.

'Well done. Right, Amy, let's hear this reading, then.'

They were settled down at the kitchen table, poring over Amy's reading book, when Nick rang the doorbell.

'I'll get it,' Ben yelled, and ran to the door.

'Hi—I thought I'd lost you,' Nick said, and his deep, gravelly voice did funny things to Ronnie's insides. She forced herself to stay there and not rush to greet him with the same enthusiasm as Ben.

She couldn't stop herself from returning his smile when he came into the kitchen, though. 'Hi,' she said softly. 'Meg had a headache—I hope you don't mind them coming here.'

'No, of course not,' he said, and settled his hips against the worktop just opposite her, brightening up her view no end. 'I hope you didn't mind.'

'Absolutely not. Coffee or tea?' she asked. 'Or wine? There might be some red in the cupboard.'

'Wine sounds wonderful,' he said wearily and, turning a chair round, he straddled it, looking sexier than he had any right to. She busied herself with the corkscrew, and then set the glass down in front of him on the edge of the table.

He smiled gratefully up at her and raised the glass, and the message in his eyes was unmistakable. She felt a terrible urge to laugh—or cry. She wasn't sure which, but there was a real feel to the situation of, 'Hi, honey, I'm home.' Any minute now she would start asking him about his day—which was absurd, because she knew all about his day. She'd been there.

Oh, knickers, she thought tiredly.

Amy was still reading out loud, her blunt little finger following the words, hesitating every now and again, and Nick was prompting her when necessary.

He was good, she thought. He didn't just tell her the answer, he helped her to work the word out, and it was obvious he'd done it hundreds of times before.

Without her.

She picked up her glass and sipped from it, and let him deal with the children. It was his job. They were his children, and they weren't ever going to be hers.

Even if she did occasionally let herself pretend they would.

'The decorators go in on Thursday,' Nick volunteered, swivelling round to see her better. '*If* the plumber's out of the way. He's being very cagey about it, and I don't know if he's just being awkward or if he really is behind.'

'Let's hope he's just being awkward. Do you owe him money?'

Nick nodded.

'Good. He's more likely to do the work if he stands to get a nice fat chunk of dosh when it's finished. Human nature, isn't it? We all need a reward, and sometimes just doing the job well isn't enough.'

She reached over and topped up his wine, and he gave her a tired smile. 'Don't give me too much—I've got to cook for this lot yet.'

'We could have pizza,' Amy suggested absently without lifting her head. 'I like chicken and sweetcorn.'

Ben and Nick turned to stare at her, but she kept her head bent over her book, her little finger moving slowly across the page, her lips silently forming the words.

Nick looked up and sought Ronnie's eyes. 'Pizza?' he said incredulously.

She shrugged and suppressed a smile. 'Apparently.'

'Fancy pizza?' he asked her.

'It's up to you. It's your supper.'

'Join us,' he said, and there was a plea in his voice she couldn't ignore. Not that she tried.

'That would be lovely,' she told him. 'Your place or mine?'

'Mine. We can put the children in the bath while we finish the bottle that way.'

Was he thawing?

Or just as desperate for her company as she was for his?

Or, in the end, would that add up to the same thing?

The pizza arrived just as they were settling down in front of the gas fire in Nick's sitting room. Ronnie had hardly spent any time there, and it seemed strange. A mirror image of her own, and furnished by the hospital in almost identical style to hers, it was bare and bleak and characterless, like a waiting room.

Like hers had been when she'd moved in, but she'd lived there for years now and had made it her own. He'd only been there five weeks or so, and for them it was very temporary. He had an excuse.

They sat round in a ring, with the pizza boxes open on the coffee-table, and pulled slices off at random, ignoring niceties like plates and cutlery. Amy's first slice had a great dangling string of cheese hanging off it, and it trailed down her chin and gave her and Ben the giggles.

It was impossible not to join in their silliness, and over their heads she caught sight of Nick's face. He looked years younger, truly happy, and she wondered if she was a part of that happiness, or still on the outside, looking in.

He leaned across the table and wiped Amy's chin gently with a tissue. 'Mucky urchin,' he said affectionately, and Ronnie felt even more isolated.

Then he looked up and caught her eye, and winked, and she felt all her worries dissolve. Give him time, she told herself. Do what Ryan said and give him time.

She settled back with her glass of wine, and watched them clean up the last few slices of pizza in no time flat. Then Nick went out to the kitchen and came back with bowls heaped with ice cream, bananas and chocolate sauce, and then, while Ronnie cleared up the mess and made coffee, Nick hustled the children through the bathtime routine and into bed.

'I'll come up in twenty minutes to put your lights out,' he called as he came down, and Ronnie looked up as he walked into the kitchen.

'Coffee,' she said, holding out his mug, and he took it, smiling gratefully.

'Lifesaver,' he murmured. 'Come and sit down.'

They sat at each end of the sofa, their hands meshed on the centre cushion, and then Ronnie turned and swung her legs up so her toes were tucked under his thigh and she could feel the warmth of his leg against her feet.

His hand came down and snuggled her ankles, and she settled her head against the back of the settee and thought that life couldn't really get much better. 'What are you doing at the weekend?' he asked drowsily, breaking the long, companionable silence.

'Working Saturday, nothing Sunday. Why?'

He gave a slow, wry smile. 'Because we're decorating the kids' bedrooms. I wondered if you wanted to help.'

She chuckled. 'I expect I might be coerced into it,' she agreed. 'Any idea what you're doing?'

'Well, Amy predictably wants yellow again, but most of her bedding is yellow, so that's fine. Ben said something about spaceships and planets, but I don't know what we can do about that.'

Ronnie sat up a little more and shuffled her bottom back against the arm of the sofa. 'How about a very dark blue ceiling?' she suggested, seeing it in her mind's eye. 'With stars and planets on it. You can get maps. My sister did it for her son a couple of years ago—she might still have the map. You have the light fitting for the sun, and work out from there.'

'On dark blue?' he said sceptically.

'Yes—almost black. You hardly notice it, it's like a stage, going up into the bit where they hang the lights and hoist up the scenery—you know.'

'Or the night sky, even.'

She laughed at the dry tone in his voice. 'Even that,' she agreed with a smile. 'And then you graduate the colour down so that by eye level it's soft grey-blue, and by the skirting board it's white. You can stencil spaceships and satellites and things in silver around the top, and it's wonderful.'

'It sounds it. Can you ask your sister about the map?'

'Sure—and now I'm going to go home and do my ironing and get an early night, because I have to be at work for seven tomorrow and you need to go and turn their lights out.'

He stood up and pulled her to her feet but, instead of releasing her, he drew her into his arms. 'I wish you could stay. I wish we could spend the night together.'

'Maybe another time,' she suggested.

'Maybe next weekend—not this one, but the one after. We'll go to a hotel—I'll treat you. We'll have a lazy, romantic dinner, and a lie-in in the morning.'

She swallowed hard. 'That sounds wonderful,' she said breathlessly.

'Good.' He lowered his head and brushed her lips with his. 'Now, go home before I do something silly and irresponsible.'

It sounded tempting, but she stepped back and made herself walk towards the door. 'I'll see you tomorrow. Thanks for the pizza.'

'My pleasure. Thanks for the wine.'

He kissed her again, right inside the front door, where the children could easily have seen them if they'd come to the head of the stairs, and then he opened the door and she went out into the chilly night, and back into her own house.

It seemed incredibly quiet and empty.

Ryan made great strides that week. Perhaps because he could sleep properly at last, he seemed to find his natural reserves and bounced back. By Thursday he was wandering around the ward, sticking his nose in everyone's notes and getting in the way.

'Do you think you should be at home?' Ronnie suggested with a smile as he gatecrashed her, giving report.

He smiled and propped himself up against the wall. 'Good heavens, no. I'd have nobody to irritate and nothing to do. I'd go crazy.'

'Well, we aren't having you in here, driving us nuts, for the next four weeks until you're fit to go back to work, so perhaps you'd better send Ginny out to buy you some jigsaws or something.'

He snorted and eased himself carefully away from the wall. 'I can tell when I'm not wanted,' he grumbled good-naturedly, and ambled off up the ward, stopping to chat to the patients on the way.

'He's going to find it very hard convalescing,' Ronnie mused, watching him.

'He'll cope. He'll have to. He's nothing like fit enough to go back to work yet,' Vicky said pragmatically. 'He'll just have to learn to amuse himself. Buy a computer game or something.'

'Or read that stack of journals. That should keep him quiet.'

They laughed and moved on to the next patient, but Ronnie kept her eye on Ryan. He went into the day room, and she made a mental note to go and see him in a while. Perhaps he needed someone from Occupational Therapy to give him something to do.

Andy Graham, Nick's first patient, came in to visit them later. He'd been transferred to Orthopaedics because one of his legs hadn't lined up well and he had to have a series of operations, and he went into the day room and found Ryan, who had been on duty when he'd come in to A and E.

Ronnie found them playing cards, both of them cheating outrageously, and she left them to it. It kept Ryan out of her hair, and Andy wasn't doing any harm and was obviously bored to death with his slow recovery.

She rang the ward to let them know where he was, and over the next few days it became a routine. It seemed to keep Ryan sane, which was just as well because he periodically spiked a temperature, and Nick was unhappy to let him go home until he was truly well again.

On Sunday morning Ronnie was looking forward to her first day off in ages. She woke up to the sound of

Nick and the children chatting in his bedroom at some
ghastly hour. She couldn't hear the words, but she
could understand the tone of voice.

The children wanted to go and decorate, and Nick
wanted to sleep. Judging by Nick's howls of outrage
and the giggles from the children, they were winning.
She turned over, snuggled down again and smiled.
She'd get up later—much later—and go and help
them...

'I don't know why you think we needed such an early
start anyway,' she grumbled, perched at the top of a
stepladder slapping midnight blue paint on Ben's ceiling.

'Perhaps by the time you get down to the skirting
boards, you will,' Nick said with a grin. He was painting the walls white so that she could bring the gradu-
ated colour down over them in a wash, and it would
have been so easy to reach over with the roller and
splat him with navy paint.

She debated it, and gave up. He was right. There
was a lot to do, and Amy was grumbling that she just
had plain yellow walls and she needed something
pretty.

'I could do a stencil round Amy's walls,' Ronnie
suggested. 'Clowns and balloons and little animals, or
something. Perhaps a circus frieze?'

'She's got sort of circus striped bedding,' Nick
mumbled from the corner. 'That would look nice.'

'Do we need to see the bedding to choose the colours?' Ronnie asked, reaching for the last bit of white.

'No, I've done it the same colour as the last room,
to make it easier.'

He straightened up, his hands on the small of his

back, and stretched. 'I'm getting too old for this,' he grumbled.

Ronnie laughed unsympathetically. 'Not enough exercise, that's your trouble.'

'No opportunity,' he said, looking up at her on the ladder with an unmistakably suggestive smile. 'Next weekend, however…'

She grinned and climbed down the ladder, brushing against him tantalisingly. 'Mmm. Lovely thought. Exercise has never been more appealing!'

'Have you done it?'

They looked round at Ben, who was standing in the doorway, looking puzzled. 'We're getting there, sprog,' Nick said affectionately. 'What do you think so far?' He peered around, his face a little crestfallen. 'I thought my walls were going to be sort of shady,' he said, and his voice was rich with disappointment.

'They are,' Ronnie assured him. 'We've just got to wait for the white to dry and we can start painting them. We're going to look at Amy's now while we wait.'

She put her roller in a plastic bag and wiped her hands on her old shirt. No matter how careful she was, she got paint all over herself always. There was probably some in her hair, and she knew for a fact there was a smear of it on her nose.

Ah, well.

She followed Nick next door into Amy's room, and cannoned into his back in the doorway.

'Oh, Amy,' he said disbelievingly, and Ronnie peered round his arm and gasped.

Amy, obviously having decided that Ben was having too much attention, had decided to paint flowers on her bedroom walls. Huge, blue and white flowers that splodged and dribbled down the walls, and had obviously splodged and dribbled down Amy as well. Paint was in her hair, all over her clothes, and after one look at her father's face she dissolved into tears and dropped the brush on her shoes.

Nick closed his eyes, leaned against the wall and counted softly under his breath.

When he was in the mid-twenties, Ronnie elbowed him out of the way and took over.

'Whoops,' she said gently, and picked the brush up off Amy's newish trainers. 'I think we need to get you and your clothes into the bath, sweetheart, while Daddy sorts out your walls. We were just talking about some circusy things—animals and balloons and clowns and big tops and so forth—does that sound nice?'

'I want flowers,' she hiccuped, and started to wail again.

'We'll discuss it. Let's get you cleaned up first. Nick, do we have hot water—Nick?' she added, a little more sharply, and he opened his eyes and scanned the room again, before focusing on her.

'What?' he croaked. If ever there was a desperate man, she thought with an inward smile.

'Hot water?'

'Oh. Um—yes, should be. Use their bathroom—the bath still needs to be restored, so she won't be able to do it any damage. Unlike the walls in here...'

'How about a nice wash over with a sponge and a bucket before it dries, and then another coat of yellow, hmm?' she coaxed, and ushered Amy into the bathroom before he killed her.

Half an hour later the miserable little miscreant was at least substantially paint-free, and so were her clothes and trainers. Everything, child included, was soggy, but there didn't seem to be any towels.

Ronnie pulled the lever that lifted the huge brass

plug out of the bath, and told Amy not to move while she found something to dry her with.

'I've got a stack of old towels for washing down the walls and things—in the kitchen in a carrier bag,' Nick told her, swiping, grim-lipped, at the tenacious flowers.

Whoops. Ronnie ran down to the kitchen, found the towels and ran back up to Amy, who hadn't moved so much as a hair. She scooped the little girl out of the bath, towelled her off and wrapped her in another one, then rubbed her hair as dry as she could.

'I don't know what you're going to wear, poppet,' she said thoughtfully. 'What about if I give you my jumper?'

She dressed Amy in her own socks and underwear, and pulled the jumper over the child's head, turning up the sleeves about six times so that the slightly blue little hands could peek out of the cuffs.

'I think you've got something to say to Daddy, don't you?' she said gently, and Amy nodded and clung to her leg.

'I wanted flowers,' she said, and started to cry again. 'Ben's having spaceships.'

'I know.' She hunkered down on the floor at Amy's level and looked her in the eye. 'Do you want flowers, or circus things?'

'Circus,' Amy said. 'With flowers,' she added as an afterthought.

'Circus with flowers,' Ronnie said in confirmation. 'Let's go and see what Daddy says.'

Daddy was putty in her hands, of course. He sighed, shook his head and held out his arms, and Amy rushed into them and buried her head in his shoulder. He straightened up, her little legs wrapped round his waist, and hugged her while she cried.

Ronnie left them to it. He was quite capable of dealing with his own six-year-old daughter, and if she was off the scene too long, Ben might start on his room and then all hell would break loose!

It took several evenings and a few more tins of paint, but by the following Thursday the children's rooms were finished except for new curtains, and they were ready to move in.

The carpet for the hall, stairs and landing, the snug and the children's rooms came on Friday, and on Saturday Nick delivered the children to their grandparents and came back.

It was the weekend of their planned getaway, and Ronnie was feeling almost sick with nerves.

'I wish you'd tell me where we were going,' she said plaintively.

He tapped the side of his nose. 'Secret,' he told her. 'I have to go over to the house for a while and talk to the plumber and the decorator—why don't you meet me there at three?'

'What should I pack?' she asked. 'How smart is it?'

He shrugged. 'It's an old inn in the middle of nowhere—just a dressy pub, really. It has a wonderful reputation for being a romantic getaway.'

'Says who?'

'The brochure. I picked it up from the tourist information office.'

She smiled. 'Dressy pub. Right. Thanks. I'll see you later.'

She spent the day pampering herself—and, goodness knows, she needed it. She'd spent all week stencilling walls and drawing clowns, and her nails were a mess, her hair was full of paint and she felt generally scruffy.

She dressed in smart trousers, ankle boots and a fine

silk blouse, and just hoped that it would be dressy enough for his 'dressy pub'.

She arrived at the house at ten to three, and found Nick on his mobile phone in the newly completed hall. He beckoned her in, finished the call and drew her into his arms. 'You look lovely—mmm, and you smell wonderful.'

'Clean, you mean!' she said with a chuckle, and looked around. 'This house is beginning to look really good. I love the carpet.'

'It's worked, hasn't it? I'm delighted. Thank you for helping me find the house. In fact, thank you for all sorts of things. Let's go and celebrate.'

He ushered her out, parked her car on the drive instead of his and shut the high gates behind it so nobody would know it was there. Secrets, again, she thought heavily. Oh, well. She didn't really want it publicised that she was going off for a dirty weekend with him. Sometimes secrecy was just another word for privacy, and they were very short on that.

The hotel was about an hour away, down pretty twisting lanes, past hedges just breaking into leaf, and when they arrived the daffodils along the drive were just beginning to open.

'Oh, it's pretty,' she said as the pub came into view. It was thatched, and the stableyard behind had been converted to form part of the accommodation. Tubs of bulbs and polyanthus brought touches of colour to the courtyard area, and more were clustered round the door.

They parked the car and took their luggage in, and were greeted by a young man behind the desk, who signed them in.

'Up the stairs, turn left and go to the end. It's the last room on the right. Dinner's served from seven till nine, and we serve afternoon tea in the lounge bar until six.

There's also tea- and coffee-making facilities in your room for your convenience. Enjoy your stay.'

'Thank you,' Nick murmured, and took Ronnie's elbow. His hand seemed to tremble slightly, and Ronnie wondered if he was as nervous as she was, or if it was just anticipation.

They found the room easily, and it took a matter of seconds to explore it. Then there didn't seem to be anything left to do to stall.

Ronnie's mouth seemed suddenly dry, and her heart seemed to be hammering in her throat. It was ages since he'd held her—three weeks since that weekend they'd spent working on the house and making love in the intervals.

A man was crossing the courtyard below them, and she watched him and wondered what she was expected to do.

'Ronnie?'

She turned and looked at Nick.

'I don't bite,' he told her gently, and with a little cry she went into his arms...

CHAPTER NINE

'MORNING.'

Ronnie opened her eyes and found Nick there, a playful smile on his lips. He was propped up on one elbow, looking down at her, and she wondered briefly how dishevelled and morning-after-ish she looked.

But only briefly, because, however she looked, it was obvious that Nick was happy with what he saw.

She reached up a hand and rubbed her palm over his cheek. It rasped on the stubble, and she smiled lazily. He looked like a pirate, sexy and forbidden, and she didn't want to move.

Ever.

Her stomach, though, thought otherwise. It growled loudly, and Nick chuckled. 'Was that you or me?'

'Me,' she confessed. 'I'm starving. I must have worked off all that wonderful meal we had last night.'

'Mmm. Me, too. Shall we have breakfast sent up?'

She stretched contentedly. 'How decadent,' she said with a smile.

'Was that a yes?'

'Mmm. Cereal and fruit juice and tea—and toast and marmalade.'

'Not a cooked breakfast?'

She pulled a face. Somehow the thought of all that greasy food curdled her stomach. 'No, not a cooked breakfast.'

'Mind if I do?'

She shook her head. 'Of course not.'

She slipped into the bathroom and showered quickly

while he phoned room service, and was just stepping out of the shower when he came in.

'It's all yours,' she told him, went up on tiptoe to press a kiss on his cheek and left him to it.

He came out minutes later, showered but not shaved, and sat on the edge of the bed. 'You look gorgeous,' he told her softly. 'Good enough to eat. I don't know why I ordered breakfast, I'd rather have you.'

'You haven't shaved,' she said, rubbing her hand over his cheek again.

'No. Do you want me to?'

She shook her head. 'I love your stubble. Very sexy. Shave later.'

He smiled, a lazy, predatory smile and, leaning closer, he lowered his mouth to hers. It was a gentle kiss at first, slow and indolent, without haste. He eased her dressing-gown open and slid a hand inside, cupping her breast, then lowered his head and took the nipple in his mouth.

So much sensation! The heat of his mouth, the firm flick of his tongue, the slight scrape of his beard against her delicate skin. She moaned softly and he shifted her, sliding her down the bed and coming down beside her so she was in his arms again.

'How can I want you again?' he groaned, trailing hot, open-mouthed kisses over her shoulders. 'You're just irresistible—delicious. Mmm.' His lips closed over her other nipple, drawing it deep into his mouth, and she arched against him and cried out softly.

'Easy, sweetheart, easy,' he murmured, and ran his hand over her hip. 'We've got time—'

The sharp tap made them jump. 'Room service—breakfast.'

He jackknifed away from her. 'Um—can you leave it outside, please?' he called, and they heard the clatter of the tray and the retreating footsteps on the carpeted landing.

She started to giggle, and after a second he joined in, falling back onto the bed beside her and pulling her into his arms and hugging her.

'Oh, dear, I thought he was coming in,' he said with a chuckle after a moment.

'Me, too. Is the door locked?'

'Yes—I locked it last night. Don't worry. Now, where were we?'

She slid her hand inside his dressing-gown and down over his hip. 'Ah, yes,' he murmured, and his lips found hers again. Within moments they were swept away again, lost in their own world—so lost that it was a few seconds before they registered the ringing of his mobile phone.

He said something that, if Ben had understood it, would have cost him dearly in the swear-box, and swung his legs over the side of the bed. 'If it's that damn plumber, I'm sacking him,' he growled, fumbling for the phone on the bedside table and finally switching it on.

'Sarazin,' he snapped, and then his voice mellowed. 'Clare—hi. No, sorry, I couldn't find it for a second. How are things? Oh, Lord. Is he all right?'

Ronnie slid up the bed, dragging the covers with her, and watched his face anxiously. 'What is it?' she asked when he'd put the phone down.

'Ben—he's fallen out of a tree and sprained his wrist. Well, they think it's sprained, but it might be broken. Clare's just going to take him to Casualty, but she wants me to meet her there.'

'Where are they going?'

'Addenbrookes. They live just outside Cambridge.'

He glanced at his watch. 'You'll have to come with me. I haven't got time to take you home.'

'You could put me on a train in Cambridge on your way,' she offered, but after a second he shook his head.

'No. Come. Clare needs to get back to Sunday school, and you could sit with Amy. We can be there in half an hour.'

'OK.' She slipped out of bed, put on fresh underwear and the clothes she'd had on last night, and packed her bag. She didn't bother with make-up—Nick seemed in a hurry to get to Ben, and she could understand that. She was in a hurry herself.

'Got everything?' he asked, and she nodded.

'Right.'

He pulled open the door, strode out—and fell headlong over the breakfast tray.

It was too much for Ronnie. She propped herself up in the doorway, covered her mouth with her hand and howled with laughter.

'What happened to your trousers, Daddy?'

Nick gave Amy a jaundiced glower. 'I tripped over my breakfast. I'd put it on the floor.'

'That was silly. Why didn't you change?'

Because he didn't have any other trousers with him—that was the simple answer, but not, of course, one he could give his daughter. Ronnie wondered what he'd say, but he got out of it easily.

'I didn't realise they were so splashed,' he lied, and his look dared Ronnie to disagree with him. She simply arched a brow slightly and looked away, biting the inside of her lip so she didn't laugh again.

It hadn't really been funny. Doors had opened and people had shushed them furiously. One couple had threatened to complain, and as they'd checked out and offered to pay for cleaning up the mess, the receptionist had explained that they'd thought he'd been an employee and he'd dropped a tray.

'We didn't know what they were talking about,' she'd said with a smile. 'Please, don't worry. I'm just glad you weren't hurt.'

Only his pride, Ronnie thought, and suppressed another smile. What a disastrous morning! And then they'd had Clare to deal with, although she'd been so relieved to see them that Ronnie didn't think she would have cared if they'd turned up stark naked!

Later, however, was another matter. They went back to the house, with Ben's sprain confirmed and his support bandage duly signed by the nurse, just as Clare and Peter were coming back from church.

'We don't have a cover story worked out,' Ronnie said out of the side of her mouth.

'Forget it. We'll say we were at the house. Hi. No fracture, just a sprain,' he said to his in-laws, and then took Ronnie's elbow and ushered her forward. 'Clare, Peter, this is Veronica Matthews, my next-door neighbour and surgical ward sister. Ronnie, you've met Clare, of course, and this is Peter.'

Ronnie, her heart pounding like that of a cornered criminal, dredged up what she hoped was a normal smile and shook their hands. 'Hello. Nice to meet you.'

'You got here very quickly—you must have been over this way,' Peter said to Nick, inadvertently wandering into the middle of a minefield.

'Um—we were hoping to look at an architectural salvage firm,' he lied.

'Oh, really? I didn't know they were open on Sundays.'

'Ah. I don't know. We were just going to try and find it,' he ad-libbed, digging a bigger hole.

'You didn't shave,' Ben said, eyeing him curiously. 'You *always* shave.'

'I forgot,' he said, and changed the subject firmly back to Ben's arm.

Nevertheless, Ronnie felt their eyes on her, their curiosity thinly veiled, and hoped to high heaven that she wouldn't turn scarlet and give the game away. She was, however, growing more and more conscious of the little patch of whisker-burn on her top lip, courtesy of Nick's stubble.

Any minute now she was going to start giggling hysterically, she thought, and bit the inside of her lip.

'So, Ronnie, the children tell me you've painted their bedrooms with spaceships and clowns and all sorts of things,' Clare said, settling in beside her as they walked up to the front door. 'That's very good of you.'

Was that a leading question? Maybe.

'It was a pleasure,' she told Clare. 'I enjoyed it. I love decorating, especially when it's interesting like that. And the children make it all worth it, they're so pleased when you've finished.'

'They certainly were pleased, they've talked about nothing else,' their grandmother confided, and Ronnie felt a flicker of alarm. Had the children inadvertently given away more than they, in fact, knew?

Holy Moses, she thought. Get out of that!

But it was easy. Conversation moved on to more general talk of the house as they all sat round the kitchen table. Clare was putting the finishing touches to Sunday lunch, to which they were all, of course, invited, and Ronnie for one was more than ready for it. Missing breakfast hadn't done anything for her, and she was feeling a little light-headed.

'Sherry, anybody?' Peter offered, and Ronnie shook her head.

'No, thank you, I won't.'

'I'm driving,' Nick said regretfully.

'Not till later.'

'Not that much later. I'd like to get back straight after lunch, if you don't mind. I've got quite a lot to do on the house still.'

'You could have a small one,' Clare coaxed. Nick shook his head. 'No, I won't. Anyway, I had quite a bit last night.'

'Oh? Celebrating the house?'

His neck coloured slightly and he avoided Ronnie's eye. 'Yes—I took Ronnie to a hotel for dinner to thank her for all her help.'

And make of that what you will, Ronnie thought with rising hysteria.

'Daddy fell over his breakfast,' Amy said, apropos of absolutely nothing, and their eyes swivelled to him. Had they linked the two?

'However did you manage that?' Clare asked in surprise.

'He put it on the floor,' Ben informed them importantly. 'He didn't realise his trousers were so splashed—that's why he's got egg all up them.'

Nick closed his eyes, and Ronnie would have laid odds he was counting. She rushed in to rescue him. 'Maybe it didn't show when it was wet,' she offered.

'It's *yellow*,' Ben said, as if he were talking to an idiot child.

'Whatever. I'm sure he won't do it again.' She shifted her attention back to Ben's grandparents. 'Have you seen the house yet?'

Peter shook his head. 'No. Nick's keeping us in suspense. He said it was so dreadful we'd have a fit if we saw it too early. I don't think he credits us with any imagination.'

Funny, Ronnie thought. I would have credited you with altogether too much. 'It's wonderful. Lots of character. It's got a lovely big entrance hall—I think that's so important, don't you?'

Nick shot her a grateful look, and the conversation ebbed and flowed as they ate their meal. Ronnie's light head settled down, and Clare and Peter stopped asking awkward questions and concentrated on the children.

'So, when are you bringing them back to us?' Clare asked as they sipped tea in the drawing room.

'Next weekend—I'm on call then—if that's all right?'

'Of course it's all right. And you'll be here for Mothering Sunday, won't you? In three weeks.'

'Yes—yes, we'll be here for that, don't worry.'

'Good.' Clare stood up. 'Come on, children, let's go and pack your things so that you can get off nice and early. You heard what Daddy said—lots to do.'

'His bedroom's a real mess, but he says he doesn't mind,' Ben told her as they went out.

'Is it?'

Nick laughed. 'Oh, yes. But it doesn't matter. It'll probably be the last thing that gets done. I need to sort out the bits people see, and the garden's clamouring for attention, too. There just aren't enough hours in the day.'

'Well, you know we're always happy to have the children so you can work late at night if you want to, but I expect you'll be moving in soon.'

'On Friday—and they have to go to school, of course, but thank you, Peter. Perhaps in the holidays— or maybe I'll get an au pair.'

Peter laughed. 'You've said that before.'

'I know. I just don't fancy having a stranger in the house.'

'You ought to get married again,' his father-in-law said calmly.

There was a second of shocked silence, then Nick let his breath out on a gust. 'Ah—I don't think so. Not yet. And, anyway, it's not a very good reason.'

'It's as good as most.'

Ronnie busied herself with her teacup and tried to be invisible. This was the *last* conversation she'd anticipated!

They were saved by Clare, coming downstairs with the children, bags in tow. 'All ready.'

Nick stood up with alacrity. 'Wonderful. Thank you so much. I'm sorry you had to take monster here to A and E.'

'Any time.' She laughed and tousled Ben's head, and he smiled up at her, clearly devoted. 'Right, let's get these bags in the car.'

They all trooped outside and without thinking, Nick opened the boot. There, as large as life and a dead giveaway, were two overnight bags.

For a moment they all froze. Then Clare looked at Nick, then at Ronnie, and smiled a gentle, understanding smile. She said nothing, just put the children's luggage in the boot, shut the lid and kissed them all goodbye. She paused by Ronnie as she opened the passenger door, and patted her shoulder.

'It's about time,' she said softly, and Ronnie felt tears fill her eyes.

She said nothing. Indeed, she couldn't have spoken if her life had depended on it. She just leaned over and gave Clare's cheek a grateful kiss, then slid into the car beside Nick. Clare closed the door and stood back, and they pulled away, the children waving through the back window.

'Whoops,' Nick muttered quietly.

Ronnie leaned back against the headrest and said nothing. She was still speechless and, anyway, she was too busy absorbing the implications of Clare's remark.

There was no opportunity for them to talk again that day—or not at length. Nick wanted to ask what Clare had said, but he had a feeling he didn't want to know—and, anyway, the children were there with their antennae going.

They went round to the new house so Ronnie could pick up her car, and while the children ran upstairs to have another look at their bedrooms, Nick put Ronnie's case into her boot to avoid another embarrassing incident.

'Do you think she realised what was going on?' he asked, in the vain hope that Ronnie would say no.

Instead she gave him a wary smile. 'Yes, she did. She said it was about time.'

He groaned and dropped his head against the roof of the car. 'Damn.'

Ronnie laid a gentle hand on his shoulder and squeezed. 'Nick, it's all right. You're a healthy adult, and it's been four years. They live in the real world. Anyway, they love you and they want you to be happy.'

'But do they want to be lied to? Because that's what I did, countless times today.'

'So ring them up and tell them, when the children are in bed. Use your mobile and go and sit in the car, so they don't hear you. Explain.'

And he would have done, if he'd felt able to. He just didn't know where to start, because the truth was he didn't know what he felt about Ronnie.

All he knew was that since he'd met her nothing had been the same, and he didn't think it ever would be again.

Ryan O'Connor went home the next day, three weeks after his stabbing, still tender but much more his old self, to the extent that Ronnie felt sure he'd overdo it.

Still, he was a doctor, an intelligent man who knew the risks better than most. She threatened him with death if he ended up back in there, but he just grinned.

'Don't fuss,' he said mildly, and carried on packing up his wash things.

'Just doing my job.'

'I know.' He lifted his head. 'So, how's it going with Nick?'

She gave a weak smile. 'His in-laws just found out about us.'

Ryan winced. 'Uh-oh. Tricky one. I remember when Ann's parents found out about me and Ginny—I thought they'd have apoplexy.'

Ronnie laughed. 'Actually, her mother was wonderful. She said it was about time.'

'Good. I agree. It's just going to be hard to make the man see it. We can be extraordinarily obtuse. Keep me posted.'

Ginny appeared then, putting an end to their conversation, and, after handing him all the necessary paperwork, Ronnie kissed his cheek and sent him home with his wife. She was sorry to see him go. He'd been an excellent patient really and, being a fellow professional, she'd been able to treat him differently.

Ah, well, she thought. There were plenty of other patients that needed her attention, and plenty who were interesting people, if you bothered to find out enough about them.

Mrs Eddison, for instance, who was back in again with her perforated bowel and stoma that refused to heal properly. She'd been a Tiller girl in her youth, and had danced at the London Palladium. Not that you'd

ever know it to look at her now, with her arthritis and
other problems, but if you sat and talked to her, Ronnie
thought, she was fascinating.

Ronnie went to see her now, to change the dressing
on her stoma and see if there was any progress in the
skin which had broken down.

'Hello, dear,' Winnie said with a cheery smile. 'Did
you have a nice weekend with your young man?'

Ronnie nearly dropped the dish of swabs. 'I had a
lovely weekend, thank you,' she replied, refusing to be
drawn. Surely she didn't know about Nick?

Apparently not. 'You must have a young man,' the
woman coaxed, but Ronnie wouldn't fall for it. Not for
the world would she discuss her private life with this
lively and interesting perpetrator of gossip! 'That
Vicky, now,' Winnie went on, 'she had a lovely weekend with David. They were planning the wedding.'

Winnie lay back with a sigh. 'I remember planning
my wedding, only I was older than her, of course. I'd
worked on the stage for eight years, so I must have
been twenty-six when I met Bob, and twenty-eight
when we got married. Just before the coronation, it
was—nearly fifty years ago. He died on our ruby wedding anniversary. It was such a shame, but at least he
made it. I would have been ever so cross if he'd died
the day before!'

Ronnie chuckled. 'I don't suppose he'd have dared.'

'Probably not! Oh, dear, I did miss him though, at
first. Still do, in a way.'

'I can imagine,' Ronnie said sympathetically. And
for the first time she began to have some inkling of
what her patients were going through when they de-
scribed feelings of grief. Loving Nick, it made her realise just what losing him would do to her. If nothing
else, then, her affair with him would make her a better

nurse and a better person, because it had given her a greater understanding.

She supposed she should be grateful. Just now, she was too busy alternating between hope and despair, like a demented see-saw.

'Penny for 'em,' Winnie Eddison said.

Ronnie laughed. 'Not likely! Well, it looks as if the skin's beginning to heal again. That's good news. Now all we need is a bit of progress on the inside, and we'll have you home again!'

'Don't hurry on my account, dear,' Winnie said. 'I'm quite enjoying myself with all this company. I hated it when I went home before.'

Ronnie carefully placed the new stoma bag, sealed it firmly onto the skin and pulled off her gloves, dropping them into the midst of all the other disposable bits and pieces on the trolley and wrapping them securely. 'Have you ever thought of going into a residential home? Not a nursing home, you don't need that, but a residential home for the active elderly? You might enjoy the company.'

'I was thinking that myself,' Winnie confessed. 'I don't suppose you could help me find out about it?'

'I can get the hospital social worker to come and talk to you—she has all sorts of contacts. I'll arrange it if you like.'

'Oh, please. It'll help pass the time if nothing else, and you never know.'

Ronnie gave her hand a quick squeeze. 'I'll see what we can do,' she promised, and wheeled the trolley back to the treatment room to clear up her debris.

Vicky was in there, doing the same, and Ronnie shot her a smile. 'I gather from Mrs Eddison that you've been planning the wedding over the weekend.'

Vicky laughed. 'Sort of. It's going to be one long

set of compromises, I can tell you. He wants this, I want that, his parents want something else, and my parents say as they're paying for it they're having it another way—I thought I was going to kill them all!'

'The joys,' Ronnie said, secretly envying her colleague. She'd have given her eye-teeth to be planning her wedding to Nick. She wondered if it would ever happen, and decided it was too depressing a speculation to waste time on. She'd live for the moment, and let the future worry about itself.

Nick and the children moved into the house on Friday. Nick took the first part of the morning off to oversee the installation of the major pieces of furniture in the right rooms, and left the removal men to it for the rest of the day.

He had no choice. He had a full list, and Ronnie could tell he was like a cat on hot bricks.

'I bet I have to move almost everything round again,' he said with a resigned smile. They were in the canteen, grabbing a quick sandwich during his lunchbreak, and Ronnie had managed to get away at the same time by a miracle.

'Are you going straight there after work?' she asked.

'Yes—well, I have to go and pick up the children.'

'I could do that for you,' she offered. 'I'll be finished at three today, I was on an early, so if it helps…'

He nodded gratefully. 'Brilliant,' he said round a mouthful of sandwich. 'That would be such a help. I can go straight to the house then. I'll ring you when I'm leaving here.'

So Ronnie went home and changed into jeans and a jumper and trainers—ideal for running up and down stairs with misplaced boxes, she thought! Then she waited for Nick to ring.

He finished at ten past four, and she went round to Meg's and told the children what was happening, and Ben cheered and ran for the door. Amy, though, walked with Ronnie, looking thoughtful, and she had a feeling something was wrong.

'What's the matter, sweetheart?' she asked, bending down to her.

'I don't want to leave you,' Amy confessed, and threw her arms round Ronnie's neck and burst into tears.

Oh, dear. Ronnie hugged her and rocked her, and told her that, of course, she'd still see her, just because they were moving didn't mean they wouldn't still be friends, and she'd come round and see them often, and, anyway, they'd still be coming to Meg every day so she'd see them then.

The crying hiccuped to a halt, and Amy lifted her tear-stained face from Ronnie's shoulder and sniffed. 'Promise,' she said wetly, and Ronnie promised.

'Now, let's go to the new house or Daddy will wonder what I've done with you.'

Ben was leaning on the car, watching this exchange, and he looked up at Ronnie worriedly. 'Is she all right?'

'She doesn't want to move.'

'I do!' Ben said firmly. 'It's a cool house, and I've got a spaceship bedroom, and a big garden—Dad says I can have goalposts in the garden to play football.'

Ronnie could already hear the tinkling glass from the broken windows, but she held her tongue. Maybe he'd kick it sideways across the garden.

'Right, into the car—let's go.'

Nick was already there when they arrived, organising the movement of a couple of large pieces of furniture, and Ronnie made herself useful with the teapot while the children ran excitedly through the house, re-acquainting themselves with all their furniture. Then at last the door closed behind the removal men and Nick turned to her with a sigh.

'Well, that's it. Everything's here, except for our clothes and bits and pieces at the other house.'

Ronnie swallowed the lump in her throat. She didn't want them to go any more than Amy did, and she was dreading the silence from next door once they'd gone. She'd got so used to hearing their voices over the past month or two.

'Come and see,' he said, and she followed him round, looking at all the furniture, the boxes, the huge amount he still had to do.

'We need curtains, of course. I don't suppose you know anybody?'

'Meg will,' she told him with a smile.

'Bless her, she's the fount of all knowledge. Well, the children go to their grandparents for the weekend, and hopefully by Sunday night I will have got the place a bit straighter and the other house cleared, even if we haven't got curtains. I'm sure I can find something to put up.'

'Do you want a hand?' Ronnie offered.

'If you've got time. I seem to be taking up all your time recently.'

She didn't know how to answer that, so she ignored it and went with the first part of his answer. 'I've got time,' she told him. In truth she had nothing else. She couldn't remember how she'd spent her time before they'd all come along. Perhaps she'd better start thinking about it!

It was an exhausting weekend. Nick was on call, and several times he left Ronnie unpacking books or crockery or such-like while he went back to the hospital.

It was strange, handling all his things. She wondered how many of them Anna had chosen, and how Anna would have felt about her. At least her parents didn't seem to object too violently. She put a handful of books on the shelf in the snug and sat back on her heels.

She'd hoped things might have moved on a little since last weekend, or that they would have talked more about Anna's parents and their reaction, but Nick had been remarkably distant in a way.

No, not distant. He'd just avoided any chances for intimacy of any sort. There had been no kisses, no hugs—not even this weekend, while they'd been alone.

She heard him come back, and quickly scrubbed away the tears she hadn't realised were on her cheeks. 'Hi—I'm in here.'

He came in and stood behind her. 'Wonderful. Thank you. It's beginning to look like a home.'

She stood up, brushing her hands on her jeans, and gave him a slightly off-key smile. 'Do you mind if I go home?' she said. 'I've got lots to do, and I've got a bit of a headache.'

'No, of course not. Thank you so much for all your help. You've been wonderful.'

He drew her into his arms and hugged her, then pressed a kiss to her brow. 'Go on, you go home. I'll be all right now. Thank you, Ronnie.'

'You're welcome,' she said huskily and, grabbing her keys from by the door, she let herself out. She managed to get home before the tears fell, but only just. Meg found her slumped over the wheel of her car on the drive, sobbing as if her heart would break. She took her friend inside and made her a cup of tea and gave her lots of sage advice while Ronnie sniffed and blew her nose and howled again.

Finally, though, Meg had to go and collect Jimmy from his father, and there was nothing to distract Ronnie from the knowledge that nothing had changed. Nick still didn't want to acknowledge her as part of his life, and Ronnie could do nothing about it.

CHAPTER TEN

WINNIE EDDISON went home at the end of the next week. She'd found a residential home that could take her from the beginning of April, and as she had her own funding, she was able to move at her own convenience, instead of waiting for the wheels of bureaucracy to turn.

Her daughter had taken her to look round a couple of times, and she'd come back from the second visit, bubbling over with excitement.

'You'll never guess—there's someone there I haven't seen for thirty years, but we still recognised each other. She used to be my neighbour, but then she moved away and we lost touch. Isn't that amazing?'

'And have they definitely got a space?' Ronnie asked, delighted to see her enthusiasm.

'Yes—I'm going next Friday. Well, if I'm all right by then. I have to have a few days at home to pack everything up and sort my things out.'

'We'll ask Mr Sarazin when he comes down,' she said. 'He'll let you go as soon as you're ready, don't worry. Have you got someone to move you?'

'My daughter—she'll help. I can have all my things. There's a big empty room, and I can take all of my personal bits and pieces with me—letters from Bob when we were courting, things of the children's—you know the sort of thing.'

Ronnie did. She had a drawer in her bedroom that was filling up with things—a note from Nick, a drawing from Amy, Ben's version of his bedroom, a thank-

170

you note from him for painting all the spaceships—all sorts of little things to get out and cry over in a weak moment.

She knew just what Winnie was on about.

'Just don't make yourself overtired, packing everything up,' she cautioned.

Winnie laughed. 'Oh, no, dear. I shall sit in my chair and tell my daughter and my grandchildren what to do!'

Ronnie didn't doubt it for a minute!

She spoke to Nick about Winnie's plans when she next saw him, and he made time to go and have a look at her and chat to her about her stoma care and the care of her bowel.

'I don't see why you shouldn't go, so long as you're careful not to overdo it,' he said.

Winnie patted his hand. 'Don't you worry, I'll be all right. It's the first time since I lost Bob that I've had anything to look forward to. I feel years younger.'

Ronnie was sorry to see her go on Friday, but glad for her that everything seemed to be turning out so well. She wished she had something to look forward to in her own life, because Nick was still keeping her at arm's length, and the house next door was unbearably quiet.

She went away for the weekend rather than flagellate herself with Nick's absence, and visited her father and stepmother in Southampton. They went to Lymington and walked along the river by the yacht club, and she assiduously avoided any personal conversation.

Until, that was, her stepmother cornered her in the kitchen after Sunday lunch. 'What's wrong, Ronnie?' she asked with typical directness. 'You've dried that plate so thoroughly you've nearly rubbed the design off it.'

Ronnie put the plate down and picked up another. 'I'm in love,' she confessed. 'He's a widower, with two small children, and he won't let me in because he doesn't want to upset them.'

Kathy sighed and rested her hands in the washing-up water. 'Been there, done that,' she said softly. 'It hurts, doesn't it?'

Ronnie looked at her in puzzlement. 'I don't understand. You were widowed when Dad met you. You got married straight away—and Martin didn't have any children.'

'Martin didn't, no, but your father did. And I wasn't a widow when I met him, I was a young woman in my late twenties, and I fell hopelessly in love, but he wouldn't do anything about it because of you and Bryony. We kept our love a secret for four years, and then I met Martin, and he offered me a chance at a real relationship, so I took it.'

'And then his heart gave out.'

'Yes. He always said I broke it, because he knew I truly belonged to your father in my heart of hearts, although I did everything I could to be a good and loyal wife to him.'

'And then he died, and by then Bryony and I had grown up, so it was all right,' Ronnie said slowly. 'But that's so silly! I would have loved to have had you as a mother then! I really needed a mother so much.'

Kathy smiled. 'I tried to tell your father, but men can be very slow about these things.'

Funny, Ryan had said something very similar, Ronnie recalled. 'Oh, Kathy, I'm sorry. All those wasted years!'

'No, not wasted,' she said gently. 'I loved Martin in my own way, and he loved me. It was just different, not wasted. And your father and I are together now.

You might just have to wait a long time for your man to come to his senses. How old are the children?'

'Six and eight,' Ronnie said bleakly. 'Twelve years till they go to university.'

'By which time you'll be forty. You have to make a decision, Ronnie. Hang around and wait, or go out and make a life for yourself without him.'

'I'll never forget him.'

'Of course not. I never forgot your father, but I had a life, a very full and satisfactory one. You just have to choose.'

It gave Ronnie a great deal to think about, and later in the week she found even more to think about.

She was cleaning out her bathroom cupboards to kill the empty hours when she found her tampons. She looked at them thoughtfully. When *had* she last had a period?

Weeks ago—before the ball. Before they'd made love. Eight weeks ago, to be exact.

She sat down with a bump. Oh, God, she thought, surely not? She stared at her watch. Seven-fifteen. The supermarkets were still open. She ran down to her car, flew round to the supermarket, grabbed a pregnancy test kit off the shelf and rushed home.

Then she closeted herself in the bathroom with the test and stared at it for ages. She read the instructions about six times, then decided there was nothing else for it. She had to do the test.

She couldn't open her eyes. She daren't look at the strip. She washed her hands, flushed the loo and sat down on the lid, still with her eyes shut. She didn't want to know.

It might be negative.

She felt sick, either with anticipation or apprehension, or even just because she was pregnant.

'You don't know that,' she told herself. 'You have to look.'

It was positive. She closed her eyes, opened them again and checked, and then shut them.

'Oh, my God,' she said softly. 'I'm having a baby.'

And then she started to cry.

'Jimmy's got football—I don't suppose you could bear to have Ben and Amy, could you?' Meg asked. 'He wants me to go and watch—it's an important match, or something, and Nick's just phoned to say he's been held up at the hospital with an emergency and won't be back for ages.'

Ronnie dredged up a smile. 'No, that's fine,' she said, ignoring the fact that it was going to tear her apart. 'Of course I don't mind.'

'Brilliant. I'll send them round. They're doing their homework, and they've had something to eat, so it shouldn't be too arduous.'

Looking after Ben and Amy was never arduous to Ronnie, but she didn't bother to say so. She just threw together a packet of chocolate brownie mix and put it in the oven just as Ben and Amy pounded on the door.

'Hi, kids,' she said, welcoming them into the hall. 'Put your coats on the banisters and come and finish your homework, and then we can watch the telly.'

'Are those brownies in the oven?' Amy asked, her radar zooming in on them.

'Yes,' Ronnie said with a chuckle. 'Later. Home-work first.'

They settled down at the kitchen table with a little grumble, and pulled out folded pieces of card and col-ouring pens.

'We have to do Mother's Day cards,' Ben said, screwing up his nose. 'We do them for Grannie.'

Oh, God, Ronnie thought, aching for them. How awful.

'I can't remember Mummy,' Amy said, sticking her tongue out of the corner of her mouth in concentration. 'I wish I had a mummy.'

'Jimmy's got two mummies,' Ben said. 'Meg, and his dad's married again, but she's bossy, he says.'

'I've got a stepmother,' Ronnie told them, sitting down at the table. 'Her name's Kathy. She's very nice.'

'I bet she was bossy when you were little.'

'She wasn't there when I was little,' Ronnie told them, wishing she had been. 'My mother died when I was eleven, but my father didn't get married again until I was twenty-two.'

'So do you 'member her? Your real mum, I mean,' Amy asked.

'Oh, yes. Sort of. I can remember quite a lot.'

'That must be nice,' Ben said. 'I don't remember much. I can remember her smell. She smelled of hospitals.'

Poor little things. Ronnie blinked. 'I'll just check the brownies,' she said, even though she knew they were nothing like ready. Anything to get away from the clear, all-seeing eyes of those children while she pulled herself together.

She could hear Amy scribbling away with her felt pens, colouring in flowers and leaves with big, wild strokes that went over the edges. Ben was being much more careful, drawing a very intricate picture of a spaceship.

'Grannie doesn't like spaceships,' Amy told him, and Ronnie intervened quickly before there was a fight.

She wondered how long it would be before her own child was sitting at the kitchen table, drawing a

Mother's Day card for her, and her hand slid down to cradle the slight bulge.

It wasn't really a bulge yet, more of a fullness, but it wouldn't be long and then she'd have to make some difficult decisions.

She'd already decided she had to tell Nick, but what happened after that, she couldn't even begin to guess at. What she didn't want was for him to marry her out of misplaced duty, and for her to spend the rest of her life trying to live up to Anna's memory.

The brownies were finally cooked, and the cards completed, and they went through to the sitting room and snacked in front of the television.

It was eight o'clock before Nick turned up, and the children were drooping and ready for bed.

'I'd invite you in for coffee, but they've had it,' Ronnie told him regretfully.

He smiled at her over their heads, a strained smile which made her think he'd probably have said no anyway, and ushered them out to the car. The silence was deafening.

Mothering Sunday dawned bright and sunny, fluffy clouds scudding across the sky, and the daffodils were nodding their heads in the stiff April breeze.

Nick was dreading the service. He'd started coming with Anna before they were married, and it had become a tradition. They'd continued to come with their own children, and since Anna's death, he'd brought Ben and Amy to put flowers on Anna's grave. It seemed appropriate, and it was a comfort to Clare because she only had her grandchildren now, and they filled the gap Anna had left.

His own mother was in Somerset, miles away and surrounded by family, so his absence didn't really hurt them and besides, he found himself locked into the ritual.

It didn't hurt any more like it had at first, but for some reason this year it seemed strange, as if they should have moved on.

He wondered if the children felt it, or if it was just him. He'd taken his ring off this week and put it away. After four years he felt it was time, and he realised he'd been hiding behind it. He was all stirred up because of Ronnie, of course. He'd been avoiding her, but it didn't make any difference. He still thought about her every minute that he wasn't with her, and the nights were getting harder and harder to deal with.

He'd thought moving to the new house would help, because he wouldn't have to listen to her through the wall, humming softly as she went about her chores, the rapid patter of her feet on the stairs, the roar of her vacuum cleaner, the clash of her dustbin lid in the garden outside.

Now he had nothing but an eerie silence after the children were asleep, broken only by the occasional car going past, and the sound of cats fighting on the fence at the bottom of the garden.

Nothing, in fact, to distract him from missing her.

He threw open the window and drew in a lungful of fresh country air. If only he could be sure their relationship would work, but he was sure Ronnie wouldn't want to take on his children. She would want a family of her own, not a man with a past and children with scars that went so deep he thought they'd never heal.

Amy had started wetting the bed again, and Ben was grumpy and difficult, despite the spaceships. They talked about Ronnie constantly, and clearly missed her as much as he did.

And he didn't know what to do about it.

He went to wake them, to take their cards in to their grandmother. Peter had just left to prepare the church for communion, and if they left it any later Clare would be busy.

He went into the room next door which had been Anna's room, and woke them.

'Rise and shine, kids. You've got to give Grannie her cards.'

Ben sat up, scrubbing his eyes and blinking, and Amy started to cry.

'I wet the bed,' she sobbed, and with a quiet sigh Nick took her in his arms and cuddled her.

'It's all right, darling. Don't worry. We'll wash the sheets for Grannie and give you a bath. Let's change your nightie and you can go and give her your card.'

'I don't want to,' she sobbed. 'I want to give it to Ronnie.'

Oh, Lord, he thought. Not this again. Her teacher had come out on Friday afternoon when he'd picked them up from school, and had smiled at him curiously. 'I gather congratulations are in order,' she said.

His jaw had dropped. 'Excuse me?'

'Oh—have I misunderstood? Amy told me she was making two Mother's Day cards—one for her grand-mother, and one for her new mother.'

He'd quickly disabused her of that notion, but Amy had been harder to persuade, and it seemed he'd still failed to get through.

'Darling, I explained this to you on Friday,' he said patiently. 'Ronnie's not your mother. She's just a friend. She's a very special friend, but that doesn't mean she's your mother.'

'But I want a mummy!' Amy sobbed. 'I want Ronnie!'

'So do I,' Ben said quietly from his bed. 'She's not

bossy. Jimmy doesn't really like his stepmother, but Ronnie's cool. She doesn't tell me what to do, and she's funny.'

Nick swallowed. 'But... I don't know how Ronnie would feel about it.'

'Why don't you ask her?' Clare said from behind him, and he looked over his shoulder and stared dumbly at her.

'Ask her?' he croaked.

'Mmm. Now.'

'Now?'

'Yes. Ring her and invite her for lunch, and ask her. Or go now.'

He looked at his watch. He couldn't go now, because he'd miss the service and, dread it or not, he had to be there to help the children through it. They always took flowers up to the altar with all the other children, and had them blessed by Peter, and then went out into the churchyard to put them on Anna's grave.

He had to be there for that.

'I'll ring her,' he said, and stood up. 'Um, Amy's wet the bed, by the way.'

'Oh, sweetheart, never mind. Let's give you a nice bath, shall we?'

He left the children in Clare's capable hands and ran downstairs to the study. It was quiet in there, and he could speak to Ronnie without interruptions.

He dialled her number, frantically trying to remember if she was on duty or not, and then nearly dropped the phone when she answered.

'Ronnie?' he said, and his voice cracked with emotion.

'Nick? What's wrong?' she said, instantly picking up on it.

'Nothing. Ronnie, can you come for lunch?'

There was a second of silence, then she said in a puzzled voice, 'I thought you were at Anna's parents'?'

'We are. Can you find it? I can give you directions.'

Did he sound desperate? It would be strange if he didn't, he thought, because suddenly it seemed as if his whole future depended on her answer.

'I can find it,' she said after a moment. 'Just remind me.'

He gave her quick directions, and then said goodbye. All he could do now was wait.

'Well?' Clare said when he went back upstairs.

'She's coming.'

The children shrieked with delight, and Clare smiled her encouragement.

'It'll be all right, Nick. You'll see.'

He hoped so. He really, really hoped so...

Nick had sounded odd. Strained, as if things were not quite right. Ronnie didn't know what was wrong, she couldn't even hazard a guess, but she knew he needed her, and that was enough.

She had a quick bath and put on a smart day dress and a cardigan. It was too warm for a coat, she thought, and looked at her watch. If she left now she would be hopelessly early, but she couldn't bear to hang around.

It only took just less than an hour to get there, and she arrived at eleven. She could hear singing in the church, and there was no sign of them. She didn't know what to do, but the chances were that Nick was in the church. Perhaps she should go in and find him?

Or just slip in and sit at the back.

Or wait in the car.

Which?

She went into the church, lit with the brilliant sunshine of the early April day, and Clare turned her head and beckoned to her.

She went, tiptoeing down the aisle at the side and slipping into the pew between Clare and Nick. He took her hand and squeezed it, and didn't let go.

That was fine. She didn't either. She sneaked a glance at him out of the corner of her eye, and saw the strain etched on his face. Whatever did he want? What on earth could be wrong?

She forced herself to concentrate on the service, and listened to the children who were gathered at the altar as they sang 'All Things Bright and Beautiful'.

It brought a huge lump to her throat, and Clare pressed a tissue into her hand.

'Thanks,' she whispered, and blotted her eyes. How silly. It had just been such a long time since her mother had died, and this service brought it all slamming back. Besides which, she was very emotional at the moment anyway.

She laid her hand with the crumpled tissue in it over her baby and hung on, watching as the children in turn took their little posies up to Peter for blessing. Nick stood up as the children turned, and she remembered that Ben and Amy were going to put their flowers on their mother's grave.

Oh, Lord.

Ronnie blinked again, and as she opened her eyes Amy saw her.

'Ronnie!' she cried excitedly, and ran and threw herself into Ronnie's arms, almost squashing her daffodils.

'Hello, darling,' Ronnie said unsteadily. She gave her a kiss, then looked up at Nick for help.

'Come on, sweetheart. Let's do the flowers. You can see Ronnie in a minute.'

He held out his hand, and after a moment Amy went,

skipping down the aisle. Ben grinned at Ronnie, and she smiled back and wondered how long it would be before she could creep away and have a good howl.

Clare's hand settled discreetly on her knee and gave it a comforting squeeze, and she blinked and smiled back and tried not to lose it completely.

Then the children came back inside, and Amy slipped into the seat beside her and pressed a daffodil into her hand. 'I saved one for you,' Amy said, and the tears refused to be held back any longer.

'Thank you,' Ronnie whispered and, closing her eyes, she let the tears slide unheeded down her cheeks. Her arm wrapped itself round Amy's shoulders, and Amy climbed onto her lap, almost crushing the daffodil as she snuggled into Ronnie's arms.

Ben wriggled up beside her, and she put her arm around him and hugged him too. 'Hi, spaceman,' she said softly, and he grinned.

She met Nick's eyes over his head, and the longing in them made her heart race.

What did he want? What could it be?

Then, finally, the service was over and, taking her hand in his, Nick led her out into the churchyard and round the corner. There was a grave there under a tree, beautifully tended, the headstone a very simple memorial to a young woman who should never have died as she had, with so much to live for.

'Anna, this is Ronnie,' Nick said quietly. 'I love her, and the children love her, and I hope she loves me, because I want her to marry me and help me bring up our children. I know you would have liked her, and she would have liked you, even though you're very different. I'll always love you, and treasure your memory, but I need to move on and so do the children. I just wanted you to meet her.'

Ronnie couldn't believe what he was saying. All you have to do is wait, Ryan had said, in one of their many conversations, but she hadn't dared believe him.

And now, today of all days, or perhaps because it was Mothering Sunday, Nick was asking her to marry him.

He turned to her, his eyes full of hope and fear and uncertainty, and looked down into her eyes.

'Veronica, will you marry me?' he asked softly.

'Oh, yes,' she said, tears welling helplessly. 'Of course I will. I love you—I love you all, so much.'

She reached out her arms and gathered the children to her side, and Nick's arms came round them all.

And then the shadow of the clouds was chased away by the sun, and the children's flowers on their mother's grave were bathed with gold...

'So, when's the great day going to be, and where?' Peter asked as they all sat round the table for lunch. 'Will you get married in Suffolk, or do you have a family home?'

'My father and stepmother live in Southampton,' she told them, 'but it isn't really home. I suppose where I live now is home, but I don't have a parish, really. I sometimes go to services in the hospital chapel, but not often. I haven't really thought about it.'

'You could get married here,' Amy said brightly. 'Grandad does weddings.'

Ronnie looked up, startled by the suggestion, and met Clare's eyes. 'You could. It's up to you, but it would be lovely if you were married here.'

'Wouldn't you mind?' she asked, thinking again of Anna.

'No, and nor would Anna. Nick's in our family now,

and we'd like you to be as well—if you don't mind, that is. Maybe you'd rather not.'

Ronnie swallowed. 'What about Nick?' she asked, turning to him. He smiled tenderly. 'Whatever you want. I just want to marry you. I'll do whatever you like.'

'In which case,' she said unsteadily, 'I can't think of anywhere I'd rather we were married than here.'

'Good, then that's settled,' Peter said, settling back with a smile.

'Um... Do you do christenings as well?' she asked, and Nick nearly choked.

'Ronnie?' he mouthed silently.

She smiled serenely. 'Yes,' she said, and watched the shock turn to joy in his eyes.

'Are we going to have a baby?' Amy asked, looking curiously from one to the other.

'Not yet,' Ronnie told them. 'We'll get married first.'

'I'd better look at my diary,' Peter said, and beamed at them. 'I wonder if I've got a space next week.'

EPILOGUE

SHE was so beautiful. Tiny features, perfectly formed, her fingers curled over his as she slept—Nick thought she was wonderful.

About as wonderful as Ben and Amy, and nearly as beautiful as her mother.

He looked across at Ronnie, slender again after the long months of pregnancy, and caught her eye. She smiled, a contented, loving smile, and hugged the children. They stood next to her, one each side, as devoted as ever and much more settled now, and he wondered how he could ever have thought Ronnie might be bad for them.

Not Ronnie, exactly, but a relationship with her. In fact, the last year had been one of the happiest of his life, and it seemed fitting that they should be gathered here—in the church where he and Anna had started their marriage, where their children had been christened, where Anna had been laid to rest, and where he and Ronnie had been married just ten months ago—for the christening of their daughter Elisabeth Anna.

She was Elisabeth for Ronnie's mother, and it had been Ronnie's idea to give her Anna as a second name.

He had been deeply moved by her gesture, more so by the fact that it wasn't just an empty gesture, it was an acknowledgement of the fact that Anna would never be forgotten, that her name wouldn't be avoided, and that her children would grow up able to talk about her freely with both parents.

Clare and Peter had been wonderful, too. They had

welcomed Ronnie into the family with open arms, and had made her totally at home. It was down to Ronnie's easy friendliness and generous nature that it had all worked so well, Nick thought, and that, instead of Clare and Peter losing him and the children, they'd gained another daughter and another grandchild.

Because the children now had three sets of grandparents, and all of them were assembled there in the church to see little Beth christened.

She started to squirm, the service failing to hold her attention, and she chewed her fist fretfully.

'She's hungry,' Nick said softly to Ronnie, and she took the baby from him, cradling the little one against her shoulder and rocking her gently.

The sun slanting through the window touched them all with gold, and as Peter drew the service to a close, Nick met Ronnie's eyes again and smiled.

'I love you,' he mouthed, and her smile softened, a light in her eyes only for him.

'I love you, too,' she replied silently.

And Beth, not to be left out, burped milk all over Ronnie's shoulder.

'Whoops,' Amy said, giggling deliciously. 'Beth's christened you now!'

Nick took his youngest daughter back while Ronnie wiped her shoulder, and she snuggled against him with a contented sigh. Wind, then, not hunger.

The service having ended, they drifted out into the churchyard and headed back towards the house. As they went, Nick glanced back over his shoulder at Anna's grave. It was bathed in sunlight, the flowers the children had put there that morning nodding in the breeze, and he felt peace steal over him.

He'd never thought he'd be happy again. Not truly

happy, like this, with a wonderful wife and another precious child, a fresh start for all of them, hope for the future.

Life truly was good...

Don't miss Pink Tuesday
One day. 10 hours. 10 deals.

PINK TUESDAY
IS COMING!

10 hours...10 unmissable deals!

This Valentine's Day we will be bringing
you fantastic offers across a range of
our titles—each hour, on the hour!

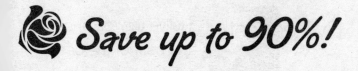

Save up to 90%!

Pink Tuesday starts
9am Tuesday 14th February

Find out how to grab a Pink Tuesday deal—
register online at **www.millsandboon.co.uk**

*Visit us
Online*

0212/PM/MB362

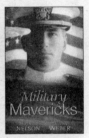

Have Your Say

You've just finished your book.
So what did you think?

We'd love to hear your thoughts on our
'Have your say' online panel
www.millsandboon.co.uk/haveyoursay

- Easy to use
- Short questionnaire
- Chance to win Mills & Boon® goodies